The Iron Tree
(Book One of The Crowthistle Chronicles)

"Dart-Thornton has crafted an impresive start to an epic journey down the corridors of myth and legend. . . . Readers looking for an intense and old-fashioned magical world will eagerly anticipate the next step in the journey."

—*Romantic Times BOOKreviews* (4 stars)

The Ill-Made Mute
(Book One in The Bitterbynde Trilogy)

"A rich tapestry woven out of the bright threads of myth and romance, imbued with the magic of *Alice in Wonderland*, Middle-earth, and a thousand ancient fairy tales."

—Susan Krinard

The Lady of Sorrows
(Book Two in The Bitterbynde Trilogy)

"Dart-Thornton has a lyric style, a gorgeous perception of nature, and a fascinating inventive world that interweaves traditional tales and balladry with some stupendously original creativity. An outstanding work!"

—Janny Wurts

The Battle of Evernight
(Book Three in The Bitterbynde Trilogy)

"*The Battle of Evernight* begins to resemble *The Lord of the Rings* on acid, passing through sinister mines and weird forests to a dark realm where I nearly expected Frodo to show up among the wights (though the special effects here are groovier than anything in filmic Tolkien)."

—*Locus*

Also by Cecilia Dart-Thornton

THE BITTERBYNDE TRILOGY

Book 1: The Ill-Made Mute
Book 2: The Lady of the Sorrows
Book 3: The Battle of Evernight

THE CROWTHISTLE CHRONICLES

Book 1: The Iron Tree
Book 2: The Well of Tears
Book 3: Weatherwitch
Book 4: Fallowblade

Weatherwitch

**BOOK THREE
OF THE
CROWTHISTLE
CHRONICLES**

Cecilia
Dart-Thornton

TOR fantasy

A TOM DOHERTY ASSOCIATES BOOK · NEW YORK

WEATHERWITCH: BOOK THREE OF THE CROWTHISTLE CHRONICLES

Copyright © 2006 by Cecilia Dart-Thornton

Edited by Claire Eddy

Map and Crowthistle logo by Elizabeth Alger

A Tor Book
Published by Tom Doherty Associates, LLC
175 Fifth Avenue
New York, NY 10010

www.tor.com

Tor® is a registered trademark of Tom Doherty Associates, LLC.

ISBN-13: 978-0-7653-5056-5
ISBN-10: 0-7653-5056-4

First U.S. Edition: November 2006
First U.S. Mass market Edition: July 2007

Printed in the United States of America

0 9 8 7 6 5 4 3 2 1

Dedicated to Courtney,
for being loving, spontaneous, keen, funny, talented,
and all things amazing

CONTENTS

GLOSSARY

Álainna Machnamh:	(AWE-lanna Mac-NAV)
a stór:	darling (a STOR)
Ádh:	luck, fortune (AWE)
Aonarán:	loner, recluse (AY-an-ar-AWN)
áthair:	father (AH-hir)
brí:	the power possessed by weathermasters, enabling them to predict and control the dynamics of pressure systems and temperature, winds and other meteorological phenomena
Cailleach Bheur:	(pronounced cal'yach vare or cail'yach vyure) The Winter Hag
carlin:	wise woman
Cinniúint:	destiny, fate, chance (kin-YOO-int)
Cuiva:	(pronounced KWEE-va) in the Irish language this name is spelled 'Caoimhe'
Earnán:	(AIR-nawn)
eldritch:	supernatural
Eoin:	(OWE-in)
Fedlamid:	(FEH-limy)
Fionnbar:	(FIN-bar or FYUN-bar)
Fionnuala:	(Fin-NOO-la)
A gariníon:	granddaughter (a gar-in-EE-an)
A garmhac:	grandson (a gar-VOC)
Gearóid:	(GA-roid)
Genan of Áth Midbine:	(AWE mid-BINNA)
gramarye:	magic

gramercie: an expression of thanks

Lannóir: (lann-OR) Goldenblade; the golden sword, the only one of its kind, slayer of goblins and heirloom of the House of Stormbringer

Liadán: (LEE-dawn)

Luchóg: (la-HOGE)

Mairead: (maw-RAID)

Maolmórdha: (mwale-MORGA)

máthair: mother (MAW-hir)

Mí-Ádh: Bad luck, misfortune (mee-AWE)

Míchinniúint: doom, ill-fate (mee-kin-YOO-int)

A muirnín: darling (mwirr-NEEN)

Ó Maoldúin: (oh mwale-DOON)

Páid: (PAWD)

Risteárd Mac
   Brádaigh: (reesh-TARD Mac BRAW-dig)

Saibh: (SAY-EVE)

A seanmáthair: grandmother (SHAN-waw-hir)

seelie: benevolent to humankind

To *sain:* is to bless, or call for protection from unseelie forces

Uabhar: (OO-a-var)

Uile: is pronounced "ille," with the "e" as in "best"

unseelie: malevolent to humankind

SOME SIGNIFICANT CHARACTERS

THE KINGDOM OF ASHQALÊTH (Capital city: Jhallavad)
Chohrab Shechem: King of Ashqalêth.
Duke Rahim: King Chohrab's brother-in-law, brother of Parvaneh.
Parvaneh Shechem: Queen of Ashqalêth.
Pouri: the youngest of King Chohrab's six daughters.
Shahzadeh: King Chohrab's eldest daughter, the Princess Royal of Ashqalêth.

THE KINGDOM OF GRÏMNØRSLAND (Capital city: Trøndelheim)
Gunnlaug Torkilsalven: youngest son of Thorgild.
Halfrida Torkilsalven: Queen of Grïmnørsland.
Halvdan Torkilsalven: second son of Thorgild.
Hrosskel Torkilsalven: eldest son of Thorgild, and Crown Prince of Grïmnørsland.
Solveig Torkilsalven: third child and only daughter of Thorgild.
Thorgild Torkilsalven: King of Grïmnørsland.

THE DISTRICT OF HIGH DARIONETH (Principal seat: Rowan Green)
Aglaval Maelstronnar (Stormbringer): Storm Lord in days of yore.
Albiona: Dristan Maelstronnar's wife.
Aleyn Cilsundror (Sky-Cleaver): bard of Rowan Green.
Alfardëne Maelstronnar (Stormbringer): the swordsmith who fashioned Fallowblade.
Arran Maelstronnar (Stormbringer): eldest son of Avalloc.

Asrăthiel Heronswood Maelstronnar: only daughter of Jewel and Arran.

Avalloc Maelstronnar (Stormbringer): the current Storm Lord and member of Council of Ellenhall.

Avolundar Maelstronnar (Stormbringer): the warrior mage who wielded Fallowblade during the goblin wars.

Baldulf Ymberbaillé (Rainbearer): "second-in-command" to Avalloc and member of Council of Ellenhall.

Bliant Ymberbaillé (Rainbearer): son of Baldulf.

Blostma: Herebeorht Miller's wife.

Branor: a spy for King Uabhar.

Cacamwri Dommalleo (Thunder-Hammer): weathermage and member of Council of Ellenhall.

Calogrenant Lumenspar (Light-Spear): the Ambassador for High Darioneth in Cathair Rua.

Cavalon: son of Dristan and Albiona Maelstronnar.

Corisande: daughter of Dristan and Albiona Maelstronnar.

Desmond Brooks: swordmaster at High Darioneth.

Dristan Maelstronnar (Stormbringer): youngest son of Avalloc.

Elfgifu Miller: a daughter of the miller.

Engres Aventaur (Flute Wind): weathermaster.

Ettare Sibilaurë (Whistles-For-The-Wind): a weathermage and member of Council of Ellenhall.

Faramond: The eldest son of Herebeorht and Blostma Miller.

Galiene Maelstronnar (Stormbringer): a daughter of Avalloc and member of Council of Ellenhall.

Gauvain Cilsundror (Sky-Cleaver): a weathermaster.

Gvenour Nithulambar (Walks-In-Mist): weathermage and member of Council of Ellenhall.

Herebeorht Miller: Osweald's eldest son.

Hilde Miller: a younger daughter of the miller.

Jewel Heronswóod Jaravhor: wife of Arran and mother of Asrăthiel.

Lidoine Galenrithar (Gale-Rider): carlin at Rowan Green.

Lysanor Maelstronnar (Stormbringer): a daughter of Avalloc and member of Council of Ellenhall.

Mildthrythe Miller: the mill-wife.

Nyneve Longiníme (Long Cloud): a weathermage and member of Council of Ellenhall.

Osweald Miller: the gentleman miller.

Tristian Solorien (Rising Sun): a weathermage and member of Council of Ellenhall.

THE KINGDOM OF NARNGALIS (Capital city: King's Winterbourne.)

Giles: Asrăthiel's butler at The Laurels in Lime Grove.

Hallingbury: The Lord Chamberlain.

Lecelina: eldest daughter of King Warwick, the Princess Royal of Narngalis.

Linnet: Asrăthiel's maid at The Laurels.

Mrs. Draycott Parslow: Asrăthiel's landlady, the owner of The Laurels in Lime Grove.

Saranna: youngest daughter of King Warwick.

Sir Gilead Torrington: King Warwick's lieutenant-general.

Sir Torold Tetbury: The Lord Privy Seal.

Walter Wyverstone: second son of King Warwick.

Warwick Wyverstone: king of Narngalis.

William Wyverstone: eldest son of King Warwick, and Crown Prince of Narngalis.

Winona: second daughter of King Warwick.

THE KINGDOM OF SLIEVMORDHU (Capital city: Cathair Rua)

Adiuvo Constanto Clementer: a druid who renounced the Sanctorum.

Almus Agnellus, "Declan of the Wildwoods": a druid who renounced the Sanctorum.

Conall 'Two Swords' Gearnach: Commander-in-Chief of the Knights of the Brand.

Cormac Ó Maoldúin: third son of Uabhar.

Fedlamid macDall: Queen Saibh's most trusted servant.

Fergus Ó Maoldúin: fourth son of Uabhar.

Fionnbar Aonarán: an enemy of Arran Maelstronnar.

Fionnuala Aonarán: Fionnbar's sister.

Gearóid: a younger brother of Uabhar.

Grak: a Marauder.

Kieran Ó Maoldúin: eldest son of Uabhar, and Crown Prince of Slievmordhu.

Krorb: a Marauder captain.

Lord Genan of Áth Midbine: a courtier.

Luchóg, a minstrel at Uabhar's court.

Mairead: a child who served at the Red Lodge.

Maolmórdha Ó Maoldúin: a king of Slievmordhu, the father of Uabhar.

Páid: a brother of Uabhar, next in line after Gearóid.

Primoris Asper Virosus: The Druid Imperius.

Risteárd Mac Brádaigh: High Commander of the Slievmordhuan armed forces.

Ronin Ó Maoldúin: second son of Uabhar.

Ruurt: a Marauder captain.

Saibh: Queen of Slievmordhu, wife to Uabhar.

Scroop: a Marauder.

The Spawn Mother: a progenitrix of the Marauders.

Tertius Acerbus: a druid.

Uabhar Ó Maoldúin: King of Slievmordhu.

Urlámhaí Ó Maoldúin: Urlámhaí the Gracious, an ancient king.

CROWTHISTLE

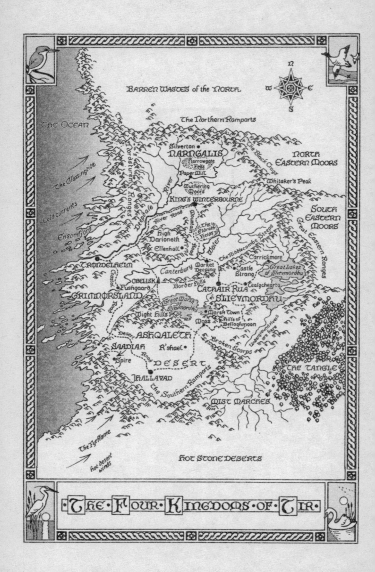

The Four Kingdoms of Tir

THE STORY SO FAR

Weatherwitch is the third book in the Crowthistle Chronicles.

Book 1: *The Iron Tree,* told of Jarred, a young man who possessed an amulet that apparently made him invulnerable. He and his comrades visited a town built among the intricate waterways of the Great Marsh of Slievmordhu, where Jarred fell in love with a marsh-daughter named Lilith.

Slievmordhu is a kingdom situated in the southeast of Tir, a continent throughout which grows a disliked but beautiful common weed called "crowthistle." Eldritch wights dwell in the marsh but seldom harm the marsh-folk, who understand them and their ways. An urisk, a seelie wight like a dwarfish man with the legs of a goat, often loitered near Lilith's cottage.

Jarred and Lilith discovered that the long-gone Sorcerer of Strang had cursed Lilith's bloodline; if she married, eventually she would fall prey to madness. When they learned, however, that marriage to Jarred—a descendant of the sorcerer, and therefore immune to most forms of harm, even without the amulet—might be a way of thwarting the curse, they were wed. Their joy was complete. They named their only daughter "Jewel," in honor of the extraordinary white jewel of Strang that had come into Jarred's possession.

The King of Slievmordhu was seeking to entrap the sorcerer's descendant in order to make him open the sealed Dome of Strang and reveal its arcane treasures. Brother and sister Fionnbar and Fionnuala Aonarán helped Jarred to escape from the king's men, on the proviso that Jarred would later leave his family and go with the Aonaráns to unlock the secrets of the Dome.

Shortly thereafter the madness caught up with Lilith despite all, and in trying fruitlessly to save her life, Jarred lost his own. Their orphaned child Jewel—who had inherited virtual invulnerability from her father—escaped from the marsh, eluding the royal cavalry.

❧

Book 2: *The Well of Tears,* told how Jewel was raised at High Darioneth, the home of the Weathermasters of Rowan Green. Ellenhall was the name of the great building in which the weathermasters held their councils. The weathermasters' leader was the Storm Lord, Avalloc Maelstronnar-Stormbringer, whose eldest son was Arran. Over the mantelpiece at the Stormbringer house hung the famous sword, Fallowblade, long ago forged to defeat unseelie goblin hordes.

High Darioneth was teeming with brownies and other eldritch wights; Jewel met an urisk and realized that it was the same one that used to belong to her mother's household at the Marsh. The urisk had followed her; yet it was most uncouth and unresponsive when she tried to draw it into conversation, and never appeared for long.

At the age of seventeen Jewel decided to journey to Strang and see if she could unlock the secrets of the sorcerer's mysterious Dome. Without her knowledge, Arran followed her, as her protector. He caught up with her inside the Dome. Together, Arran and Jewel lit upon a book that told of certain Wells, each of which held a few drops of the Water of Eternal Life.

After a long journey they found the Well of Rain, but at the last moment Fionnbar Aonarán appeared, seized the Water of Life, and drank it. His accomplice Cathal Weaponmonger ascended the Tower and destroyed the dry Well, but fell to his death. Enraged by the loss of Weaponmonger, with whom she was in love, Fionnuala blamed Arran and tried unsuccessfully to shoot him with her crossbow.

Later, just as Arran found the Well of Dew, Fionnuala and her henchmen attacked him. They were about to slay him and make off with the Water of Life. In his extremity Arran had no option but to swallow the Draught himself. When he finally returned home he and Jewel, who had fallen in love, were wed.

Jewel and Arran had a baby daughter. They named her Astăriel, and the impet Fridayweed informed them she had inherited immortality from her father. Arran and Fridayweed went to seek the last well, the Well of Tears. After many difficulties they discovered it, but alas! ancient upheavals had destroyed it. The well was empty and dry.

Visualizing a future in which he lived eternally without Jewel at his side, Arran was gripped by rage. He swore vengeance on Fionnbar and Fionnbar's half-sister Fionnuala. After embarking on a hunting trip he trapped Fionnbar in a cave in the far northeastern mountains of Slievmordhu, telling his prisoner that he must dwell there forever, immortal, suffering loneliness and exile.

Fionnuala Aonarán hated Arran. She knew she could no longer harm the weathermaster, so decided to do harm to the one he loved best. Having learned the secret of Jewel's bane, she wounded her. Jewel, however, was the mother of an immortal child; therefore she did not die, but instead fell into a deep and lasting sleep that resembled death. The beauteous sleeper was placed on a silken couch on the glass cupola atop the Stormbringer house. Wild roses entwined their stems about the cupola, framing the eight panes with leaves and their five-petaled rosettes.

Declaring he would scour the unknown lands until he discovered a way to waken his bride, Arran abandoned his child, his home and his inheritance, including the golden sword Fallowblade, leaving them all with his father, Avalloc.

By then, Jewel's young daughter Astăriel had encountered the very same urisk that used to be attached to her grandmother's cottage in the Marsh. Towards the end of *The Well of Tears* the girl and the wight sat companionably together in a high place, looking out at the distant lands.

The story closed with these words:

The child . . . had lately come from the glass chamber where her mother lay like a porcelain doll among the flowers, and thoughts of the loss of both her parents had cast her into a doleful, yearning mood. A broken line of birds passed swiftly and noiselessly overhead, the last swallows migrating south . . . Yet Astăriel's father had set out in the opposite direction, and as she gazed northwards, a terrible wistfulness seized her heart. She longed to take wing, to fly from her perch out across the vaporous lands to the northern mountains and beyond.

"Your sorrowfulness is irksome," commented the urisk.

She replied, "If you do not like it, you need not stay."

"Be of good cheer."

"I will not."

They reverted to silence and sat beneath the pink-streaked sky, watching the sun melt in a glorious pyre behind the mountains. Soon it would give way to the solemn majesty of the stars.

"If you choose melancholy," said the urisk, "then, the more fool you."

She said, "It is easy for you to say those words, ignorant immortal creature. You cannot know what it is to forever lose someone you love."

The wight, a being that was unable to lie, who had existed for many lives of men and accumulated more knowledge in those lifetimes than could ever be measured, said pityingly, "It is you, not I, who is ignorant. You fail to understand. Loss may be reversed. Even death is not the story's end."

Weatherwitch

PROLOGUE

In the darkness deep beneath the icy mountains of the north,
something alive was delving, as it had been delving for
years; digging through caverns and tunnels, scraping and
scrabbling at small openings, making them large enough to
push through so that it could continue on its journey. Its
hands were torn from constant clawing at jagged rock. They
had bled many times and half-healed, only to be wounded
over and over. Repeatedly thwarted and aborted, the mending of the tissue had begun to go awry. The fingers, hard and
blackened, now resembled talons.

To make its progress easier, the thing that dug sometimes
made use of the traffic-ways of mining wights and other
dwellers in the cold deeps: subterranean roads, ramps,
bridges and stairs both ancient and new, by which those
small immortal creatures traveled through the hollows of the
underground. Yet the wights themselves were shy of this
burrower, and seldom allowed themselves to be glimpsed.
Generally they tolerated no commerce with foreigners, and
if an accidental encounter occurred they swiftly hurried on
their way. They were busy enough with their own tasks. The
rumor of their industry echoed through shadowy labyrinths
of stone; hammerings, scrapings, bangings, the clatter of a
bucket drawn up by a windlass, a babble of outlandish jabbering and jarring, shrill laughter. It would appear to any onlooker as if the eldritch wights were hard at work.

With the hubbub of mining echoing behind and ahead, the
burrower approached a cavern in which three *knockers* were

assiduously occupied. Members of this species of mining wight were truly dedicated laborers. Gap-toothed and straggle-bearded, the dwarfish ore-getters customarily clad themselves in moleskin trousers held up by braces strapped over their shirts. Some wore red and white spotted kerchiefs tied akimbo on their heads, lending them a piratical air. Large feet were thrust into capacious boots. Their torsos were strong and nuggetty, their limbs as wiry as the roots that grasped the loam and stones far above their heads. Ragged fringes of hair bristled from beneath their conical caps; tousled, shaggy locks, roughly chopped as if shorn haphazardly with knives. Ceaseless was their toil, yet they did not labor under some ancient curse, nor did they need to earn a livelihood, for they were not subject to death. Mining was what they did; it was their eternal obsession, and they were as incapable of abstaining from it as ordinary human beings were incapable of living without sustenance.

The knockers had the faces of hearty old diggers, and their shirtsleeves were rolled up to their elbows. One was hacking at a rock-face with his pickax, another was shoveling mineral fragments into a bucket, and a third was sharpening his tools. Before the black-handed burrower passed by, the wary trio had, not unexpectedly, disappeared.

Sometimes, from dim underworld lakes and rivers, naked female forms of waiflike delicacy would arise; lovely, despite their unhumanness—the chins perhaps a little too narrow, the jawbones a fraction too delicate and piscean, the bone structure of the lower half of the face conceivably thrust a little too far forward, as if about to extend further and metamorphose into a muzzle . . . yet lovely, somehow; graceful as reeds, with long, swaying backs and plenteous, shining hair that draped, dripping, down over their marble-white shoulders and arms into the flood. Unspeaking in the gloom, these wild water-wights would stare at the passing burrower with large and luminous eyes before sinking down once more into their habitat.

While the water-girls gazed and the knockers delved, many other kinds of wights lingered down there in the eternal darkness. The creatures known as "the Fridean" were so elusive as to be almost indescribable. A grinning leer from a crevice in the rocks, the sudden wink of a knowing eye deep in the shadows, a knobbly-fingered hand reaching around a stone—that was about all that could ever be seen of them, but it was said they snatched crumbs dropped by picnickers on the sunlit upper surface, and at times their eerie bagpipe music drifted up to the ears of the burrower from beneath the floors, or wafted in spine-chilling wails from far-off halls and cavities.

Haunted were the northern mountains, and honey-combed with the workings and dwelling places of eldritch incarnations.

Yet, amongst the activity of strange diminutive beings, the black-handed burrower moved differently. Here was an entity that worked almost as ceaselessly as the little tin-miners, but in solitude. Always alone, for it was not of their kind. It was much larger than the wights, and could not fit its frame through all their doorways and gates. Sometimes its progress was swift, but often it went slowly, meandering in three dimensions; upwards, downwards, sideways. No matter what obstacles it encountered, it never gave up. It was forever moving, except when it slept; yet its slumber was never long. It moved relentlessly, as if mechanical. It was, however, no engine of steel, but a man.

More accurately, it had once been a man. . . .

I

Comrades and Foes

The world, a sphere of metal and rock scarfed in water, turned.

Above the churning vapors of the troposphere, stars appeared to glide across the heavens from east to west; from High Darioneth, across the Snowy River to the western shores of Tir. There, in Grïmnørsland, a hunting lodge perched on a stark crag, looking out over the ocean. Surf pounded the cliffs and a blood-biting wind howled in from the sea, smacking of brine. Around this building the landscape ramped into the stormy distance; gaunt and wild, rugged, roaring with cataracts, roofed by racing clouds in full sail, battered by salt winds, lapped by mists. This was a realm of black rock, grey sky, and silver water, where dark green conifers, rank on rank, stalked up mountainsides to pierce steaming skies.

The hunting lodge belonged to the King of Grïmnørsland, Thorgild Torkilsalven. From here, on the twenty-first of Mai, five princes set out: Halvdan and Gunnlaug, the second- and third-born sons of Thorgild; Kieran and Ronin Ó Maoldúin, the eldest sons of Uabhar of Slievmordhu, and Walter Wyverstone, younger brother to Crown Prince William of Narngalis. Thorgild had invited the royal scions of his neighboring kingdoms to be his guests in Grïmnørsland, where they might participate in games and divertissements, celebrating the season and reconfirming the bonds of solidarity between the realms. The monarch himself remained with his queen, their eldest son Hrosskel and their daughter Solveig at Trøndelheim, attending to matters of state, while the rest diverted themselves with blood-sports.

Low in the sky rode the evening sun, drifting on a band of persimmon cloud. The five princes, accompanied by their retainers, moved on foot through harsh terrain, clambering up the sides of dim vales and following narrow tracks through forests of spruce, pine, birch, and larch that soared out of shadow. The topmost tapered tips caught the last bright gleams of sunlight so that they glistened like miniature trees dusted with gold. Against the glimmer of sunset the black silhouettes of wind-gnarled branches wove elegant patterns. Falcons with outstretched wings hovered over sharp-toothed crags; Steinfjell, Isfjell and Galdhøpiggen, Sterkfjell and Skagastolstindane; heights with towering, majestic names.

"It is a fact," Prince Gunnlaug Torkilsalven was instructing Walter of Narngalis, "that some archers conceal themselves in thickets to ambush whitetail deer, or crouch behind woven blinds near lakes and streams to waylay roe deer as they come down to drink. The second approach is never successful after rain. Game will not visit watering places when there are small puddles to drink from. Therefore, the truly versatile huntsman must perfect the art of stalking on foot."

Walter nodded brusquely, his lips compressed in a thin

line. He found it insulting to be lectured on a topic he understood well, but was too courteous to protest.

"Hounds would have been useful, of course," continued Gunnlaug, "yet a man must learn to hunt without hounds, in case he ever finds himself alone in the wilderness."

Gunnlaug of Grïmnørsland was a brawny youth, somewhat shorter in stature than his elder brother Halvdan, who walked ahead. His features were coarse, his pockmarked skin reddened and roughened by much exposure to wind and sun. Like his sibling he was flaxen-haired and hazel-eyed. As he and the other huntsmen made their way in single file along a precipitous goat track he was sweating copiously, and to Walter's joy, after some time he began to lag behind.

"There's a big-antlered beauty up there in Hoyfjell's crags, thinking he's too clever for me," Gunnlaug called out, wheezing slightly. "But I shall nail him. He shall be no match for Gunnlaug Torkilsalven. I'll put him down for good and get a fine trophy this evening."

"Make speed, Gunnlaug," his brother Halvdan called back over his shoulder.

"There is no need to scuttle forward like a frightened pig," panted Gunnlaug. "We have plenty of time. The sun is yet a thumb's breadth from the horizon."

"If you had not swallowed so much beer last night you might find it easier to keep up," said Halvdan, but he said it in an undertone. His younger brother was easily provoked to wrath, and his inevitable outburst of rage would spoil the atmosphere of comradeship. Gunnlaug, perhaps guessing Halvdan's thoughts, turned his head and spat upon the ground in a gesture that might have been either a cleansing of the palate or contempt. He flicked sweat-drenched strands of blond hair from his eyes.

The huntsmen leapt from rock to rock and scrambled down scree slopes.

"We have timed our excursion well," said Conall Gearnach, mentor to the princes of Slievmordhu. "If we keep the sun behind us we can use the low light to our advantage. It will dazzle the eyes of our prey." Gearnach, a doughty warrior who had weathered about forty Winters, was commander-in-chief of Slievmordhu's crack corps, the Knights of the Brand. Having earned himself a formidable reputation as a fighting man, he had risen to the position of one of King Uabhar's most highly respected knights. His nickname was "Two-Swords Gearnach," for he was as well able to use his left hand as his right, and he had taught himself to wield two blades simultaneously, making him an opponent to be reckoned with.

Although Conall Gearnach was liegeman to the King of Slievmordhu, and performed the duties of guide and counselor to his sons, he was well acquainted with the princes of Grïmnørsland also. King Uabhar's eldest son Kieran had spent two years of his boyhood dwelling in the household of King Thorgild. The young prince had been under the auspices of Gearnach, who in those days held the second highest office of the Knights of the Brand: that of captain-general. During that period Kieran had formed a fast friendship with Halvdan, second son of Thorgild. By chance, the two had been born on the same day, and they were like-minded in a great many ways: both enjoyed shooting at targets, and wrestling, and balladeering, and fishing in the deep fjords of the west coast. Both were young men of fearless honesty, who loved duty and honor as much as they loved good fellowship. Kieran Ó Maoldúin, a youth of considerable height, possessed a mane of dark brown hair that flowed down upon powerful shoulders. In looks he took after his mother; his nose was straight and thin, and his oval countenance sharp-lined with the clean contours of late adolescence. Tall and blond was Halvdan Torkilsalven, with a muscular torso; a physical match for Kieran. When the two wrestled, the outcome could never be predicted.

"Continue to keep watch for unseelie wights," Gearnach reminded the equipment-laden retainers as the party crossed the vacillating suspension bridge over the gorge of the great river Fiskflød. Far below, the torrent was gushing rapidly; droplets sprayed up like fans of threaded sequins as the water smashed against rocks in midstream and swirled around snags, gurgling and rumbling. Clinging onto the hand-ropes to keep their balance, the huntsmen eventually reached the

other side of the chasm. There, on the grassy flank of an out-
flung spur of Hoyfjell, grew the stands of ancient spruce
trees for which they had set their course. For a few moments
the party halted beneath the needlelike foliage and swigged
a draught from their water-bottles. The bearers and equerries
handed to three of the huntsmen their arrow-packed quivers
and tautly strung hunting-bows. Princes Halvdan and Kieran
had carried their own gear, as had Gearnach.

Having outfitted themselves, the party moved quietly in
amongst the rough-barked boles. They were wearing close-
fitting garments dyed with greens and browns, to blend in with
their surroundings. Soft-soled boots shod their feet, and they
sought to avoid stepping on twigs or dry leaves, looking for
mats of fallen spruce-needles, or short turf on which to walk.
A steady breeze rustled the fragrant foliage, creating a continuous whisper of silvery sound against which the hunters' slight
noise of passage might pass unmarked. Branches dipped and
swished as a couple of squirrels scampered by.

As they neared the high clearings where wild deer grazed,
the huntsmen continually monitored the direction of the air
currents, that they might approach the animals from downwind. "The evening breeze generally blows downhill," Conall
Gearnach murmured to Prince Ronin of Slievmordhu, who
clambered close behind him. "We are still climbing. All is
well, so far."

Ronin—second in line to the throne of Slievmordhu—
was of middle height, and, like his father, had a somewhat
square face. His nose was wide, with flared nostrils, and jutted above a downy upper lip. "I wish I were not downwind
of Gunnlaug," he commented with a wry grimace. "He
stinks of stale sweat and beer."

Gearnach chuckled quietly. As they climbed the spur,
with the wind in their faces and the sun peering over their
left shoulders, the knight hitched his baldric to a more secure position on his shoulder. He put on an extra burst of
speed and pulled ahead of the group. Instinct warned him it
would be wise to scout in advance.

His intuition proved well-founded. From the corner of his

eye he spotted movements that seemed out of place, above them on the slope and to the left. Instantly he extended his hand in a prearranged signal. The gamekeepers and other attendants, always alert to Gearnach's commands, took heed and relayed the message through the party: *Possible danger ahead. Take cover.*

The huntsmen made themselves inconspicuous behind boles and fallen branches, and crouched, watching. If Gearnach had signalled "peril," it was likely that unseelie wights lurked nearby.

From the northwest, a line of stooping figures came loping swiftly and quietly through the woodland. They were moving across the spur, keeping to the south side, just below the crest of the ridge and parallel to it. It was an old huntsman's trick, staying out of sight beneath a ridgetop to avoid being outlined against the horizon. Gearnach counted twenty of them.

Yet, these were not wights.

They were men: gigantic men, slow and strong as oxen; uglier than diseased toadstools. It was also said they were as stupid as cabbages, but never to their faces, for they were utterly without compassion. The recognition startled the watchers. It was not often that Marauders were spied at such great distances from the eastern ranges of Slievmordhu. The Grïmnørslanders amongst the party knew also that on the other side of the spur the land dropped quickly into a valley, where the village of Ødegaard nestled in a bend of the river, and it was toward that isolated hamlet that the Marauders were making. There was no doubt they intended to despoil the village; it was ever their way.

"My heart yearns to pin those freaks with my sword," muttered Gunnlaug. "This will prove a better day's sport than I had hoped."

Gearnach, who had crawled speedily back to join the hunting party, whispered, "My lord Gunnlaug, you and the other princes must not endanger your lives by challenging these creatures. As your fathers' heirs you bear that responsibility to your people."

"Nay, Two-Swords," Halvdan said quickly. "It is there you

are mistaken. Leaders who are not prepared to defend their subjects are unfit to rule them."

"Aye," brothers Kieran and Ronin said together.

"Indeed Halvdan is right," Walter of Narngalis agreed.

For the blink of an eye Gearnach held still, while a thousand concerns whirled through his mind. He was aware that if they were to strike the Marauders they must strike soon, or they would lose the advantage. The five sons of kings under his care were fearless; he had guessed they would refuse to be left out of any action, and as their vassal he was in no position to gainsay them. Making one last attempt to do what he considered to be his duty, he said, "We must let them pass, but send messengers to the village to raise the alarm."

The princes would not hear of it.

"Quit your dawdling, man!" said Gunnlaug, seething. "Let's skewer them."

If the knight was nettled at the prince's insulting tone, he was too disciplined to show it. Besides, his thoughts were occupied with matters at hand. All members of the hunting party were trained fighters. It was part of a princely education to study the martial skills, and the gamekeepers and equerries who accompanied the princes on hunting trips had also been tutored in combat, for they additionally performed the role of bodyguards.

Conall Gearnach rapidly calculated the odds. The hunting party numbered only a dozen, but he reckoned he could personally take on two foes at a time. Furthermore, if the Marauders were allowed to reach the spur's furthest outpost and begin descending into the valley of the Fiskflød he and his companions would gain an extra advantage; not only would they take the brigands by surprise, they would be attacking from higher ground. There would be an opportunity for some archery before they engaged in hand-to-hand combat.

The knight made his decision.

"Follow me," he said. "Keep low and be silent. When I give the signal, move quickly to the attack. Loose your arrows. Keep shooting until they either scatter and flee, or rush us. If they advance, draw your blades for close work."

The huntsmen crept up the slope in the wake of the Marauders. Soon the brigands reached the eastern end of the spur, where it began to fall away into the dale. They commenced their descent. At their backs, the huntsmen quietly congregated along the very spine of the ridge, looking down upon their foes. Trees were sparser on this northern incline. Spruce gave way to ivy-carpeted birch-woods, their delicate boughs in early bud. In the wooded valley at the foot of the spur, mist was rising from the broad and winding river. Through the trees on the far shore, the slate roof of a tiny cluster of houses could be glimpsed. Tendrils of smoke trailed from their chimneys. Sunlight snagged like filaments of glitter on the topmost crags of the mountains that rose behind the village. The huntsmen drew arrows from quivers, nocked them to the bowstrings, and stealthily moved forward. Calculating his moment, Gearnach sketched a quick downward stroke through the air, and the skirmish ensued.

Prince Gunnlaug's arrow was first to spring from the bow; he had not waited for Gearnach's downstroke but had let fly as soon as the knight raised his hand. The shafts of his companions were not far behind, and three huge Marauders lay writhing, mortally wounded by the time the remainder realized they were under attack. During the ensuing moments another four suffered injury and fell screaming to the ground. Some of the brigands dashed for cover while others ran up the incline towards their assailants, who continued to loose their arrows. The Marauders were drawing knives from their scabbards as they charged.

"These two are mine!" Roaring at the top of his voice Gearnach sprang forward to meet the leaders, both his swords at the ready. Faced with the unexpected sight of the twin blades whirling and flashing like the spokes of interlocking wheels of light, the Marauders momentarily balked. In their instant of hesitation Gearnach was upon them. As he fought, more Marauders bounded up the hill to join the fray, one by one, like nightmarish giants. Their group was scattered, with some sheltering from the barrage behind trees, while those who had been furthest down the hill were still scrambling back up to join their fellows. This meant that those who arrived first were outnumbered. The huntsmen cut them down; then, leaving Gearnach to dispatch his opponents, they plunged down the slope to engage the balance of their enemies. Having ascertained that he himself would be in no great danger, Prince Gunnlaug leaped down at the heels of his companions, yelling and brandishing his sword. On reaching the wounded swarmsmen he hacked them to death where they lay.

Conall Gearnach, wiping the blood of his defeated opponents from his eyes, raced down the hill to join his charges. As he ran he tried to scan the scene. Trees blocked his view, but he calculated that twelve of their foes lay dead. Suddenly he flung himself to one side, somersaulted and nimbly rolled back onto his feet. Two Marauders had jumped out at him from behind the trunk of a forest giant. Having barely evaded their first assault Gearnach set to, defending himself, his swords arcing and slicing, no longer bright but dark with gore. Yet he remained partly blinded by blood and sweat, while his assailants, who had been in hiding, were clear-sighted and vigorous. The knight found himself hard-pressed. Only capable of peering from one bleary eye, he was forced to give ground. Focusing all his attention on the struggle, he could not spare the breath to shout for help, but he was aware that unless he received aid, he would soon be cut down. Having parried the swarmsmen's blades, he simultaneously locked swords with them both. With his single sighted eye he saw a knife being driven towards his heart. In that flash it was clear that by the time he had unlocked his own weapons it would be too late to deflect the blow. Driven by desperation, the knight dropped one of his swords, intending to make a last-ditch attempt to ward off the lethal stroke with his bare arm; but there was no time. Gearnach knew he was about to die.

As he steeled himself to be riven by the final wound another blade entered his field of vision. Halvdan was there, thwacking the knife aside with the flat of his sword and sending it spinning. Gearnach swept his remaining weapon in an upward arc, slitting open the belly of his nearest oppressor. Having finished off one opponent he turned to the other, but the fellow, perceiving that reinforcements had turned the tide, had already taken to his heels.

"Thirteen down!" bellowed Gearnach. "Seven to go!"

He passed his sleeve across his eyes to wipe them clear, and when he looked again Halvdan was gone; but there was plenty of action further down the slope in the twilight, so he took himself amongst it.

Soon the fight was over. By the time the last brigand had been slain or driven off, young Ronin of Slievmordhu, white-faced, was seated on the ground with his elbows on his knees and his head in his hands. Around him the slender birch-trunks glimmered palely in the gloaming. Evening moths flittered on the edges of vision, like half-forgotten thoughts. Gunnlaug stood with feet braced apart, shooting arrows at any movement amongst the trees, no matter that it was only the wind, while the equerries, bearers and other attendants collected fallen arrow-shafts and counted the corpses of sixteen Marauders.

"No stomach for blood, eh?" Gunnlaug said to Ronin, guffawing.

"Four have got away," growled Gearnach, wiping his sword-blades on the grass. "But they'll not forget this encounter."

"They shall think twice before they venture onto Grïmnørsland soil again!" yelled Gunnlaug, wasting more arrows.

"What are our casualties?" Conall Gearnach asked one of the gamekeepers.

"Five wounded, one slain, sir. Prince Halvdan's page lies dead. Their royal highnesses are unhurt."

"Tend to the wounded." The knight slid his weapons into their scabbards, one to each side of his body.

"This is a great pity," said Walter of Narngalis. "Garth Carter was a fine lad. His mother will grieve." The prince's voice sounded hoarse; he was indeed deeply moved by the death of the youth. Swiftly he crouched beside one of the injured men, who had been groaning in pain, and began to give him water from a flask.

Kieran of Slievmordhu was leaning on his sword, breathing heavily. "Where is Halvdan?" he asked.

The huntsmen looked about. King Thorgild's second son was nowhere in sight. It came to Gearnach like a stone hitting him in the heart: he had not set eyes on the flaxen-haired prince since the incident in which Halvdan had saved his life.

"I saw him over there, near that fallen tree swathed in moss," Walter said, but there was doubt in his voice. Raising his finger, he pointed.

Almost before the words had left the prince's lips Gearnach had hastened over to the spot, and was kneeling on the greensward. "There are tracks," he said urgently. "Many marks of boots in the soft ground, and long grooves, as if something has been dragged along." Next instant he was off again, leaping over fallen boughs and tussocks, heading in the direction indicated by the grooves. Before his companions fully understood his purpose he had disappeared into the birch-wood.

"He'll need support. I shall go after him," said Kieran, picking up his sword.

"I too," said Walter. He jumped to his feet.

Kieran's equerry made protest to his lord. "Nay, Your Highness, begging your pardon," he said, " 'Twould be folly. We no longer have the advantage of surprise. In those woods ambushers might pick off any man with ease. Your father would not forgive me, were you to be harmed. I am somewhat skilled in healing, which may be of use. I beseech you, let me go in your stead."

The gamekeepers volunteered to join him, but Kieran, his eyes alight, would not be swayed. "I will aid Halvdan!" he cried, quickly tucking a full water-flask into his belt-pouch.

Moving closer to his lord, the equerry murmured rapidly, and in low tones, so that none might overhear, "Sir, I pray, look about you. Your brother's face is milk-white, and I fear he feels somewhat faint. Prince Gunnlaug wishes only to find more heads to break. Prince Walter is concerned for our wounded, and I ween he would thank you, were you to take charge for now, in place of Prince Halvdan. Gearnach and the gamekeepers are woodcrafty. If they cannot discover the son of Thorgild, then no man can."

Reluctantly, Kieran acquiesced. Gunnlaug, who had flung himself down on a carpet of ground-ivy to rest, said, "Two-Swords knows what he is at. I daresay he will rescue my brother and soon return with him. But if you fellows are so keen on this mission, then hie hence." Not to be outdone, to his own equerry he said, "You, Riordan, accompany them."

Unaware that several of his companions were following him, Conall Gearnach careered through the canting woodlands. The light was fading, but he was tracing a conspicuous trail of broken twigs and crumpled vegetation. The sweet fragrance of crushed mint-bush scented the air, and the dainty rich purple petals of royal bluebells flew up from his running feet.

Presently the trees opened out, and he burst into a glade. He slewed to a halt. Before him two lumbering Marauders, as tall as horses, were hauling the limp form of Prince Halvdan between them in a strenuous effort to cross the clearing and reach the shelter of the trees. The moment they spied the avenging knight they let fall their burden, but it was too late. Whipping out his knife, Gearnach fearlessly leapt upon one of the brigands. Locked together, they crashed to the ground, tumbling over and over in a desperate struggle until, with a lightning movement, Gearnach slashed his throat. Confronted by this apparently berserk fiend, the other fellow made off in reckless haste.

"Are you alive?" Gearnach said, dropping to his knees beside the prince.

Halvdan, barely conscious, nodded weakly. He lay spent but living, amongst the prickly spears of alpine crowthistle. Crashing noises issued from the woods behind them, and Gearnach jumped up. He whirled to face whatever new danger threatened, this time drawing his swords. On spying the three retainers who emerged into the clearing he sheathed the blades once more, barking, "Tend to his highness. Do not wait for me. I will meet you at the lodge." He dashed off again in the wake of the fleeing Marauder.

"Bide!" Halvdan weakly called after the knight, but to no avail. Gearnach, moving at speed, was already out of earshot.

"Your Highness!" exclaimed the Head Gamekeeper.

"I am hale," said Halvdan, dismissively waving a hand. His appearance belied his words; he was spattered with ichor and grime, his garments ripped to tatters. "It is Two-Swords for whom you should be concerned. Darkness is nigh, and the woods wallow in shadow. To pursue a lone brigand is not only perilous but also bootless. I would have stopped him, if I could. It is sheer folly."

"Lord, it is our duty to bring you safely back to the hunting lodge," said Gunnlaug's equerry, Riordan. "Come, let us bear you to your comrades."

The retainers half-carried Halvdan back to the scene of the skirmish, where the rest of the hunting party waited. Joyously they greeted the prince, but their delight turned to dismay when they heard of Gearnach's grim and reckless quest.

"Alone at this time of the evening!" exclaimed Walter. "Unseelie wights will soon be out and about."

"In the darkness a man might easily lose his footing," said Ronin of Slievmordhu.

"Let us hope that common sense prevails," his brother Kieran said, "and Gearnach soon abandons this mad mission. Halvdan, my friend, let my equerry bandage your wounds. I cannot tell you how glad I am to see you!"

"There is no need for fuss," said Halvdan, swaying as he stood.

"Lo, this one is still somewhat quick!" cried Gunnlaug. He began to kick one of the dying Marauders in the ribs and skull, until Walter of Narngalis pushed him aside and with one clean blow of his sword severed the ill-proportioned head of the suffering colossus.

"We are not unseelie wights," he said coldly to Gunnlaug. "We do not torment our enemies. It is the duty of honorable men to grant mercy. We owe our fellow men a clean death, at least, be they ever so ill-made."

"It was only sport," the Grïmnørslander retorted sourly. "Let's go hunting the rest of these filth. That was the best amusement I have had since I speared that big boar in the Forest of Svalbard."

"Nay, Gunnlaug. Darkness falls, and they are gone," said Ronin.

"In that case, let us hunt game!"

Walter said, "There are some few injured men here, in addition to Halvdan, and we must bear them to shelter. Besides, with all that shouting, the quarry will be far away."

"Then let us bring our wounded to the village down there in the valley," Gunnlaug said. "We might get us some beer and enjoy some wenching."

Wearily, Halvdan clapped a scored and bloody hand on his brother's shoulder. He shook his head. "Come away, Gunnlaug," he said. "Come away, come back to the lodge. This night's work is done."

Gunnlaug sneered and scowled, reluctantly acquiescing to the decision of the majority.

Prince Kieran's equerry, skilled in healing, bound the bleeding cuts of the injured men. The other attendants fashioned makeshift litters from birch-boughs to carry their dead and wounded.

⁂

The sun had set, leaving a pale orange smear across the roof of the ocean. Lit by the soft radiance of afterglow, the burdened men trudged back to the hunting lodge. The Steward of the Lodge and his staff rushed out to meet the returning party, proffering aid.

Halvdan, who had managed to stay on his feet, his arm across the strong shoulders of Kieran, said, "Send messengers to my father and Hrosskel at Trøndelheim, and to the village of Ødegaard beyond the Fiskfløed. Tell them Marauders roam in these parts."

By the time they reached the threshold there had as yet been no news of Gearnach. He had not returned. White stars blazed over the sky-stabbing crags, and still there came no sign of the avenging knight.

While the rest of the wounded were being doctored, the five princes bathed and put on fresh garments. Afterwards they dined together in a long room warmed by a bright hearth-fire. Lost in their thoughts and their exhaustion, they conversed very little. The only sounds to be heard were the clatter of cutlery, the roar of the blaze in the fireplace and the eerie cries of the wind careering in from the ocean, which plucked at the eaves and rattled the panes. Once, Walter of Narngalis broke the silence.

"I cannot help but wonder why those cave-dwellers traveled so far west."

"'Tis not out of character," replied Kieran of Slievmordhu. "Marauders prefer to prey in regions they have previously left alone, where villagers are unsuspecting and unwary. It is known also that some amongst them are wont to travel and explore, perhaps in search of new lairs."

Following this brief exchange, silence again stole over the fellowship. As they hearkened to the wind's lonely lament their thoughts fled into the darkness beyond the lodge's thick stone walls. Somewhere out there in the distance was a lone knight, perhaps wandering lost, perhaps lying dead. They listened for any hint of Gearnach's return, but all they could hear was the incessant wind, and the scrape of a twig against the roof-shingles, and the sudden sputter of sparks exploding in the grate.

Evening dragged into night. The heads of the royal youths began to nod, and, wearied by their exploits of high adventure the princes took themselves to their couches to rest. Still no tramping footsteps echoed on the steep path leading up to the lodge, signaling the return of a weary knight. Throughout the lightless hours there came no knock at the door, no voice calling out from beneath the windows; only the screech of a passing owl, the disquieting high-pitched laughter of eldritch wights and the sobbing of some mortal sleeper in the lodge, trapped by evil dreams.

Beyond the walls, mighty breakers pounded the cliffs all night, and the wind barreled in over the brine, sharp with salt and ice. When the princes awoke at first light there was yet no word of their missing comrade.

"Get up a search party," Halvdan Torkilsalven commanded his retainers. They hastened to obey, but no hope shone in their countenances.

The faces of Halvdan's companions were also grave. "He was a valiant knight," said Walter of Narngalis.

"The best of warriors," said Ronin.

"Aye," said Gunnlaug. "None shall dispute his worthiness."

"But many shall mourn," said Kieran of Slievmordhu. "Many shall mourn."

&ea;

It was just as the search party was mounted and accoutred and about to depart that Gearnach came back. The knight arrived haggard, bloodstained and weary at the door of the hunting lodge, in the cold, cobalt light of early dawn. Triumphantly he held aloft a gruesome object; the severed head of a Marauder, which he gripped by the roots of the hair.

"I took him!" he proclaimed, his voice rasping with fatigue. "I took him."

He staggered, and fell into the arms of the attendants, who bore him indoors to ply him with wine and water. The princes were avid to hear his tale, and indeed the knight refused to eat a bite until he had recounted the story, with the bloody head propped up before him on the table, its eyes glazed and its jaw horribly askew.

"I pursued him without rest," Gearnach said grimly. "Through thicket and briar, over tor and down dale, though it seemed every unseelie wight in Grïmnørsland was abroad— duergars lurking behind every rock, hobyahs crouching on every bough, drowners beckoning from shadowy streams, fuathan pinning me with their unwinking stares as I ran by. A waterhorse came at me from a black pool deep in some ferny hollow. Once, three maidens in misty robes beseeched me to join their dancing beneath the trees, where human bones, paler than their gowns, lay glimmering. I am too canny to be tricked, but never have the charms I carry stood me in such good stead—my amber talisman, my steel weapons, the four-leafed clover and red verbena stitched into the hem of my shirt, and all the rest. No wicked wight could stop me. All night I hunted him, and at the end I had my way." He downed a swig from his tankard and wiped his mouth with a filthy sleeve. "I would not let him escape," he informed his enthralled audience. "Had I not caught him I would be roaming the wildwoods seeking him yet. A wrong has been righted."

"Why so zealous, Two-Swords?" Gunnlaug asked. "You might have let the cur go, and saved yourself some trouble."

Gearnach turned to the questioner and fixed him with a flinty gaze. "My Lord, he tried to abduct one who was in my charge. No thing, foul or fair, man or un-man, shall do dishonor to me or mine and not suffer for it."

Gunnlaug barked out a short laugh of approval at this vindictive creed.

When the tale had been told, a basin of clear water was fetched. Conall Gearnach laved his bearded face and brawny hands before falling ravenously on a repast of bread and meat. Meanwhile four of the princes went out deer-hunting. Out of respect for Halvdan's deceased footboy, Walter, Kiernan and Ronin had been reluctant to embark on the jaunt, but Gunnlaug was insistent and eventually proved persuasive.

Halvdan remained at the lodge, his arms and ribs bandaged. He watched his brother and companions disappear down the gravel path, the golden glow of morning stretching their shadows long upon the ground. Afterwards he went to the stables to greet his horse and ensure that it was comfortably housed. Many thoughts were disquieting him, and his wounds throbbed painfully.

He was concerned about the intrusion of Marauders so far west, and wondered what had given rise to their enterprise; but more than that, as he ran his mind over the trials he had endured at the hands of the brigands, he mused upon what would have befallen had Conall Gearnach not come to his rescue. His death would have been certain, the length of his suffering open to conjecture. To the knight's sheer stubbornness and impetuous courage he owed all. Two-Swords could be violently impulsive at times, but that trait could actually be an advantage in a warrior. Moreover, the knight was amongst the most chivalrous of men. Indeed, in Halvdan's opinion Gearnach was more honorable by far than the master he faithfully served, King Uabhar of Slievmordhu. Thorgild's son had been privy to certain tales of savagery, and he was not blinded to Uabhar's character by filial loyalty, as his friend Kieran was. The King of Slievmordhu, Halvdan privately judged, was two-faced; dangerously so.

Continuing to ponder these matters, he returned to the warmth of the lodge's main chamber.

Illuminated by radiance brightening through the cracks of the shutters in addition to the flicker of lanterns and firelight, Conall Gearnach was still seated at the table, finishing the last crumbs of breakfast. Halvdan rested troubled eyes upon the man who had rescued him from harm and avenged his abduction. Gearnach's unhesitating altruism had moved him profoundly. As the knight rose from his seat and made to ascend the stairs to his bedchamber, Halvdan addressed him quietly, his voice steady.

"Conall Gearnach, I shall never forget your deeds of this past night," said the prince. "I will be your friend for my life."

The knight hesitated, clearly taken aback. His cheeks reddened. "I pray thee sir, say no more!" he murmured. "There is no need for gratitude. I merely did my duty."

"I saw also how valiantly you fought throughout the entire skirmish," Halvdan continued, his visage graven with earnestness, "and I have not forgotten that from my boyhood days you have upheld fairness and justice without faltering.

When I was a lad I wished to be such a one as you. That, I still hope for. In my judgment there is no man more just and valiant, more honorable and skillful than you. In my childhood you tutored me, and all the lessons you taught me are the ones I now know best, and love best, such as the names of the trees, the most cunning dueling tricks, the way to tame horses without violence, how to find food in the wild forest."

"Nay," Gearnach said, executing an awkward bow. "Nay, lord, you have the wrong man. It cannot be myself you are speaking of." He did not add, *When I was about to die under the Marauder's knife you risked your life to save mine. No man has ever done me such a service—no peasant, let alone a prince.* The warrior did not utter these words but Halvdan read them in the depths of his eyes. He gave a small nod, and an unspoken understanding passed between the two men.

The prince made himself smile at the knight's halfhearted jest. "Pray go now to your rest, Gearnach. I will detain you no longer."

Having bowed a second time, the knight departed.

❧

Whether brought on by recent tribulations, or by the continual thunder of wind-churned waves upon the cliffs and the rattling of shutters and panes, or by the rich sauces served at dinner, that night the slumber of Prince Ronin of Slievmordhu was greatly disturbed by visions of the past.

Some weeks before he had set out for Grïmnørsland, thousands of his countrymen had assembled just outside the city of Cathair Rua, at the command of his father. King Uabhar had been inspired to create a new feast-day in Slievmordhu— the Day of Heroes. As the first of these feast-days had dawned, the cadets, the reserves and the standing army had gathered in the Fair Field, lining up behind the ranks of the famous Knights of the Brand, to renew their oath of allegiance to king and country. The troops were outfitted in dress uniform, the harness worn only for parades; ornate, brightly polished, never dented by battle—indeed, during the last couple of

centuries or so of peace in Tir they had only waged real
conflict against Marauders or unseelie wights. The locks of
the Slievmordhuan soldiers—ranging in tone from light
brown and chestnut to the color of walnuts—streamed from
beneath shining helms. Their gauntlet-clad fists firmly gripped
the poles of their numerous standards, which bristled into
the blue sky like a mass of gigantic bulrushes. From the
tops of these poles long, tapering pennants rippled, as
bright and lively as fishes swimming upstream. The warriors' banners, their cloaks and plumes and their flowing
manes were all fluttering along the course of the wind;
solemn were their faces, yet the spark of patriotic pride
glinted fiercely in their eyes. A kind of hush rested upon
them. The only sounds were the ringing of metal, the clank-
ing of jointed armor plates, the occasional heavy stamp of a
booted foot, and the soughing and snapping of flags in the
breeze. Sunlight glanced from burnished lames and steel
vambraces, flickering like silver sparks as each man shifted
balance slightly, or turned into the wind, never taking his
eyes from the platform whereon his sovereign presided in full
panoply beneath the venerated emblem of the Burning Brand.
The High Commander of the Slievmordhuan armed forces
stood at King Uabhar's left hand, while the Commander-in-
Chief of the Knights waited at his right, ready to speak. The
voice of Conall Gearnach was powerful, and he possessed
the knack of broadcasting his messages over a vast area. In
this, today, he was aided by the direction of the blowing
airs.

The flags having been lowered on every city building,
Gearnach stepped forward, drew breath and launched into
his monologue. Uabhar himself had written the speech for
the knight to memorize word for word, and it was an oration
so awe-inspiring, yet somehow *disturbing*, that it made
Prince Ronin Ó Maoldúin review every precept on many an
unquiet night from that hour. The utterances haunted him
ever after, but he could not really say why.

"Sons of Slievmordhu," Gearnach had cried in stirring
tones, "thousands of you are gathered here upon the Fair

Field of Cathair Rua. On this day, you will together swear an oath of loyalty and obedience to King Uabhar Ó Maoldúin.

"You are swearing your oath on a feast-day that Slievmordhu celebrates for the first time—the Day of Heroes. We lower our flags in remembrance of those who lived as heroes, and died as heroes. We lower our flags in memory of the giants of our past, the countless numbers who fought for Slievmordhu in the Goblin Wars.

"Woe to the country that fails to honor its heroes, for it will cease to bring them forth! A country without heroes is a country without leaders, for only a heroic leader is truly able to withstand the challenge of difficult times. The rise or fall of a realm can be determined by the presence or absence of a great king.

"Slievmordhu demands loyalty from you, not only in deed, but in character. Loyalty in character is a heroic virtue; unbreakable loyalty, a loyalty that knows no weakening. Loyalty in character means absolute obedience that does not question the results of an officer's command, nor its reasons, but rather obeys for the sake of obedience itself. Such obedience is an expression of heroic character when following orders leads to personal disadvantage or even seems to contradict one's personal convictions. King Uabhar Ó Maoldúin must know that when he commands, or allows a command to be given, that every man will obey absolutely, down to the last drummer-boy.

"Sons of Slievmordhu, you have given the same absolute loyalty to our king that Slievmordhu's warriors gave long ago during the Goblin Wars, which demanded their heroic deaths for the good of the kingdom. You have the great fortune to live in a realm that the best soldiers of that era could only dream of—a kingdom that for all eternity will remain strong and united if you do your duty. For you, doing your duty means: Obey the king's orders without question! Thereby you will be the best living memorial to the dead heroes of past wars.

"Be ever aware that you owe thanks to King Uabhar Ó Maoldúin, for his government enables victory and prosperity. Whoever you are, be you high or low, work for his ideals, and therefore for Slievmordhu. The reward for your labors is knowing you have done your duty for all that is right. It is an honor to fight, suffer, risk, bleed and sacrifice for our country's future. You will earn the thanks of all who enjoy the advantages of life in this kingdom.

"Sons of Slievmordhu! You will now take an oath to King Uabhar Ó Maoldúin! You have the joyful privilege of taking an oath to a king who is a paragon amongst rulers, who always acts with honor and dignity, and who always chooses the right path, even when at times some of his advisors fail to understand why.

"You take an oath to a king who follows the laws of providence, upon which he acts independently of the influence of worldly powers. Through your oath you bind yourselves to a king who was sent to us by way of the grace and generosity of the Four Fates who rule our lives. He who takes an oath to King Uabhar takes an oath to great Slievmordhu! Make the vow! I swear upon my life that I will obey my king without question!"

Throughout the Fair Field the troops, rank on rank, repeated the oath, after which trumpets sounded, the flags were raised in the city and Conall Gearnach cried, "We salute the king!"

Dreaming in King Thorgild's hunting lodge, Prince Ronin of Slievmordhu moaned and tossed upon his feather bed, slicked with sweat. His nightmares changed; not for the better.

One afternoon several days after the oath-taking Ronin and his three brothers had been strolling with their mother beneath the sun-flecked elms in the palace gardens. Presently their lauded father had joined them, shadowed at a judicious distance by his usual entourage.

The king of Slievmordhu, a man of middle height with powerful, sloping shoulders, had thrived throughout forty-one Winters. His face was square, the jaw flabby and beginning to sag. The broad, mottled forehead was molded by salient brows. His wide nose and flaring nostrils jutted above a mustachioed upper lip. Firm and rounded was his chin, his cheeks somewhat puffy. He was in a jovial mood, and anxious to announce the reason for it, so that his progeny might understand his achievements to an extent over and above the considerable degree to which he had astounded them in the past. Of his wife he took little heed.

"Lord Dubthach MacRoigh is no longer a thorn in our side," Uabhar proclaimed, grinning broadly, "and never more will be."

Queen Saibh stifled the look of horror she had spontaneously directed at her husband. Her fragile grip tightened on the arm of her eldest son, and her step faltered, but she spoke no word. The party came to a halt beneath a leafy bough as the youngest prince, Fergus, exclaimed, "Well, is it done, then, Father?"

"It is indeed, my son," Uabhar affirmed, scratching his nose with an air of smugness. "The wretch admitted to treason not an hour since, under the diligent questioning of my inquisitors—just in time, fortunately, for shortly thereafter he passed from this life." Gleefully he rubbed the back of his neck. "Which saved the cost of an execution," he added. "Once again, justice prevails!"

"And MacRoigh being guilty of treason, his considerable estate is forfeit to the crown," said young Fergus, not without delight.

"His lands and all his possessions," Uabhar said, shrugging, "according to law."

"Such a windfall will certainly swell the royal coffers," Prince Kieran commented, "for which we must be grateful. However 'tis a pity it happens at the expense of a man's life. Until the last twelvemonth, MacRoigh's reputation was impeccable. Who could have foreseen such an unaccountable alteration?"

"If not for Father's excellent spies, the man's plotting would never have been uncovered," said Prince Cormac.

"Indeed, loyal lad," the king said approvingly. "I am not suspicious by nature, as everyone knows, for I myself am as honest and forthright as the day is long; yet I yield to the counsel of those who are more distrustful than I, and sadly my beagles sniff out rotten meat occasionally."

Ronin said quietly, "Like you, Father, there are many who would prefer to believe no ill of their fellow men. The weathermaster Ryence Darglistel, who testified in favor of MacRoigh's character, seemed always to hold that the charges of conspiracy were trumped up."

"Trumped up by whom, I'd like to know?" his father said. "Who would do such a thing? But that is typical of the way the weather-meddlers ride roughshod over us these days, endeavoring to seize the reins of our own kingdom and thwart us at every turn. By the Axe of Doom, they hold a much-inflated opinion of themselves. Their heads have swelled as huge as their hot air balloons, and need a good pricking."

Ronin had been taken aback by the vehemence of his father's denouncement of the widely revered storm-mages. He felt a twinge of uneasiness—which vanished as abruptly as it had appeared, for all his life he had been taught to invest great faith in his father's judgment, and supposed he must be right.

"It is of no consequence in any case," the king went on, "for all doubt on MacRoigh's account is now swept aside. Full confession has been heard from the man's own mouth. Although," he added, stealing a sidelong glance at his wife, "he was somewhat toothless and my inquisitors had to lean closely to decipher his mumbling, after his screams died down." Uabhar examined his fingernails, apparently oblivious of Queen Saibh's reaction. Ronin knew that his brother Kieran shared his discomfort on their mother's behalf as the king launched into a description of the methods used to extract MacRoigh's acknowledgment of guilt.

Conall Gearnach approached the party, striding across the lawn. A scowl flitted across his features as he entered within earshot under the trees, but on meeting Kieran's friendly glance of greeting a warm light kindled in his eyes. His demeanor returned to neutral, however, as he waited at a few paces distance until his sovereign had finished expounding; then he bowed low. King Uabhar gave him permission to

speak, whereupon the knight presented his salutations and
begged for a private audience with his liege on some matter
of military business.

Still in high spirits, Uabhar assented readily. He quit the
gardens with Gearnach, accompanied also by Princes Cormac and Fergus, and the shadowy retinue. Kieran and Ronin
resumed strolling through the grove alongside their mother,
whose delicate face had grown ashen.

"Mother," said Ronin, "Pray, do not be distressed if our
father fails to comprehend your disposition as we do. It cannot be his fault that by nature he is unaware of feminine
sensibilities."

Indeed, that Uabhar was incapable of fathoming the depths
of women's subtleties had been plain to Ronin since the day
Kieran had been sent to dwell for two years at the court of
King Thorgild. Saibh had wept and wrung her hands, begging Uabhar to change his mind and let her dear boy stay by
her side, but Uabhar would have none of it. "You would tie
my heir to your apron strings and make a milksop of him," he
said, laughing heartily at his own wit. "I would make him a
man. Let him go into the world and stand on his own feet! Besides, he should become acquainted with his bride-to-be, so
that his eyes may be open when he is of age to wed. Many an
honest man has been lured into marriage with some stramul-
lion whose maidenly artifices have disguised her true nature.
Let him not be one such hoodwinked victim!"

Ronin tactfully refrained from pointing out that since
Princess Solveig of Grïmnørsland had been betrothed to
Kieran at the age of three months, she could hardly be ac-
cused of employing petticoat wiles to snare a husband.

"It is bad enough that you send him away, but to dispatch
Gearnach with him! That man is a fire-eater!" the queen
protested in tears. "Let not my boy be assigned to the care of
a daredevil!"

"Two-Swords will make a fine nursemaid," the king rejoined with a chuckle.

At the time, it had been Uabhar's dismissal of his
mother's entreaties that had led Ronin to believe his father

was inherently numb to her passions. In later years, as he approached maturity of understanding, the prince had come to conjecture that just *possibly* his father had been blind in another way entirely, and that he himself had also been taken in. For it occurred to him, from a casual word dropped here and there, that his mother had actually *engineered* Kieran's sojourn in Grïmnørsland. She never admitted to it, and he never quizzed her, but he knew full well that she looked with satisfaction on the years his elder brother had spent in the western kingdom, quietly pleased that at least one of her sons had, for a time, escaped what she considered to be a stifling atmosphere, and a hotbed of machinations and base influences: the court of Slievmordhu.

Beneath the rustling elms Ronin spoke gently to the agitated queen, as if in apology. "Father means well, Mother," he said. "He has taught us the value of honesty and openness; he has instructed us to be loyal, and never to lie to him, wherefore we have grown up to be honorable men."

Saibh nodded. She swallowed her queasiness and managed to smile wanly. "Indeed you have both grown to be men of principle," she said, "and loving sons also. Some day you will make fine husbands." To Kieran she said, "Solveig Torkilsalven will be a happy wife."

But Ronin, asleep in the hunting lodge thought of his brother's promised bride with a pang of love and longing. Sweetened by an image of her pretty face in a cloud of golden hair, his visions faded into slumber.

❧

In Grïmnørsland a band of Marauders lay dead, but far away on the other side of the Four Kingdoms, the main clan thrived. The Great Eastern Ranges, which separated Slievmordhu from the uninhabited South Eastern Moors, were perforated with a complexity of excavations and natural warrens. Many of these caverns sheltered groups of human creatures loosely connected by amorphous and slippery social bonds. Supernatural wights were scarce in the Eastern

Ranges, and seldom troubled those cave-dwellers. Human they were, these troglodytes, but bizarre and un-human in aspect.

Marauders were outcasts. Their ancestors had been outlaws and misfits seeking secret places to hide, using them as bases from which they could launch surprise raids on the law-abiding citizens of the Four Kingdoms. As years passed, the descendants of the original population became altered in appearance and personality, growing ever more bellicose, brutish and fierce. Why this should be so was not certain, but it was said that some vile poison, or unseelie force, or toxic gas, slow-simmered beneath the mountains in that region, and it was further reckoned that this mysterious influence seeped gradually into the flesh and bones of those who dwelled in the caverns, twisting them, misshaping their offspring, until the population came to resemble nightmares rather than ordinary humankind. Some of them had grown unusually gigantic of height and breadth, and as strong as oxen or draught-horses. Although the alterations made them as hideous as the most repulsive of eldritch wights, the Marauders remained human, and possessed not a whiff of supernatural power or immortality.

In the Main Cave of a network of interconnected ventricles infested by a loose-knit clan, or comswarm, that frequently, but not invariably, called itself "The Sons of Blerg," two Marauder captains were planning their next foraging foray into the countryside. The cavern, although draughty, cold, damp and bereft of creature comforts, teemed with men and youths. Unwashed, clad in an assortment of filthy animal skins and stolen finery, they squatted around small fires playing at knucklebones, sharpening weapons, picking their remaining teeth or multiple rows of fangs, or brooding in sullen silence. Smoke collected in suffocating billows beneath the high ceilings. Now and then an unexpected gust of wind from some rocky orifice would send the fumes blasting down to the cavern floor, where it swirled amongst rising clouds of ash and sparks, engendering bouts of coughing and cursing and slapping.

"Oi still say we should 'it that village jest across the Ashqalêth border," Captain Ruurt was saying to his fellow captain. "Last toime we got good pickin's there. Cracked a lotta heads, too. Good sport."

"Nah, that's too far away, ya block'ead," replied Captain Krorb. "Go fer somethin' closer, I say. Loike some place on the Mountain Road or the Lake District." He scratched at his third ear, a sanctuary for fleas.

"We orways go for *them*," argued Ruurt, spitting into the fire. "Too much work, not enough fun. They got their defenses built up, these days. They got their lookouts, and sojers."

"Not fer much longer, if them soft'eads can be trusted to keep their word, eh?" Krorb uttered a cackle of laughter.

"Can't depend on that. Gotta try further off. That swarm from up Capstone way, whadda they call 'emselves? The Seed of Havoc?"

"Yeah, Seed of Havoc. Good name. Better than 'Sons of Blerg.'"

"Yeah, them. Some 'o their gangs go out as far as Grïmnørsland, I 'eard."

"The further off we go the more loikely we'll be spotted boy some nosy weather-squeezer in one o' them sky-balloons."

"What's the matter? Lost ya nerve?" The color of the bulbous growth on Ruurt's forehead transmuted from raw pink to congested purple, always a sign his temper was on the rise.

Krorb was in the process of formulating a suitably scathing response when a terrible scream ripped through the local smoke-haze. Heads jerked in the direction of its source, and there was a sudden flurry as men leapt to their feet—or other extremities used for locomotion—and fled away from the darker recesses at the back of the cavern. They huddled in fear, as far from the back wall as they could get, cowering and staring into the gloom.

Whispers rippled amongst them.

"The Spawn Mother . . . "

A second wild yell pierced the air, growing fainter as if traveling fast-paced along a tunnel that led away from the

Main Cave, which in fact it was. The Spawn Mother had abducted yet another unwary man.

Marauder women were as pleasant to look upon as the men. In character they tended to be a little less violent; were this not the case they would eventually have slaughtered their own issue, and the comswarms would have died out years before. Most of the women—who lived communally with their brats, in caves separate from the men—possessed sufficient nurturing instinct to care for their offspring until they were old enough to fend for themselves.

Not so the Spawn Mother.

This gigantic progenitrix lived in a deep cave, and stole men as she pleased, when they ventured into the lairs near her abode, or when she wandered the network of tunnels. Most often, these abductees were never seen again. The litters haphazardly produced and abandoned by the Spawn Mother had to be removed by the other ghastly females while she was sleeping, or she would devour her own progeny as she probably devoured their fathers. Her children grew up to be the largest, fiercest, most demented killers amongst the Marauders; so berserk they had to be raised in cages to ensure the longevity of the community.

Silence now reigned in the Main Cave.

"Reckon that was fat-for-brains Scroop," muttered a voice. "I seen 'im go over t'wards the Steep Passage not long ago."

"No, it wozzen me," shrilled an anxious second voice, apparently belonging to Scroop. "Reckon it woz Grak."

"'Twozzen me noither," quavered the equally timid Marauder known as Grak. In an attempt to appear insouciant he shrugged lopsided shoulders. "Dunno who."

After a long while the men began to breathe easily again. They shuffled back to their fires and resumed their previous occupations, but presently their tranquillity was disturbed once more, this time by Captain Ruurt, who barked, "Look sharp, slag-piles, we gotta head down to the lake camp. Gotta moiting with them soft'eads."

❧

Stars were putting forth their glittering needles in the eastern skies and hanging suspended above the wooded shores of one of the Great Lakes of Slievmordhu, where stood the ruins of a mighty fortress. Argent light frosted broken battlements and walls of crumbling stone. Ominous shadows huddled in interstices. On the north side, the waters dimly mirrored the decaying shell of the stronghold, which long ago had been the bastion of some proud chieftain. This was the meeting-place near the lake camp of the Marauders.

That same night, at this secluded location, far from the clustered habitations of humankind, a secret meeting commenced to take place. Dimly against the tranquil lapping of the waters there came a tintinnabulation of bridle and stirrup. A small party of armed horsemen arrived from the west, moving warily through the smashed architecture to halt beneath a corroded tower. Their clothing was nondescript; dark-dyed cloaks and hoods covering yeoman's garb; yet, curiously, they rode in formation and sat their steeds with uniform ease and grace. Most remained astride their horses, while their captains dismounted and held discourse with the leaders of a second company, which had approached from the opposite direction.

Those with whom they rendezvoused were grisly of face and form. If the identity of the riders was veiled, the pedestrians, at least, were easily recognisable as Marauders out of the eastern caves, swathed in their clots and membranes of rags and millinery and assorted haberdashery, and well accoutred with weapons. To the rear of the group, Scroop and Grak, the timid pair, furtively jostled for last place.

The leaders of each party faced one another, mutual loathing evident in every line of their posture. Yet they were treating together almost as if they were allies instead of traditional enemies.

"As promised we will arrange for security to be lax during

that period," the drab-cloaked captain of the riders was saying. "If you attack before or after, you will face much stiffer opposition. Therefore it is in your interests to be punctual. Have you any further questions?"

Stone-faced, the leader of the Marauders, who towered over the man, gave a grunt and extended an acquisitive talon. "Where's the gold?"

"You will be reaping a fortune in bounty from your raids," the foremost horseman said. A bold fellow, he stared scornfully up at the hulk who loomed over him. The Marauder's height, like that of so many swarmsmen, was close to seven feet. "Do you really expect us to *pay* you for it?"

Captain Ruurt of the Sons of Blerg scratched his head with his claws. As he did so, his upper eye rolled uncontrollably in his head, like a stray marble at the bottom of a moving donkey cart. "Orroight," he said, "it's a deal. Ya know what'll happen if ya ever double-cross us."

The expression on the horseman's face did not alter. Straight-backed and austere, he stepped away from the Marauder captain. "We expect your cooperation," he said formally. "Good evening."

"Good evening, *sir*." The Marauder captain was unable to suppress the hint of a sneer, but the rider appeared oblivious of it. He turned and sprang up on the back of his mount. With a gesture of command to his men he led them out of the tumbled stones, away into the benighted woodlands.

The Marauders too turned their backs on the ruins and began to make their way through the trees along the lakeshore toward their local bivouac. Scroop and Grak scuttled ahead, eager to place as much distance as possible between themselves and the horsemen. Ahead, the crescent moon hovered above the mountains.

"Yer makin' us into puppets of that misbegotten pukestockin'," Krorb muttered into an aperture in the side of Ruurt's head. "Oi don't wanna be that."

"Are you mad? The fools are payin' us to do what we do best. What more could we ask?"

"Oi don't loike it."

"Well it suits me roight enough. It's easier, plunderin' this way."

They reached their bivouac before dawn and threw themselves into their purulent bedrolls. When the morning sun flared, and a flock of crows passed overhead, they were still snoring.

II

Mai Day Eve

Who mines within the mountain's heart, beneath the flinty
    ground,
And wakes the silence of the deep with hammer-tapping sound,
Where precious stones and fossil bones in rocky tombs lie
    curled?
Brisk knockers and quaint coblynau; wights of the Underworld.

Who winds distaff and spindle in caves hidden from the sky,
Or in old courses, waterworn, now rockfall-dammed and dry,
Where rivers subterranean through dim defiles once swirled?
The spinning-crones, the busy wheel-wives of the Underworld.

What motley creatures lurk throughout those cold and sunless
    halls,
Where limestone columns loom like wraiths, and gems encrust
    the walls?
Last midnight blue-caps flitted by, Fridean bagpipes skirled,
And gathorns prowled with bockles in the eldritch Underworld.

To loiter near dark pools in hollow places is not wise.
There, comely damsels swim, watching with green,
    remorseless eyes.

They'll beckon you and drown you, cruel seductive water-girls,
Ye mortals, dare not venture down into the Underworld!
—"THE UNDERWORLD," A SONG FROM SILVERTON, IN NARNGALIS

*The Northern Ramparts, beneath which the burrower stub-*bornly toiled, formed a natural barricade between the king-doms of Tir to the south, and the so-called Barren Wastes to the north. In the west, the mountains joined the cold uplands of the Nordstüren, an alpine region whose boundaries seemed to mimic the shape of a dragon. The sinuous neck of the sim-ulated beast stretched northwards along the rugged coast, while the serrated backbone, with crags jutting like pyrami-dal dorsal plates, curved down in a southerly direction between Narngalis and Grïmnørsland, ultimately coiling back on itself to form the Mountain Ring. That dragon's-tail circle of mighty peaks, or "storths," protected a high-altitude plateau at the heart of the Four Kingdoms, known as "High Darioneth."

Leafy roads and lanes crisscrossed the farmlands between the untamed forests of this plateau, winding amongst or-chards of nut trees, across swift-running streams, from ham-let to mill to schoolhouse to farmstead. Along one of these byways, late in the afternoon of Highland Mai Day Eve, sev-eral conveyances were being driven at a leisurely pace. A woman was directing one of the traveling-chaises, while a younger woman walked alongside. The latter was flanked by two children: a boy and a girl. As they walked the lad clapped his hands in time to some unsung tune that carouseled in his head, while the girl stared inquisitively at every passing butterfly and winged beetle, every miniature wren that darted in and out of crevices in the dry stone walls, every dipper that plunged into the fast-flowing alpine streams. In this she was encouraged by the young woman.

Across these high-altitude districts the warmth of Spring-time arrived later than in the lowlands beyond the Mountain Ring. For this reason, Mai Day was traditionally postponed to a later date in the highlands. If not, too few Spring flowers would be found. Only now had the blossoms reached the commencement of their full abundance, and it was time to go maying in preparation for the annual festivities, the celebration of the new season. At this time eldritch wights both seelie and unseelie were prone to increase their activities; therefore it was deemed wise to simultaneously collect rowan and birch to repel the wicked and mischievous amongst them.

The convoy steering a course along Mill Lane included many of the young folk who dwelled at Rowan Green, the Seat of the Weathermasters, that vast shelf of living rock jutting from the flanks of Wychwood Storth, more than three hundred feet above the plateau. The travelers were on their way to join some of the youths, damsels and children who lived on the steadings and crofts of the high plain. Plateau dwellers and cliff dwellers ever mingled freely, although to the outside world it would seem that the weathermasters' status—like their abode—was far above that of the rest. The ethos of High Darioneth was such that variations in status and wealth made scant difference to friendships. Neither jealousy amongst the plateau-dwellers nor arrogance from those who lived at greater heights were tolerated.

As she walked beside the chaise, lifting her skirts over the worst of the muddy patches in the road and satisfying the little girl's enquiries about the ubiquitous wildlife, the younger woman surveyed her surroundings with evident pleasure. Shadows were lengthening, as if arising from their graves. The mists of evening were already ascending, curdling to opacity. They swathed the treetops and softened the distance with subtle veils. Overhead, between the evergreen boughs of snow-gums, clouds blew raggedly across the sweeping arch of the heavens. A flock of scavenging ravens soared and dived, possibly clustering above the site of a wolf pack's kill.

Rocks glistened with condensation. There had been rain earlier that afternoon; all leaves were glossy, new-washed. The air itself was incense, each breath like a clear draught of water tinged with the flavour of eucalyptus, palest green and bubbled right through with the smoke-blue haze of misty mountains. And always, on the horizon's rim, there reared up against the welkin like great glittering crystals suspended from above—watching, vigilant, seemingly eternal—the rugged, snow-topped peaks known as the storths.

The eyes with which this damsel looked upon the world were like the Summer sky's pure essence. Her lids, when closed, resembled the two wings of the bluest of butterflies; it was as if the dust of powdered lapis lazuli had been brushed on to them. Her hair, mostly caught beneath a voluminous velvet cap whose color matched her eyes, was as black as an underground river, the locks wisp-ended and tapering. Long and narrow was her waist, and supple as a serpent. Her name, as given her by her parents, was Astăriel, meaning "The Storm" or, literally, "The Storm Wind," but on the day she had watched her father depart on his impossible quest she had declared to one and all that henceforth she would be known as "Asrăthiel," "The North Wind"—for, said she, it was the cold, strong wind from the north that would some day bring her father back, bringing also the precious prize he sought.

In the year 3491 the mode for everyday wear in High Darioneth tended towards simplicity of design. Women and girls wore sleeveless surcoats that reached to mid-calf. Beneath the surcoat was an ankle-length, long-sleeved kirtle. A belt cinched the two garments at the waist. To keep out the chill of the highlands, women also wore soft leggings beneath their skirts; these were tucked into supple slippers for indoor wear, or boots, or pattens for walking on muddy roads. Their heads were warmly wrapped in the folds of woollen caps and hoods, often lined with fur. Sweeping, fur-lined cloaks draped from their shoulders. The grey and azure raiment of the blue-eyed damsel, however, sported no fur trimmings and was perhaps lighter and less cumbersomely voluminous than that of other women, as if she did not suffer from the cold as greatly as others. Even her hood was pushed back from her head and lay across her shoulders, revealing the pretty cap of velvet. The icy wind, sending shivers through the trees, lifted escaped strands of the damsel's night-colored hair, and unfurled them along its currents.

The small boy trotting at her side—the son of her uncle Dristan—was dressed in thick trousers and sturdy boots, a tunic hemmed at mid-thigh and clasped with a narrow belt, a knee-length cloak and a hood of the type called the *cucullus,* often worn by shepherds and travelers. Beneath the hood his hair, like that of his sister and mother, was as brown as walnuts, glossy and well tended. His cheeks were red with the kisses of the glacial breeze as he made his way along the miry track, now forgetting about his silent tunes and turning his attention to the conversation.

"Well, if you insist upon hearing yet another story," the blue-eyed damsel was now saying, as she ducked beneath the overhanging boughs of a beech, "I shall tell you a tale about my father's impet."

"Nay! Asra, prithee do not tell us of the impet," protested the little boy. "I know all about it. Grandfather has told us many a time. Uncle Arran's impet never did anything to be much frightened of."

"We want a story to make us scared," the boy's twin sister affirmed earnestly. She skipped over a stone in the middle of the road. "Tell us about the field called Black Goat, and the wicked things that lurk there."

"Your mother would not be well pleased with me, were I to give you nightmares!"

From the driver's seat of the traveling-chaise, the children's mother laughed. "Indeed I would not!"

"That story would not give us nightmares," the lad declared boldly.

"In any case," reasoned his sister, "everyone is forever telling us about drowners, and how they reach out their long claws and drag unwary children into pools. That demonstrates we are allowed to hear about fearsome things."

"My sweet Corisande, people only tell you about drowners in order to warn you against swimming in the wild pools and streams," said Asråthiel.

Corisande reflected on this statement for a moment, then

her eyes lit up. "If you tell us about goblins we won't go near the places they dwell," she exclaimed. Turning to her brother for support she added, "Will we, Cavalon?"

"Never," agreed the lad, shaking his head vigorously. "By talking about dangerous things you are in truth keeping us safe."

With the reins held lightly in her hands the children's mother spoke from her perch. "You know full well that goblins have been extinct since the Goblin Wars ended," she said, swaying from side to side as the equipage rattled along the rutted track. "Since they are all gone, there is no need to warn children about them."

Perceiving that the battle was almost lost, Corisande rested her small, gloved hand coaxingly on Asráthiel's forearm and peered tragically into her face. "Prithee," she crooned beseechingly, "Prithee, Asra, tell us a scary tale! We won't be scared," she subjoined in a reassuring manner, inadvertently contradicting her own words.

After glancing down at the hopeful countenances of her twin cousins, Asráthiel relented. "Very well," she said, heaving an exaggerated sigh, "if you wish, I will tell you some fearsome tale to satisfy your unnatural cravings for dread."

"Not too fearsome!" their mother admonished. "Dristan shall call me to question when he returns, if he finds out I allowed you to frighten them from their wits!" The woman was smiling as she spoke: her husband was the mildest of men and in any case, she had complete faith in Asráthiel's judgement where the children were concerned.

"Give me a while to think of something," Asráthiel said to her gleeful cousins. She ran a slim white hand, gloveless, through escaped strands of her hair as she examined a few of the old tales she held in her memory. After choosing one, she reviewed it, making mental notes of ways in which she might doctor the true history, taming the visceral horror of the events that had played out so long ago that they were now no more than tales for children.

"Goblins it is," she began, in a tone of deliberate ominousness, and her cousins squealed. "The goblins," commenced Asräthiel, "as you know, were the most malevolent of all unseelie wights, and they lived in dark, dirty holes deep beneath the ground. They were small and stunted—about the same size as our household brownies. About the same size as you two, in sooth! And they looked somewhat like little men, but they were oh! so ugly, so grotesque that nobody who was unfortunate enough to set eyes on them could mistake them for true men at all. The wars started because the goblins were wicked and cruel, and longed to exterminate humankind. Many battles were fought. One of the greatest was the Battle of Silver Hill, and afterwards the bards made a song of it. . . ."

Her words danced on invisible waves, amongst tiny golden insects that hovered above the road like spangles of winged light. Sounds of laughter and chattering could be heard from ahead and behind, as the other Mai Day revelers joked and conversed amongst themselves. Tiny bells were ringing, as protection against unseelie forces, and someone was tootling happy tunes on a whistle. The horse clip-clopped onward, pulling its burden; the walkers stepped briskly, and the children became engrossed in the story. With the telling of the tale, time passed unnoticed.

Long crimson-gilt rays of the setting sun sliced through gaps in the clouds and reached out across the countryside. They emblazoned the westerly facets of the storths and stretched across the valley of the Canterbury Water many miles away to the east, before sliding their tines through the Riddlecombe Steeps and staining the walls of the Great Eastern Ranges, where the Marauder comswarms dwelled. Runnels of water trickled from the heights, finding their way into fractures and fissures. The runnels joined to form rivulets, which in turn became tributaries of underground waterfalls cascading down to subterranean streams. Converging, the streams created a river that flowed eastward beneath the Lake District of Slievmordhu. As it followed the inclines of vast slabs of buried strata, the river ran beneath the Riddlecombe Steeps, under the valley of the Canterbury Water and far, far below the Mountain Ring on its way to the sea. Wights of the water swam therein; some seelie, others wicked. Of the procession that went maying in High Darioneth that same afternoon, perhaps only one was a weathermaster powerful enough to be aware—albeit dimly—of such a great body of water flowing along so many fathoms down beneath their feet.

The afternoon was waning, and the sky became overcast. Meadow-pipits were settling to roost, and every copse and thicket was raucous with their chatter. Pausing at a crossroads, the convoy's members lit their lanterns against the gathering gloom. At this point Asrăthiel and her family parted from the rest of the reveling Mai Day Eve procession, which turned down a byway leading to a great meadow bordered with flowering hawthorn hedges, glimmering in the dusk like pale galaxies of stars.

The journey of Asrăthiel and her companions took them instead past the meadow, and along lanes hedged by the tangled razor-wire hoops of leafless sweetbriars. Through barebranched nut-orchards they passed, where chaffinches chased one another from tree to tree, and through appleorchards whose twigs were punctuated with tiny buds, and over bridges spanning swift, cold streams where water-voles lurked, and past fields lying fallow. Grass-blades shivered as dormice did some last-minute foraging amongst their roots before nightfall; the countryside teemed with life, and Asrăthiel comprehended it keenly, rejoicing in the natural marvels of the world.

She rested her eyes pensively upon young Corisande and Cavalon, who were laughing in excitement as they embarked upon the annual celebrations, and a sudden wave of nostalgia swept over her. The children's minds were as yet untroubled by loss and grief, and they were secure in the knowledge that both their parents—as well as numerous other relatives—watched over them, ever solicitous for their well-being. A loving family also surrounded Asrăthiel, but her own dear parents were beyond reach. The damsel wondered how it would be for her if her mother's suspended life were restored, and if her father came home at last, after questing long in the uncharted lands of the north. An ache centered itself beneath her ribs as she pictured her forthright and vivacious mother, Jewel, wrapped by death-like sleep within her glass-walled, rose-entwined bower. Visions of her father also formed: Arran, strong and umber-haired, solemn and steadfast, a man of integrity and wisdom, undemonstrative in public yet unreservedly loving to his closest kindred. She had lost them both in the year she turned ten Winters old, and this year, on the twenty-eighth of Aoust, she would be nineteen. There had been too many Mai Days without her parents, and she sighed, missing them anew.

"My legs are tired," said Corisande, breaking into her aunt's reverie. "Let us climb up into the chaise."

"You may do so if you wish," said Asrăthiel. "For myself I prefer to walk."

"Why walk when you can ride?" the children's mother called out. She was teasing, for she knew the answer.

"I would rather not make poor old Dobbin work any harder than he is doing already, Albiona!" Asrăthiel said in reply.

Albiona said, "Old Dobbin won't mind—he's used to it. In any case, you are only a feather's weight—he'd never notice if you climbed aboard."

"He may well be used to pulling loads, but that does not make it fair to use him so. Have you not observed the way he rolls his eyes and flattens his ears when he's made to step backwards into the shafts?"

"But he enjoys his labor!"

"Does he indeed? The language of his body indicates otherwise. See how he plods."

"Everyone has to work for their keep," said Corisande sagely, walking at Asrăthiel elbow. "He ought to work for his, too."

"But what right have we to keep him in the first place?" asked Asrăthiel, "to own him? Surely if he were not forced into service for us, he would be away on the grassy plains of the lowlands amongst the wild herds, galloping freely across the meadows, unhaltered, unharnessed, unconfined, feeding on green grass and drinking from clear streams. He does not need us to keep him, and I'm certain he would be happier if we did not."

"You are making me feel sorry for Dobbin!" Corisande accused fretfully. "I'll not want to ride in the chaise any more."

"Do as you see fit," said Asrăthiel, twitching the hems of her skirts as she stepped over a fallen pinecone. "However," she added, "do it with wisdom and compassion, above all."

"What use is wisdom when your legs are tired?" groaned the boy.

"Much use," answered his cousin. "Dobbin is wise, and I can recall at least one way in which the wisdom of horses has proved beneficial to both equine and human animal."

"But horses love people! They enjoy being ridden."

"Do they? If left to their own devices, do horses seek out saddles and wriggle their way beneath them? Do they search for metal bits to bite on? The way mankind treats horses can be summed up in one word, which we use when their wild spirits have been utterly defeated and we have made them *broken*."

Albiona had lost her bantering mood. She leaned down from her elevated seat to pour words into Asrăthiel's ear. "Please stop this lecturing, Asra," she hissed in low tones. "You are upsetting the children. Live and let live, eh? Can you not be satisfied to abide by your own principles without pushing them on others?"

Right now you are pushing yours onto me! Asrăthiel thought, but diplomatically she refrained from saying it aloud. Averting her head so that her aunt would not bridle at the sight of her frown, Asrăthiel said, "Everyone has the right to hold their own views, Albi, but intellectual liberty is very different from freedom of conduct. People may believe whatever they wish, on condition that they do no harm to others. Those who judge that mortal creatures should be abused and slaughtered do not own the moral right to act according to those convictions! History teaches that society at large once condoned wife-beating, human slavery, bigotry, witch-burning, the labor of children in mines, and many other practices that are now universally recognized as wrong. If we do not tell people how to act with kindness, if we do not speak up on behalf of reform, then how shall reform happen?"

"Hmph! Let me inform you, some people are beginning to view you as didactic. Your preaching does nothing to endear you to others."

"I hope I have a grander purpose in this world than to win some popularity contest," Asrăthiel replied stiffly. "Of course it is important to me to be accepted and loved, but I am prepared to risk becoming controversial and falling into disfavor and being called a pedant in the cause of justice, though I gain nothing material by my stance."

Albiona fell silent, and Asrăthiel feared that her aunt had taken insult after all. Though the two women were generally on good terms, a certain tension underlay their relationship. Yet, despite her desire to preserve family harmony, Asrăthiel would never apologize for her outspokenness on this topic. If necessary she would give way on every other matter, but not this, the fierce desire to bring equity to all mortal creatures, a passion that seemed fused to the very essence of her existence.

The damsel had been ardent for this cause from her very earliest childhood days, when she had begun to observe the wild creatures of mountain, woodland and stream, and marveled at their attributes. Their navigational skills, their speed, their finely honed senses and their elaborate social interactions had astonished and fascinated her. Later, in the lowlands, she had seen birds trapped in cages, beating their wings against the bars in a frenzied effort to be free; and bears forever chained, and dogs beaten until their bones broke, and starving horses straining to pull heavy wagons, and live deer being ripped apart by eager hunters. These acts and worse were accepted as "normal" by people who seemed, in most other respects, quite decent. Her heart had hardened implacably against cruelty and she had toiled to rescue as many creatures as possible, while broadcasting enlightenment far and wide.

The hedgerow rustled. A startled currawong arrowed

across the lane to avoid the party that had disturbed it, and stationed itself in an overlooking spruce tree.

"Ryence says 'tis nigh impossible to live without using animals," said Cavalon.

"Once I breathed in a midge," Corisande said. "I could not help it."

"And back there, by that mossy stile, I accidentally stepped on a beetle," her brother said.

"Well, it *is* impossible to live at all without causing *some* harm," Asrăthiel responded, "but that does not give us the right to do it deliberately."

"Ryence says it is animal abuse to name a horse 'Dobbin,' or a dog 'Rover,'" Cavalon declared.

"Cousin Ryence will have his little jests," murmured Asrăthiel.

"Or a parrot 'Polly,'" the little boy supplemented. "Or a cow 'Buttercup' . . ."

Breaking her silence Albiona said abruptly from the driver's seat, "How can it be fitting to make such efforts to save animals when so many destitute *persons* need assistance?"

Reluctantly but adamantly her niece replied, "At the risk of appearing disagreeable and being seen to moralize excessively, I put it to you that the world is full of troubles that merit our response, and barbarity towards nonhumans is but one amongst them. We ought to endeavor to relieve distress in all situations, if 'tis possible." She was growing tired of having to defend herself.

Corisande lifted her piping voice. "But Ryence says—"

"Look there!" cried Asrăthiel. "The roof of the Mill is showing between the trees, gleaming in the twilight. Can you see it?"

Albiona flicked the reins and with a jerk the chaise picked up speed, heading along Old Horse Lane on the last leg of the journey, until at last they arrived at the High Darioneth Mill.

The Mill was a roomy, three-storied edifice built of stone, with living quarters attached. In the walled yard stood an assemblage of outbuildings including a byre, stables and a kiln. Substantial and imposing, the manufactory nestled below the weir on the millstream. When the chaise approached, the incoming party could hear the rhythmic splashes of the great waterwheel as it turned. Black water, silver-polished, surged down the head-race and through the wooden gates that controlled the flow. As it entered the wheel-pit, it cascaded into the long buckets fastened to the outer perimeter of the mighty wheel, which turned in a direction opposite to the water's flow. Weighed down, the full buckets sank, spilling their contents at the lowest point of the wheel's rotation. The water then surged away down the tailrace, returning to the stream at a junction below the mill buildings.

Wheat, barley, oats, rye and other cereal crops would not thrive at these high altitudes. This was not a flour-mill but a nut-mill, and its water-driven machinery powered not only the massive grindstones for making nut-meal, but also the shell-cracking rollers.

A family owned and ran the works. Their name, coincidentally, was "Miller," and they had been friends to Asrăthiel's family ever since she could remember. Throughout her childhood Asrăthiel had accompanied her parents and the large Miller family at the annual celebration of Mai Day. Now that she was eighteen, for old times' sake she continued the tradition.

Asrăthiel and her young cousins ran ahead of the traveling-chaise as it bowled through the gates of the millyard, keeping their distance from the mud thrown up by the wheels. Primrose lamplight spilled from the windows of the building. Seven white geese scattered, honking, from Dobbin's hooves, and a thick shaft of radiance shot from an aperture as a door was flung open. A few ghostly feathers drifted in the air while the eldest son of the current millmaster came striding out to welcome the visitors. He was a young man of three-and-twenty Winters, and his name was Faramond. In his wake his siblings, aunts, uncles, cousins and parents issued from the building calling out greetings. The newcomers entered and, after they had partaken of some steaming hot soup, they and the willing members of the assembly set forth into the gloaming, lanterns held high, dragging small sleds or carrying baskets.

All across the plateau folk bearing lanterns were bringing in the mai, collecting the spume-froth of hawthorn-flowers from the laden hedgerows. The darkling woods rang with laughter and cries of delight, which were not always associated with finding good specimens of flora; Mai Day Eve was a time of unbridled fun, for which reason many parents forbade their daughters to participate in the overnight flower-gathering.

Mai Day Eve had an alternative name: "Mischief Night." During these sunless hours, eldritch wights were wont to play practical jokes on humankind. Taking advantage of this phenomenon, pranksters of the human variety indulged in an annual prodigality of lawlessness, during which their pranks, being blamed on mischievous wights, might go unpunished. It was a night for knocking on closed doors and running away, for blocking chimneys, abducting and hiding garden gates, pretending to smash windows by smacking them with the palm of the hand while breaking glass bottles, and blowing smoke through keyholes. In his youth, Asrăthiel's cousin-once-removed, Ryence Darglistel-Blackfrost, had perfected a cunning device made of buttons and string which, when hooked up correctly, could be used to tap on windowpanes from afar. He had taught the trick to several of his young relations, and still delighted in helping them confound innocent householders.

The hawthorn blossoms appeared luminous against the evening shadows; in less than an hour their shimmering pallor filled basket and sled, and Asrăthiel's companions, their lanterns swinging like pendant jewels, were wending back to the mill to partake of more refreshments. They were secure in the knowledge that the mill had been well guarded from pranksters; the miller himself, and several stalwart mill-hands, had made certain of it.

Mead and ale flowed freely, and much jollity was enjoyed.

Afterwards the family's hearth fire was extinguished with due ceremony, in the tradition of Mai Day Eve. As soon as their tankards were empty and the hearth-fire embers hissing their last gasps of steam, the Millers hitched two pairs of horses to their barouche and joined their visitors on the journey along the byways of the plateau to Greatlawn Common. On the way the two conveyances met and merged with convoys of other revelers, on foot or in carriages. The full procession, lighted by bobbing lanterns and heralded by mirthful singing, arrived on the common well after the sun had set.

Resplendent firelight flickered through the trees. On Greatlawn Common the Mai Day Eve bonfire was beginning to burn. Almost all Asrăthiel's kindred and friends were present, the people who filled her life with unswerving love, occasional selfishness, kindness, thoughtlessness, friendship and evanescent quarrels. In a wide circle around the contorting flames the folk of High Darioneth mingled, regardless of worldly status, their cheerful faces painted with flickering red light. The weathermasters amongst them were of goodly bearing and appearance. Most were garbed in richly patterned clothing of various colors. The elder weathermasters, however, no matter were they man or woman, were invested with splendid raiment in many shades of grey; storm-cloud, ash, iron and slate. These were the mages. Their garments of voluptuous velvet and copiously embroidered satin were emblazoned with the emblems of their calling: the runes for Water, Fire and Air: ¥, Ψ and §.

The brí, the innate ability to sense and affect the weather elements of air, fire and water, was a gift passed on through generations of weathermasters. As brí-children grew to adulthood they became prentices, learning how to master their abilities and being schooled in the ethics of weatherworking. Successful prentices were permitted to become journeymen. When they had satisfactorily completed their studies—usually at the age of twenty-one—journeymen were deemed ready to pass the ultimate test and become full-fledged weathermages; only then did they receive the final secret of weather-wielding. Asrăthiel was a journeyman, yet the brí was potent in her and she had sped through her lessons at an unprecedented rate. There was talk of her achieving early mage-hood.

The schoolhouse down on the plateau, Fortune-in-the-Fields, provided education for the plains-dwelling children; but Rowan Green perched on its high shelf had no schools. Personal tutors had the job of teaching all brí-children, prentices and journeymen, and at this period Asrăthiel's grandfather was her mentor. As the Mai Day Eve bonfire flared, the damsel smiled upon him; Avalloc Maelstronnar-Stormbringer, the Storm Lord, aquiline of feature and grey-maned. He was surrounded by family and friend; his daughters Galiene and Lysanor with their husbands and grown-up children; his sister Astolat with her grandchildren; Lynley and Baldulf Ymberbaillé-Rainbearer with their son Bliant and his wife and youngsters; the venerable members of the Council of Ellenhall; Ettare Sibilaurë, Gauvain Cilsundror and Engres Aventaur; the new carlin, Lidoine Galenrithar; and the farmers, orchardists and tradesfolk of the plateau. While Asrăthiel cherished them all, it was at celebrations such as this that she mourned her parents afresh, longing for her mother's touch, her father's smile. Her smiles concealed a sorrow that never melted away.

Calling on her powers of fancy and her weather-senses, she listened a while for signs of things and places unseen. Out at the edges of the night, far from the circle of firelight and the rejoicings of humankind, screech owls and other nocturnal creatures were awakening. Eldritch wights such as grigs, spriggans and siofra stirred amongst banks of early-flowering crocuses and anemones, while songbirds, lynxes, and marmots were settling down to sleep in their nests and burrows. All seemed at rights; however Asrăthiel was insightful enough to understand that all was never completely at rights, that appearances could often be quite shockingly deceptive.

Deep beneath the world's surface many kinds of phenomena were slowly evolving, as ever; vast networks of fungi filaments infiltrated the soil, worms nourished their long pink bodies, roots drilled, dark rivers flowed. Miles underground iron boiled, and magma bulged toward crustal faults. Aloft, amidst the surrounding peaks of High Darioneth, the ambient temperature dropped below freezing point. Water from the air condensed and froze in the crevices of the mountains' upper battlements. As seams of ice expanded, their pressure cracked the stone; the sharp reports of shattering rock echoed and ricocheted between the mountain walls and down steep, profound gullies. Asrăthiel, had she wished, might have extended her weather-senses further and known the deep cold of the high crags.

But on Greatlawn Common there was laughter, dancing, and song through the night. The youths and maidens and younger children spent the early morning of Mai Day in woods and fields seeking more flowering branches to carry home in triumph at sunrise; foamy snowdrifts of hawthorn blossom, sprays of rowan and boughs of birch; basketfuls of wild primula from the corries, explosions of pink cinquefoil from the scree slopes and buttercups from the banks of the mountain streams; apronsful of alpine poppies, still in bud, and alpine daisies like surprised faces, and gentians like flakes of the sky fallen into the lap of the mountains. These blossoms and branches were used to decorate the exteriors of houses, or woven into garlands with marsh-marigolds from the highland bogs. Colorful flowers were also employed to deck the interiors of the houses, yet in no case were any white flowers used for that purpose. To bring white flowers indoors was to invite the wrath of unseelie entities, and attract ill fortune.

A roguish group calling themselves the "Mai Birchers" sang uncouth songs as they traveled from house to house bestowing floral decorations on the thresholds of their neighbours:

"Pear for the fair,
Hawthorn for the well-born,

Plum for the glum,
Alder for a scolder,
Bramble if you ramble."

One youth shouted, "Nut for a slut and gorse for the whores," but he was pounced upon gleefully by several of his companions, carried bodily to the nearest duck-pond and hurled into the half-frozen mire.

As the sun rose higher the clouds blew away, leaving only a few languid wisps wreathed around the pinnacles. The spirits of High Darioneth's denizens soared with the sun, whose rays seemed to reach into their hearts and open the doors of jollity. Curlews gave warning of a sparrowhawk in the vicinity with their bubbling cry, and magpies warbled greetings to the morning. Human songsters with flowers twined in their hair tramped from house to house while the day aspired to noon, and they were greeted with gifts of food in return for the vegetation they proffered. Yet, for all the fires and the flowers, the parading and the songs, the apogee of Mai Day was the Mai-pole.

With the greatest veneration this perennial icon was brought to Greatlawn Common. Twenty yoke of oxen, each with a nosegay of fragrant flowers adorning the tips of his horns, hauled the straight-grown birch-tree trunk. The Mai-pole, painted all over with gorgeous colors and decorated with flowers and herbs fastened with twine, was hoisted into position. The handkerchiefs and flags tied to the top fluttered in the breeze. Folk strewed straw all around it, and upon the straw they begin to dance while the band played merrily. It was as if the Mai-pole were itself the stamen of a great flower, and the dancers that encircled it were living petals, gaudy in their festive colors. In addition to dancing they participated in sports and simple plays. Over all the Mai games reigned the Mai Queen, a democratically elected schoolgirl clothed in fine costume.

By the evening of Mai Day the revelers were exhausted from their merrymaking. They wended their way to their separate houses, some of which had recently received the attentions of pranksters such as Ryence Darglistel and his cohorts, who had generously been painting whitewash over the windows while the householders cavorted on Greatlawn Common.

The weathermasters returned to Rowan Green, the wide shelf atop the cliff. Some proceeded to their homes, but others went to Long Gables, the great common-hall of the Seat. It seemed they were reluctant to allow the night to conclude, unwilling to go straight to their beds: to do so would be to admit that the festival was over for another year. Inside the hall a fire was burning low in the grate, and in the half-light human forms could be glimpsed, draped here and there on cushioned settles and in chairs or on the thick rugs scattered across the floor. Amongst them was Asrăthiel.

Snippets of desultory conversation crisscrossed one another. One of the prentices plucked three notes on a stringed instrument. At length a voice inquired, "What is your favorite tune?"

Another responded, "I enjoy the funny drinking songs, especially the one about the rooster in the yard."

Lazy laughter upwelled and trickled away, but with the fire mellow on the hearth and wine ruby in the glass a sated lethargy had stolen over the gathering, and no one felt inclined to the exertion of belting out a rollicking tavern ditty.

"I have always liked the melody of that old song about Fallowblade," said a third speaker. "It is plaintive yet thrilling."

"Ah yes, *Fallowblade*," said the first, "a wistful strain in sooth, as pleasing to the ear as its subject is to the eye, or so I am told, for in fact I have never seen the fabled weapon drawn from its sheath."

Several persons looked to Asrăthiel, who rejoined, "As one who has seen the golden sword, I can tell you he is fairer far than any music, except perhaps the music of the *baobhan sith*, who lure men to dance in mushroom circles."

"Some day," a fifth speaker put in, "I would like to behold Fallowblade wielded in combat. Only in rehearsal, of course." This pronouncement was greeted with approval, and a rambling discourse about the sword's history ensued.

The companions were weary, however, and eventually the conversation petered out.

Someone began softly strumming a lute. Presently, the musician began to sing:

"A wondrous sword was Fallowblade, the finest weapon ever seen;
Forged in the far-famed Inglefire, wrought by the hand of
    Alfardēne,
Famed master-smith and weathermage. Of gold and platinum
    'twas made:
Iridium for reinforcement, gold to coat the shining blade,
Delved from the streams of Windlestone; bright gold for slaying
    wicked wights,
Fell goblins, bane of mortalkind, that roamed and ruled the
    mountain heights
Upon a dark time long ago.

To forge the mighty Fallowblade upon the peak of bitter snows
The Storm Lord labored long and hard. The heights rang with
    his hammer blows,
Hot sparks flew up like meteors. A lord of fire was Alfardēne;
With power terrible he filled the sword. And all along the keen
And dreadful blade he wrote the words in flowing script for all
    to find:
Mé maraigh bo diabhlaíocht—'I am the Bane of Goblinkind.'
Upon a dark time long ago.

When weatherlords to battle fared, the glinting of the yellow blade
Was spied from far off. Wild and strange the melody, the blood-
    song played
By winds against the leading edge. The wielder of the golden
    sword
Smote wightish heads, hewed pathways of destruction through
    the goblin horde.
Their smoking blood blacken'd the ground. Unseelie wights
    were vanquished. Then,
 'To victory!' sang Fallowblade. 'Sweet victory for mortal men!'
Upon a dark time long ago."

As the singer's words rose from the hearthside like clear sparks and whirled away through the windowpanes into the starlight, Astăriel-Asrăthiel, granddaughter of the Storm Lord, felt a terrible restlessness sweep over her, as if her heart yearned to leap from her ribcage; and as the last chords of the lute died away she moved to stand beside one of the window embrasures.

Out across the roofs of the compound she gazed, and through the budding branches of a rowan tree, and past the parapet bordering the cliff edge. To the left, the fertile plateau of High Darioneth stretched away toward the far side of the mountain ring. To the right, towering steeps soared up like a colossal palisade. The lofty waterfall that cascaded down Wychwood Storth was making its own music. Dark, double-bows of bird-shapes were circling in a sky that seemed impossibly huge; deepest indigo sprinkled with a salting of stars. When they flew closer, one could see that they were bats, black as blowing ashes against the beaten silver of the starfields. Behind the cloud-wrapped peak of Wychwood Storth, the sickle moon was floating. On the plateau more than three hundred feet below, feather-down mists lay peacefully across dim fields and orchards.

Somewhere to the southeast the ruins of the Dome of Strang lay brooding in the mists of Orielthir. That desolation claimed Asrăthiel's attention from time to time; she could not rid herself of the tug of the past. Her mother and father had told fascinating, fearful tales of the place. She wondered whether any trace of the sorcerer's reign still lingered undiscovered amongst the tumbled stones. . . .

As ever, Asrăthiel turned to face the north. The crags of Wychwood Storth loomed, as implacable as ever, a sentinel against what lay beyond. Stars winked out, then materialized again as some other winged thing flew across the night sky. Beyond those crags, into the unknown lands her father had passed, striding away on his long legs with a bundle on his back and purpose in his heart. Would any news of him ever come back? What would it be like to follow after him, to seek him out—impossible in those vast, unmapped tracts—and to join him in the search? What unimaginable adventures waited beyond the Northern Ramparts, the loftiest and loneliest mountains in the Four Kingdoms of Tir?

In a melancholy mood the watcher murmured to herself as she leaned yearningly across the sill, "Upon a dark time long ago . . ."

III

Conversations

She dreams in lonely splendor, while the seasons of the year
Ornately alchemize the hues of mountain, wood and mere,
And daylight flits through walls of glass like yellow butterflies,
Or grey moths, when the wind draws ragged clouds across the
    skies.

By night the silver moon and stars reflect from crystal panes
That shelter this fair sleeper from the bitter winds and rains.
She slumbers in tranquillity, untouched by time's decay,
A figurine of porcelain, though warmer than the clay.

Her lids, two azure petals, rest upon her raindrop face.
Her hair, nocturnal filigree, entwines like silken lace.
And round about her bedchamber a wondrous web-work grows,
Of thorns and blooms and twining stems—the gorgeous briar rose.

The briar rose; a living cage, a leafy, fragrant bower
Each blossom tinct alizarin, each bud and full-blown flower
Aglow with vibrant reds, a fitting canopy for one
Who dreams in lonely splendor 'neath the pathways of the sun.

The secret of how she may be awakened, no one knows
So she sleeps on, amid the tangles of the briar rose.
   —"THE SLEEPING BEAUTY IN THE BRIARS," A POEM BY ALEYN
      CILSUNDROR-SKYCLEAVER, BARD OF THE WEATHERMASTERS

Floral confections adorned the houses and halls in the precincts of Rowan Green. Garlands of vestal hawthorn decorated front doors; nosegays of gentians and primula nestled on window-ledges; crisp bouquets of daisies burst from stone jars placed upon the copings of wells.

The first caress of the newborn sun gilded the walls of the nine imposing half-timbered houses built of granite blocks and roofed with slate. They were arranged around the boundaries of an expansive village-green, wherein almond-blossom drifts of geese and ducks congregated at a pond. Atop the roof of one of the houses sat a glass cupola, wreathed with a fine basketry of intertwining stems. The stems were black, hazed with the pale green of new buds. Between the houses grand rowan trees, far taller than the rowans of the lowlands, put forth their boughs.

Taller even than the rowans was the semaphore tower. Almost a decade had passed since the semaphore line system had been invented—in modern times a network of relay leagues, or hilltop signal towers within sight of one another, ranged across Tir, augmenting, rather than replacing, the old arrangement of carrier pigeons and post-riders. With the building of enormous signal-arms and the use of spyglasses, stations could be positioned as much as twenty miles apart. This was a considerable advantage in rough and mountainous terrain, where the construction and maintenance of post-roads was costly. The speed of the lines varied with visibility, which was affected by the weather, but a typical message could take a mere half an hour to travel one hundred and twenty miles, passing through fifteen forwarding stations. The capital cities, and several of the major towns, all commanded their own towers.

Pigeon-post was not redundant, however, especially over

shorter distances. Some of these birds now orbited overhead, abruptly raining down like scraps of bleached muslin to alight in lofts atop the stables, set apart from the dwellings. Their smooth cooing honeyed the air from high on the crag overlooking Rowan Green, the waterfall draped its silken threads down jagged precipices. Glittering, it bypassed the apron on which the houses stood, hurtling straight down to the flat lands at the foot of the cliff, where it ran, burbling, away amongst the orchards.

In the middle of the green, abutting an octagonal tower, stood Ellenhall, a long building constructed of the same materials as the houses. A slender belfry-turret topped the gable. The larger shape of the common hall, Long Gables, was set at right angles to the first, and somewhat apart. At one end stood three elegant chimneys with translucent hair of blue smoke.

It was here at the Seat of the Weathermasters that Asräthiel Heronswood Maelstronnar abided, in the house of Avalloc Maelstronnar, her grandfather. She also shared that rambling, cupola-topped dwelling with her uncle, Dristan— who was currently away on a weathermastery mission—and his wife and children.

On this fine Mai morning Asräthiel, garbed in robes of linen russet, entered the Maelstronnar dining hall: a wide, low-ceilinged chamber paneled with walnut, and comfortably furnished with solid oak settles and tables. Peach-topaz daylight slanted in at the windows. As ever, her eyes were drawn to the familiar spectacle of the impressive sword in its scabbard hanging on the wall above the mantelpiece. Everyone knew the weapon by reputation, of course; it was renowned far and wide. Here was Fallowblade, called *Lannóir* of yore: the golden sword, slayer of goblins, and heirloom of the House of Stormbringer.

As a small child, Asräthiel had asked her grandfather, "Why is it called 'Fallowblade'? I thought that 'fallow' meant 'resting,' like the fields farmers leave lying uncropped throughout the year, to let the loam regain its goodness."

He had answered, "The word has two other meanings besides. It describes the color of pale reddish-gold, such as the shade of poplar leaves in Autumn, and the hide of small deer, and the stubble left behind in a meadow after the hay-making."

"Then it means Goldenblade!" Asrăthiel cried. "What else?"

"Have you ever heard a ploughman speak of 'fallowing a field'? No? To *fallow* the land means to break up the hard soil. During the wars, Fallowblade was a superior breaker of hard things, such as goblins' heads."

"Why *do* ploughmen break up the soil?" the child wanted to know.

"For the same reason Dristan turns over the garden beds with his spade and fork—to make it ready for sowing seeds, and to destroy weeds."

"Fallowblade destroyed all the goblin weeds," Asrăthiel had responded with glee. "That is a fitting name!"

From beyond the casements came the musical notes of small songbirds twittering, and the soft cries of children playing on Rowan Green. The mountain wind, ever unquiet, sighed and murmured as it prowled the eaves and ruffled the rowan-twigs with cool fingers. For a long moment Asrăthiel stood motionless, looking at Fallowblade.

It was the song she had heard on Mai Day that sparked her memories about the famous weapon, inspiring her to go and look at it again this day. Her underlying restlessness also played a part—Fallowblade, with all its accompanying accounts of magickal forging in hidden werefires, and unguessable properties, and heroic deeds, symbolized adventure. Adventure, exploration, travel in search of the unknown—that was what she craved.

Avalloc Maelstronnar had always adamantly affirmed that Fallowblade would eventually be bequeathed to his eldest son, Arran. Upon the Storm Lord's death the famous weapon was to be held in trust by Asrăthiel until her father, Arran, should claim it, if ever he returned—which, as everyone knew, was a thin hope. If Arran never came back, the weapon was to pass into the keeping of his only child.

Long had Asrăthiel wished to obtain the training necessary for employing this unique weapon. No man-in-the-street could wield it without coming to harm. The sword itself could destroy anyone who was not strong of limb, a blood-heir to the brí, and drilled in mastering its peculiar features. Except once, it had not been used for centuries, not since the goblin wars; merely brought forth now and then to be admired and polished and handled with extraordinary wariness before being restored to the sheath above the mantelpiece.

The sole exception to Fallowblade's long disuse had happened more than a hundred years earlier. Aglaval Maelstronnar, the Storm Lord who led the weathermasters at that time, had lent the blade to Tierney A'Connacht, another of Asrăthiel's distant forebears. A detailed written account of this adventure was stored in the Maelstronnar library. Knowing the weapon's fearsome reputation, Tierney's two brothers had refused to use the sword, but had eventually perished. Tierney, the youngest—no weathermaster, but a man of great courage—had been willing to risk wielding Fallowblade for the sake of the woman he loved. He had lopped off the hand of the sorcerer Janus Jaravhor and successfully rescued his sweetheart from the Dome of Strang.

Storytellers had fallen out of the habit of explaining that the two brothers had elected to use their own weapons instead of Fallowblade simply because they had been afraid to touch the golden sword. The brothers understood its properties very well. It was blindingly swift and lethal, but because of the manner of its forging, Fallowblade would hurt anyone who seized hold of it, had that person ever deliberately caused injury to any living creature. No mortal man was innocent in that respect, though some claimed to be, and when they assayed to pick up the sword their flesh was burnt, or they underwent agonies to varying degrees of excruciation. Tierney A'Connacht was not immune, but he hung on to the sword despite the torment, and thereby overcame the sorcerer's might. Ever afterwards he was crippled in his sword arm; however, that fact was not made common knowledge.

Only the influence of the brí, the potent talent possessed by weathermasters, could begin to tame the moral peculiarities of Fallowblade. Those in whose blood the brí flowed had a better chance of being able to handle the legendary blade. Only family members were permitted to touch the weapon at all, and only a fully trained swordsman who truly understood its qualities might properly wield it. To do otherwise was likely to bring great harm upon the user. In the rosy days before the dart of mistletoe had almost slain Asrăthiel's mother, her father had been wont to speak of his desire to someday employ the golden sword according to his birthright.

"Not that High Darioneth is in any danger of being attacked," Arran had added with a laugh, "but in memory of he who wrought the sword, my ancestor Alfardēne, I would like to use Fallowblade as he is meant to be used, rather than relegate him to the permanent status of wall-decoration." Albeit, before he had fulfilled his wish, tragedy had struck and he had quit the Four Kingdoms.

In the Maelstronnar dining hall, Asrăthiel carried a three-legged stool to the hearthstone and set it down. After hitching up her skirts she clambered onto the seat, placing one foot on the mantelshelf for balance. Leaning forward she reached up with both hands and lifted the heavy weapon off the wall, then carefully, awkwardly, climbed down. When she stood again upon the floor she drew the great blade from its sheath. A pang sizzled up her arms; she quieted the effect with a coolly muttered word.

What is it about polished gold that so fascinates the eye? It holds the luster of mellow Summer days; of brandy-wine in a glass, struck through by a spear of sunshine; of candlelight gleaming on brassware; of amber firelight; sparkles glinting in the hair of a girl; richness; the fruitfulness of ripe corn; the lubricious sweetness of syrup. Gold's warmly shining beauty promises wealth and contentment. It invites caresses, attracts the touch of hands, fills the mind with wonder.

The fluted tongue of Fallowblade was a slender pillar of flame. Gripping the hilt firmly, Asrăthiel held it vertically in front of her body, the point turned upward. White-gold spangles ran up and down its glimmering length. The atmosphere seemed to sing with arcane voices, as if the exquisitely sharp edges of Fallowblade severed the very air, particle from particle. Gently Asrăthiel hefted the sword in her hands, swishing it slightly, almost imperceptibly, from side to side, her gaze never shifting from the blaze of aureate loveliness. She was careful to limit the sword's range of motion, and refrained from performing any battle-moves such as feinting, thrusting or sweeping.

Fallowblade was fashioned of gold, platinum and iridium—that much Asrăthiel knew. During its forging the metals had been enlaced with the power of the brí, imbuing them with qualities they could never possess naturally. She was aware also that the sword had hewn off the head of many a goblin; that its like had never been seen before and never would be seen again in the four kingdoms of Tir. But what more was there to learn about this beautiful, shimmering, lethal thing?

While Asrăthiel stood, as transfixed by admiration of the weapon as if it had impaled her, Avalloc entered the room.

A timeless quality clung around Asrăthiel's grandfather, as around most weathermages. His eyes were the color of jade, and hooded by deep lids; his nose hooked, like the beak of a bird of prey. Straight-spined and frost-haired in his grey robes, he seemed as enduring as an oak-tree. His face, molded and engraved by the kneading fingers of age, bore the stamps of patience and wisdom. Since the day, nine years ago, when his eldest son had packed his rucksack and disappeared into the desert wilderness of the remote north, the Storm Lord had borne his accumulating birthdays as if they were as weighty as tombstones.

Avalloc's family name, *Maelstronnar*, meant Stormbringer, and he had been freely elected Storm Lord of Ellenhall and High Darioneth. He was the most authoritative, and until recently the most powerful of all weathermasters. His eyes darkened to thoughtful olive-green as he looked at his grandchild standing before him, holding the sword. Here was one who, he suspected, had the potential to command the power of weathermastery—even beyond his own capabilities. He had lost his son and his beloved daughter-in-law, but the dark, empty place that gaped in his psyche was illuminated by his joy in their child.

"Good morrow to thee, Grandfather."

"And to thee, dear child. Fallowblade shines as bright as ever on this day."

"Indeed, sir, and fain would I put him to the test." Lambent radiance, reflected from the blade, skittered around the walls and across the features of Avalloc. He squinted to avoid the glare. Asrăthiel did not notice—the sight of the golden sword still held her in thrall. It seemed to gather brilliance to itself; to string nets of sticky light about its axis, like golden cobwebs. "Fain would I," she continued, "learn how to wield him suitably. I believe that now I am ready." Turning to face her grandfather she added, "Therefore I am asking for your permission."

The Storm Lord regarded Asrăthiel with grave intent. He said, calmly and deliberately, "That is no insignificant request."

"Of that I am aware, and I do not undertake to ask it lightly."

"I know that you are one of the few, Asrăthiel, who have the potential to wield the golden blade in combat, yet you must understand that you are entreating my approval for one I hold most dear to indulge in a dangerous enterprise. You ask a great deal from me."

"How dangerous can the sword be to me?" The damsel did not add, *I am immortal and invulnerable,* but they both knew what she meant.

"Who knows? Fallowblade's capabilities have never been fully catalogued. Conceivably they are measureless."

At the end of a few moments' pondering, Astăriel said, "Well, if there is a risk, I am willing to take it. What say you, Grandfather? Will you give your consent?"

She looked so proud and zealous, standing before him with the extraordinary weapon in her hands, as if she had broken off a piece of the sun, that Avalloc's manner softened. He had long guessed that one day she would petition him for the use of Fallowblade and, having thought it over, had decided to grant her wish. Graciously he inclined his head. "You have my permission." A faint smile flickered across his mouth. "Under one condition," he added, "and that is, you must promise not to engage in combat rehearsal until your swordmaster judges your ability to be outstanding in every way. You will need more than common competence if you are to handle this perilous blade."

The damsel's face lit up with pleasure. "I promise! Gramercie! Well, Fallowblade," she said, beginning to slide the sword back into its sheath, "you and I shall soon have some dancing to do."

When she drove home the hilt, the chamber seemed to grow dim. Together, Asrăthiel and Avalloc replaced sword and scabbard in their usual position above the fireplace.

"You must break the news tactfully to your aunt," the Storm Lord advised. "She will not be happy; you know how she feels about your inheriting the blade."

"Of course I shall be gentle with her!"

"Fallowblade has other names," Avalloc informed his granddaughter as they finished the task and stepped back from the fireplace. "He is called also 'Frostfire,' because he burns like both ice and flame, and his color is of the sun. In the speech of the Gwragged Annwn, 'Frostfire' is translated as 'Síoctine,' which men were wont to render as *Shockteen*."

"A curious name. And what a curious song it is, Grandfather," said Asrăthiel, "the song about Fallowblade. All my life I have listened to it, from time to time, and yet there is much about it I do not understand."

"Ask me. It will be an excellent commencement to your further training."

"Everyone knows," Asrăthiel began, "that our famous forefather Alfardēne was a master-smith. Everyone knows that hundreds of years ago he forged the blade in the famous Inglefire, which burns to this very day beneath one of the mountains in the Northern Ramparts. But what *is* the Inglefire? Where exactly does it lie? What makes it extraordinary?"

Avalloc offered Asrăthiel his arm and they sat down together on the seat by the open window, surveying the sunlit panorama of glistening snowy peaks as they conversed. "The Inglefire," said the Storm Lord, "is no common conflagration, but a 'werefire,' an ancient, everlasting blaze of gramarye that burns deep beneath a certain mountain, in the far north. It is called 'Inglefire,' but that name is a corruption of the old word, 'Aingealfyre.' Aingeal, you see, means 'light.' As the song tells, it is there that the sword Fallowblade was forged. That fire is anathema to unseelie things, therefore after Fallowblade was made the goblins posted guards around the werefire so that no more swords like him could ever be created. The goblins themselves could not abide the fire; could not even go near it. It is said that the Inglefire burns out wickedness. That is why the sword is pure and smote goblins so well."

"Did the goblin guards not suffer from the fire's proximity?"

"The goblins themselves did not guard it. They set their kobold slaves to the task."

"But they dispersed and fled into hiding when the goblins were defeated. What guards it now?"

"Unseelie wights of other varieties, so it is told. Nobody has sought the Inglefire for many a year. There is no need. These days we have neither living master-smiths as great as our grandsire Alfardéne, nor any real need to fashion more swords like Fallowblade. Unseelie wights are kept at bay by repellents such as bells and iron and rowan, or by the use of the brí; or chiefly by educating mortalkind to beware of the haunts of wicked entities, and shun them."

"Well, it is a shame there will be no more swords like Fallowblade, for he is beautiful."

"Aye, that he is, and perilous also."

"Such a strange heritage is mine," mused the damsel, leaning her elbow on the windowsill and resting her chin in her hand. "A golden sword, the power of the brí, eternity, a ruined fortress . . ." For a while she was silent, while the two of them watched the clouds roll by. Then she sat up straight. "The Dome," she said. "The ruined Dome of the sorcerer Jaravhor—it is mine by law, is it not?"

"By the laws of Slievmordhu and Narngalis, it belongs to you and your mother, dear child. You and Jewel are apparently the sorcerer's only living descendents."

"Yet King Uabhar, without permission from the rightful owners, had it dismantled and ransacked," Asrăthiel said discontentedly. "In the process it was destroyed. All that remains are heaps of broken bricks and stones, swarming with crowthistle and other weeds. The once-great Dome of Strang is now just a pile of rubble."

"Even the stones might have been removed by now," said Avalloc.

"People do not go there to steal building materials, because they are afraid that the blocks might have malign spells on them, some lingering curse," said the damsel.

"You have never published your claim to the estate, my dear. Then again, why would you wish to do so, hmm? As you say, it is worthless." The Maelstronnar appended, "Your mother ended up hating the place. There were all those skeletons and what-have-you concealed in the walls." He waved a hand airily.

"But Grandfather, who knows? There might still be some precious secrets hidden at the site, perhaps buried underground."

"Uabhar's servants dug and pried for years, until the cellars and foundations resembled a rabbit warren. They were meticulous in their search, but they found nothing of value, which is why they abandoned it to the weeds."

"The king's servants are stupid. Besides, they don't have the brí flowing in their blood. If secrets are hidden there, it will be weathermasters who find them, not Uabhar's henchmen. I shall publicly claim the ruins of the Dome as my own, by the laws of inheritance."

The light of good humor disappeared from Avalloc's eyes. "I do not understand your attraction to that place," he said sternly. "It was the same with your mother. She seemed drawn to it, yet in the end, it gave her only pain and trouble."

"The Dome was the key to my father's immortality," said Asrăthiel.

"Aye, but he never asked for that. And was it boon or bane to him, my dear, hmm?"

A shadow flitted across the damsel's face. Meditatively she looked down at her hands, resting in her lap. What was boon or bane for her father also applied to her. She did not like to contemplate her immortality; it set her apart. At times the natural desire to *belong* made her agonize over being thus isolated, in a state neither eldritch nor fully human, but somewhere between.

Her unique condition was kept secret from the wider world. The Councillors of Ellenhall were privy to it, of course, and the carlin; also some members of the royal family at King's Winterbourne, whose discretion could be depended upon. Were the public to be apprised of it they might respond with any combination of fear, jealousy, awe or resentment. Almost certainly they would not greet the revelations with liking or acceptance. The mere *mention* of her situation—no matter how obliquely, no matter that she was in the company of a trusted confidant—made Asräthiel feel uneasy. Were it to become common knowledge that she could not die, some madman might perchance take it into his head to put her invulnerability to the test, making her the target of assassination attempts. Even though such attempts must fail, they could endanger those who surrounded her, and cause untold havoc in her life. Conversely, if she ever found herself in some extremity, deliverance might depend upon her deathlessness being unrecognized by the enemy. Keeping it secret was like concealing an ace in her sleeve while playing at the card-game of life.

"I do not know," Asräthiel replied to her grandfather's question in soft tones. Looking up, she continued impulsively, "All the same, the Dome is mine and my mother's, and I intend to make public our claim. Nobody else wants it, after all."

"And what shall you do with it?"

"Explore!"

"When will you have time to do so?"

"Even if I am too busy with my studies and my work, I am certain some of the prentices and journeyman will be ardent to see what they can find. I shall let them make their excavations, if they so desire."

"Are you bent on this enterprise?"

"I am."

"Then I suppose you had better do it," the weathermage said mildly, "for I know full well I will not be able to dissuade you."

"What harm can come of it?"

"Who knows?"

"I have no fear of any lingering spells left by the dead Sorcerer of Strang," said Asrăthiel. "Throughout the whole of his infamous lifetime he managed to execute only two momentous deeds—the laying of the curse on the descendants of Tierney A'Connacht, and the benison of invulnerability on his own blood-heirs. Most of his other so-called spells were mere trickery."

"He had also managed to keep himself alive far beyond the normal span of years."

"True, yet in the end that feat brought him no reward. He was really not as powerful as he would have had people believe—even his apparently ever-burning flames were fueled by gas piped from underground, which eventually caused an explosion." Before Avalloc could make reply, a movement from outside the window caught Asrăthiel's eye. "Look, Grandfather! The arms are moving!"

Within the semaphore station, signalmen had descried changes in the angles of the movable wooden limbs on a distant tower. Pulling on a couple of handles, they were sending the "message received" symbol.

Avalloc shaded his eyes against the sun. "I believe you are right, dear child. I wonder whether our sharp-eyed lads have received notification about the approach of sky-balloons. Perhaps Dristan is returning with his fleet!"

Eagerly Asrăthiel and her grandfather hastened to the launching and landing place of the sky-balloons. At the northern edge of the shelf it lay, overlooking the stupendous torrent of the waterfall; an apron carpeted with small-leaved creeping mint. In recent times the weathermasters had acquired more sky-balloons. For many years they had owned a maximum of four of the great aerostats. These days there were twelve, and two more were being constructed as fast as the spidersilk farms could supply materials for the envelopes. The increase was due to demand. Across the four kingdoms of Tir the weather had grown more violent during the last decade. Weathermasters freely used their skills to prevent damage to life and property; however, they too must earn a living. The wealthy and influential, who were the least inclined to tolerate the vagaries of the atmosphere, traditionally sponsored them; gigantic spidersilk balloons were costly in the extreme.

The air-filled balloons, lifted by the heat of sun-crystals and guided by winds summoned by their pilots, could carry weathermages swiftly to wherever their skills were required to calm the atmosphere, invoke rain during drought, or stem flood-causing deluges.

Avalloc's guess had been correct. In the distant skies three moonlike spheres could be seen approaching. A small crowd had assembled at the landing place. The return of sky-balloons was a commonplace occurrence, but Dristan Maelstronnar and his crew had been absent for several days, and their friends and family were eager to greet them. On hearing about the semaphore signal, Albiona had fetched the children and run to the balloon-port to meet her husband.

Soapbubble, *Silverpenny* and *Dragonfly* landed with precision, one by one, on the wide apron of mint. There was much welcoming and embracing of the new arrivals; it was always a relief when crews returned safely from a mission. Asrăthiel kissed her uncle and greeted him with "Sain thee!" She smiled to see him hoist both his children onto his back, so that they squealed and protested in delight at being thus squashed like a stack of pancakes, but as she turned away to accompany them home she caught sight of the last deflating balloon, and was arrested in her tracks.

That familiar feeling of restlessness overcame her yet again; an unbearable desire to be on the move, to leap into a balloon-gondola and release heat from the sun-crystal so that the envelope swelled tight; to rise above the ground and leave it all behind; floating into the sky and summoning a wind, a *southerly* wind, to sweep her away.

After a final glance at the balloon Asrăthiel returned to the house of Maelstronnar and climbed the spiral stair to the rooftop cupola. The small room, walled with glass, was bright and warm. To the west, a sweeping vista of the plateau showed through the intricate weavings of rose-stems that framed the panes. In this pleasant bower two women sat serenely, their hands busy with fancy needlework. They greeted Asrăthiel as she entered. She returned their salutation and crossed the floor to the great, canopied couch that dominated the chamber. There, upon shimmering draperies and cushions of rubicund fabrics, lay a porcelain doll, or else the effigy of a beautiful woman. Yet it was no effigy but a living being who slumbered there as if lifeless; Jewel, the mother of Asrăthiel.

Her skin was smooth and pale as ivory, her cheeks and lips tinged with a faint flush. It was as if twin petals of jacaranda blossom had drifted down to rest on her eyelids, whereupon they had thinned to translucency. Against the pillows, her black hair spread out in delicately vaned fans.

The young weathermaster stroked her mother's hair, kissed her brow, and looked upon her with utmost tenderness. As always she wondered whether her absent father would ever discover a way to waken his wife from her enchanted sleep. But her father was immortal; he would seek forever; until the end of time, if necessary. He would search, and he would not return home until he found an answer. The damsel stood, unspeaking, by the canopied bed for some while, then turned away. After a polite nod and a word to the two women who kept vigil, she returned downstairs.

The unquiet mood would not leave her. Later that morning she took herself on a solitary walk, climbing the precipitous path to the weathermasters' cemetery on Wychwood

Storth. The road mounted pine-clothed slopes, crossing bridges over gullies and rocky gorges, ultimately leading her to the small and tranquil dale that cradled the graveyard. There she halted a silent while beside a black headstone. A honeysuckle-like plant was growing on this grave, twining its slim stems between the miniature wildflowers that quilted the plot with rainbow stitchery. Tinkling twitters chimed up and down the brittle air; the call of Blue Honeyeaters. A single feather lay in the center of the grave. It shimmered with every shade of blue: lapis lazuli, sapphire, cornflower, antique ice, oceans, skies, sorrow, tranquillity.

Once her mother had lain in this grave. That was before the scholar Almus Agnellus had discovered, from some mysterious source, that she lived yet, caught in an enchanted sleep; whereupon with the greatest haste she had been raised from the loam and taken to the cupola.

After a while Asräthiel moved on. Instead of continuing to climb to the boulder above the cemetery, one of her favourite lookouts for surveying the countryside, she turned downhill and went amongst the trees.

Sudden rushes in the undergrowth indicated shy creatures of the wild fleeing from her approach. The chirping of insects counterpointed the long-drawn sigh of fern-hidden streams flowing over rocks. Her booted feet trod upon the twigs that strewed the ground, and mosses, and scatterings of small stones. Sometimes she came upon fine strands of brilliance strung across her path: the gossamer threads of spiders glinting in limpid daylight. It felt good to stride out, with a long, easy walking pace along those dappled trails.

Clouds blew across the face of the sun, and the day darkened. Asräthiel had paused to stand beside a fast-flowing stream when she looked up and saw the urisk watching her.

This reclusive member of an innocuous species had been part of Asräthiel's life since childhood. Sometimes she glimpsed it here and there, near water, or in high places on cloudy days, or in shadowy forests. Other times it would not be seen for months. Its appearance did not alarm her. She was accustomed to eldritch wights. Indeed, a domestic brownie was attached to the House of Maelstronnar; at nights it emerged to clean up the domicile and efficiently set everything to rights. All that the brownie received in return for its labor was a dish of cream and a small loaf, but that was the traditional habit of its breed. If anyone tried to offer them greater rewards for their pains, they would invariably, inexplicably, depart. Furthermore, when Asrăthiel had been very young, her father—before he went away—had adopted, or been adopted by, a small impet by the name of Friday-weed. The presence of seelie wights such as the impet, the brownie and the urisk did not disquiet the damsel.

Other folk seldom caught sight of the urisk. It was a secretive entity, generally shunning human company and behaving unlike the rest of its kind. Common wisdom held that urisks were a type of wild brownie, bringing luck to any house to which they attached themselves. Farmers, in particular, considered themselves fortunate if an urisk should come to dwell on their land, for the wights were skilled at herding cattle and performing general farm labor. According to lore, when not working, urisks preferred to haunt desolate pools, but occasionally they desired the company of human beings, and had been known to tag along behind folk who traveled by night. If the travelers halted, so it was said, the typical urisk would shyly approach in the hope of striking up a conversation. If not, the wight would continue its optimistic pursuit all through the night, inadvertently terrifying the wayfarers who, blinded by the darkness, presumed they were being hunted by some unseelie monster.

An urisk's appearance, however, was not monstrous. Above the waist they resembled somewhat uncomely little fellows whose ears ended in pointed tufts, whose nose turned up at the tip, and whose eyes slanted in a way that gave the features an elfin aura. Two small horns jutted from their curly manes. As usual this particular urisk was wearing a decaying jacket and ragged waistcoat. Frayed breeches covered the shaggy goats' legs, but there were no shoes on the cloven hoofs.

When Asrăthiel encountered the wight she would attempt conversation with it. Whether any speech passed between them depended, apparently, on its mood. At times it exhibited a fair degree of sullenness and morosity. On other occasions it could be so merry and lighthearted that the damsel would wonder whether this was, in fact, the same urisk. Eldritch wights were incapable of lying, however; therefore if ever she was unsure of its identity she only had to ask: "Are you that same urisk who was acquainted with my mother and my grandmother?" And if it condescended to respond at all, it would reply, "Indeed, I knew them both." If any doubt remained in her mind she would persist, "Are you the one to whom my grandmother proffered the fishmail shirt?" "I am," the wight would reply—impatiently and acerbically, for it had made it plain that it detested the dullness of human beings who could not tell one wight from another, and that her distrust was an affront and her barrage of questions irksome.

The entity's surliness failed to bother Asrăthiel. She considered the urisk to be a precious link with her family history on the maternal side, for it had known her mother and her mother's mother long ago, when they had dwelled in the Great Marsh of Slievmordhu, and, in fact, her grandmother's mother and any number of other forebears. Lilith, Asrăthiel's grandmother, had once given the urisk a shirt made of fish-scales, which was reputed to have been fashioned by a mermaid. The urisk had eventually returned the artifact to Jewel, Asrăthiel's mother, and the shirt had remained in her keeping, an heirloom to be passed on to succeeding generations.

On this morning in Mai, as she stood on the banks of the stream, Asrăthiel was about to speak to the urisk when it spoke first to her.

"Weatherwitch," it said, "how farest thou?"

"I fare well enough," she said, seating herself on a fallen log and propping her elbows on her knees. "I have not seen you of late. Where have you been?"

"I journey about."

"Where?"

"Far and wide."

"How wide?"

"Very. Also very far." When the damsel looked dubious the wight added, "Typically you misconceive how swiftly my kind can pass across the countryside."

"Doing what? How do you occupy yourself on your travels? You do not help anyone, I daresay."

"I avoid your tedious kindred. To keep myself amused I scare a few frighteners."

Asrăthiel stared skeptically at the wight's puny frame. "How do you scare them?"

"Creep up and say 'boo.'"

The weathermage burst out laughing. "To be sure!" Chaffingly she added, "Why, perhaps I have underestimated you, urisk! You make it easy for me to forget you possess a sense of humor." Laughter had relieved her melancholy mood, and for this she was grateful. Sometimes the urisk could be good company. It occurred to the damsel that she knew very little about this peripatetic creature who could amuse or annoy or astonish her without notice. "In sooth, you are a big perplexity for such a little thing. I have scant knowledge of you. What do you eat? You do not help humankind, so you are not rewarded with our food. How do you survive?"

"I am immortal, fizzwit, or have you forgotten? Lack of victuals will not kill me." The wight stared straight at Asrăthiel with its disconcertingly numinous eyes. "I am like you. You know what you are, although you insist on trying to pretend otherwise."

Discomfited, Asrăthiel looked away. Why did the vexing creature have to spoil everything by referring to a subject that she assiduously tried to avoid? That it was aware of her immortality was no surprise; it had been hanging around long enough to have ferreted out all the family secrets; besides, eldritch wights had their own arcane ways of discovering things. Worse than alluding to her immortality, how could the urisk possibly compare itself with her? An ill-humored, goat-legged wight that was of no use to anyone, insinuating that she and it had something in common! Its presumption would have been laughable if not so irksome.

She deflected the topic. "Oh, so I presume it was not you who thieved a cooling dish of gooseberry fool from the kitchen windowsill last Salt's Day se'nnight."

"Of course 'twas I. I take what I want."

"And give nothing in return?"

"Why should I?"

"Because it would be mannerly to do so."

"Spare me the lessons in etiquette, Weatherwitch. You are in peril of becoming as tiresome as the rest of your kind."

Asrăthiel shrugged. "If I weary you, seek other company," she said, rising to her feet and brushing scraps of damp moss from her skirts.

"Be certain I will. For the present, you have failed to weary me."

"I shall be forced to try harder."

"Come now! You are too disconsolate. Instead of remaining with your family to celebrate your uncle's homecoming, you wander abroad, alone, as if something bites you." The wight began to saunter away, along the forest path beside the stream. Asrăthiel followed, keeping within earshot.

"You seem to know all about the affairs of Rowan Green," she said as she walked. "It's intriguing, how you come to discover our business."

"It is scarcely difficult. Three of your air-bubbles make show of themselves across the skies, and the whole world is forced to learn of your transactions."

"It is true, my uncle Dristan has come home from Grïm-nørsland." The damsel sighed. "He traveled there with his fleet, to appease a violent storm that blew in from the ocean. If I am disconsolate, it is due to his tidings. While he was on this mission he saw a small fishing-village that had been half-destroyed by extreme weather conditions. Roofs had been blown off, houses flooded. Most of the meager posses-sions of the villagers had been destroyed or washed away. If Dristan and his crew had not come to the rescue, the weather would have waxed more savage and the damage been worse. But even the brí of nine weathermasters could not entirely turn aside that powerful sea-storm. My uncle told us that after the wind and rain had abated he saw druids' henchmen going amongst the destitute folk, telling them that the Sanctorum would intercede with the Four Fates on their behalf, if only they would give the druids their last few coins to indicate their trust in the Fates. I stayed to hear most of his news, then I felt driven to go out. It irks me every time I learn of druids exploiting gullible folk. I could endure such tidings no longer."

Like liquid glass, swift-flowing water combed over the rocks in the riverbed. The sound of it bubbling and gurgling was a delight. Asräthiel watched the water flowing into the shadows beneath the tree ferns that leaned out over the stream. She watched, but did not see, for her thoughts temporarily distracted her.

"It does not take exceptional wit to see through the wiles of the Sanctorum," she said angrily. "There are no such entities as the Fates. 'Tis nought but superstition to keep people under the thumbs of the druids. 'Tis all for money and power. The druids assure people they will beg the Fates to improve their luck. And for an extra fee, the druids will ask the Fates to ensure a blissful afterlife. There is no afterlife! Corpses return to rain and dust. Consciousness is nullified."

"These destitute Grïmnørslanders," said the urisk. "Did the words of the druids' henchmen bring them joy?"

"Why yes, I suppose so; those who believed them, at any rate. I've seen it before. The druids give false hope."

"Hope can heal," said the urisk. "A madman can be happy. You ask why should anyone have hope? I ask, why not? How can you be so certain of the future?"

The wight stopped in its tracks, so abruptly that the damsel almost tripped over it. Without turning around, it said, "Even misplaced hope, or what may appear to *some* to be misplaced hope, is better than none."

To that statement, Asräthiel could devise no reply.

The wight and the girl walked on without speaking, while the many tongues of water, woodland and wind sang all around. The path meandered, sometimes running along the banks of the stream, other times winding away amongst the trees. Whenever it approached the stream, the sound of running water became louder; a laughing sound, murmurous, melodious, lilting. As it moved away, the sound faded to a hushed murmur.

At length, Asrăthiel spoke again. "You are lucky."

"How so?"

"You may travel at whim, wheresoever you wish to go."

"Ah yes. How remiss of me not to recollect my good fortune."

Overlooking the creature's asperity, Asrăthiel resumed, "I long to travel past the boundaries of the kingdoms of Tir. I am eager to learn what lies beyond."

"If you are so ardent to depart, then why not do so?"

"I feel obliged to stay until I am older; at least until I have repaid my grandfather in some measure for his care of me throughout the years." The damsel glanced at the wight with an inquisitive air. "The lands beyond the borders are passing strange, so it is told." When she received no response, she pressed, "Have you ever seen them? The Stone Deserts? The Mist-Marches? The Barren Wastes of the North?"

"Urisks favour domestic situations, can it be you are unaware? Urisks prefer herding cattle and mending ploughs to adventuring in the wilderness."

"But you—you are not like others of your species."

"With how many other urisks are you acquainted?"

"I confess, none; but the lore-books in the library describe the customs and characteristics of your race, and the books were written by the most excellent of scholars."

"Ah, the lore-books. Infallibility can be most inconvenient."

"Sarcasm can be most vexing."

"Weatherwitch," said the urisk, "vexation can be most tedious."

Moving on in silence, they arrived at a stone bridge that spanned the stream.

"Can you cross running water, creature?" inquired the girl.

"What do you think?" The wight had apparently lapsed into its customary irritable mood.

The damsel surmised that the urisk might be unable to cross the bridge but unwilling to admit its shortcomings. Deciding to allow it to retain its dignity she said, "In any case, it is time for me to turn back for home," and began to retrace her steps.

Fleeringly, the urisk leaned on the parapet of the bridge, making no move to accompany her. Behind her back she heard it say, "Go back to the confines of your walls."

Scowling, the damsel rounded on the wight, ready to snap a retort. But the goat-legged fellow was no longer where it had been a moment before. All that leaned on the parapet was a diaphanous reflection of light from the stream, and a lucid shadow of ferns.

۹۶

A breeze came out of the west. It picked up spores released earlier by those very ferns, and whisked them away. For days, and weeks, it carried them. Sometimes the spores would be blown back on their own tracks. Other times they would reach breathless heights, only to spiral slowly down. Eventually the living cells were caught in a rain shower and came to rest in a water-meadow, where some of them germinated. Through this region an old and unkempt man was plodding.

Many miles to the east of High Darioneth the long coach-road between King's Winterbourne and Cathair Rua passed through a wide variety of landscapes. Along this route trudged the man, heading south toward Slievmordhu in his ceaseless quest for different people from whom he might cadge food, drink, clothing or shelter. The skies were ragged with fast-moving clouds. The beggar lifted his stubbled chin and cocked his head as if listening. He fancied he could hear, faint on the west wind, the bass *clang* of a bronze clapper striking some hollow metal device. Hastily he raised a skinny, age-blotched hand, sketched an aerial sign to ward off wickedness, and hurried forward as fast as his limping gait would allow.

The highway wandered through the ancient flood-meadow carpeted with a wealth of buttercups and tiny ferns whose spores had blown from distant places, before ascending into woodlands clotted with bluebells, lily-of-the-valley and wild garlic. Cuckoos uttered their distinctive call from high in the boughs of oak, beech and alder. After passing through the woods, the road emerged into farmlands, where thick white blossom slathered the miles of hawthorn hedges bordering each field.

After brushing a stray harvestman spider from his tattered sleeve, the beggar scratched at a wart on his neck. He could hear the sound of singing coming along the road behind, growing louder; a chorus of voices accompanied by the dislocated twanging of some stringed instrument and the tinkling of small bells. Behind the singing, the rattle of wheels and the clopping of hooves could be discerned. The voices gave the impression of being jovial, so the old man made a decision based on years of itinerant living, and chose not to run away or hide. Instead he composed his decaying features into their most pitiable expression and trudged on at a slower pace, until the travelers caught up with him.

The singers were nomadic merchants, journeying in five covered wagons pulled by hard-working horses. A flock of children walked alongside the vehicles. Many of the travelers were kitted out in the old-fashioned traveling-cloaks known as *sclavines,* characterized by wide, elbow-length sleeves, buttons down the front from neck to hem, and an attached hood.

"Sissa! 'Tuz a biggar," exclaimed the man driving the lead wagon.

"Odds bodkuns!" cried a woman who had poked her head out from the lead wagon's canopy, " 'Tuz Ket Soup humsilf, uff I'm not mustaken! Hey there you old perasite, what's afoot?"

"What's afoot?" repeated the old man, staring blearily at her. "Blisters is afoot, missus." He sneezed juicily.

"Sain thy five wuts, Soup," a second wagoner shouted. "Hop aboard!"

Ponderously, the convoy rolled to a halt. It comprised several families of itinerant cobblers and traders, returning from their biannual bartering-trip to King's Winterbourne. They spent much of their lives on the road, and during their travels they had encountered this particular tramp on more than one occasion. They knew him to be penny-wise, squalid, sly, a fine storyteller, and very, very old. Over the years, desultory familiarity had bred a kind of affection.

"Hop aboard," yelled the second wagoner again. "We'll save your feet, you old sponge. But make certain you repay us wuth a tale!"

The beggar needed no further urging, even though he did need a helping hand to haul his bone-bag body up onto the vehicle. He sat next to the driver of the second wagon, a grey-haired fellow whose nose appeared to have been smeared sideways across his face.

"Eat!" said the grizzled wagoner, passing a hunch of soft bread across to the beggar as the drivers yelled commands at the harnessed mares and the wagons rolled forward again.

"By the Star of Ádh and the Axe of Míchinniúint, Squüdfitcher, you're a generous man," gushed the beggar, enthusiastically clamping his gummy jaws around the loaf.

The vehicles of the west-coasters were festooned with bells and other wight-repelling talismans. An odor of hempseed oil clung about them, and they were littered with the fibers of hempen rope, sacks, coarse fabrics, sailcloth, and packing cloth. Having rid themselves of the items manufactured in their native land, the Grimnørslanders had piled their wagons with boxes of produce purchased in the north: silvered mirrors, prismatic cristalle vessels, sharp knives of Narngalis steel, tableware, plate, buttons, buckles, cups, soap, fine linen and woolen cloth.

As they bumped along the road, Cat Soup fell asleep, tumbled backward into the wagon's interior and lay snoring, like a festering scrap heap that quivered with insect life. That evening, however, as he sat around the campfires in the company of Squüdfitcher, Squüdfitcher's wife Heidrun, their children and grandchildren and numerous other members of the wandering family, the beggar rewarded his hosts with a story.

"There used to be tin-mines up Riddlecombe way when I was a lad," said Cat Soup. "Greatly rich in ore was that ground, and the biggest mine of all was Ransom Mine. Called that because 'twas said there was a king's ransom worth o' tin in the lode. And the knockers knew it to be true, because they were always plenty active in Ransom Mine, with their digging. You could hear their chippings and chopping in every part o' the mine, but most especially you could hear their noise up the east end. Everyone reckoned there must be great riches in that part o' the lode, yet despite the captains of industry offering the miners extra pay and tremendous inducements, no pair of men had courage enough to venture into the territory of the bockles."

"I thought you sid they were knockers," interrupted Heidrun Squüdfitcher, a stickler for accuracy.

"Knockers, bockles, Small People, 'tis one and the same," answered the beggar. With speckled and grimy fingers he plucked a stray hair out of his tankard. "By any name they are seelie wights and skilled miners, but beware those who fall foul of them."

"Where do those mining wights git their clothes from?" one of the children asked.

Having been asked this question before, Cat Soup already had an answer prepared. During long hours of tramping on the road he had honed his reply until, in his opinion, it sounded rather lyrical. "Maybe from the hides of excavating animals that have died underground," he intoned, "or from threads spun by eldritch spinsters in darkling caverns, whose wheels hum night and day like the mutter of distant crowds. Perhaps they bargain for cast-off raiment stolen from humankind by sly trows. Their source of materials, like their dreams and desires, remain incomprehensible to mortal beings."

"Oh, viry nice!" the wagoners said approvingly.

"Anyway," said the beggar, whose burst of poetic inspiration had come to an end, "Let me get on with the story.

There was an old miner who lived with his son at Trenwith in the Riddlecombes, and some folk said these two were possessed of some secret by which they could communicate with the Small People."

"Will, were they?"

"How should I know?"

"I fency you might know more then what you're tilling, Mester Soup."

"That's as may be," replied the beggar cagily. "Howbeit, one Midsummer Eve this father and son went out around midnight and hid themselves near the top of a shaft, and kept watch until they spied the Small People bringing up the gleaming ore. Then they stepped from their hiding place, much to the astonishment o' the bockles who, like all wights, greatly mislike being spied upon.

" 'Whae d'ye be aboot, carls?' demanded the little miners. 'For why sould we nae strik' ye doon wi' foul fortune seen ye clappit yer een on's?' "

" 'Twas then that the two men made haste to explain themselves, you can be sure. With great couthness in their mouths and bending many a civil bow, they said, 'Kind sirs, we offer to save you all the trouble of breaking the ore out of the ground. We will bring to grass for you one tenth of the richest stuff and leave it properly dressed, if you will quietly give up to us this end o' Ransom Mine.' "

"What does ut mean, 'brung to grass'?" the Squüdfitcher grandchildren wanted to know. "And what does ut mean, 'properly drissed'? Did they hev to put jeckuts on ut?"

"It means hauling the stuff up out of the ground and sorting the good from the dross and washing it clean."

"Right enough," said Squüdfitcher. "End what dud the luttle min say to thet?"

"They considered the proposal, and muttered amongst themselves in their own jargon awhile, and then there was some dickering about the terms of the agreement, but at last the bargain was struck. The old miner and his son took the pitch and worked hard, and 'twas not long before they had accumulated to themselves a great deal of wealth. All the while the old man never failed to keep to the agreement and leave a tenth portion of the ore for his benefactors."

"What about the son?"

"He did as his father bade him."

"So they both became ruch gintlemin, eh?"

"Aye, and they lived in a grandhouse, waited on by more servants than you could count on both hands, and there were fine horses in the stables."

"Thet's not a proper tale," complained one of the grandchildren.

"'Tain't finished yet," said the beggar promptly. "The old miner got older, so old that he died. The son took to thinking, why should he work hard for the knockers—"

"Or bockles," interjected Heidrun Squüdfitcher.

"—or bockles, and leave a tenth of the precious ore all nice and clean for them when he could have it all to himself? And so he sought to cheat the little miners, and day by day the portion he left for them became smaller and smaller, but he thought, 'They won't notice the difference, the little chewets; anyway, how can they know how much ore my men bring to grass each day?'"

"Oh!" said the grandchildren. The light of foreknowledge dawned on their features. They were fully cognizant that wights had their own mysterious ways of finding out information. "But he was mustakin, was he not?"

"He was indeed. His own greed and foolishness it was that ruined him. Wights are canny. The lode failed, and from that time on nothing answered with him. In his disappointment he took to drink, squandered all the money his father had made, and ended up a beggar."

"Like you, Master Soup," piped one of the children.

"Aye," said Cat Soup, nodding sadly, "like me." And he swiveled a bloodshot eyeball to stare thoughtfully into his tankard.

"Lit thet be a warning to you, my led," admonished the child's father, seizing this handy opportunity to lecture his son on moral principles. "Do not be greedy or you might ind up ez a useless old biggar."

"Useless?" the storyteller swiveled his eye again, fixing it on the speaker. "Old I am, but useless, no."

"Storytillung passes the time, Soup, but 'tuz hardly *useful*."

"I do more than amuse people with my tales. I *see* things," said Cat Soup, and he tapped the side of his nose with an air of secret knowledge. "I see things what others do not see. I hear things, too." He paused for dramatic effect. "And that can be *very* useful." The old man leaned forward with a confidential air, as if about to impart a momentous secret, although if he had expected everyone to inch closer in order to catch every word he was disappointed, for they recoiled from his fetid breath. Undeterred he murmured, "Last time I was down south in Cathair Rua I heard some gossip; ill-natured gossip."

The old man seldom passed on information without weighing it thoroughly in advance, to ensure it contained nothing that might prove injurious to him. This unsubstantiated rumor seemed to fit the bill, and it would certainly elevate his status among the wagoners as a repository of knowledge.

The children gazed at him, wide-eyed. Their elders looked expectant.

"Scandal and defamation," said Cat Soup with significant nod and a twitch of his scraggy eyebrows, "a nasty buzz such as there ain't never been before, not in my memory."

"Well?" his hosts demanded impatiently after a pause.

"They *say*," said Cat Soup, quickly glancing over his shoulder to enhance his dramatic role, "although I do not believe it for a minute, that the weathermasters, of all gentlefolk, are turning greedy and lazy! That they are setting exorbitant prices for their services and not doing half so good a job as what they used to do! They *say* the weathermasters are no longer honorable and worthy of esteem. Personally I believe it is all false report. I am only telling you what I heard; the word in the street so to speak."

Astonished, the elder wagoners proceeded animatedly to discuss this bizarre news among themselves. The children, however, dismissed the matter after scant deliberation and requested another story.

Far away in the night, golden-eyed frogs were performing creaky refrains.

❧

Nine days later, on a Moon's Day, as the sun began yet again to fall from its apogee, the convoy of wagons passed a fork in the road called "Blacksmith's Corner." While the wagons continued their journey south, the branch to the right turned away west, leading to the mountain ring. Up to the gates of High Darioneth it climbed, zigzagging steeply up the mountainside through tall forests of eucalypt and fern.

Clouds had cleared from the skies above the high country, and the afternoon was bright. In Long Gables, the Great Hall of the Weathermasters, the tables and settles had been pushed back against the walls. Cold and dark gaped the fireplaces. They had been swept clean of cinders, and kindling had been laid in readiness for the next blaze. The chandeliers on their hoops of marigold brass remained unlit. Daylight streamed in at the windows, laving the hall's spacious interior with ripples of light distorted by flawed glass panes.

The swordmaster's apprentice lolled at one end of the chamber. In the center of the floor of polished boards stood Asrăthiel, dressed in the usual costume of the heavy-weapon duelist; gloves, boots, light helm, cuirass, gorget and mask. Her sleeveless doublet, close-fitting her whiplash waist, reached to mid-thigh. At each flank it was slit from hem to belt. The loosely flowing sleeves of the drop-shouldered shirt were gathered at the cuffs, and the trousers were tucked into supple knee-boots. She had laced a cuirass of thick leather over these garments. Her hair, spun strands of shadow, had been bundled up with pins and thrust beneath the fencing-cap. Her legs too were armored, and a swordbelt girded her narrow hips. From it hung a scabbard intricately carven with intertwining foliate patterns. A small shield, carried on her left forearm, completed the set of equipment.

The swordmaster stood facing her, on guard and similarly armored. His lean features, visible before he lowered his mask, were furrowed and scarred, indicating middle age, wiry strength and much combat practice. He was neither tall nor stout, but he exuded the poise of a fighter with many years' experience, and balanced on the balls of his feet as if prepared to spring into the air or leap in any direction without notice.

He nodded.

Simultaneously, he and the damsel reached their right hands across their bodies, grasped the hilts of their weapons and withdrew them from the sheaths. A subtle shift took place in the demeanor of the swordmaster's apprentice. His stance altered from relaxation to vigilance. Loudly he shouted, "Lay on!" and the lesson commenced.

The swords were made of wood; this was, after all, a practice session. For a few moments student and tutor circled one another warily, their weapons held at the ready, each scrutinizing the other for evidence of some weakness, trying to estimate the timing of the other's intention to strike so that it might be preempted, and advantage thereby gained. Losing patience, Asräthiel decided to attack. She drove a thrust forward. Her opponent stepped aside, pivoted on his heel and struck a glancing blow off her shoulder.

"One!" he called out, even as she danced out of his reach. "I have severed the sinews in your left arm."

Asräthiel pursed her lips in an expression of combined resolution and deliberation. The duelists held each other at bay for another instant, before the swordmaster feinted to mislead her, following the feint with a straight thrust. She parried and counterattacked; he took her blade in a circular movement and swept it aside, but before he could profit from her vulnerability she ducked, dodged and jumped backwards.

"There is no use playing by the rules," said the swordmaster. "When you are fighting for your life, there are no rules."

"I would not know," his opponent replied, between arrogance and bitterness. It was unclear whether the swordmaster understood the strange truth about her; that she was immortal and invulnerable. Perhaps Avalloc had informed him.

"Make believe," said the swordmaster, and suddenly he attacked with great speed and ferocity, lunging again and again, driving her back. The shields and wooden palings clattered against each other. Asrăthiel fought with strength and determination, focusing her mental energies, endeavoring moment by moment to foresee his moves and counter them.

At last her tutor performed an expert *prise de fer*. Asrăthiel's weapon flew from her grasp, skidded across the floor and rattled to a stop against a table. Momentarily disconcerted, she lost her balance and stumbled. The swordmaster executed a flying *flèche*, the point of his sword arriving on her ribs well before his feet touched the floor.

Asrăthiel glanced down. The sword was a sharpened stake pointing at her heart.

"Two," said her tutor.

He paused for effect, before withdrawing his blade and holding it vertically in front of his face, to salute his defeated opponent.

They bowed to one another, and then he sheathed his weapon while Asrăthiel ran across the floor to retrieve hers.

"You fought well," the swordmaster complimented her.

"Not well enough," she said.

They spent the remainder of the afternoon hard at work, he demonstrating how she might improve her technique, she relentlessly practicing until she knew she had mastered each maneuver, then continuing to practice, as though she strived for nothing less than perfection.

At the close of the day, after they had ceased their drill and parted company, Asrăthiel returned to the House of Maelstronnar. Just before sunset, the never-sleeping wind of the highlands began to blow harder. Having bathed, the damsel took herself to the covered and colonnaded ambulatory that ran along the walls of the courtyard. In the center of the court a stone lion spouted water into the basin of a fountain. Nearby, five carved pedestals supported ceramic urns, from which spilled filigrees of foliage. She seated herself upon a wooden bench, drying her hair in the wind, resting after the bout of exercise and untangling the smoky abundance of her locks with her silver comb.

Dusk intensified. Thick layers of cloud swarmed across the stars, obliterating them. The air was chill but Asrăthiel, although barefoot, felt no discomfort. In the shelter of the court the fountain chimed glassy notes, its droplets sparkling in the mellow radiance spilling from the lamp-lit windows, while outside the walls the cries of birds returning to their roosts tore through the moaning of the wind. The air was redolent with the thick aromas of baking and stewing that wafted from the kitchen.

As she combed her hair, the damsel pondered on her training session that day. Having made mental notes to herself about her performance, she turned her attention to the fact that her claim to the estate of the Sorcerer of Strang had recently been published through the correct channels in both Cathair Rua and King's Winterbourne, and so far nobody had gainsaid the declaration. It appeared she was to officially inherit the site of the old Dome in Orielthir. The thought pleased her, although she could not explain why. Anticipating success, she had already informed the prentices and journeymen of Rowan Green that they might travel to Orielthir whenever they had the time and the inclination, to fossick amongst the ruins. Dristan had promised his children he would take them to Strang so that they could see the remains of the famous fortress for themselves. Asrăthiel intended to journey there eventually, after she had finished her studies, celebrated her nineteenth birthday and precociously received the title "Weathermage."

At length her mind drifted on other pathways, wandering to meditations about the goat-legged wight, with which she had not exchanged words for some weeks. It would be a pity, were it to permanently shun her company. The creature was a type of heirloom, and she would resent being deprived of it. She had spied it, now and then, lurking in various locations not far from the Maelstronnar house; near the Tower of the Winds, or by the entrance to the underground storehouses and smithy, or upon the leafy margins of the launching place.

Through the shining curtain of her tresses, as she raked

them, she caught sight of an alteration amongst the low shrubs of lavender bordering the cloisters. A transition shivered through the leaves, and the urisk, coincidentally, was manifest.

"Oh, 'tis you," Asrăthiel commented. Disguising her smugness she resumed her combing. "How are the frighteners these days?"

"There's no knowing," said the urisk in the lavender. "You might ask them."

Rich lamplight bloomed in more windows of the house. The odor of roast beef pervaded the courtyard.

"Faugh!" snorted the urisk. "The stench of charred flesh is offensive."

"We call it 'cooking,'" Asrăthiel said dryly. She shook her head. Droplets flew. "Yet I agree, the smell of meat is distasteful. I never eat flesh." Sensing the customary discontent of the shaggy-haunched manikin, she tacked on a casual effort to mollify him. "The cook, however, prepares delicious recipes of vegetables, and the most splendid puddings. Come with me into the kitchen. I shall find you a dish to your taste."

"That's unlikely."

"Do you not need anything?"

"Perhaps."

"You never ask for so much as a scrap."

Apparently afflicted with ennui, the wight merely lounged against a column with his arms crossed, as he had leaned on the parapet of the stone bridge.

"And," Asrăthiel continued, "I have noted that when you are given a gift, you are wont to return it. As I have mentioned before, my mother told me the tale of the Heronswood coat of fishmail, and the Jaravhor jewel. You refused them both."

"Does my failure to behave as your dependent inconvenience you, weatherwitch?"

The damsel glared at the hairy-shanked incarnation. His dreary garments flapped in the breeze. She might claim him as an heirloom, but he was only a diminutive domestic wight after all, and a useless one at that. Too frequently he overlooked his inferior station. At this moment his patronizing tone grated on her self-containment.

Placing her silver comb on the bench beside her, she said coldly, "I believe that sometimes you forget whom you are addressing! I was born with powers that can only be guessed at by the likes of you. Invulnerability runs in my blood, inherited from my ancestors. My father made me heir to the power of the brí; furthermore, I am immortal."

It did not matter, after all, declaring this to a wight. He, too, was deathless, so he would hardly think of her as a freak. Besides, he seemed to have been aware all along that she could not die or suffer hurt, and it had made not a jot of difference to him.

The urisk, still lolling against the pillar, said provokingly, "How impressive. What's the weather forecast, witch?"

Driven by a sudden urge to prove herself superior, Asráthiel ignored his insolence and initiated her weather-faculties, sending them probing into the mercurial gradients of pressure, temperature and humidity that surrounded her. In the courtyard the ambient air was cold—about beer-cellar temperature. Her senses roved outwards, to the snowy peaks of the storths where the atmosphere's currents blew much colder and stronger. Further and higher, she detected a trough moving across the High Darioneth region. A band of precipitation had already developed over the ranges, and with the temperatures so low, it would almost certainly soon be falling as snow on the heights. The moderate to fresh northwesterly winds would shift toward the west following the change, and then southerly later in the night. Bitter weather would develop, with snowfalls continuing. War's Day would again be chilly, although snowfalls would become more isolated, clearing early on King's Day as a weak high pressure ridge moved across the region. Another front was likely to arrive on Thunder's Day, bringing more showers, tending to more snow at higher elevations.

"The night will continue to be cloudy," she said aloud, "with rain developing after midnight. Snow will fall on the high crags, and the northwesterly winds on the heights will blow at gale forces until midnight, when they will ease slightly but remain strong and gusty. Down here inside the mountain ring the winds will ease to moderate." She concluded with, "Tomorrow morning, rain will be followed by an overcast day with light to moderate northwesterly winds on the lowlands, gusting up to about fifty knots in the ranges." Asrǎthiel cast a look of complacency at the urisk.

The corners of the wight's mouth twitched upwards. Was there a tinge of irony in that smile?

"Those who make your acquaintance are fortunate," he said. "They will always know whether to bring an umbrella."

His mocking tone was insufferable. Asrǎthiel's temper flared.

"If I had an umbrella I would knock you on the head with it, you considerable fool! You make light of that which you cannot understand. The potency of weathermastery is vast beyond your reckoning."

The eyes of the urisk darkened, as if the creature suddenly stood beneath a different sky. He pushed himself away from the pillar and poised upright on his cloven hoofs. For the first time, Asrǎthiel became uncomfortably conscious of the *otherness* of this wight, and experienced a jolt of fear. Urisks were seelie, but they were no less arcane than wicked wights. They were akin to water, wood and stone, rather than hearth and table. They belonged to the night.

"It is you who have but a slight notion of greater forces," the wight said softly.

Asrǎthiel's fear subsided, but she could not help feeling somewhat wary of the wight. It was as if she had picked up a familiar ornament, only to discover it had a secret catch which, when triggered, opened the item to display strange internal workings that had been there all along. The urisk's intentions in paying visits to her were unclear and his comments were obscure—but then; it was useless to ponder on the ways of eldritch creatures. Their minds, their purpose— all were unfathomable to most human minds.

That there *was* some purpose, however, she was beginning to suspect.

Suddenly a loud and crashing boom reverberated through the courtyard; a cacophony like crushed brass.

Asrăthiel jumped. The urisk winced.

Somewhere in the core of the house the dinner-gong had been struck.

The clamor and its echoes broke the uneasy tension. However, when the damsel looked again, the urisk was—naturally—nowhere to be seen. He had disappeared without taking his leave, as was his custom.

"Dinner!" someone called out.

In the tarnished light, the courtyard appeared to be completely devoid of wights. The creature was as absent as he was mysterious. Why he had attached himself to her family in the first place was a puzzle, and why he called on her was beyond understanding. According to received wisdom, urisks were customarily attached to certain *places,* rather than to families. Tribes and clans of mortalfolk might come and go, but urisks were wont to frequent age-old watery places such as wells, and shady pools, rarely consorting with humankind at all. Of course there were always exceptions to any rule, and this, evidently, was one such case. Asrăthiel wondered why.

Slowly the damsel stood up and ran her fingers through her tousled hair. She picked up her silver comb and left the gloomy cloister, making her way indoors, where lamplight enfolded her like a saffron robe.

IV

Philosophies

Riders of night mares, ugly and vicious,
Ruthless and wicked, fell and malicious
Lurk in the dark hours, sniffing and sneaking;
Pounce on the hapless, squealing and shrieking.

—"GOBLINS," A RHYME

Midsummer's Day passed, celebrated with the usual festivi-
ties throughout the Four Kingdoms. Some two weeks afterwards, a wisp of swifts in chevron formation flew over the
long-deserted lake-camp of the Marauders. The birds
crossed the Border Hills and winged their way toward the
Mountain Ring.

It was early in the month of Jule. A caravan of itinerant
peddlers from Cathair Rua arrived in High Darioneth, bringing their wares and tidings of doings in Slievmordhu. Marauders had raided the hamlet of Carrickmore, they said, with
great loss of goods, and some lives. Most of the villagers had
fled when the attackers struck. Many of those who stayed to
defend their homes had fallen to the cruel axes of the raiders.
In Cathair Rua, the palace had announced that the defense
levy on all households in the kingdom would be substantially
increased, to pay for better fortifications and more numerous
troops to protect outlying towns and villages. Poverty was on
the rise, for the rustics were hard put to meet the new taxes.

The peddlers were fearful. Their wagons bristled with
weapons, and they had hired their own mercenaries to
strengthen their escort. They were of the optimistic opinion,
however, that traveling convoys did not appear to be attacked
as frequently as villages these days.

At High Darioneth the plateau-dwellers and the denizens
of Rowan Green inspected the wares of the peddlers, making
a few purchases and listening, grim-faced, to the news.

On a Summer dusk, another flock of birds—swallows this
time—passed over the lichened roof-tiles of the houses on
Rowan Green. Their calls flooded through the open windows
of the library in the house of Maelstronnar. Hearkening to
their stridor, Asrăthiel lifted her head and focused the hyacinth lenses of her eyes, as if her gaze could pierce the ceiling and the steeply pitched roof to the skies above, and the
stars on the other side of the universe.

Avalloc, Storm Lord of High Darioneth and most eminent
weathermage in all of Tir, occupied the library also. He had
returned that very morning from a visit to his friend, the
scholar-philosopher Almus Agnellus, who was dwelling, in-

cognito, in a lonely and humble abode near the borders of the Wight Hills. Together, Avalloc and his granddaughter had been discussing the progress of Asrăthiel's studies in weathermastery. Having exhausted that topic for the moment, Asrăthiel turned to another.

"Grandfather, what lies beyond the borders of the Four Kingdoms?"

Asrăthiel asked questions like these from time to time. Avalloc was aware that despite having traveled all over Tir throughout her life, his granddaughter was far from content, and wished to reconnoiter beyond the fences. He pondered. "We cannot be certain. To my knowledge, no adventurers have ever come to Tir from the lands beyond."

The damsel persisted, "In all the tomes and scrolls in the libraries of High Darioneth, and many of the collections and stacks belonging to noblemen and royalty in the great cities, there is little to be told of those regions, save for their various names and sparse description of their hither marches. I should very much like to take a sky-balloon and go exploring."

Her grandfather observed her thoughtfully.

"You understand, dear child, that is impossible," he said. "Our fleet is larger these days, because the worldwide climatic pattern is altering. Our services are more in demand than ever. Bear in mind that the weather is wilder and more fickle than in earlier times."

Asrăthiel said, "You and I, grandfather, can extend our senses great distances into the atmosphere, predicting the weather far in advance. When we augur that the atmosphere will be relatively tranquil across the kingdoms for a few weeks, leaving at least one balloon idle, I could go exploring!"

"Even the most proficient weathermaster," Avalloc countered," must acknowledge that he or she is ultimately fallible, and that the atmosphere is as capricious as any tricksy wight. Emergencies sometimes arise, and we must be prepared. Balloons and crews cannot be spared for adventuring or exploring."

"But do you not wish to know what lies past the borders?" A hint of pleading had entered Asrăthiel's tone.

"You and I both understand the nature of the weather systems that prevail over the closer areas of those outlying regions, at the furthest limits of our weather-senses. Is that not sufficient, hmm? Besides, all evidence indicates those lands are not inhabited by humankind, nor are they habitable at all by our race—" the Storm Lord checked himself, then amended, "by *mortal* men of our race, I should say. Too many perils and vicissitudes beset far-off places; if not heat and drought then icy cold, or unseelie wights in their hordes, or wildwoods impenetrable, or the hostility of landscapes wind-scoured and barren. To explore those strange countries would require a well-provisioned expedition, and I doubt not 'twould take many a long day—months or years; perhaps decades. And no guarantee of a profitable outcome, or indeed of a safe return."

"Knowledge is profit!"

"Exactly my point, dear child." Avalloc wagged an earnest finger. "There's no guarantee an exploratory expedition would discover any information of value. Writers of the lore-books surmise that the acres of desert or snow or tangle surrounding the Four Kingdoms extend for league upon league, until they simply come to an end at some far-off shore."

"Well, I consider the prospect of exploration to be exciting, "Asrăthiel replied obstinately. "I daresay there are wonderful discoveries waiting to be made."

"My dear child, what are you hoping to discover?"

"I should like to diagnose the purpose of the universe, and learn the manner of its birth, and what we are made of, and how to banish wickedness."

Avalloc's eyes twinkled. "That is very right-minded of you, to be sure. The druids would say you only have to pledge loyalty to the Sanctorum and be generous with donations, and you shall achieve all your goals."

"And why should we doubt their word?"

Their laughter mingled, as so often. Conversation turned to the subject of the latest "prophecies" from the Sanctorum, which in turn led Asrăthiel and Avalloc to discuss the violence being stirred up throughout the Four Kingdoms by the now-frequent schisms within the druidic brotherhood.

"I would that they might all exterminate each other in battle," said Asrăthiel tartly. "Then we might live free of their strictures and blind bigotry. May the Sanctorum and all its rotten branches wither!"

"And yet," said Avalloc, shaking his white-maned head, "people have a profound need to trust in something beyond themselves. Hope, no matter how illusory, is preferable to despair."

Asrăthiel threw him a quick look. "How odd," she said, "someone else made a similar statement to me, not long ago."

Their conversation continued until at length, when the moon's white-bone face was peeping through the multiple glass panels of the windows, Avalloc decided to retire to his bedchamber, leaving Asrăthiel alone in the library. Curled up in an armchair she commenced perusing a book, with eager intensity, as if words were the air she must inhale in order to stay alive. So intent was she on her reading that she was oblivious of all things around. The wall-paneling squeaked, leaded panes rattled in the night breeze, broken patterns of moonlight slid across the floor.

As Asrăthiel turned a page it came to her that the broken patterns of moonlight had conceived a shape. Or rather, a configuration that was an absence of light.

A shadow.

She started. The book slid from her knees to the floor, landing with a thump.

"Fie on thee, thing!" cried Asrăthiel, springing out of her seat in amazement and outrage. "How came you in here?"

"And a good evening to you too, witch," the urisk said, giving her an urbane nod.

"It should be impossible for you to enter here. You cannot cross the threshold of any house unless invited!"

"You invited me."

"I did not!"

"Your words were, *Come with me into the kitchen. I shall find you a dish to your taste.*"

Slowly, wonderingly, the damsel stepped back and re-seated herself in the armchair. "Well, so I did," she said softly, shaking her head. "So I did."

Abruptly she laughed. Her smile was a flash of pure white. Her face, when she laughed, shone as if lit with a golden radiance. She felt rather delighted at the wight's impudence in interpreting her offer of food as a literal invitation to enter the house. Of course, the creature would still be unable to come inside if wight-repellent talismans were hanging over the doors and windows, but houses that harbored domestic brownies did not guard their entrances with wards and charms.

"Why do you not appear before other folk?" she asked, secretly pleased that the urisk had returned after their quarrel in the courtyard. "Why to me alone?"

"Humankind is, by and large, a tedious race. Of all its members, you are perhaps least so."

"Why, thank you! I am pleased to learn I approach a chance of being tolerably tedious. I shall strive to achieve this goal, while hoping you do not perish of boredom in my company."

The last of the smile lingered, tugging at the corners of Asrăthiel's mouth. The creature could be entertaining, in spite of his vexing ways. Moreover, she was beginning to discover he was surpassingly knowledgeable. When he deigned to be in a reasonably pleasant mood, she was usually able to learn a great deal from this supernatural manifestation; after all, he had lived for an immeasurable span of years, and his store of lore must be greater than the greatest library of humankind. When he sank into an intemperate humor, however, he would tell her nothing.

"You arrived at a convenient moment," said the damsel, "for I am rereading Master Clementer's speculations on the durable nature of Life. The writer used to be a druid. *You* seem to know much about the druidry."

"If so, it is merely because I have existed for so long."

"It is unfortunate the druidry has existed for any length of time at all."

The wight seated himself, cross-legged, on a woven mat. "Apparently you detest them."

"I wish them all exiled forever." Asrăthiel picked up the book that lay sprawled at her feet, smoothed the pages and closed it. As she walked over to the shelves to return the volume to its place she continued, "Once you claimed, 'Even false hope is better than none.' Since then I have mused often on the matter. I do not begrudge people their hope of an afterlife, or of happiness in this one. 'Tis those who would wield that hope as a weapon to enslave others whom I detest. That is what the druids do."

"Would you shatter the comforting illusions of the populace?" asked the urisk. The window behind him framed his head. The silver moon seemed pincered between his horns.

The damsel detected that his interest was purely academic; nonetheless she was passionate enough about the subject to press on. "No, but I would take away the lies and power-mongering that the Sanctorum has chained to those pristine hopes of happiness."

"Oh, it has ever been a tradition amongst your kind, political elites exploiting human emotions in an attempt at subjugation. How would *you* present hope to your countrymen?"

Impetuously, Asrăthiel dropped to the floor and knelt, not close to the urisk but low, so that she could speak to him face to face. He regarded her intently. "In this," she said: "I would give them hope without the dogma. That is the hope I cling to, whenever I long for—" she hesitated and drew back, embarrassed to find herself on the verge of vulnerability in the presence of this alien personage. "No matter." After pausing to organize her thoughts, she explained, "Life is tenacious. The scholar Adiuvo Clementer learned that it survives deep beneath oceans under enormous pressure, where no light can reach; even in the superheated vents of submerged volcanoes."

She had spent untold hours at her mother's bedside, puzzling over whether there was some profound meaning to Life, and if so, how it was to be found. It was a topic that fascinated and frightened her. Motivated by the urisk's intelligent glance and contemplative attention, she added, "Life exists even at the bitterest ends of the world. It can survive in the harshest of environments, if water is present. Is that not marvelous?"

"Certainly."

He was not being sarcastic, for once.

Asräthiel paused. At length she said huskily, "Clementer has written that at the dawn of time the dormant seeds of life came to our world across the airless void of the heavens, through a cold so profound we have no words for it, riding on the backs of falling stars."

Beyond the windowpanes, as if in response to her words, a meteor traced a luminous stripe against the constellations. While watching the bright arc swiftly fade, Asräthiel said, "It moves me deeply to understand that the universe wants Life to be. As long as the universe exists, so will Life, in some form—even if not necessarily a form with which we are familiar." The damsel glanced back toward her listener, who was still seated on the mat, self-contained and typically aloof, though patently missing nothing.

"It is indeed a fact," commented the urisk, "that the first motes of Life alighted on this world after voyaging through the Void on fragments of broken planets—as fevers and agues travel from sufferer to sufferer on a handkerchief, or through the air. Life germs discovered a victim to infect, a host in which to breed—the world of Tir. They proliferated and, out of the resultant purulence, humankind arose. Indeed," said the wight, "the *germs* of humankind were aptly titled. They were, in truth, specks too small to be descried by human eyes, whose pathogenic cousins, to this day, make war on your kindred as your kindred make war on each other. The plague called humanity has much in common with other diseases. You act like your festering and destructive forebears because it is in your nature to do so."

Ignoring the wight's sardonic tone, Asräthiel said pensively, "Perhaps Master Clementer's apocalyptic vision is right, and in the distant future Tir will no longer be fit for Life to inhabit. But the seeds of Life are tenacious, and if they once spread to this world, there is every reason to believe they have spread to other worlds, and will go on spreading forever, whether or not Tir falls into the sun."

On the mantelpiece, a lighted lamp guttered. The wick hissed.

"Even so," the urisk acknowledged. "The Uile is made up of matter, energy and life. Matter and energy cannot be created or destroyed, merely changed. It is the same with Life. Like matter and energy, it is perpetual."

"So if Life is 'Good,'" Asrăthiel philosophised, "then we may rest assured that Good will *be,* throughout eternity. With the power of the Uile driving every living entity, how can there ever be an end to the essence of mortal creatures? I would give people *that* faith," she concluded, "and then they would have no need for these fabricated icons, the Fates."

Now the lunar dazzle from the windows had concentrated itself into a glaze of glittering quiddity, which sparkled in the eyes of Asrăthiel. Her lower lip trembled. She gazed at the urisk, almost beseechingly, hoping for some validation of her reasoning. The moon seemed to melt into the horns of the wight, and flow down into his curly hair. It limned his silhouette with metallic glimmers. Beholding the small figure wrapped in moonlight and shadows, Asrăthiel was brushed by the wings of awe.

"I doubt whether they would ever lose that need," said the urisk. "Evidence indicates humanity requires some anthropomorphic idol to turn to at times of despair and abandonment. That is why they invented the Fates."

Asrăthiel sighed. "Yes," she said. "And for that I can find no remedy."

"Perhaps there is one."

She glanced sharply at him. "You astonish me, condescending to seek solutions to benefit humankind."

"My consideration is merely a whim."

"Of course. It has not escaped me that your disdain for my race is exceeded only by your contempt. But prithee, state your case."

The urisk was no longer sitting cross-legged on the mat. He stood upright; a small, somehow indistinct figure in the tenebrous chamber. The yellow light from the lamps glinted on brass fire-tools and the gilt-embossed spines of books, but did not seem to have the power to touch him.

"No thing that lives," he said, "is ever alone. Most mortal creatures can read the maps and make sense of them. Many of the human variety, however, no longer remember how to draw wisdom from the current of life."

"Tell me how!"

"*You* know already. Meditate, or write, or speak softly, from the heart, into the world that exists behind the eyes. The answers are all ready and waiting to be found."

Unexpectedly, an aching pressure arose within Asrăthiel's chest. She was taken by surprise, and fought to suppress a dry sob.

"Life is without you," said the urisk, "and within you. Ultimately," he concluded, "it holds all its own explanations. It is complete, question and answer both. I would say *that* is the remedy."

Asrăthiel quickly turned away and hid her face.

"Why do you weep?"

"I do not," she replied in muffled tones. "I cannot. Or if I do, I weep no tears. Immortal human beings are unable to shed tears. Did you not already know that, wise urisk? Perhaps you did not, since only two such beings walk free on the face of the world. Did you know that when people speak of matters close to their hearts, they may sometimes cry, even if no tears fall?"

"I did. I do."

"Then you are indeed wise." This time, when she said it, she was in earnest.

She found that she was, however, discomposed by having been so profoundly affected in front of the urisk, notwithstanding that the lapse had been but momentary. Upon regaining her composure she spoke again, affecting a nonchalance she did not feel, in order to dilute her discomfort. "I value your insights, of course. You have traveled hither and thither in the world accruing erudition, while I am obliged to remain within the Kingdoms. Your visits are welcome, although—" A thought struck her and she swung around to face the wight. "I have never understood why you do pay me this courtesy. Tell me, why did you attach yourself to my family so many generations ago, and why do you remain with us after all this time?"

The wight uttered a short, cynical laugh, which, for the most part, was what Asrăthiel had come to expect. Nevertheless, he gave reply.

"For many years I wandered aimlessly," he said, watching the shadows as if they reflected the distant past. "The tedium half drove me mad. It chanced that I stayed awhile by a western seashore, and it was there that I witnessed an event that stirred my jaded curiosity for the first time in ages, though only to a trifling degree. A mortal man, a boat-builder, rescued a stranded mermaid, carrying her down to the sea's edge from which the waves had cast her. It was then common knowledge—and remains so to this day—that he who does a good turn for the mer-folk is entitled to three wishes; albeit, this man refused to demand his payment. Some weeks later the sea-girl gifted him with that shirt fashioned from the armor of sea-fish, and he was too polite to return it."

"Oh!" exclaimed Asrăthiel, thinking of the shimmering garment she had inherited from her ancestors. At long last she understood how the strange artifact had fallen into the hands of the Heronswoods.

Her companion continued, "The boat-builder's surprising stupidity—doubtless some would call it "altruism"—interested me a little, and for want of any better purpose I came to look in on him and his family from time to time. I followed them when they migrated to the Marsh, then stayed there. It seemed as good an abode as any. Also," the urisk appended, "I came to hear certain stories about the exploits of your forebears—stories I found somewhat inducing."

"*Inducing?* Why?"

"Indeed, I cannot say."

"Cannot or *will* not?"

"Conjecture as you please."

Asrăthiel pondered, but could make nothing of the creature's oblique references. A cloud drew its veil across the moon, and the library darkened. The oil lamp by which the damsel had been reading was burning low; the wick needed trimming.

When the damsel looked around again she could barely make out the shape of the eldritch presence in the gloom. She shook herself, as if ridding herself of cobwebs. Unaccountably she once again felt ill at ease with the wight. To conceal her awkwardness she yawned. Rising to her feet she said, suddenly formal and impeccably polite, "The hour is late. I am weary and must seek my couch. Now that you have been so impudently artful as to interpret my remark as an invitation, I suppose you may stay or go as you please, for my word, apparently, is given; therefore I cannot prevent you. Nevertheless, whenever you are in this house be aware we have a brownie of whose welfare we are solicitous, for it performs all the onerous household tasks during the night when we sleep, and it is a most cherished member of our household. No doubt it is lonely, being the only wight around here. I daresay it might enjoy your company from time to time, when you are gracious. Good night."

She departed swiftly, quietly closing the door after her.

The library appeared to be empty. Only starlight glittered at the window, and a few motes of dust shifted on the floor, eddying in a draught that stole in under the door.

V

Strategies

Commoners are as worthy of life, joy and liberty
As men who are kings by right of birth.
Non-humans are as worthy of life, joy and liberty
As creatures who are human by right of birth.

—ASRÃTHIEL'S MOTTO

Summer had at last truly arrived in the highlands, and crowds of bees were thriving in the blossoming nut orchards. In the House of Maelstronnar, Dristan's wife, armed with a notebook, was seated at the kitchen table consulting with the cook, while the butler stood to attention close at hand. "Pea soup," proclaimed Albiona, enumerating dishes for the evening meal and crossing them off her list with a crayon, "followed by boiled hare garnished with small vegetable marrows, bacon and beans. For dessert, black-currant pudding with custard. Of course Lady Asrăthiel will not be having the meat, so ensure there is nut bread on the table, the butterless variety."

As her name was pronounced, Asrăthiel, in search of viands, happened to wander through the kitchen on her way to the larder. Her cheeks were still flushed, she having spent the morning in the vigorous practice of swordplay, and her eyes shone a clear blue, like burning gas.

The mistress of the house interrupted her task of annotation and looked up. "Asra!" she cried, "I am glad to see you. Pray, let me take a moment of your time." The cook curtseyed to Asrăthiel, while the butler politely tugged his forelock. Dristan's wife, clearly troubled about some weighty issue and determined to speak her mind, bade the servants leave the room temporarily so that she might engage in private discussion with her niece.

"Sit down with me at the table!" Albiona invited, and when Asrăthiel had obliged, the mistress of the house commenced to explain the cause of her dissatisfaction. "How ever did that urisk get into this house?" she demanded.

This question took Asrăthiel unawares. "Urisk?"

"The creature does not help around the place. In fact one might say it hinders, because it frightened Cook out of her wits when it appeared unexpectedly by the inglenook one evening, and she spoiled the dinner."

"'Tis seelie. 'Twill not hurt any of us."

"That's as may be, but seelie domestic wights are supposed to help with household chores, and it does nothing of the kind."

"It does no harm, either."

"That is a matter for debate. But 'twill do harm if it disturbs our friendly brownie, he that scrubs the kitchen floor and sweeps the hearth every night, and sets the fires ready for the morning and works all through the sunless hours to make this house spick and span. If your urisk goes upsetting the brownie there'll be trouble all around."

"Why do you call him *my* urisk, Albi? I have no governance over him, or any other eldritch wight."

"He *is* yours, is he not? He was associated with your mother, so I understood."

"Well then, in a manner of speaking I suppose he could be called mine. He was attached to the house of my maternal forebears. He's a kind of heirloom, one might say, like the fishmail shirt and the gem, and even the sword that hangs above the fireplace."

At the mention of Fallowblade, sparks snapped in the eyes of Albiona. Asrăthiel immediately wished she had not referred to the sword. Albiona wanted it bequeathed to Arran's brother Dristan, later to be passed on to their son Cavalon. Dristan, however, was content to lack inheritance of the sword. He was a good weathermage but far more interested in gardening than fighting, or even than weathermastery. As for young Cavalon he admired the golden blade, like everyone who set eyes on it, but he showed no inclination to wield it.

"Should I spy the urisk," Asrăthiel said, with an awkward attempt to be conciliatory, "I shall remind him to be courteous to the brownie." She added, determined to ensure that Albiona was aware of her competence, "As I have done already, in the past. For now, Aunt, I must distract you no longer from your tasks."

The damsel left the table and visited the adjacent larder, from which she subtracted a platter of raisin tarts and a flagon of elderflower wine before departing.

She carried the refreshments to the dining hall, where, after sparing a keen glance for Fallowblade suspended in its usual position above the mantel, she set them on a table. The room was bright, the air perfumed with the scent of blossom. Outside, swallows were twittering. Through the open casements she could see, in the far distance, the snowy cones of cloud-wrapped mountains upholding the sky. The alpine wind, ever unquiet, keened and caroled as it swung upon the green boughs of the rowans, which were bedecked with their corymbs of white flowers. The damsel fetched two wooden goblets from the sideboard and filled them with clear, golden wine.

Soon her grandfather entered the chamber. Old man and young woman seated themselves near the window, within arm's reach of the sweetmeats. Fresh breezes eddied in, plucking at their hair and sleeves.

"Dear me, it seems not so long since I first interviewed your mother in this very room," the weathermaster said pensively. "At the time she was close to the same age you are now. I have a vivid memory of her standing over there, looking up at Fallowblade. She had requested an audience with me. It was then that she let me in on the secret of her invulnerability."

"Not so invulnerable after all," said Asrăthiel sadly.

"Never lose hope, dear child," said her grandfather. He took a draught of elderflower wine and replaced his drinking vessel on the table. "Now, let us to the matter at hand. It is to be your nineteenth birthday in a few weeks' time, as no doubt is uppermost in your mind."

Gravely, the damsel inclined her head. They had met here to discuss her future, and she had expected preliminaries of this nature. She too sipped from her goblet.

"It is unusual for a journeyman to become a weathermage before the age of twenty-one; however you are an unusual child, in many ways. You were not only born with the brí, you were born with your father's other gift; that old age will not wither you, nor be the agent of your demise. As far as anyone can guess—for of course you are the first human being ever to be born immortal, and we cannot yet *know*—once you reach the full flowering of maturity the aging process will cease. And you have proved outstanding at your lessons. As you progressed from brí-child to prentice and thence to journeyman, you passed every test of ethics and skill with ease. Indisputably you are ready to face the ultimate test, to become a full-fledged weathermage and be awarded the final and most puissant secrets of weather-wielding."

Asrăthiel fastened her eyes on her wine-cup. Her grandfather was merely confirming what she had already guessed.

"You will wield enormous power, Asrăthiel," said the Storm Lord.

So rarely did he call her by her name that it came as a surprise. She met and held his gaze.

"And *that* you merit," he said, nodding to emphasize the point. "That, you merit."

"Gramercie, sir."

"What will you do with it, hmm?"

"I have not altered my intention. I should still like to diagnose the purpose of the universe, and learn the manner of its birth, and what we are made of, and how to banish wickedness."

Avalloc slapped his knee and uttered a short laugh. "And I *still* say, that is very right-minded of you!" he said. "But what of weather-working?"

"That will always be my duty and my delight," she said, flashing a brilliant and loving smile, "and I am looking forward to piloting my own flights, you may be sure—but Grandfather, you of all people know I would fain explore faraway places, particularly towards the north. When I am a mage, I would like to break with the tacit tradition of using Rowan Green as my base. Our people have ever been loath to leave the mountains—perhaps it is some unguessed quality of the brí that anchors us here, but for some reason, maybe because I am—" she hesitated, "*different,* I do not feel that same tug."

Avalloc said, "Granted, 'tis possible your immortality is the wellspring of your desire to spread your wings; we have no way of knowing. You have forever been a restless one, like a bird in a cage."

"Restless forever, but not yearning to be away forever.

Wherever I go in the Four Kingdoms, I will return often to spend time with you, and you must also call on me."

"Of course!"

Asrăthiel added wistfully, "And bring the rest of the family with you. Perhaps matters would be better between Albiona and myself if the two of us did not dwell beneath the same roof. She can never be easy about the inheritance of the sword, and my ideologies concerning rights for nonhumans, and the urisk nuisance. . . ."

"Perhaps you are right, dear child. Now, listen well. Bearing in mind your oft-declared desire to move northwards, I am about to make certain arrangements. If the proposal pleases you, then after you achieve the rank of weathermage you shall become High Darioneth's new representative at King's Winterbourne."

"The proposal pleases me indeed!" exclaimed Asrăthiel, sitting bolt upright. "It is an excellent idea! King's Winterbourne is the fairest and most commendable of cities."

"And since you would be residing there, you might as well take the official title of resident weathermaster, weathermage to the King."

"Resident weathermaster! There have been few who ever held such office in any city. The last was many decades ago, as I recall."

"You recall rightly, my dear. It has been as long as that since any mage could be coaxed to dwell away from Rowan Green."

"I love my home, too, but I am not bound to it. I should very much like to take up this position."

"I had an inkling you would agree. Capital. We will notify the appropriate officials forthwith. The king will be overjoyed, and our own council will be glad to have a representative in the capital."

Asrăthiel clasped her hands tightly, as if all her poise was contained between her palms and she must protect it from her exuberance, which threatened to break it asunder. "And while I dwell at King's Winterbourne," she began, "I might take advantage of the numerous private libraries—"

She broke off as a small, nondescript figure shot into the

room, sprang onto the table and jumped out the window. It vanished from sight, leaving only a thin shriek bleeding along the wind.

"Great heavens!" said Avalloc, rising to his feet and peering over the sill in an effort to spy the escaper. "Was that not our brownie?"

"It was," said Asrăthiel, equally astonished. She joined him at the window. They could find no sign of the wight on the lawns outside. "'Tis most unusual for it to be abroad in daylight."

"I have never known it to act thus," said Avalloc, stroking his beard musingly. "I wonder what's amiss. What was that word it shouted?"

"I am not certain," replied the damsel. "It sounded like *'crowthistle,'* but why should the wight screech the name of a weed? I see no crowthistle growing in our lawns, to prickle its soles!"

The sound of running feet drew their attention to the door, and presently Albiona burst in, her face pinched with anger. "Asrăthiel, your urisk has been oppressing the brownie," she cried without preamble. "Just now I opened the door to the still-room and there was our poor wight cringing in a corner. I asked what ailed it, but it gave a terrified yell, sprang past me and fled away like a streak. When I turned around, there behind me stood the urisk, leaning against the doorframe, as nonchalant as you please. He startled me so much I was lost for words, but before I could find my tongue he had turned the corner and vanished from my sight. I am certain it was that useless creature who caused the brownie's distress."

Asrăthiel opened her hands in a gesture of helplessness. "I am sorry for our faithful helper, but what can I do?" she asked. "I have no power over the urisk."

"It was you who let him enter in the first place, was it not?"

"I suppose so, but I did not intend . . . it was not my fault. . . ."

"You must do what you can to make amends. The wretched creature only ever speaks to you. Persuade him to let the brownie alone, or preferably, to leave this house."

I doubt whether anyone could persuade the urisk in any way whatsoever, Asräthiel thought to herself. Aloud she meekly said, "I will try." Even though she had not intentionally invited the surly urisk to cross the Maelstronnar threshold, she felt culpable, and somehow responsible for his deeds. It irritated her, this attachment to the annoying wight; for it *was* attachment she felt, in spite of his troublesomeness; no doubt of it. "I shall endeavor to rectify the matter," the damsel reaffirmed, in an attempt to placate her incensed aunt.

"Thank you," said Albiona stiffly. She bowed to Avalloc, adding. "Pray pardon me, sir, for interrupting your meeting."

The Storm Lord nodded. "You are pardoned, my dear," he replied mildly. "As mistress of the house it is your duty to see to the servants, whether human or eldritch. It is understandable you are concerned for the welfare of our industrious sprite." Albiona departed, leaving Asräthiel and Avalloc to resume their discussion.

During the following days Asräthiel found herself caught up in her studies and in preparations for her birthday celebration and the conferral of weathermagehood. She was so often occupied with urgent business that the matter of the urisk and the brownie slipped her mind. From time to time Albiona would bring it up, and the damsel intended to act on the matter, but the urisk was being elusive; she seldom spied him, and when she did, he failed to remain in view for long, and would not speak to her.

She could not help being troubled about Albiona's blaming her for the brownie's plight. It was bad enough that Asräthiel's aunt failed to see eye to eye with her about the inheritance of Fallowblade, or her stance on equal rights for all animals, without another grievous fault being added to the catalogue. Furthermore she was indeed sorry for the poor bullied brownie, for she empathized with all things that lived; and she tried to think of some way to aid the wight.

❧

Pollen and petals from the last of the roses that bloomed around the cupola on the house of Maelstronnar were dislodged by the wind and blown away. The petals landed on Dristan's neatly scythed, weed-free lawns. Three tiny jots of gold whirled through the eastern gate of High Darioneth and across the tops of the alpine forests, until they drifted over the junction of the byway and the highway: Blacksmith's Corner. There, one minuscule mote alighted upon the helm of a passing knight, while the others floated on.

The warrior was Conall Gearnach, commander-in-chief of Slievmordhu's Knights of the Brand. He led a company of chivalry from the Red Lodge, King Uabhar's fiercest and most loyal fighting men. They were traveling northwards, on their way to practice martial maneuvers amidst the harsh and frigid steeps on the marches of Narngalis. Most rode on horseback, their mounts champing on the steel bits that ruled them by way of their sensitive mouths. The emblem of the burning brand illustrated the scarlet tabards of the knights, and their uniforms were resplendent with crimson, vermilion and madder. Yellow bronze damascened their helms of steel. Beneath their tabards they wore the breast and back plates of cuirasses. From their shoulders flowed carmine cloaks that covered both the rider and the haunches of the horse. War-chariots and supply-wagons were hauled by sweating draught-horses whose hides bore cross-hatchings of whiplash scars.

After they had passed Blacksmith's Corner, where the side road branched off to High Darioneth, they rounded a bend and encountered a group of horsemen coming from the other direction. No sudden panic overcame them; only a sharpening of wariness. The Knights of the Brand, heavily armed and honed in the skills of fighting, were fearless.

In any case, those who approached appeared harmless; a band of men who, by their salt-white hair and beards, all looked old enough to be grandsires. They were clad in civilian garb, and would doubtless move aside and give up the road to the military cavalcade.

As they came near, Gearnach hailed the civilians. "Ho,

men of Narngalis!" He raised his hand in a signal to his troops. Both parties reined in their horses.

"I am Conall Gearnach of the Red Lodge," said the knight. "What news of Narngalis, good citizens?"

"Conall Gearnach! Hail! Your fame precedes you, sir," one of the travelers answered courteously. "The commander-in-chief of the Knights of the Brand is widely renowned. My name is Tsafrir. I was once Captain of the Guard to the Duke of Bucks Horn Oak, and I remain in service to his household. We are the duke's liegemen." The look in his eye clearly showed him to be honored that Two-Swords Gearnach would speak to a band of humble retainers.

Recognizing a fellow soldier in this grizzled cavalier, Gearnach gave a curt nod of acknowledgment. "Well met, Tsafrir."

"You ask for tidings, sir, but I must tell you there are few. Narngalis is a peaceful land." As he said this, bold Tsafrir deliberately let his gaze wander over the shining steel of chariot and helm.

"And shall remain so," said Gearnach, noting the direction of the man's gaze. "King Warwick grants us leave to practice the arts of battle amongst the steeps of Ironstone Pass, the better to accustom ourselves to harsh conditions. What news of Marauders along the road ahead?"

"None, sir. We were not harassed."

"That is well. But look to your weapons and your watch if you intend to cross into Slievmordhu. Marauder raids have become frequent throughout our realm. King Uabhar sends out his troops in ever-increasing numbers, to keep the savages in check. Slievmordhu's eastern borders are vigilantly patrolled. Despite these measures—" the knight's voice roughened "—despite these measures they continue to wreak havoc. Three days ago we happened upon a small settlement under attack." Beneath his helm, the eyes in the soldier's weather-beaten face hardened like splinters of flint, and abruptly he fell silent. Clearly, what he had witnessed caused him distress.

"I thank you for the warning, sir," Tsafrir said respectfully. "Our ultimate destination is Ashqalêth, but we shall bear in mind your timely rede."

Gearnach nodded again. "Derry Meagher is the place I speak of. Good day to you, Tsafrir of Bucks Horn Oak."

"And to you sir. Fare well."

Tsafrir and his companions moved to the side of the road as the squadron of mounted knights cantered by, their harness jingling, their chariots and wagons clattering. When the last of the warriors had passed, the liegemen resumed their journey southwards.

"I rejoice that I do not have to cater for such a large quantity of hungry soldiers," observed a deep-chested fellow with grey whiskers. He and Tsafrir looked to be about the same age—close to sixty Winters. "It is enough that I cook for the household of the duke."

"For my part, Yaadosh," said a third man, "I rejoice merely that your culinary skills have improved vastly since your youth."

Yaadosh tapped the side of his leathery nose. "Ah, but when a man is employed in the work he relishes," he said, "one cannot help but raise one's skills to a more excellent quality. Much as your juggling has mended, Michaiah my lad, you having spent years as conjurer and entertainer."

Tsafrir, who had remained silent since their brief exchange with the knights, now spoke. "Such a wonder!" he exclaimed. "We have met Two-Swords Gearnach. Everyone speaks well of him, from Narngalis to Grïmnørsland. He is reputed to be an honorable man, fiercely loyal his sovereign. King Uabhar instills into his troops, indeed into his own family, the precept of 'Loyalty Above All,' and Gearnach is a paragon of that precept."

"I deem he is also a man of compassion," Yaadosh observed.

"Compassion, yes," rejoined Tsafrir, "for recall the tale from some years ago, about how he cut down the assassin who tried to hang herself from the Iron Tree in Cathair Rua, and thereafter the woman was rehabilitated, and she made the great Garden for the good of all, and became the Crone of the Herbs. If not for Two-Swords she would have died and the Garden would never have grown in that wasteland."

Ahead of the travelers, masses of grey clouds billowed slantwise through the sky, as if tightly massed chimneys from acres of manufactories were pouring out smoke. The highway meandered through a lush water-meadow before climbing a wooded slope. Blackbirds were warbling in oak, beech and alder. Red admiral butterflies dodged through the leaves.

"I would that we might hasten our journey through Slievmordhu," said Michaiah, whose nag plodded laboriously. "Everybody we meet informs us of the increase in attacks from the mountain clansmen. I am too old to be beating off bandits. I've already done my fair share of hewing ugly heads. These visits to R'shael seem more arduous every year. I am always pleased to see our old friends, but I'd just as soon be home amusing the grandchildren with sleight-of-hand."

"Ach!" Nasim snorted. "You are talking like a greybeard!"

Michaiah's eyes crossed as he looked down at his own chin. "A greybeard is what I am," he said. Then he added, wonderingly, "Where did the years go?"

❧

A few days later they crossed the hills into Slievmordhu. Bordered by luxuriant oak woods, the road climbed a low ridge. As the riders breasted the rise, catching their first glimpse of a small village about half a mile away in the valley below, a band of armed men sprang out from the trees to bar their way. The guards wore Sir Réamonn Meagher's coat of arms, for he was lord in those parts and they were in his service. They challenged the newcomers and would not let them pass until they were satisfied as to their identity and the peaceful nature of their business.

"We wish to break our journey," explained Tsafrir, "mayhap to take a drop of ale at your inn."

"The inn at Derry Meagher was lately burned to the

ground," the patrol captain grimly informed the visitors.
"But you can get ale at the brewer's house."

The travelers turned off the highway onto the meandering
byroad and made for the settlement. Beyond the hills on the
horizon, massed rainclouds were still blowing across the
skies, and a scattering of dark birds winged eastwards.
Cloud-reflections drifted beneath the glassy surface of a
duck-pond.

As the vista opened out, the riders could see in the distance an ox-drawn wagon jolting along a winding lane, over-
taking a goose-girl who was supervising her flock. A woman
carrying a wooden yoke across her shoulders, a pail suspended at each end, was delivering milk up to the manor
house, while two young men hauled sacks of oats from the
granary to the mill.

Berries were ripening on the hawthorn hedges, and star-
lings were squabbling beneath the eaves of stable and byre.
The village's three large fields flanked the road. It was close
on harvest-time; wheat and rye hazed the north field with a
pale yellow mist; oats, barley, peas and beans thrived in the
home field strips, while three or four cattle grazed under the
chestnut trees bordering the fallow southern field. Children
walked up and down the furrows scaring off the birds. When
they spied the riders they ran away, shouting in fright, de-
stroying the impression of a peaceful idyll.

Derry Meagher with its mill, its small brewery and its inn,
was a settlement inhabited by about one hundred and eighty
people. The mill and a row of thatched wooden cottages
lined the stream at the bottom of the valley. Larger cottages
clustered along both sides of the main street, flanking the
walled demesnes of the slate-tiled manor house, the only
stone building. Each dwelling, surrounded by gnarled apple
and plum trees, occupied its own yard. Toddlers played
amongst the chickens and dogs; they, too, fled when they
caught sight of strangers riding into town. In the crofts behind the yards women leaned on their hoes, warily watching
the riders from amongst rows of turnips and parsnips, beans
and peas, onions, cabbages, and clumps of sage and thyme.

The travelers passed a skinny fellow with the dazed demeanor of the slow-witted, who was sitting cross-legged by the roadside playing a merry tune on a bone pipe. After removing the instrument from his lips he sang,

> "Poor folk in hovels,
> Charged with children and overcharged by landlords,
> What they save by spinning they spend on rent,
> On milk, or on meal to make porridge."

"Can you not get it to *rhyme*?" Michaiah the songmaker muttered intolerantly as they went by.

"Poor Rori and Cluny and Tipper, lyin' cold in their graves," the fellow sang heedlessly, before putting the pipe to his mouth and resuming his incongruously happy tune.

As they passed along the main street the liegemen found themselves audience to the sound of low sobbing, which emanated from one of the houses. Men with fresh cuts and scratches on their faces and hands were mending a splintered door and affixing iron bars to windows. A linen bandage wrapped the head of one worker. Burdened by a bundle of kindling-twigs, a hunchbacked woman trudged past, one arm in a sling. Across the top of the main street, beside the grassy common dotted with sheep, a third group of cottages had been built. At the end of this row stood the inn, the brewery and the brewer's house. Where the inn had once been, however, there was now nought but a blackened ruin. Most of the burned timber had been cleared to one side, and men were already beginning to reconstruct the building on its original chalk footings. Using a block and tackle, they were hoisting the first of several enormous pairs of wooden crucks, whose bases were to rest on large padstones built into the foundations.

The first raindrops of a light shower commenced to patter down, and the visitors were glad to find shelter within the brewer's house. Dark and warm was the interior; a long room with a byre at one end, occupied by a few sacks of barley and several twelve-gallon vats, and a half-height chamber containing sleeping quarters at the other. Smoke from the open fire pit escaped through a hole in the roof. A deep stew-pot cast in bronze hung from a tripod over the coals. The rafters of the great crucks arched overhead, while underfoot the hard-packed clay floor was well swept.

Within this house the visitors found hospitality and good brown ale. Oonagh the brewer served them; a rosy-cheeked woman with the stamp of good nature on her countenance, overlaid by recent woe. Her sleeves were rolled up to the elbow, revealing the raised red weals of her scalded arms, a mark of her profession.

"I would like a rissole," Yaadosh began without preamble, for his stomach rumbled. "You say you have none? What about sausages, do you make sausages? Are there any eggs? Chicken?"

"I have no penny to be buyin' pullets," Oonagh responded matter-of-factly, "nor geese nor pigs, but I have two green cheeses, a few curds of cream, a cake of oatmeal, two loaves of beans and bran, baked for my children; and I have parsley and pot herbs and plenty of cabbages. There's pottage warmin' on the hearth; take a bowl and help yourselves!" And with that, Yaadosh and his friends were satisfied. They fell to with good appetite.

"We heard your village has lately suffered a fearful raid," said Tsafrir, while Oonagh slammed extra wooden spoons and trenchers onto the tabletop one by one, as if striking down imaginary enemies.

"Aye," said the brewer, "and we are all on the lookout for Marauders. By the Black Dice! If they return they will not be farin' as well as they did the first time."

Yaadosh dunked a hunch of rye bread into his pottage. "Why? What happened the first time? Did nobody raise the hue and cry?"

"It was gettin' dark," Oonagh said. "The monsters came creepin' through the oak-woods, where some of our youngsters were out late, gatherin' kindling. The poor little tykes saw them comin' and oh, they were so scared they hid themselves without makin' a sound. Slevin spied them, too, the swineherd; he was herdin' his pigs back to the sty, but he was not swift enough to bring the news before the raiders reached the village, for he is somewhat crippled in the legs, and then Renny the goose-girl was goin' home along Thatcher's Lane flickin' that old tardy gander with her switch and she clapped eyes on what was comin' and dropped her hazel stick and started screamin' and the geese ran all about honkin' madly, but by then they were already upon us."

"What did they take?"

"They took three lives, that was the worst of it, the trio of brave men who tried to stand against them, Rori and Cluny and Tipper, and they hurt some others badly, and they made off with livestock. They ransacked the blacksmith's, stealin' spurs, arrowheads, scissors and knives, they broke into the granary and carried off sacks of grain, they beat the baker to within an inch of his life and stole as much bread as they could lay their hands on. I had three fat hams curin' in the smoke above this very fire. Gone, all gone."

The visitors expressed their sincere sympathy.

"I was hearin' the geese, and Renny's screams, and I ran to look out the winder. I shall never forget what met my eyes—" the woman sketched a lucky sign in the air "—for I am still sick from the sight. There was poor Rori, and those giants pushin' him to the ground with his arm all bent up behind his back, and then one o' them seizes a milkin' stool that had been propped against Rori's house and brings it down over the poor man's head. Rori's face gets all over splattered with blood and this murderer, he scoops the blood in his claws and smears it across his ugly muzzle like some trophy he's proud of, and another picks up the stool all splintered, and licks the blood off it like it was delicious as honey, and then both of 'em rolls their eyeballs up inside their sockets till only the whites is showin', and lifts their upper lips and bares their fangs like crazed dogs, all the while standin' over poor Rori dead on the ground. In the name of the Spinnin' Hag, I ain't never set eyes on anythin' so disgustin'." For a moment Oonagh could not bring herself to say any more without breaking down, and fought for composure. Presently she went on, "I just had enough time to bundle my youngsters and myself into our hidin' spot beneath the trap-door before the monsters burst in. Oh, but I wish I'd had a vat on the boil; I'd have been after pourin' the lot over them. Our lord Sir Réamonn says he will go to the city Sanctorum to make generous offerin's to the Fates on the village's be-half. Our lord says we must have displeased them somehow, for by unlucky chance it was just after the king's garrison had withdrawn from Meagher Manor's demesnes that the at-tack was sprung. Had the raiders come just a sevennight ear-lier the king's soldiers would have been here to protect us." After drawing a long breath the brewer went on, "But our lady declares the Fates were not displeased and Sir Réa-monn should be savin' his tithe-coin, for in the middle of the attack who should come gallopin' into Derry Meagher but Two-Swords Gearnach himself, and a whole column of ex-cellent knights at his back!"

"Praise Ádh!" Michaiah said. He swigged from his tankard.

"They thrashed the reavers all right, and put an end to their pillagin' and murderin'. Most of the monsters fled, and Gearnach's men rode them down; some escaped though. One who went after them was slain, it was Lieutenant Mac Seáin, Gearnach's second, also a lifelong friend of his, so we found out after, but Two-Swords was lively with the battle-lust hot in his blood, and when his men brought word of his lieutenant's death, he got into a fury and leaped upon his horse and galloped up Main Street, screamin' blue murder. He leaned from the saddle as he rode, and snatched up a fiery brand—oh, by the Bell of Míchinniúint, he was like some madman, spittin' blood and foam. I think he had lost all reason in that moment and did not know where he was, for as he passed the inn, he plunged the torch deep into the dry thatch shoutin', 'This place I name the bane of Mac Seáin, for had he never come here he would still be livin'!' And our inn went up in flames."

The visitors exchanged glances of astonishment. "Were any lives lost in the burning?" asked Nasim.

"Not a one, thank Fortune. And oh, but Two-Swords was most repentant afterwards," said the brewer. "After he had cooled off no man could be more repentant than he. 'Alas, for I am cursed with a terrible temper,' said he, and he swore to make full reparation. Then and there he handed our reeve a full purse, with the promise of more to come from his personal coffers, which he sent for from the city. Gearnach is famous for bein' a man of his word, and when the gold arrives we shall have enough to rebuild the inn better than ever it was. So you see, as trade for a little inconvenience, *that* part of the doin's has turned out for the best."

Some more swapping of news took place, which included, to the surprise of the visitors, the revelation that in Cathair Rua of recent times, public slurs had been cast upon the previously immaculate reputations of the weathermasters.

"What can the citizens be thinking of, to believe any slander about the most admirable benefactors of Tir?" Yaadosh cried indignantly.

"The knowledge of that is not at me," said Oonagh, "but where there's smoke there's fire, as they say."

"They also say," said Tsafrir, "those who speak ill of others reflect badly upon themselves."

After paying the woman and thanking her for her kindness the liegemen took their leave, for the rain-shower had dwindled and passed. The fellow with the stunned demeanor tagged after them awhile, playing his bone whistle, as they walked their mounts along the byway leading out of the village.

"The king's much-vaunted parades," the whistler sang out unexpectedly, "Of guards are charades/It is naught but a token/Be careful what is spoken."

In surprise, the travelers turned around to stare at the speaker.

"The garrison mysteriously withdrew/Just before the raiders came through," the fellow persisted, undaunted.

"What are you raving about?" demanded Tsafrir.

"Occasionally one or two/Marauders are caught and hanged, 'tis true," said the whistler, "But in confidence I tell ye/The hangings are staged mere-lee/To justify higher protection tax." He waved a dirty hand as if merely bidding the party a cordial farewell. "Do not dare suggest that to loyal Gearnach," he added in his singsong fashion, regaling them with a gap-toothed grin.

"My friend," said Tsafrir wearily, "it is to be hoped your loose tongue—"

"—and abominable attempts at poetry," interjected Michaiah.

"—will not repeat such rumors in the company of others. It is better not to even *entertain* such thoughts, lest you spill them inadvertently when you are in your cups." Tsafrir tossed the whistler a brass farthing.

"Be not troubled once ouncel," the songster said happily, pocketing the farthing. "I can keep close counsel." He fell behind, still waving. Turning their backs on him the liegemen resumed their journey. When they reached the highway they heard the piping of the bone whistle, rare and desolate through the oak-woods.

"Quite the social reformer, is he not?" Nasim observed.

"Why is it that fools always play some sort of musical flute?" Yaadosh mumbled into his beard.

Michaiah, who was still wincing at the memory of the worst doggerel he had ever heard, made no remark.

"More to the point, why is it that so many apparent fools are so wise?" Tsafrir returned darkly.

"What?"

"He suggested something I have long suspected."

Yaadosh, who had survived several battles and many Winters, shivered as the full implications of his companion's words sank in.

❧

The road ahead of the liegemen stretched all the way to Cathair Rua, the royal city of Slievmordhu. There, upon the three crowns of the highest hill rose three clusters of stately buildings: the palace citadel of King Uabhar Ó Maoldúin, the Sanctorum of Slievmordhu, and the Knights' Hall—of strong, ruddy oak—known as the Red Lodge. As twilight closed in, the windows of all these structures glowed like eyes of flame.

Within the palace two men sat at their ease around a table of polished mahogany in a splendid chamber overlooking the grounds. Soaring stained-glass windows depicted one of the former kings of Slievmordhu kneeling at the feet of Ádh, Lord Luck, the Starred One, who rested his benevolent hand on the king's bowed head. The star bound to the brow of the Fate was a glittering topaz set into the leadwork. Beyond these intricate panes, the city was laid out beneath the clear evening sky, a jumble of red rooves and towers.

Magnificently furnished, the chamber was lightly cluttered with objects. Sideboards gleamed with polish, their shelves covered in small ornaments, candlesticks, tapers, candle-snuffers, wick-trimming scissors, writing equipment, jars of sweet-smelling dried petals and other bric-a-brac. The largest adornments were marble statues of the four Fates: comely Ádh with his winning smile; stalwart Míchinniúint, Lord Doom, hefting his twibill; the sly siren Mí-Ádh, Lady Misfortune, accompanied by her malicious feline companion; and the scowling crone Cinniúint, Lady Destiny wielding her spinning-wheel and shears, ready to snip the life-threads of men.

Uabhar brusquely dismissed the attendants in red livery who had been serving wine and pastries. The majority backed out of the chamber, bowing effusively yet barely noted, leaving a solitary butler who stood to attention by a sideboard occupied by goblets and decanters. With hands clasped behind his back, he stared blankly at the wall-paneling as if seeing nothing, hearing nothing. His manner was impeccable.

The king of Slievmordhu was gorgeously attired in habiliments lavishly trimmed with fur, and his dark brown hair was immaculately coiffed. He wore it in the fashion of his youth, combed off his face and tied at the back of the neck with a thin band of velvet. A jeweled cap topped his head.

"My dear friend," he was saying to his confabulator, "as

you know, I am as famous for justice and impartiality as I am for open and honest dealings with my neighbors. If there is one species of man I cannot endure, it is a liar and a cheat. Like you, I am a straight-talker. In fact, you and I are so similar in this respect we might be brothers."

Uabhar's demeanor was authoritative and self-assured, but as he spoke he avoided meeting anyone's gaze. He picked at a loose thread on his raiment, apparently fascinated by it.

"Yes indeed," agreed the recipient of his wisdom. Chohrab Shechem II, King of Ashqalêth, was one year older than his interlocutor; however, he had the air of being the more naive. His chin, sprouting a few straggling hairs, receded into a drooping throat that segued with his neck. Narrow and hunched were his shoulders; his cheeks and belly swollen with excess fat. Like his fellow ruler he was clothed in magnificent garments, but his chosen colors were the shades of a sunburnt land; brown and copper, contrasting with oranges and yellows.

"And, as your *brother,* Chohrab," continued Uabhar, peering at a blemish on the back of his own hand, "I wax wrathful, on your behalf, when my spies constantly inform me of Narngalis's secret plans to annex your kingdom. I can scarcely sleep at night. How dare Warwick contemplate such an atrocity!"

"How dare he indeed," repeated the Ashqalêthan king. After a moment's reflection he subjoined, "But though you are certain of his duplicity I have yet to be convinced of it."

"Alas, a good man is only too ready to believe the best of others. Like you, I could not credit it at first." Uabhar gestured emphatically. "You, my friend, are a paragon amongst men. For fidelity and sincerity there is none as pure, unless it be myself."

"Yes."

"And, as so often, Warwick of Narngalis takes advantage of your openness, reviling you behind your back, accusing you of being *weak,* and *easily led*! Oh how my heart ached to hear of such vile and patently false accusations."

"What insolence, to make such claims! But surely your spies must have been mistaken. Perhaps he spoke in jest."

"I wish 'twere so. My gravest fear is that Warwick tries to turn the tide of opinion against you, so that the machinery of his plans to overrun Ashqalêth may be oiled."

"May the Fates forbid it!" cried Chohrab, and he took a long swig from his goblet as if his life depended on the draught. His companion eyed this behavior with a certain curious satisfaction.

"Warwick preys on the weak, and if anyone is weak it is Thorgild," said Uabhar, leaning closer to his guest while simultaneously signaling for the butler to top up the contents of Chohrab's cup.

"Thorgild of Grïmnørsland?" After his swallow of wine, Chohrab seemed, for an instant, confused.

"The very man. Lo! Here is an example of your sagacity, for you have instantly penetrated my meaning. Aye, Thorgild of Grïmnørsland, who plays games of his own, and who foolishly hearkens to the poisoned words of Narngalis."

"But I thought your own sons were firm in friendship with the sons of Thorgild!"

"Thorgild has his own reasons, I doubt not, for endeavoring to cultivate the good favor of my sons," said Uabhar, nodding sagaciously. "It begins to dawn on me that perhaps he too is a schemer. Fortunately you and I possess enough acuity to ultimately penetrate any stratagems he might concoct—but *his* wit is no match for the ingenuity of cunning Narngalis. Why, it is possible that Thorgild is this very moment being won over to the north-king's side. Chances are they are making a pact of alliance even as we speak!"

"By Axe and Bell, I hope it is not so!" Dismayed, Chohrab II stared at the ruler of Slievmordhu, his eyes round and vacuous.

Uabhar sipped his own wine, which, unnoticed by Chohrab, had been poured from a different decanter. "Pray do not stint yourself," he said, waving an expansive hand. His guest gulped another mouthful. "But tell me," said Uabhar conversationally, as he set his goblet on the table, "for I

value your advice—what can be done to defeat their reprehensible schemes?"

"I know not. Maybe we could parley with them. . . ."
Chohrab floundered. He seemed bewildered again. A drop of
wine, red as blood, trickled from the corner of his pudgy
mouth into his beard. Suddenly he put a bloated hand to his
forehead and said thickly, "I am fatigued. I must retire at once."

Uabhar's discomfit was obvious, though only for an instant. "But brother, the hour is yet early!"

"No, no. I must lie down. Parvaneh waits for me. . . ." Un-
steadily, Chohrab heaved himself to his feet. Perceiving his
guest was not to be dissuaded, Uabhar sent for Chohrab's attendants, for the King of Ashqalêth liked to be carried about
in a litter, as befitted his status and his varicose veins. Courteously Uabhar bade goodnight to his guest and watched him
closely as he departed.

Next evening they were back in the same chamber attended
by the same butler, this time accompanied at the table by two
additional dignitaries. These supplements were listening intently to the conversation, but like the servant they seemed
to be paying attention to the window, the walls, the statues;
anything within view except Uabhar and Chohrab. One was
the druid known as "The Tongue of the Fates," Primoris Asper Virosus, Druid Imperius of Sanctorum in Tir. A short,
slight figure, with a caved-in chest, pinched features and
eyes like augers, he was clad in robes of pristine white ar-
mazine interwoven with gold thread. At the age of seventy-
six he had lost all the hair on his head, but having lately
revealed to the public that the all-powerful Lord Ádh of the
Fates required druids to be tonsured, he did not seem as bald
as before. His exposed skull housed faculties of artful sub-
tlety. The fourth man at the table was both younger than the
druid and larger in all dimensions, a military officer of
supreme rank, the High Commander of the Slievmordhuan
armed forces. His name was Risteárd Mac Brádaigh.

The sociability between the kings was continuing from where it had left off the previous evening. Similarly, the drinking; Chohrab had declared himself very keen to taste more of his host's astonishingly excellent liquor. He seemed extraordinarily thirsty.

"Indeed the Starred One favors you, neighbor, with your obedient queen and beautiful daughters," Uabhar was gushing. "I *do* hope they are comfortable in their apartments here. How favored *I* am, also, having fathered such loyal sons. When I think how stupid and hotheaded one's own kin can be, I consider myself doubly fortunate!" he exclaimed with feeling. "Take, for example, my dear departed brothers— Gearóid the violent and impetuous, who was, after me, next in line for the throne, and Páid, the weaker of the two, but perhaps the more subtle. From their boyhood days, intense hatred existed between them. 'Tis scarcely to be wondered at that during later life they met with tragedy."

"Páid poisoned your youngest brother, did he not?" Chohrab mumbled.

"Aye, with *tardigrade* toxins. Gearóid, discovering the scheme too late, murdered Páid by stabbing him to the heart, before the poison took hold and brought about his own demise. A double tragedy. Ah, my poor mother."

"I daresay it was that sad event," Chohrab said, making an attempt to appear solicitous, "which ultimately tipped the dowager queen over the brink."

"Oh yes, she's completely insane, the old crow. Broods incessantly, as if each day is a funeral for the day before." Uabhar sighed. "Nonetheless, one must cheerfully bear the burden of one's relatives." A short silence ensued, which he curtailed by saying, "But now to the urgent business of the danger Ashqalêth faces. Last night, Chohrab, you suggested negotiation, but alas, judging by the latest reports from my spies, Warwick and Thorgild are by now past all reasoning. I'll answer for it that the schemers are hot for action, not words. 'Tis feasible they are already building up their armies, setting events in train for the invasion of your fair realm. I ask again, what can be done to defeat their reprehensible plans? When one's enemies take up arms to fight against one, what can one do?" He screwed up his face in an expression of puzzlement and chewed his fingernails.

"We must build up the defenses of my country. . . ." The Ashqalêthan king's declaration died away as his burst of impulse lapsed into irresolution. He stared perplexedly at his cup. "How I dislike being presented with these conundrums. It reminds me of the schoolroom. I always detested the schoolroom when I was a lad. Butler, fill my cup! Do you know, Uabhar, I always feel so much better after taking this drop of yours. I believe it has medicinal qualities. You must allow me to bear a quantity of it back to Jhallavad with me when I return home. Never in my life have I tasted such fine liquor. It is as if the cares of the world lift away from me with every sip. Perhaps there is some pharmacopeia in it, yes?"

"Dear brother!" Uabhar said hastily, "I could not so much as *think* of adulterating good wine. Naturally it would make me the happiest of men to gift you with the best my cellars have to offer, but I hope you remain much longer beneath my roof, for your companionship is dear to me."

Chrohrab looked gratified.

"You speak of building up Ashqalêth's defenses," Uabhar went on briskly, "but for how long would fortifications and suchlike keep Narngalis and Grïmnørsland at bay?" He stood up and began pacing the floor, apparently deep in thought. The silk linings of his embroidered robes rustled as he walked, and his boots scuffed the sweet rushes strewed upon the parquetry. The instant he left his seat, Mac Brádaigh rose also, and stood to attention beside his chair as befitted his station. The druid primoris might be permitted special dispensation due to his age, frailty, and authority, but the only others in the kingdom who were allowed to remain seated while Uabhar was standing were members of royal families.

"Not long I suppose . . ." bleated Chohrab.

"I understand your point," Uabhar said. "You are saying defense is not enough, yes?"

"Yes."

"That your methods of repelling invasion must be more vigorous and effective than mere fortification, yes?"

"Yes . . ."

"Of course, you are right, my brother. But by the Axe-Lord, what method can be more vigorous and effective than defense?" Uabhar halted in his tracks and scratched his head, evidently stymied.

Risteárd Mac Brádaigh bowed deferentially. "My Liege, may I put in a word?" he petitioned his sovereign.

"You have my permission."

"Many are the historical battles I have studied," said the soldier, directing his carefully chosen words to Chohrab Shechem with the most respectful of demeanors. "I have long desired to make known to you, Majesty, how impressed I was to read of the military triumphs of your forefathers in Ashqalêth; in particular King Firouz IV who, upon learning his enemies were about to fall upon him, sent forth his armies to assault them before they could make the first move. An eminently successful tactic."

"Yes, yes," Uabhar said dismissively. "You are well-intentioned, Mac Brádaigh, but this is hardly the time to be expounding upon your favorite reading material. The king has more important matters to ponder."

"But wait!" cried Chohrab, his watery eyes gleaming in his wide and doughy face. "I have a notion."

Uabhar seemed to freeze. He turned an inquiring eye upon his royal guest and nodded encouragingly. "Prithee, good neighbor, speak your mind."

"You ask what method can be more effective than defense," Chohrab said excitedly, like a child who has discovered a long-lost toy. "I propose we should attack Narngalis before Warwick has the opportunity to invade Ashqalêth!"

The expression on the visage of Uabhar was one of sheer astonishment. He thumped the table with his fist. "Ádh's name, Chohrab, you are right!" he shouted. Throwing himself once more into his chair he planted his hands on the tabletop and pronounced with energy, "As ever, I bow to your superior judgment! It would indeed be in the best interests of your subjects to overthrow Narngalis and Grïmnørsland!"

Looking delighted, the king of Ashqalêth gazed around at the approving smiles of his three companions. Then a thought seemed to strike through his pleasant reverie. "Overthrow Grïmnørsland?" he began; but his sentence was cut short by the enthusing of his host.

"Chohrab, my brother in all save blood, your family and mine have been the closest of friends for years. My sons greatly admire your six lovely daughters and, I daresay, would make them all queens, if 'twere possible. Many's the gift Slievmordhu has been honored to be able to bestow upon Ashqalêth, simply to indicate our respect and admiration. We shall do all we can to aid your plan. Together, you and I shall vanquish the enemies of peace and justice! Now let us drink a toast to our alliance." Uabhar picked up a handbell and swung it furiously, so that it clanged like a thunderstruck arsenal. Chohrab flinched at the cacophony. "More wine!" Uabhar roared.

Two butlers and a ewerer hurried in bringing additional supplies of liquor, while the druid and the soldier—now seated again—congratulated Chohrab Shechem on his astute reasoning. The king of Ashqalêth found himself raising his goblet and drinking to the glory of a war he was beginning to be persuaded he had suggested.

After many toasts had been performed and several inspirational speeches orated, most of the menials were banished once more, and the four conspirators resumed their conniving. They agreed amongst themselves that the need for absolute secrecy was paramount at this stage. Only the most trustworthy and high-ranking members of their households and armed forces would be allowed to know the truth for fear that word would get back to Warwick of Narngalis and Thorgild of Grïmnørsland. Enormous advantage was to be gained in taking the enemy by surprise. Meanwhile, the armies and knights of Slievmordhu and Ashqalêth, under the guise of stepping up their drill for the purpose of defense against a possible concerted attack by Marauders, would in truth be gearing for war. After that decision had been taken, Chorhab Shechem took to his suite, complaining of sudden overpowering fatigue.

Alone in the council chamber the king, the druid and the soldier continued to converse in muted voices. "Chohrab seems most keen to go to war," the Druid Imperius said, ostensibly without sarcasm. When he spoke his thin lips revealed wedge-shaped teeth the color of aged amber.

"Ah yes. He does indeed," said Uabhar, smirking. "And of course we are ever jubilant at being given the chance to aid a friend."

"What of Chohrab's brother-in-law, Duke Rahim, he who has ever appeared distrustful of Slievmordhu? Has he yet been lulled?"

"I believe so," the king replied, absentmindedly cleaning his fingernails with an ivory toothpick. "Chohrab seems to know little about his own agents, but from all reports our operatives have been successful in feeding false information to Ashqalêth's spies in Narngalis. After much effort, the canny duke is being duped at last. Our operatives have proved to be most diligent and steadfast—I daresay they remain mindful of the rewards promised for success, and the penalties to be dealt to their close kindred if they disappoint me. They are resourceful spies, those men you selected, Mac Brádaigh. 'Tis pity they must be dispatched after their tasks are completed, but the risk of secrets slipping out must at all times be avoided." The soldier responded to the compliment with a bow. "Gearnach's Knights of the Brand are in fine fettle," the king continued, by way of deflating the soldier's conceit and infusing him with a dose of jealousy. "What of the warriors under your authority, eh Mac Brádaigh? Is Slievmordhu's army equipped for action at short notice?"

"Thanks be to the Fates, my Liege, our troops have never been feater or more ready for the field." Smug in the knowledge that he himself had been priming Slievmordhu's military host for several months, the High Commander ignored the reference to Gearnach, whom he considered to be one of his greatest rivals for the king's favorable regard.

Uabhar nodded approvingly, then turned to address the primoris. "Let us hope Ashqalêth's military forces are as well prepared to prove themselves my allies as your operatives at the Jhallavad Sanctorum would have us believe, Virosus."

Mac Brádaigh grinned into his mustache at this jibe against the competence of the druid. The old man's extraordinary influence was, in his opinion, ill-deserved, for he held office by puppeting the fear in men's hearts, not by means of hard thews, military discipline, the courage to fight on in the face of agony, and red-blooded prowess with sword and mace. He could have knocked the papery old sage to the floor with a blow from his little finger if given the chance, like brushing off a gadfly, and relished the accomplishment.

"I have no reason to suspect they would mislead us," the druid replied to his king. "Jhallavad Sanctorum is as eager as you and I to see Narngalis and Grïmnørsland brought to their knees. The northerners' slide from proper humility is beyond endurance; with every passing day they lose more respect for the brotherhood. As for the fishmongers in the west, they are so barbaric they have *never* appropriately honored the Sanctorum. United under one ruler, they will soon answer correctly to the Tongue of the Fates."

"Ah yes, the fishmongers," said Uabhar. "When I, as High King, place a loyal son on every throne in Tir, the Grïmnørslanders will hardly be able to argue, for their new ruler will be wedded to Thorgild's daughter. Besides, if they *do* rise against me, the wench will become my hostage."

"Your most royal sons, my Liege—have they yet been informed of the great plan?" asked Mac Brádaigh.

"Of course not. They know naught of any of this. I do not judge them ready, thus far. When all is assuredly under way and there can be no turning back, then I will apprise them of it; perhaps young Fergus will be first to know. They will all obey me, oh yes, but sometimes their qualms can provoke me to impatience. Gearnach, too—he shall not be told until the last moment, lest he become confused, to the detriment of his prowess on the battlefield."

Triumphant at this reminder of his special status in the

king's eyes, Mac Brádaigh inclined his head reverentially and murmured, "I am honored my lord condescends to admit his humble servant into his confidence." Deeming this to be an opportune moment to broach an equally complicated matter of politics, he said, "Your Majesty, it is my unfortunate duty to inform you that your subjects continue to vent their dissatisfaction about the increased frequency of Marauder attacks."

Uabhar's brows shot up. "But how appalling!" he barked. Then he broke into guffaws, saying, "You have done well, my man, you and that stealthy lieutenant of yours. The bandits eat out of our hands like tame dogs, striking where and when we tell them. Let the peasants be afraid! We shall be forced to raise taxes again, if they beg for armed protectors."

"Taxes to pay the costs of future war," the primoris commented dryly, "and worth many times more than it costs in lives and trouble to strike deals with the monsters. Let no man say King Uabhar does not plan with foresight."

Mac Brádaigh said, "My lords, some of the villagers are saying they would rather arm themselves and protect their own domiciles than be subject to higher taxes."

"Discover their names." The king smiled again. Under his breath, so softly that his words were barely audible to his advisors, he murmured, "There will be no complaints when I am High King of Tir." Louder he said, "Virosus, do your druids continue to search for interesting simples? I remain favorably struck by the galenical mixture you call *shape-mind*. It seems to be having the desired effect on our guest."

"Ah, yes, a blend of powdered seed of thorn-apple, mawseed and dwale," the old man said, as if reciting a favorite poem, "lythcorn and hennebelle, feltwyrt and pipeneale. A pinch of wolfsbane, the same of hemlock and hellebore; two measures of sowthistle and dried celandine . . ."

Mac Brádaigh said chattily, "Thorn-apple, eh my lord Virosus? I have heard that robbers spike the beer of their intended victims with thorn-apple, reducing them to witless idiots, unable to defend themselves."

"Well, well," was the druid's only response. He turned his shoulder to the High Commander and addressed his king.

"The search for useful medicines proceeds apace. Of late the Sanctorum has interviewed a young apothecary from the Lake District. He has discovered a certain plant, the leaves of which produce a particularly potent effect when smoked or otherwise inhaled."

"A lethal effect perhaps?" Uabhar asked.

"Nay, not lethal. The fumes cause irresistible drowsiness. This herb might be used to numb the pain of soldiers hurt in battle and facilitate the healing of their injuries, so that wounded fighting-men might sooner be returned to the fray."

"If such substances fell into the wrong hands they might be used against us," said the king, fidgeting. "We must ensure all newfound wisdom is kept secret!"

"You may be sure of that," replied the druid, lacing his hands in front of his thin chest. A chill draught moaned at the windows and sent currents to flutter the tapestries. The aged man pulled his robes closer about his coat-hanger shoulders. "Curse the north wind!" he muttered in septic tones.

"I do not curse it," said Uabhar, jumping up and striding across the room to stare out of the window. "I care so little about it that when I rule Tir I shall take King's Winterbourne as my abode. Though the bitter north wind blows through its streets, the capital of Narngalis is well constructed. I like it better than this red city. From Warwick's castle I shall found a dynasty."

"Many will oppose you for a long while after the war is won," the druid said.

"Those who stand against me," Uabhar replied, turning to face him, "shall be cruelly punished. Oh, depend upon it, I can be quite inventive."

Even the pitiless and unimaginative druid winced at the recollection of some of Uabhar's punitive inventions. "Speaking of wind and weather," he said, changing the subject, "never forget that Ellenhall stands in the way of your annexing Narngalis. The weathermasters are a power to be reckoned with, and loyal to their sovereign. When war begins they will stand against us, alongside Warwick. Their weapons are formidable indeed—we cannot match their bolts and gales and fires. You know you could never win in outright battle against them."

"Fortunately the air-blowers are sworn never to wield the brí directly against their fellow mortals," said the soldier.

"Unless in defense of lives," the druid appended smoothly. "In any event, doubtless they would soon be forsworn, like many a man before them."

"Of course they will break their oath, or claim it is in defense of lives that they throw storms at us," Uabhar said with irritation, "for they are duplicitous scoundrels." Toying with a silver candle-snuffer he had picked up from a sideboard, he went on, "The puddlemakers, with their independence and considerable influence, have always posed a threat to the stability of government. Some fools amongst the common populace view them as challengers to the Sanctorum; indeed, even as rivals to the Crown. We are all agreed that they block our path to success. Virosus, your secundi are having success with their new assignment, I presume? They are swiftly learning to predict and control the weather so that *we* may take over when we have put the puddlers out of the picture?"

"It is no small task as of course Your Magniloquence knows," the druid said, pursing his lips primly, "but they and their subordinates are directing all effort towards developing the necessary solutions."

Mac Brádaigh, who was once again standing to attention beside his chair, said, "My Lord Primoris, the fog-gatherers have been thorns in the side of the Sanctorum for years, have they not? You would fain see their power diminished in Tir, would you not?"

"They undermine the teachings of the Fates," replied the old druid, "with their worship of the elements."

"Worship?" echoed Mac Brádaigh. "I had not heard that they actually *venerate* water and the other constituents of weather."

"Near enough."

"But their appreciation of water is not a creed."

The Tongue of the Fates fastened his heavy-lidded stare upon the soldier. "Of course not, Mac Brádaigh. Even *they* know that there is only one true creed."

The druid and the soldier eyed one another with mutual dislike. Both smiled politely, and the latter dipped his head in a perfunctory bow, ostensibly of respect to the supreme hierophant of the Sanctorum.

"My Liege, if I may venture to say so," Mac Brádaigh said to the king, "they ought to be rendered powerless before we make our first move."

"Yet to do so without public approval would turn the populace against our cause," said Uabhar, "which risks insurrection, or even some attempt at a military coup. The status of the weathermasters must first be abrogated, their authority invalidated! I have already sowed the first seeds of a venture to topple the weathermasters from their pedestal of public esteem. My assistants Gobetween and the Scandalmaster have been busy. No doubt you have both been audience to the first whispered fruitings of the crop."

"Indeed, my Liege!" Mac Brádaigh answered briskly, saluting his king.

The druid imperius lengthened his mouth like a well-fed cat, and inclined his tonsured head. "Indeed."

"And after the mighty have fallen," said Uabhar, "they shall be swept away like dung before a rake."

Shortly thereafter, the three men vacated the conference chamber. Uabhar strode along one of the lofty galleries of his palace, flanked by Virosus to his right and Mac Brádaigh to his left, the sage matching the pace of his younger companions with surprising ease. This trio swung around a corner and continued down a second arcade, at right angles to the first. Courtiers scurried in their wake, keeping at a respectful distance so that they would not be accused of eavesdropping, the penalty for which was execution.

From beyond the walls of the palace, the breeze brought the high, thin jangle of a bell, and a far-off voice: one of the town criers shouting the latest news. Uabhar cocked his head to one side and skidded to a halt, as if listening. Stopping in their tracks, the druid and the soldier observed the king. A kind of radiance, as of revealed knowledge, appeared to dawn on their lord's broad brow.

"You have been inspired, perhaps?" the primoris said sourly, his bald pate shining in the illumination from the arched window by which the three dignitaries stood.

"I believe so," the king said smugly. "I believe so! Never fear, Virosus, there will be no need for outright battle against the weathermasters. There is more than one way to vanquish an enemy. Soon the wheels will be set in motion!"

"Perhaps you will enlighten me as we walk on."

"And perhaps not. You have enough of your own business to mind, Primoris, without minding mine." When the druid scowled, Uabhar bridled, adding, "I am only being considerate for your comfort."

The three continued on their way, their plotting temporarily abated.

❧

At the conclusion of his three-week sojourn at Cathair Rua, King Chohrab Shechem II departed for his palace in the south, accompanied by Queen Parvaneh and their six daughters. High Commander Mac Brádaigh and several other high-ranking officers made the journey with the royal family, to provide assistance—as a token of friendship and alliance between the two realms—in readying the army of Ashqalêth for future conflict. An emissary from the druid primoris would follow the same route within seven days, bearing lavish gifts and even more lavish words of advice, selective truth and exaggerations to the Sanctorum of Jhallavad.

The evening after the departure of the primoris's emissary, Queen Saibh was seated in the royal family's dining room. She was embroidering a cambric pillowcase for her husband while waiting for him to arrive so that dinner might be served. The room was gorgeously decorated; rosewood paneling lined the walls, glistening with dark polish. So delicate were the queen's features that they resembled a shell cameo sculpted against the background of carved furniture, tapestry hangings and heavy draperies of red velvet.

A nightingale huddled in a gilded cage suspended from a hook, perhaps dreaming of freedom in leafy woodlands he had never known. Upon a long couch near the fireplace lay the old queen, the mother of Uabhar, clothed all in black. At the age of seventy-five she was completely insane, and stared vacantly at the flames bouncing in the hearth.

Recently Uabhar had ordered new weapons and a shield struck for his personal use, and these were displayed prominently on the end wall, in pride of place. No expense or effort had been spared in the forging of the arms. "Behold the symbols of the power of Slievmordhu," Uabhar had told his sons upon exhibiting them for the first time. "They are the best in Tir, the finest ever made. You shall learn their names." Holding them up one by one, he pronounced, "My shield, Ocean; my knife, Victorious; my spear Slaughter, and my sword Gorm Glas, the blue-green." His sons had hearkened respectfully to their father's words, as they had been taught all their lives.

The four princes of Slievmordhu, having recently returned from their travels, gathered for the evening meal. First came Kieran, the eldest, crown prince. His thicket of dark brown hair, unkempt and straggling past his shoulders, was worn loose; only the tresses at the front had been caught up and tied in a knot at the back of his head to keep them out of the way. Ronin—second in birth order—was also the second to appear. After Ronin, Cormac entered, and after Cormac the youngest, Fergus. After entering the dining room they greeted their mother, kneeling before her and kissing her hand. They went next to their wizened, bejeweled grandmother and made their obeisance to her, although she had no idea who they were or what they were doing.

In the dining room, the family waiting for King Uabhar conversed in subdued tones. Kieran, Ronin and Cormac stood apart from their mother and younger brother. Their discussion centered around their country's penal system and taxation laws. To question these policies at all implied criticism of their father, so the princes kept an eye on young Fergus, for if he overhead such a conference he would trumpet the news to Uabhar without a qualm, and it was their ardent wish to avoid their father's disapproval.

"Increased levies and harsh penalties are essential if this realm is ever to be free of raiders and felons," Cormac argued in support of his father's government. "Mercenaries must be hired to guard the villages. Would-be seditionists must be discouraged. You *know* this."

"Yet the common people are hard put to feed their children," murmured Ronin, "without added tax burdens. And as for our harsh sentences—for convicted men to be flayed alive, why, only the most baneful of unseelie wights would mete out such a punishment!"

"I comprehend your arguments, Ronin," said Kieran said, "for I too have wrestled with uncertainty."

"Fie upon your doubts!" Cormac admonished. "Think on the Day of Heroes speech. There you will find strength!" Their father had made them learn the speech by rote.

"It is the exhortations of that speech that have troubled me most," answered Kieran, "for I have always struggled with the idea that 'obedience is an expression of heroic character when following the order leads to personal disadvantage or seems even to contradict one's personal convictions.' "

"Sometimes I, too, find it hard to accept," said Ronin.

"Our father would not make these edicts, were it not fitting and appropriate," Cormac said reproachfully. "I, for one, cannot wonder at them. No loyal son could."

"I wish I still owned the faith that was mine as a lad," Ronin said, "for it is a sore trial to me, this new sense of uncertainty."

Kieran nodded. "For one's head and one's heart to be at war—it is like some sickness. I shall strive to be more worthy."

Cormac chided, "He is our sovereign and sire. It is our duty to support him without question."

"You are right," said Ronin, shaking his head as if trying to rid his mind of the detritus of folly. "Of course you are right. Our father is king among kings; his leadership is an example to us all. And yet—"

When her husband suddenly strode through the open door Saibh jumped, unintentionally pricking her finger with her sewing needle. She suppressed a gasp, and was soon seen to be smiling as she welcomed Uabhar. Seating themselves around the table, the royal family took their meal; venison soup, roast kid, baked heron with ginger mustard sauce, capons dressed with a green garlic seasoning, veal in pepper gravy, rabbit in wine with almond milk sauce, and currant custard tarts. The old queen's personal handmaidens served their mistress with a variety of dishes as she reclined on her couch, but as usual she took only a pinch here, a peck there.

"I trust, sir," Kieran said courteously to his father, "that the meetings with King Chohrab proved to be both pleasant and fruitful?"

"Chohrab is a sly fellow," said Uabhar, heaving a sigh. "Sadly, I am beginning to suspect him of belligerence. Lord Ádh knows, I am fond of my fellow monarchs despite the games they play, for I overlook faults in others, being as I am of a generous nature."

"King Thorgild, at least, seems honest and upright," said Ronin. "He is loud in his praise of you, sir."

"Indeed and I think highly of Grïmnørsland in return," said Uabhar, "as demonstrated by my promotion of your brother's connection with Thorgild's daughter. Nevertheless, Ronin, recall that you are yet youthful and have much to learn. When you are older, you will come to penetrate the subtle arts of deception practiced by most men who wield power. Rare indeed is the man of royal blood who adheres to high principles. My own family is among the virtuous exceptions."

"Halvdan Torkilsalven is a man of high principles," stated Ronin, almost, but not quite, challenging his father's words.

"Of course!" the king replied lightly. A sunny smile played around his lips. "By all accounts Halvdan is a good son who honors his sire, and that is most commendable of him indeed. A man shall be judged on his loyalty to his country and to his father. Yet I daresay there is no family in Tir as fair and upright as my own. I have taught the principles of filial duty to all of you. You have been raised to be as straightforward as I am myself."

"Always we strive to be our best for you, sir," said Kieran, sincerely.

"Excellent!" Uabhar beamed. "Solidarity is an ever more precious commodity nowadays. These are vexing times, what with squabbles amongst the druids, and the Marauders escalating their raids. We are forced to raise taxes and as a result some of our more shortsighted and ungrateful subjects wax restless, but what can I do? We must collect revenue to pay the mercenaries."

"Perhaps you might arm the villagers themselves," Queen Saibh ventured timidly.

Uabhar rounded on his wife. "What? Give them weapons and encourage them to start a rebellion next time they take it into their heads to dislike some tax or other? By the bones of Míchinniúint, woman!" The king laughed immoderately. Winking at his sons, he said to them, " 'Tis little wonder the Fates decree that women must stay by the hearth and eschew the council table. Why, these ladies, they would bring the kingdom to ruin!"

Saibh colored, and stared into her goblet. Of the rest of the family only the youngest, thoughtless Fergus, joined in the king's laughter. Kieran smiled diffidently, avoiding his mother's gaze, while Ronin and Cormac frowned.

"Mother," Ronin murmured, "would you like me to help you to another slice of the fowl? I think it is your favourite."

The queen declined his offer with a wave of her hand and a grateful smile for his kindness.

Tucking into his meal with gusto, the king forked a gobbet of flesh into his mouth. As he chewed he said loudly, "I suppose you have all heard the claims by the weathermasters that the site of the ruined Dome of Strang belongs to them?"

"That we have, sir," said Kieran, spooning gravy over a capon. "The claims have been made public, in accordance with the law."

"Yet my men of law would assert," said Uabhar, still masticating, "that the site is the property of the Crown. When the sorcerer died, no trace could be found of his heir within seven days. Generally, such assets automatically became possessions of the state."

Kieran replied, "If the Crown does not deny the claim and fails to assert its own right, then after ninety days the weathermasters' claim will be validated. Ownership of the site will pass to the granddaughter of the Maelstronnar, she who is the scion of the sorcerer."

"Hmm," mumbled the king. He swallowed his mouthful and swigged a draught from his goblet. "Unless, of course, the late sorcerer could be proven to ever have plotted against the Crown. Perforce, one of the penalties for treason is forfeiture of all property, with no rights passing to the heirs." After sprinkling a pinch of salt over his meat, he continued, "When first it came to light that the weathermasters were making these demands, Mac Brádaigh urged me to assert the Crown's rights and dispute the claim. Yet I desisted. 'Let the weathermasters have the land,' I said. Mac Brádaigh believes I am overly magnanimous."

"Verily, you are generous, Father," said Fergus.

"Liberality is as much a part of my nature as candor."

"But what value has the land, sir?" Ronin asked. "Every grain of soil has been sifted in the search for treasure."

"As a matter of fact, it is fine country for grazing."

"Yet the ruins cover a large area, and only weeds grow, and no laborers can be found who dare to remove the stones."

"Still, it is prime land. But as Fergus asserts, I am generous. Let the weathermasters have it, and much good may it do them!" said the king, his cheeks swollen with food. He appeared to be remarkably convivial that evening.

After the family had concluded their repast and removed themselves into the adjoining parlor, Uabhar, whose particularly buoyant spirits continued unabated, called for a minstrel.

"Let us have melody," he cried jovially. "I will hear one of my favourites. Strummer, play that jolly ditty my boys were taught in their nursery days. You know the one I mean—the song of filial loyalty. It has a tune fit to set one's toes tapping."

Bowing low, the musician let his fingers pluck the strings of his gittern. In his finely controlled tenor voice he sang:

"There is virtue in allegiance to one's comrades,
And love's loyalty, all honest folk admire.
But of all the deeds that show if he is worthy,
A man's honor lies in duty to his sire.

The obedience of sons decrees their value,
And throughout their lives it never must expire.
Those who strive against their patriarch are abject.
A man's honor lies in duty to his sire.

All good sons, show gratitude for your begetting—
Never question, quarrel, argue or inquire.
For your father's word is law. You must defend it!
A man's honor lies in duty to his sire."

Across the chamber the king's mother, upon her couch, began clapping her hands raucously. Accustomed to her inappropriate outbursts, most of the family ignored the racket. Handmaidens twittered nervously around their mistress.

"Keep her quiet," the king said over his shoulder.

Abruptly the dowager cackled, "Is that rain I hear? What will the weather will be like next War's Day? What will it be like, eh? Will someone tell me that?"

"I told you to keep her quiet," the king said in a louder voice.

Immediately, Queen Saibh rose to her feet and glided to where the old queen lay. "Be at peace, Majesty," she said. "We shall find out the forecast for you. Tomorrow morning we shall receive a semaphore message from High Darioneth."

"Semaphore? What is that?" quacked the black-clad queen, but already she had forgotten what she was asking. "Oh Luchóg, where is Luchóg? Will he not play for me?"

"Get her out," said her son. "Allot my deaf lackeys to wait

on her, those I keep to serve me when I am discussing state secrets. Ha ha, that way no one will be driven mad by her clacking!"

Saibh had no intention of sentencing the old woman to such a fate. "Come, Majesty, it is time for you to retire to your bedchamber," she said, and she stood by the old woman murmuring soothing words as the maidservants helped her into her litter and four footmen carried her away.

VI

Household Strife

The urisk is a useful wight
Who diligently works all night,
And has a meager appetite.
(He never eats more than a bite.)
With stubby horns and shaggy legs
He sweeps the floors, empties the dregs,
Then scrubs the dishes till they're bright
And tidies everything in sight,
In shabby clothes, all threads and rags,
His goat-hooves clicking on the flags.
Sometimes he'll be the farmer's friend—
He'll plough the fields from end to end,
Then sow the seed and reap the corn—
He never stops from dusk till dawn!
A solitary wight, he's fond
Of sitting, brooding, by a pond,
Yet, craving human company,
He does not mind the drudgery.
The urisk lends a helping hand;
A boon to housewives through the land.

—"THE URISK," A CHILDREN'S RHYME

Every day, messages passed down the line of twenty-six sem-
aphore stations between Cathair Rua and High Darioneth,
giving the regional weather forecast for the following day.
Similar arrangements benefited the economies of all four
kingdoms of Tir. Farmers and graziers, in particular, relied
upon the meteorological predictions to let them know when
to sow or reap, when their stock would need shelter, or when
to batten down in preparation for storms.

The sun was two fingers' width above the horizon next
morning when, atop the Royal Signal Tower of Cathair Rua,
a blackbird that had been perched on the mast took fright
and flew off. The two huge arms had begun to rotate. Signalers were hauling on long ropes, moving the booms into
various positions that symbolized runes or phrases. The
receivers, in their tower-eyrie, had just finished inscribing
the information from a recent transmission into their record
books, having descried through their spyglasses a signal
from the neighboring station. It was the incoming weather
report for the following day: ATTENTION: CATHAIR RUA.
WARM, SUNNY MORNING. NORTHERLY WIND INCREASING TO
GALE FORCE AFTER NOON. COOLER GUSTY SOUTHWEST
CHANGE TOWARDS EVENING. SHOWERS AND POSSIBLE THUN-
DERSTORMS. END. HIGH DARIONETH.

In response, the signalers communicated the following:
ATTENTION: HIGH DARIONETH. MESSAGE RECEIVED. IF THUN-
DERSTORMS SEVERE DO NOT SEND WEATHERMAGE. END.
CATHAIR RUA. It was a frequent response. Most often King
Uabhar, who was mindful of keeping bullion plentiful in the
royal coffers and begrudged admitting any need for help
from Rowan Green, would refrain from requesting the ser-
vices of the weathermasters.

The receivers watched through the round lenses of their tel-
escopes as the neighboring station arced into action. It was
passing the information back along the line. Beginning at
Cathair Rua, from hilltop to hilltop the message was relayed
twenty-six times; past the green and rolling meadows of
Orielthir, through the Border Hills, across the valley of the
Canterbury Water to the mountain ring. There the receivers at

High Darioneth semaphore station took heed, writing it all down in their record books and forwarding a note to Ellenhall. Afterwards they settled back to their watching and waiting.

Amongst the high peaks and alpine valleys the day waxed and waned, and deepened into darkness.

The moon, an eaten-out globe of alabaster, shone down on the House of Maelstronnar as a soft cry issued from the nursery. Young Cavalon, the son of Dristan and Albiona, had woken in the night. Allowing the exhausted nurserymaid to sleep on, his mother shrugged on a dressing gown and tiptoed to his bedside. "Hush," she whispered. "All is well."

"But the dream frightened me. I will not be able to fall asleep again!"

"I shall fetch a cup of warm milk. Then you will sleep soundly."

Albiona picked up her lantern and made her way downstairs to the kitchen.

As she passed the door to the scullery, she caught a peculiar noise, and paused. As quietly as possible she dimmed the lantern and tiptoed close to the scullery door, which stood ajar. Peering through the crack, she saw the household brownie standing on a stool in front of two wooden tubs on the sinks, one full of suds and the other containing clear water. He held a brush in his wizened hand, and had obviously been scrubbing pots and pans.

Between the door and the brownie, with his back turned to the spy, stood a familiar goat-legged figure. Albiona compressed her lips in disapproval, but kept silent and listened.

"O despiteful tidings, 'tis you, you wretched drudge," the urisk was saying. "Making yourself useful, are you? Hurry along, there's a good fellow. There's plenty more to be done before sunup in this nook-shotten crib."

As the listener bit her lips to prevent herself from blurting her indignation, the brownie nervously scrubbed harder at the pots.

"You have a pretty situation here, haven't you?" the urisk continued pleasantly, "an agreeable family dwelling in a comfortable house, a delicious morsel of new-baked bread every evening and a stoup of fresh cream—what more could a fellow want by way of pampering?" Casually, the urisk began to stroll around the small room. His hoofs tapped on the flagstones as he peered at various objects, lifting lids, running his fingers along edges, examining small utensils. The brownie's eyes slid sideways. He watched his persecutor but said nothing.

"And what other feats do you perform in this house, eh?" the urisk said suddenly. "How do you occupy yourself here when all the housework is finished? Do you curl up to sleep in the chimney, or do you prowl and spy? Do you go sneaking about the house in the dark when they cannot see you? Do you listen at the doors to hear their conversations?"

Albiona shifted uncomfortably.

"Do you spy upon them as they dine at table, or sit in the parlor? Do you observe every look, every innuendo, every silence, every act of courtesy that passes between them?"

"Nay sir, wit ye well that is not my way, I do ensure thee," the brownie piped up stoutly. The mistress of the house, squinting from her vantage point, thought the sprite looked hurt. "No mischief would I perpetrate upon mine own household. All good chivalry do I maintain, sir, as has been my wont since the dawn of days."

"Well, mind that you continue to be so noble of conduct, for if ever you do not—" The urisk never completed his warning, for his words were drowned out by the crash of a copper kettle slamming into the stone floor. "Alack! Lo, 'tis all bent," the urisk said sadly. "They shall probably blame you, my good fellow. You'd better mend it. Cry mercy! There goes another. How clumsy of me."

A brass colander flew past the door and smashed into the wainscot. The brownie uttered a howl of fright, whereupon Albiona threw open the door and burst in, but already the urisk was nowhere to be found and the brownie, ever secretive, was scuttling away into some hidden niche.

Grimly, Albiona surveyed the damage and collected up the fallen kitchenware. Over the coals of the cooking-fire she heated a concoction of milk and cinnamon. She carried the beverage upstairs and gave it to her son, but although Cavalon was soon a-slumber, his mother was unable to follow suit, and lay awake, seething, until morning.

At breakfast the following day Asrăthiel's aunt confronted her with the story.

"He's a spiteful knave," Albiona complained vehemently. "Clearly he despises our dear brownie. Have you yet remonstrated with him?"

Assuming an air of calm self-possession to conceal her sense of guilt, the damsel replied, "Nay, the chance has not yet presented itself. Prithee be assured I shall do so at the earliest opportunity."

"That is what you always say! If we are not careful, the vagabond will chase away our helper entirely!"

Asrăthiel considered her aunt's fears to be exaggerated, for surely eldritch wights were accustomed to playing mischievous tricks among themselves, not only upon humankind. She was angry with the urisk for bullying the brownie without mercy, and regretted the plight of the domestic helper, yet she believed the skirmish was unlikely to lead to any serious consequences. Nevertheless she tried her utmost, all day, to contact the urisk. In the courtyard she sought him, and in the library, the still-room and the scullery—in every place he had ever been known to appear. Softy she called to him, but there was no reply. By nightfall she had had no success, and went to bed feeling dissatisfied. She did not delude herself, however, with the notion that he had departed from the premises.

Next morning the household woke to discover that, for the first time in memory, not a single domestic task had been accomplished between sunset and sunrise. Straightaway the mistress of the house flew into a panic, while Asrăthiel stood by uncomfortably, not knowing what to do.

"The brownie's gone! It's fled!" Albiona wailed. "It's been scared away! O ill-dispersing wind of misery!"

The disturbance could not have occurred at a worse time, for next month would bring Asrăthiel's birthday-party and magehood ceremony. Lord Avalloc had invited a vast number of guests, to whom Albiona's household was to play host for a full week. King Thorgild and his sons would be amongst the visitors, and the princes of Narngalis also, and there was no doubt all royal personages would be accompanied by considerable retinues.

"This is disastrous!" cried Albiona.

"It cannot be such a calamity," Dristan said comfortingly to his wife. "We have servants aplenty. Besides the butler and the cook, there are the housemaids, the grooms and the coachman."

"Dearest," said Albiona despairingly, "I suspect you have no concept of the amount of work it takes to run a household like ours on an ordinary day, let alone leading up to an important occasion. Our zealous brownie performed the work of many servants. It took on the duties of pantryman, laundry-maid, maid-of-all-work, still-room maid and scullery maid, as well as some tasks customarily assigned to a footman and a housemaid. We must find the darling sprite. We must get it back!"

"'Twill not be difficult to locate the wight," said Dristan, ever-encouraging. "It will be lurking close by, I am certain. After all, it has not been laid by a gift of clothing, so it remains, by the eldritch code, connected to our household."

"It has vanished! Vanished!" lamented Albiona, refusing to be soothed.

"While we wait for its return we should all help with the domestic tasks," said Dristan.

Asrăthiel quickly agreed. "Most certainly," she said, spotting an opportunity to redeem herself in her aunt's opinion. "I, for one, am happy to do my share."

Albiona recovered her composure and turned her attention to the task in hand. "If these premises are not to go to rack and ruin we shall all have to work hard," she said sternly. "Today, Dristan, when you fly off to do your weatherworking near Orielthir, I shall send Corrie and Cavalon with you so that they will not be bothering me. Meanwhile, Asrăthiel, prithee work all your wonders and try if you might bring back our beloved helper."

や∂

Two days afterwards Avalloc Maelstronnar was seated at the desk in his study, writing a letter. As he dipped the quill in and out of the ink-pot he was oblivious of the strong high-altitude winds at their blustering, the rattle of glass panes in their leaded frames, the scratching of the nib on the paper and the usual creaking of the wall-paneling.

Brisk footsteps grew louder along the hall. The door was flung open without ceremony and Asrăthiel stormed in, her beautiful face smudged with dirt, her apron stained and her long black hair tousled. Uttering an oath she collapsed into an armchair.

"Housework is dirty and tedious," she declared. "I have had my fill of it. Fire and flood! I had no idea how much work the brownie did every night! Albiona has not yet hired a scullery maid or a chambermaid or any other form of maid because Dristan is convinced our helper will return. The servants are simply overwhelmed. Albiona and I have been forced to help dust the chimney-ornaments, take up the hearth-rugs and beat them clean, trim the lamps and sweep the stairs, wash greasy pots and scrub tables. Aside from that there is the mending of linen and lace and the removing of any spots, which is only the beginning of the saga of the laundry. The clothes then have to be washed, starched, dried, pressed and folded. Can you imagine how tiresome such tasks can be? It ought to be mandatory for everyone in the kingdom to wear the same garments for at least a month at a time."

Avalloc looked up and blinked at his granddaughter in astonishment. She went on, "I am polluted from head to toe after cleaning the fireplaces. It is necessary to sweep out the ashes and deposit them in the cinder-pails before black-leading the grates. But even before *that,* one has to *manufacture* the ghastly blacking by mixing up asphaltum, linseed oil and stinking turpentine. For, if one does not black the grates they begin to rust, yet every time a fire is lit, it burns away the blacking. Furthermore, Grandfather, it was never before plain to me how many ordinary objects have to be polished. Not only the boots but the candlesticks, the silverware, the furniture, the handrail of the banisters, the lamps and the looking glasses. As for sweeping, the catalogue is endless!"

"And a good afternoon to you too, my dear child," said Avalloc, his eyes twinkling. He replaced the quill-pen in its holder, blotted his letter with sand, and leaned back in his chair. "Contrary to your probable expectations I do comprehend the rigorous nature of daily housework," he told his granddaughter. "I have not lived for seventy years without finding out something about the matter. It is tedious, aye, and time-consuming. Benevolent domestic wights are a boon to housekeepers everywhere. It is a great shame that ours has disappeared. It had been attached to the family for generations."

Asrăthiel picked up a corner of her apron and began rubbing at various stains on her hands. "I have searched high and low, I have left enticing morsels, I have called and wheedled and made every effort to fetch our helper back, all to no avail. I cannot even find the urisk these days, let alone the brownie, which has always been far more reticent. Everyone seems to believe that the dratted urisk is *mine,* and that therefore I ought to feel guilty about the catastrophes brought about by his meddling. But he does *not* belong to me! He belongs to nobody; he is accountable to none! I am not responsible for his misdeeds and I wish everybody would stop blaming me." She gave up scrubbing and threw down her apron. "All this trafficking with dirt makes me squeamish. I am tempted to abandon all housework and let this place accumulate dust until it turns into a hill and sprouts vegetables." Her tone was pettish.

The Storm Lord regarded her calmly, hiding the beginnings of a smile behind his hand.

"Oh, Grandfather, I am sounding spoiled and selfish, am I not?"

"You are."

"Forgive me. It was but due to the heat of the moment, I hope. Really, I am sorry all this has happened; you know I am. Indirectly it *was* my fault. Now that I comprehend how hard the household staff must work I am doubly sorry. Even with the help of the brownie their labors must have been protracted and arduous. I shall never understand wights! How brownies could actually enjoy all that hard work is completely beyond me."

"Whether they do enjoy it or not," remarked the Storm Lord, "no one knows for certain." He stretched out his arms to rid them of cramps, then clasped his hands behind his head in a relaxed pose. "Do you recall," he went on, "the tale of Alainna Macnamh, your great-great-great-grandmother?"

"You recounted it to me when I was a child."

"I learned the tale thoroughly, for 'twas passed down from my ancestors to me. I heard it many times, because it involved my own forefather, Aglaval Stormbringer. When Alainna Macnamh was but a young maiden she was stolen away by the sorcerer Janus Jaravhor, who carried her off to the Dome of Strang. Three brothers set out to rescue her: Turlough, Teague, and Tierney A'Connacht. The first two failed but the third was successful—and why, hmm?"

Asrăthiel replied, "Aglaval Stormbringer told them all to cut off the heads of whomsoever they met on their journey of rescue. Turlough and Teague did not heed his words, but Tierney, the youngest, used Fallowblade to lop off the heads of the disguised servants of the sorcerer, and thereafter he won Alainna for his bride."

"Precisely. And what then is the lesson of this story?"

"That Fallowblade is useful for beheadings?"

Avalloc cocked an amused eye at her.

"That sometimes one must overcome pain and squeamishness to achieve a goal?"

"Precisely. And at the moment our goal is to keep the premises clean until help arrives. This situation with the brownie has evolved from your actions, in a roundabout way. I am glad to see you taking responsibility and learning from it."

The damsel sighed. "I will bear that in mind next time I find myself on my knees beside the cinder-pail, smothered in ash."

❧

At the end of a week without the brownie Dristan hired a footman, a bold young man from the plateau. To the household's butler, a grey-haired man of strict standards, fell the task of showing the new servant his duties.

"This is the pantry," said the butler, ushering the fresh-faced newcomer through a crowded chamber with its long stone shelves arrayed with covered pantry boxes, its dough bowls and herb grinders, its cupboards and benches, trays and trenchers, sugar boxes and candle boxes. They entered the adjoining room. "After each meal, your place is here in the scullery, young man," the butler instructed. "Here, perfect order should prevail—a place for everything and everything in its place. See, there is a sink, and plenty of wooden tubs. Have one of the tubs three parts full of clean hot water; in this, wash all plate and plated articles which are greasy, wiping them before cleaning them with the brush."

The new footman nodded cheerfully. "Right you are, sir!"

"You must be methodical in arranging your time," the butler said sternly, as if disapproving of such extravagant displays of merriment. "All your rough work must be done before breakfast is ready, when you must appear before the family clean, and in a presentable state. After breakfast, when everything belonging to the scullery and pantry is cleaned and put in its place, the furniture in the dining- and drawing-rooms will require rubbing. Towards noon, the parlor luncheon is to be prepared. At all times you must keep flesh and fowl separate from the other victuals, otherwise the Lady Asräthiel will not touch her dinner."

Undaunted by his tutor's grave manner the footman said confidentially, "Ah, yes, upon that matter, sir. With respect to the Lady Asräthiel, I cannot understand why she refuses meat on principle. After all, animals have to die eventually, so what is wrong with eating them?"

"Keep your voice down, young man! It is not fitting to discuss members of the household at all, let alone to shout about them!"

"Your pardon, sir. I am somewhat deaf," the new servant said truthfully, "and cannot measure how loud I am speaking."

Deciding to accept this as an excuse for the time being, the butler sighed and leaned against the edge of one of the stone thrawls to take the weight off his aching hip. After brief deliberation he concluded it would be prudent to explain the philosophies of his employers, in order to prevent possible awkward misunderstandings. In a low but earnest tone he said, "My lady argues that human beings die, too, but that does not give us the right to kill them or cause them suffering. This reasoning has won over several members of the household and now I, too, shun the eating of flesh."

"Methinks the lady is overly zealous in her philosophies," the new footman said, with the air of one whose common sense abhors radical thinking. "Animals slay other animals to devour them, so why should we not do the same?"

"Most animals who kill for food would be unable to survive if they did not," the butler patiently replied, displaying the self-possession of the well-informed. "The same is not the case for humankind."

"If we grew only crops, people would go hungry!"

"Quite the contrary, young man. My father was a farmer. I was raised on the land and I know about agriculture. There would, in fact, be a greater abundance of food for all, because grazing occupies far more arable land than the cultivation of crops." At the footman's gratifyingly astonished look the butler added authoritatively, "You have a lot to learn. And keep your voice down!"

The scullery's mysteries having been fathomed, the older man beckoned for the younger to follow him. They proceeded to step through the door into the buttery, still conversing.

"Well, at least we can eat fishes in good conscience," the

footman whispered very audibly. "Fishes do not feel fear or pain, therefore they do not suffer when they are killed."

At that very moment, Asrăthiel entered the buttery from the opposite doorway. Having caught this comment she stopped in her tracks. Exasperatedly, she threw her hands into the air. "Where do people get these ideas?" she cried, frowning at the shrinking footman. "If fishes felt no fear or pain they would not be motivated to flee from danger, and they would all be extinct! Your name, sir, is Henstridge, is it not?"

His self-assurance somewhat deflated, the new servant mumbled an affirmation and bowed.

Asrăthiel continued, "Master Henstridge, I have studied the natural history of fishes. Pray allow me to inform you, their brains and nerves are of a similar pattern to our own. Their mouths, in particular, are sensitive; they use them in the same way we use our hands—to catch or gather food, to build nests, and to hide their babies from danger. Some fishes even tend their own underwater gardens, believe it or not, as you will! Fishes are far more intelligent than people wish to accept. To hurt them is as unvirtuous as it is to hurt any living being."

Henstridge looked humbly apologetic. He also looked to be quite struck with admiration, and for some time afterwards the butler was not able to get a word out of him, although he proved to be a conscientious worker.

Another three days of helping the servants severely tested Asrăthiel's patience. Every evening she searched for the urisk in his accustomed haunts, calling to him. After sunset on the third day, she sprawled half-asleep on the hearth-rug beside an open book, alone in the library. The fire was smoldering low. She had kindled it not for warmth, but for the pleasure of watching the diaphanous flames as they danced, in shades of lilac, marmalade, and cramoisy. Blue-black clouds had amassed over the Mountain Ring, and heavy rain pelted against the dormer windows. Against its muted background roar, a runnel in the roof gutters was playing a musical melody, counterpointed by the sharp *plink, plink* of droplets falling somewhere nearby. Lulled by the murmur of water and fire, Asrăthiel had begun to doze. On impulse she opened her eyes, only to behold the urisk standing near, weltered in shadows.

"By my troth! 'Tis *you*, creature!" she cried, sitting up and instantly coming to her senses. "You have materialized at last!" Contrary to her words, the wight seemed almost insubstantial, as though he hovered between the real world and some unseen realm. The damsel's words tumbled forth. "Nay, do not depart I beseech you! I am glad to see you, glad and sorry—nay do not turn away, I meant no offense—prithee stay, for I need your help."

"If you intend to ask me to grovel in the grates as you do these days," said the urisk, "think again."

"Hoy-day, wight, you are too provoking! If not for you, I would not be groveling in the first instance. You have chased away our brownie, and now everyone is forced to rub their noses in dirt and dust."

"Housework is evidently beneath the dignity of petulant witch-princesses," the urisk commented with a mocking smile.

Without paying heed to the gibe Asrăthiel continued, "Fie upon this execrable deed of yours. If not for your incessant hounding of the obliging fellow we would be living in ease and comfort, as we were wont. What say you to that?"

"'*Obliging fellow*' be hanged. I say you all seem overly concerned about having to exert yourselves a tad more than usual. The wretch was a tiresome prig, and conceivably over-inquisitive, but 'tis no fault of mine if it took to its heels. I never told it to leave."

"You frightened it away. Where did it go?"

"How should I know?"

"We are in a sorry plight, urisk. I am deluged with chores from morning till night. In a few short weeks numerous visitors will arrive, having been invited to join us in celebration and enjoy our hospitality. Allow me to acquaint you with the importance of this occasion. It is to be no ordinary coming-of-age, because I have reached it precociously, and because

I am the Storm Lord's granddaughter, and not least because I possess—yes, I am no creepmouse modestly hiding my assets in the wainscot—because I possess innate powers greater than any known in living memory."

Seizing a pamphlet from a nearby shelf the urisk began fanning his face with it as if afflicted by an unconscionable blast of heat. "The extent of your consequence overwhelms me."

"And so it should!" In an attempt to thwart his sarcasm Asräthiel deliberately interpreted his words at face value. "The princes of Narngalis and the royal family of Grïmnørsland, amongst others, will expect a cordial and generous reception. We are to entertain no end of aristocrats and attendants for an entire week. Since the *other* domestic wight has departed," said the damsel, intentionally lingering on the term 'other' because she could not resist wanting to nettle the maddening creature, "perhaps you might see your way clear to helping us prepare the house."

The flesh prickled on the nape of her neck as she wondered how the urisk would respond to the challenge and the oblique chaffing. Sometimes, inexplicably, she feared the ungracious wight, and this was one of those moments.

However he said, "I'faith! Trifles discompose you astonishingly! But your *domestic wight* shall condescend. Lo! Shall the scullery become my palace?"

A freezing gust spiraled down the chimney. The fire on the grate grew dark for an instant, and the lamps guttered. By the time the chamber had brightened, the only souvenir of the urisk was the library door, half-open and swinging on its hinges, and the discarded pamphlet riffling its pages on the floor.

Asräthiel jumped to her feet and ran downstairs, her heart pounding in dread of what the urisk's words might signify. As she neared the scullery she was partially deafened by the strident dissonance of breaking crockery. She flew into the room, only to behold a washtub filled to the brim with greasy plates, many of them shattered into small fragments. Apparently the urisk had halfheartedly thrown the tableware into the receptacle as if about to begin cleansing it, instead smashing most of it out of carelessness, before thinking better of the task and making off.

The damsel fought an inner battle to contain her exasperation. "Why can you not be cooperative, like normal household wights?" she shouted at the unresponsive walls. Not unexpectedly, there came no reply. After sorting through the crockery and disposing of the broken pieces, Asrăthiel trudged upstairs to bed. As she drifted into sleep, she despaired of ever persuading the urisk to help with domestic chores.

Yet next morning the house was clean all right—far *too* clean and uncluttered. Clothing, footwear and hats, jewellery boxes, brushes, combs, books, lamps and candles, tack from the stables, even some musical instruments— portable objects from almost every room had been hurled roughly into a huge pile outside the back door. The interior of the House of Maelstronnar was more than clean—it bordered on bare, empty and austere.

Albiona flew into a rage, bewailing this new calamity at the top of her voice. She exhorted the servants to act with utmost care in extricating objects from the pile of clutter. As she herself retrieved each battered item she brandished it high, shrieking her wrath. "Look at this! My ivory jewelcase all slippery with lamp oil, and the feathers in my best hat all stained with cochineal! Every candle snapped into bits! My necklaces broken and the pearls scattered every which way. We shall never find every one!"

No one doubted it was the work of the urisk. Perplexed, Asrăthiel picked at random through the untidy stack. "Lo! Candles are here, yet not the candleholders," she said wonderingly. "Certain garments, but not others. Behold, the wight has tossed out some of our possessions while leaving the rest undisturbed. Pots and pans, buckets and barrels, dishes and plates in the kitchen have been left untouched, but drinking vessels, wineskins and foodstuffs from the larder have been dumped without ceremony. Tables and chairs—a few have been hauled forth, most left in place. And it would have been easy for the mischief-maker to tear down the draperies, yet he has not done so. There is neither rhyme nor reason to his antics."

Her aunt Albiona was in no mind to inquire as to the rationale behind the incident. "The horsehair couch all covered with *soap*—how such a heavy piece of furniture was carried out here is anyone's guess!" she fumed. "And Dristan's boots filled with last night's gravy . . ."

This escapade of the urisk's was the final affront, the last of a series of annoyances that took those responsible for the household to the limits of their patience. The day was spent removing objects from the tangled heap, cleansing them of lamp oil, foodstuffs, spilled glue and other contaminants, and replacing them in their customary locations. That evening Albiona laid out several spare sets of children's clothing in the hope that the urisk would disappear with them and never return. As an added precaution against trouble, Avalloc bade the servants keep watch throughout the house all night.

"This is really all your fault, Asrăthiel," Albiona cried for the umpteenth time. She was flushed with anger. "The least you could do is show more remorse."

Incensed by the injustice of this remark—and feeling some guilt which she tried to quash—Asrăthiel felt obliged to defend herself. "It is *not* my fault! I did not *deliberately* invite the urisk across our threshold. He twisted my words!"

"Your mistake was far too grave," responded her aunt, shaking her finger at the damsel. "Such an invitation cannot be retracted unless the creature agrees to it. The thing will plague this house forever! You must have a confrontation with it!"

"I shall do what I can, but I tell you, he is such a perverse and wanton thing I daresay he will not appear tonight," Asrăthiel warned the family. "Or if he does, it will be to me alone. That has ever been his way." She could see how her actions, while innocent, had hurt her family and she felt a great sadness.

"We can only wait and see," her grandfather said with his usual serenity.

When the dark hours came stealing over the Mountain Ring, nocturnal creatures of many species commenced their habitual activities under wood and water, upon hill and stone. On Rowan Green the windows of the House of Maelstronnar glowed softly with the dim radiance of part-shielded dark-lanterns and solitary candles. Asrăthiel did not sleep. She stayed for a while in the library, but inasmuch as no goat-legged visitors appeared, she transferred her vigil to the courtyard, and thence to the scullery. Just before midnight, she wandered outdoors again, drifting to the garden bed that ran along the house's exterior wall. In this very plot grew the roots of the briar roses that climbed to the cupola, where her mother lay in a trance.

At midnight it appeared; the urisk.

The air was quite still—only a light breeze played amongst the briar stems, flicking at the leaves and flowers. The rose-petals gleamed argentine in the starlight.

"So, you have escaped the walls," remarked the wight, with no preamble, as if nothing untoward had happened and he had not discommoded the entire household.

"The walls contain my home, and you have caused mischief therein!" Asrăthiel said indignantly.

"Why not? It is a loathsome place."

"What?" The damsel could not be sure she had heard aright.

"Utterly nauseating. The kitchen and the library in particular."

Boiling anger arose in Asrăthiel. "I will not ask you to explain to me why you insult my home. I no longer wish to have parlance with you," she said between gritted teeth. "Except to make one final request. Send the brownie back; we'd rather have it than you. It helps, while you only hinder."

The wight scowled. "If you do not like my methods I shall take my leave."

"That is the best news I have heard in ages!" flared the damsel. "Begone, then! Begone and never return here! You cause only discord."

Next moment, Asrăthiel threw up her arm and ducked, screwing shut her eyes. The urisk had tossed a handful of leaves into her face. When she looked again, he had, naturally, vanished. "And tell the brownie to come back!" the damsel shouted into the night.

No reply came from the darkness, but then, she had expected none. The argentine rose-petals shivered as a breeze shirred through.

In the morning, the brownie was found whimpering, curled up in an empty barrel in the cellar. When freed, it declared that it had been told to stay in the House of Maelstronnar and perform its duties as before.

But of the troublesome urisk there was no further evidence. Clearly, it had departed for good.

Asrăthiel surprised herself by feeling disappointed at the lack of the wight.

Notwithstanding, there were myriad events to fill up Asrăthiel's days and push thoughts of the departed visitor from her mind. It was the middle of the month of Jule, and the hour of her birthday celebrations was approaching apace. Furthermore, tidings had recently come to High Darioneth out of Orielthir in Slievmordhu, where several enthusiastic prentices and journeymen had been fossicking for hidden wonders amongst the decaying remnants of the Dome of Strang. Three of them, armed against highwaymen, had ridden back to the Mountain Ring, bearing with them a small but well-wrapped bundle.

"Lady Asrăthiel, I come to you at Lord Dristan's behest," said the senior journeyman. "It seems that your ruins have yielded a prize after all!" Handing her the package he explained. "Lord Dristan was weatherworking in Orielthir, accompanied by his children. After the task was finished he landed his sky-balloon at the Dome site, and let the children wander at will. While exploring, your young cousin Corisande spied something lying on the ground, amongst the rubble, half covered by broken pieces of mortar. It looked like an item of no value—a thing so blackened with grime and encrusted with growths that it barely resembled its original form. Yet the brí is strong in Lord Dristan's daughter, and she recognised it as a thing of gramarye. She picked it up and took it to show her father, and when 'twas cleaned we perceived 'twas a comb of outlandish workmanship, fashioned in dark silver. Lo!"

He ceased speaking, for Asrăthiel had opened the parcel. The article lay gleaming on the creamy linen wrappings.

Tall it was, with long, slender daggerlike tines, nineteen in number. The design—filigreed, engraved, knurled and embossed—was incredibly intricate and opulent. A narrow frieze depicting ugly, glaring creatures squatting in a row topped the tines. These grotesqueries bore on their shoulders a slim band of patterned silver, and out of this band sprouted an asymmetrical woodland scene of trees with intertwining leaves and boughs, in exquisite detail, about half the height of the prongs. It might have been beautiful, were it not insidiously disturbing.

"This is a potent thing," said Asrăthiel, turning the comb over in her hands. It was not hollow but solid, and as intriguingly wrought on one side as the other. The somber metal prickled her fingers where they touched it.

"Aye," said the senior journeyman, "but we have no idea what powers it might possess."

"I, for one, am not about to secure my hair with such a comb," said Asrăthiel. "It looks like something that might send down its metal roots to infiltrate one's brain and suck out one's wits. On the matter of what it is capable of, I shall consult the Storm Lord."

Avalloc, however, could not explain the comb's arcane purpose, and neither could Lidoine Galenrithar, the carlin of High Darioneth, or any of the Councilors of Ellenhall.

"There is only one man I know who might be able to crack the riddle of this thing," said Avalloc, "and that is my old friend Almus Agnellus."

"Fortunately he will be amongst us any day now," said Asrăthiel, "for he is one guest expected to arrive early."

The wandering scholar-philosopher appeared at the Seat of the Weathermasters several days before the party was to begin. At sixty-nine years of age, Agnellus was still a sprightly man. Although totally devoid of hair on his head, of recent times he made up for the lack by sporting copious quantities on his chin. His beard reached to his waist. Clad in simple, rustic garb of brown homespun he arrived on the back of a mule, accompanied by two loyal aides; a scribe and an apprentice scribe. Like his disgraced mentor, the missing ex-druid secundus Adiuvo Clementer, Agnellus had once been a member of the druidic brotherhood but, disillusioned, had resigned in order to pursue his interests independently. Few people who had known him during his tenure at the Sanctorum would have recognized him now in his disguise. As an added precaution, he went by the vague pseudonym "Declan of the Wildwoods."

The history of both men was well known in the House of Maelstronnar. By Ninember of the year 3471, Clementer had become so zealous about his new philosophical insights that he took the daring step of publicly rejecting his faith in the actuality of the Four Fates. Jeopardizing his personal safety, he openly disseminated his opinions. This behavior by anyone, let alone an ex-druid, was intolerable to the Sanctorum. The Druid Imperius took immediate reprisals, sending a band of ruffians in the night, to apprehend Clementer as he lay sleeping. They captured him, confiscated his possessions, and hauled him away.

Naturally the Sanctorum denied all knowledge of the abduction.

Nobody could find out for certain what had happened to Clementer. His assistant Agnellus, who had escaped the same fate only by chance—he had been lodging elsewhere that night—sought information in vain. It was later rumored that the venerable gentleman had been thrown into a dungeon, there to languish for the remainder of his life, or that his throat had been cut.

Outraged and terrified, Agnellus fled into hiding at a remote hermitage in dangerous territory near the borders of the Wight Hills. The brutality and unfair circumstances of his mentor's downfall fixed his purpose; partly in retaliation against those wrongs, and partly because he believed in Clementer's cause, he determined to actively promote the ideas of the vanished scholar. These days, he and his own squire passed their days immersed in study in the seclusion of his secret abode, or traveling the Four Kingdoms discreetly promulgating Clementer's insights, gathering lore, and sometimes inveigling consultations with eldritch wights of the seelie kind. Always they journeyed in disguise, to avoid being recognized and betrayed to the Sanctorum; the punishment for defection was life-imprisonment or death.

"What prompted Clementer to forswear the Fates?" Asräthiel had once asked her grandfather as they engaged in one of their discussions in the library. "When he left the Sanctorum and first took to his wandering life he still believed in them, did he not?"

"He did. It happened this way: After he parted from the druids he spent much time pondering the nature of morality. At first he postulated that, in essence, 'good is the sustenance of life, while evil is its destruction.' Later he felt obliged to admit that for living creatures in general, both sustenance and destruction are essential. Death nourishes Life."

Asräthiel nodded, not without a twinge of unease that she herself was exempt from this natural law. "Go on," she said.

"Clementer began to travel further abroad," said the Storm Lord, "learning as much as possible about living organisms. He began to perceive the greatest Good as being the safekeeping of Life itself, rather than the preservation of individual living creatures. After investigating Extinction, he concluded that *that* must be the greatest evil."

"His further research," Avalloc continued, "led him to augur that millions of years in the future, the world would slow in its orbit and fall into the sun. Then he suffered much, picturing all life on Tir having been snuffed out by the raging inferno." Both Avalloc and his granddaughter grew pensive. "He arrived," the Storm Lord said eventually, "at the belief that it would not matter so much if the human race became extinct after all, as long as some form of life remained in the world."

"That would certainly be an unpopular tenet amongst most people!" Asrăthiel commented with a wry smile. "Clementer seems destined to choose friendless doctrines. Where did his cogitations take him from there?"

"Do not be misled into thinking he was comforted by his conclusions! The world and all life seemed doomed. Convinced of the inevitability of apocalypse and the annihilation of our species, he toppled to the nadir of despondency. For many months he remained at a point of despair. He retired to a simple cottage near Tealgchearta, abandoning his scholarly investigations and spending most of his days in bed. Ultimately our good friend Agnellus persuaded him to climb from his pit of languor, and in a final desperate search for hope, Clementer began again to sally forth, time after time, employing every means possible to gather more information from eldritch wights. He questioned them closely, knowing that their answers were all true—or at least, the truth as the wights believed it."

Asrăthiel pictured the two weather-beaten sages in their travel-stained robes, trudging through the night along some woodland track; perhaps entering a moonlit glade wherein a haunted pool glimmered, and seating themselves at the brink; perhaps setting out some gifts of food or silver trinkets, and waiting patiently in the hope of glimpsing and hailing some eldritch personification—a trow, maybe, or a spriggan, or one of the elusive woodland guardians. The scholars were venturesome gentlemen, and over a long period their enterprise had been rewarded.

"They told Clementer," said Avalloc, "of life existing in secret places; the deepest and the highest, the hottest, and the ends of the world where ice never melts. My learned friend began to understand how tenacious life is; how it can and will survive in almost any environment, no matter how extreme. It needs only one element—water."

Asrăthiel, who had been intent on her grandfather's monologue, broke in. Clapping her hands impetuously, she exclaimed, "As ever when we speak of Clementer's discoveries, I am delighted! It is always splendid to be assured that Life is *not* a fragile thing. I myself ponder much over this same matter, amongst others, as I sit at the bedside of my mother."

Her grandfather had nodded. "I am aware that such thoughts have often occupied you, my dear child." She had smiled lovingly at him, comforted by his sympathy.

Their discussion had ended here. As the first day of Asrăthiel's party approached, Clementer's protégé Agnellus came, in person, to High Darioneth, and when he first set eyes on the comb he recoiled as if bitten by a snake. On recovering his composure the sage spread his fingers and tapped the fingertips of his right hand against those of his left—a habit of his—saying in wonder, "Well, well. I never thought to see such a thing in all the days of my life."

"I gather it is something noteworthy," commented the Maelstronnar.

"My dear Avalloc," the scholar replied, "I cannot say for certain, but this might well be an artifact written of in one of my old master Clementer's rarest and most ancient tomes of lore. I believe it might possibly be the Sylvan Comb, a long-lost thing of goblin make."

"What are its properties?" asked Asrăthiel.

"It is impossible to be sure, my lady, until I try it out."

Dristan, who had lately returned from the Dome site, interposed, "Would that not be a perilous undertaking, Agnellus? One supposes that goblins would be hardly likely to fashion items that did not pose some sort of danger to humankind."

"Certainly. Be assured, sir, I will perform the trial with utmost care. But first, I must send my apprentice back to my lodgings to fetch that ancient tome of which I spoke. For on its pages is written a Word of Mastery, and I shall need that Word if I am to test this thing."

The apprentice was duly dispatched. Meanwhile, Rowan Green buzzed with activity as the day of the party drew nearer.

A lavish junket was to be held at High Darioneth, to celebrate Asrăthiel's birthday. Guests arrived in a timely fashion; the houses of the weathermasters were filled with royalty, aristocrats and commoners scattered their pavilions across Rowan Green, and before long the Seat of the Weathermasters resembled a fairground. Even sturdy octogenarian Earnán Kingfisher Mosswell made the long journey from the Great Marsh of Slievmordhu to attend, accompanied by Cuiva Featherfern Stillwater, the carlin of the Marsh. Although he was no true blood relative of hers, Asrăthiel accorded Earnán the status of great-grandfather. He had been the second husband of her great-grandmother, Liadán, the grandmother of Asrăthiel's mother, Jewel. For the sake of her mother, Asrăthiel had paid a few visits to the Marsh over the years. She had grown fond of the ancient eel-fisher, and also of Cuiva, a wise woman who had been her grandmother's friend. As for Avalloc, he esteemed the marsh-man and the carlin highly, and the three spent many hours in conversation.

On the twenty-eighth of Aoust in that year, Asrăthiel Heronswood Maelstronnar turned nineteen, and the final secrets of weatherworking were conferred on her with all due ceremony.

First, she had to fast and meditate overnight, alone, and custom dictated that this be done in Lord Alfardēne's Reflectory. Behind the houses on Rowan Green, a twisting path climbed steeply through the dim light beneath overhanging pines and across bridges spanning deeply cloven gorges, until it arrived at the tranquil dell, high on Wychwood Storth, that cupped the cemetery of the weathermasters. Central to the elegant tombs and mausoleums stood a building of vaulted stone. Here was the reflectory; a haven of serenity and seclusion; a sanctuary in which to reflect and ponder. The shining water-pools encircling the exterior held perfect images of the surrounding snow-capped peaks, wreathed in cloud. Before sunrise a group of women came to terminate Asrăthiel's lonely vigil—weathermages all—but not a word was spoken by anyone, for this part of the ritual was performed in silence.

At the heart of the building stood a great silver-lined bowl, kept clean and filled with pure water, and it was here that Asrăthiel's handmaidens bathed her. They arrayed her in ceremonial robes and dressed her hair, after which they gave her the traditional spiced bread and seasonal fruits with which to break her fast.

As the sun peeped over the horizon, Asrăthiel's attendants left the reflectory. Her tutor, Avalloc, took their place, speaking words of formal greeting. The Storm Lord taught his pupil the final secrets of weatherworking—long, intricate phrases and gestures that affected such powerful and potentially catastrophic phenomena as the world's magnetic fields, the major ocean currents, and the large-scale wind systems.

By evening the arduous lesson was over. Then Asrăthiel was conveyed down the mountain path on a litter, beneath a trellised double arch decked with the flowers and leaves of late Summer, carried high on the shoulders of eight stalwarts.

The magehood ceremony took place in Ellenhall, the belfried meetinghouse at the seat of the weathermasters. In attendance were the councillors of Ellenhall and a vast audience comprising all the denizens of Rowan Green and their guests. There was not room enough to hold everyone who wanted to view the proceedings. People from the plateau, who had journeyed up the cliff road for the occasion, crowded around the doors and the open windows, craning their necks and straining their ears.

Words were uttered and further rituals were performed, witnessed by all. At the end, Avalloc, in his role as Storm Lord, officially awarded Asrăthiel the title of weathermage, and the spectators gave a loud shout of delight, accompanied by the waving of scarves and general acclamations.

The festivities continued for four days. It was a blithe period for Asrăthiel—one of the happiest times in her life—however, she was unable to prevent some slight impatience for the conclusion, so that she would be free to claim her adult independence. The party did eventually come to an end, and most of the guests duly departed. Asrăthiel then began to make her preparations for taking up her new post as representative of High Darioneth and resident mage at King's Winterbourne.

Nine days after the party, Agnellus's apprentice returned from the scholar's lodgings, bearing the tome of lore his master had requested. Agnellus rifled through the pages, found the Word he was seeking and returned the book carefully to its velvet-lined box.

"I am ready," he announced, "to test the artifact from the Dome of Strang."

Avalloc, Dristan, Asrăthiel and the carlin Lidoine Galen-rithar accompanied the aging savant to a wild and uninhabited corner of the mountain plateau, near the steep chasm where the Snowy River broke through the Mountain Ring and thundered down in savage cataracts over the border into Grïmnørsland.

"We must carry this thing well away from the dwellings of humankind," Agnellus had warned. "There is no knowing how far its influence might reach."

They gathered on an open tract of smooth, green sward starred with tiny alpine flowers and dappled with the shadows of fast-moving clouds. Drifts of thistledown went gusting past like crowds of tiny, fleeing ghosts—perhaps the airborne seeds of crowthistle. On rafts of vapor high above and close by, the frosted tips of the mountains glittered. They hung in the sky as pristine as white jewels rinsed in rainwater.

From somewhere near the river, a kingfisher uttered a note.

"I must advise you," Agnellus told his companions, "that if anything strange happens you must on no account believe your eyes. Do not panic, but stand fast."

With that, he threw the Comb to the ground, articulating the Word.

The nineteen sharp prongs stuck into the turf, and the Comb stood upright. At once a silvery forest, weird and mysterious, sprang up all around the weathermasters. The tree boles resembled the tines of the Comb, their bark whorled, engraved, chased and twisted. The company was enclosed within a landscape of argent trunks and glimmering whispering leaves. Smoky shadows or shadowy smoke roiled, as if alive, between the trees. Other movements hinted at entities moving deep in the woods; possibly a glimpse of a slender horn, or a pearly hoof, or inscrutable eyes watching. The sibilance of whispering and the murmur of the wind was all around, so that the weathermasters were completely disoriented, as if they found themselves in an unearthly world, a place that existed on another plane entirely. A certainty of imminent peril seized them, laced with astonishment and curiosity.

Then came a feeling deep in the bones, like a thrumming vibration so low as to be inaudible, striking the universal note of terror. It entered the soles of the feet, climbed up through the limbs, and seized control of every bodily organ, seeping finally to the brain, where it sent rapid shoots along primordial pathways of utmost fear and madness. Those who were its prey experienced heightened awareness of every detail in their illusory surroundings. All seemed to threaten horror and death; the trees to crush with their boughs, the leaves to gust into every orifice and suffocate, the horns to pierce, the hoofs to trample, the wind to exhale poison, the shadows to dissolve everything they touched, leaving no sign aught had ever existed. . . .

Agnellus bent down and picked up a thing that lay glinting on the ground, and in an instant the forest had completely disappeared, and he was putting the Comb back in his pocket.

The audience stood stunned.

"That," said Avalloc quietly, voicing the opinions of all, "is an extraordinary object."

❧

Looming above the weathermasters, the mountains—so magnificent, so formidable, they seemed like the very ramparts of the world—ranged out to the south and the north. Mystically blue were their steeps, as if veiled in translucent blue-dyed gauzes. Somewhere beneath the northern ranges the busy burrower continued to delve, as ever, pushing forward persistently in the dark.

Amongst the numerous species of subterranean wights, the coblynau were famous for manifesting extravagant displays of labor and producing nothing. Many underworld caverns were illuminated by tiny lanterns grasped by milling throngs of these diminutive manlike beings. Each of the wights was about eighteen inches in height, with skinny limbs, disproportionately large hands and feet, and stout, bulbous trunks. Their faces were wide-mouthed and grotesque, their noses elongate. In shape, their ears resembled those of donkeys. Their pupils were large, dark and gleaming, filling the whole eye so that no whites showed, like the orbs of dogs and horses. Cheerfully they bustled back and forth, carrying picks and shovels and crowbars across their shoulders, or pushing barrows, or lugging buckets on poles.

If any human intruder ever caught them unawares, the coblynau would recover from their surprise in time to trick the spy with their simple catchphrase, "Ooh, *Mathy,* what's that behind ye?" As soon as the intruder took his attention off the wights, they vanished. A moment later, if the visitor turned back, not one of the miners was to be seen. Only their miniature tools lay where they had been discarded, haunted by a fading memory of sniggering and twittering. It would have been useless to try to catch them a second time. The supernatural creatures were now aware of the spy, and would be gone in a puff of dust before he could so much as wink an eye.

As the black-handed burrowing foreigner moved on, the wights boldly emerged behind its back, even before it was wholly out of sight, and returned to their ceaseless, useless travail. Although these small folk seemed very occupied with the business at hand, their buckets and barrows were empty of ore, and, despite all the wielding of picks and shovels, not one of the little miners had been actually digging. There was no tangible sign of their work.

The coblynau vacuously playacted, the fridean scrabbled

furtively, and unnameable underground dwellers shot away from the edges of vision with abnormal speed. Ignoring these manifestations, shunned by them, the anonymous burrower dug relentlessly on. It had no way of knowing it was heading straight towards the location of one of Tir's greatest secrets.

VII

Princes

Knights of the Red Lodge, knights of the Burning Brand,
Bright helms a-glinting, sworn to defend our land.
Hark ye the trumpets, hark ye the singing;
Songs of high glory on the wind winging.
Knights of the Red Lodge triumph are bringing.
Spears rank on rank, gay pennants blowing,
Splendid the colors flashing and glowing.
Mighty the horsemen, sword-blades a-ringing.
See, from our footprints red roses springing!
Matchless in courage, loyal and handpicked,
Skillful with swordplay, dauntless in conflict.
Ours is the victory, ours is the plunder.
Knights of the Red Lodge riding like thunder.

—A BATTLE SONG OF SLIEVMORDHU'S RED LODGE

*Before she set out to take up her new post at King's Winter-*bourne, Asrăthiel climbed the stairs to the rose-wreathed glass cupola where her mother lay in a charmed sleep. She seated herself beside the couch and sang a lilting song, as was her custom from time to time. Then she leaned and kissed that immaculate brow, whispering, "Farewell, dearest. I am going away, but I will come back often and visit you."

Lingering a while longer, loath to depart immediately, she reflected on the step she was about to take; the new pathway that was opening before her feet. Her life, until this moment, had been sheltered by the mountainous bastion of High Darioneth and succored by the dependable comfort of the weathermaster families. Now she was to set out on her own. Her excitement at the possibility of future adventure was tinged with her never-fading sorrow at her parents' misfortunes. This moment would have been so much more rewarding had they been there to proudly acknowledge her achievements.

A convoy of coaches carried Asrăthiel's relatives and friends, including several Councilors of Ellenhall, from High Darioneth to their destination, the capital city of Narngalis. Along the winding Mountain Road they traveled, through a changing landscape: precipitous fern gullies alive with falling water; towering forests where crescent-shaped leaves fluttered down in sporadic showers, in whose clearings charcoal burners stoked their fires and the axes of timber-getters rang; hillsides covered with a patterned knot-work of grapevines; fields of yellow stubble dotted with hay bales like fresh-baked loaves of bread. Hawthorn hedges, blood-spattered with early-ripened fruit, bordered dandelion-freckled pastures stretching away to grassy ridges in the middle distance.

As for the new weathermage to the king, she traveled to her post in a small sky-balloon. Its name was *Lightfast*. The fabric of its envelope was woven from plant fibers—not as strong and light as spidersilk—and it had been custom-built to carry no more than three people. The other two aboard were her own chosen crew-members; not weathermasters but robust, eager youths from the plateau who wanted to see the world.

"When I abide in King's Winterbourne," Asrăthiel had said to her grandfather long before her departure, "I will not keep horses. As you know I dislike harnessing any sort of animal to haul me about when I can just as easily walk. This will have the added benefit of reducing my expenses, for the cost these days of maintaining stables and a carriage, not to mention the wages of coachman and grooms, is not inconsiderable."

"My dear child," Avalloc had said somewhat testily, "it will be looked upon as eccentric if you walk about the city streets. All the highborn city ladies have their own carriages, or at least their own chairs."

"I would not mind traveling the city streets in a chair," said Asrăthiel, "for chairs are borne by men, who have a say in the matter of whether or not they will do the job. But I will not have a carriage."

"Well, you might get away without employing horsepower while you abide in the city and its precincts, but you will have to hire a post chaise, I daresay, whenever you return home to visit us. We cannot spare balloons and crews to ferry you. To walk from King's Winterbourne to High Darioneth would take weeks, and the roads are dangerous. Surely you are not suggesting that you make such journeys on foot!"

"When I travel long distances I will do so in my own aerostat, with my own crew. And before you remind me, dear Grandfather, of the cost of lightweight envelopes and suncrystals, let me point out that I have a way of offsetting that cost."

She opened her hand, which had been clenched. There on her palm lay a concentrate of silver-white, a mote of dazzling light the size of a cat's eye. It was as if moonlight were being sucked into this scintillant and condensed to its purest essence. The jewel from the Iron Tree gave off sparkles of reflected radiance, pure, yet flashing with every color.

"As you know, Grandfather, my mother gave me this," said Asrăthiel. "It is an heirloom, but I understand she was never fond of it. She would not mind if I sold it. I have never seen or heard of its like. I daresay it is valuable and will bring a good price. Some noble family will wish to own it."

Avalloc looked long and hard at his granddaughter. "No," he said at last, "you must keep the jewel. You are right—your mother never cared for it, even though she was its namesake. Yet I perceive that in your heart you think of this stone as a memento of her days of wakefulness, and you will grieve a little if it is lost to you. Let your sky-balloon be a parting gift from me."

The damsel thanked him joyfully, and kissed his grizzled cheek, and put away the ornament.

Asrăthiel's luggage was not abundant, consisting mainly of books packed into canvas bags and loaded onto *Lightfast*. She had taken lodgings in King's Winterbourne, at a large house in Lime Grove, on the east side. The building, known as The Laurels, belonged to Mistress Draycott Parslow, an elderly woman who had stumbled across good fortune in her later years. The widow now dwelled in a small but comfortable cottage on the grounds, having decided to let her house to "a tenant of good propriety."

By the time the overland convoy had arrived in the city, Asrăthiel had already alighted at The Laurels in order to supervise the unloading of her belongings. She was to be assisted in her new position by a small domestic workforce and an even smaller clerical staff: a personal maid, a butler, the two stalwart lads of her balloon-crew, who could act as chair-bearers and even as bodyguards if necessary, and a secretary to tally up accounts and write letters. Provender for the household would be provided by Mistress Draycott Parslow's cooks. Leaving her household staff at the lodgings to prepare everything according to her specifications, the Storm Lord's granddaughter ordered her chair to be brought around to the front door. Her four bearers, two crewmen and two footmen, conveyed her down the gravel driveway and out the gates of the estate, turning off Lime Grove into Eastcheap and continuing along Great Castle Street, to Wyverstone Castle where the other members of her weathermaster coterie were bound.

The City of King's Winterbourne occupied an area of approximately three square miles; almost two miles from east to west, one and a half miles from north to south. Housing a population of about one hundred thousand, it had long since expanded beyond the limits of its original walls, with their twelve gateways. The civil precincts clustered along the northern banks of the River Thyme, with a small settlement across the river in Southborough. The Port of King's Winterbourne was always busy with river traffic from Grímnørsland and outlying regions of Narngalis, and ferrymen continually plied their trade. Winterbourne Bridge spanned the broad river, carrying on its back Walkwood Street, the main thoroughfare. It was constructed of stone, and eight of its twenty arches sheltered huge waterwheels that powered water pumps and corn mills. After Walkwood Street crossed the Thyme and plunged through the heart of Southborough it split in two, becoming the Mountain Road that ran south and the River Road heading east.

In the city's west lay the inns of court and chancery, hostels for lawyers and students, the colleges of history, music and art, the public library, the museum, and Westleigh Sanctorum. Magnificent as these buildings were, it was not for them that King's Winterbourne was famed, but for its palaces of basalt. There were, throughout the city, more palaces than in the other three capitals put together. Aristocrats had built them for use as townhouses, ensuring that they were spacious enough to quarter the entire retinue of a noble family, which might comprise as few as two hundred or as many as eight hundred liveried servants. Other buildings of prominence included the many guildhalls scattered throughout the municipality, and the imposing Asylum for Lunatics, tucked away at the edge of town. The trades had bestowed their names upon many of the thoroughfares: Threadneedle Street, Carter Lane, Candlewick Way, Cornhill, Cordwainer Row. To the east stood the only three fortified buildings in the city: the Tower of King's Winterbourne, Essington Tower and Wyverstone Castle, the chief residence of the royal family. It was within the latter, amidst barbicans and turrets of battlemented stone, that the large company of weathermasters attended a welcoming celebration given by King Warwick, in honor of Asrăthiel's new appointment as resident weathermage.

Grand and dignified was Wyverstone Castle, its magnificence matched by the somber splendor of the royal family and courtiers. Although the fabrics were sumptuous, their raiment was designed with relative simplicity and restraint. They favored dusky hues and intense sable, contrasting with vivid flashes of jewels, brocade, or embroidery; or rich, lively colors crawling with the intricate scrolls of blackwork. In particular, Narngalis fashion inclined towards dark violaceous tints of heather, lavender and hyacinth, accentuated by the contrasting pink-purple of martagon, fuchsia and damson.

Older noblewomen customarily wore the gabled headdress, or soft veils of lace encircled with elegant chaplets of silver wire, rather than the strenuous steeples and butterfly hats of the Slievmordhuan court, the horned headgear of Grïmnørsland, or the plumed turbans of Ashqalêth. Younger woman adorned their heads with jeweled cauls, their hair hanging down their backs. Men hatted their long locks with capuchons in myriad varying designs, complete with attached scarves, pleats, or folded brims.

Many of King Warwick's knights were present at his court at this time. Remote of demeanor and steely eyed were they; clad in chain mail and cloaks of deepest indigo. Their tabards of velvet and silk brocade were lined with linen, and appliquéd with heraldic designs. These warriors, Companions of the Cup, were as honorable and learned as they were stern and battle-ready. Highly esteemed, they were popularly considered the best knights in Tir.

At the welcoming feast the revelers lacked for naught to divert and sustain them, and the festivities lasted throughout the night. Performers entertained the diners between each course. Asrăthiel sat at the right hand of William, eldest son of King Warwick of Narngalis, a comely young man with merry eyes and light brown-gold hair whose shining strands draped across his shoulders. He was dressed in a calf-length doublet of flowing pattern, beneath which his white linen shirt showed at the neck. His sleeves were tight, concluding with a long cuff over the backs of his hands. The loose white linen undersleeves appeared in small puffs along the back seam, which was not stitched but held together at wide intervals with buttons and loops. The Crown Prince had not accompanied his brother Walter on the hunting trip to Grïmnørsland the previous Spring, despite being as fond of outdoor recreation as any of his peers. He had, instead, been attending to matters of state. He was assiduous and earnest by nature, and desired to learn as much as possible about the management of the kingdom so that Narngalis might continue to profit from equitable and merciful government, and that by excellent statesmanship he might uphold the honor of the family name when it came to be his turn to rule. William often attended Privy Council meetings with his father, who valued his opinion and encouraged him to exercise his judgment.

The Crown Prince and Asrăthiel had last seen one another at Rowan Green, during her coming-of-age celebration, but since their childhood they had been often in each other's company. Visits between King's Winterbourne and Rowan Green occurred several times a year for various reasons, including festivals, conferences, weddings or funerals, or when Asrăthiel or Avalloc accompanied an aircrew to the capital city on a weather-taming mission. High Darioneth was, after all, part of Narngalis, and it was natural for Wyverstone Castle and Ellenhall to associate frequently. During their acquaintance William had never made a secret of his high regard for the Storm Lord's granddaughter. She was aware his esteem had turned to love a year or two since, and she loved him in return, although not in the way he hoped; rather as a sister loves a brother. It pained her to be the inspiration of anyone's suffering; she could only hope that the passage of time would modify his partiality.

"I hear you have become even more proficient with the sword," said William as he helped Asrăthiel to a bowl of makerouns. "I would fain witness you at practice."

"Oh, but that would be profitless, sir!" she responded. "You must not merely *see* me—you must play the role of my opponent!" Having broken apart a bread roll, she dipped it in one of the sauces.

The prince was amused. "You jest. You know I would not spar with a woman."

"Ah," said his companion, "but I will give you no quarter!"

At that he laughed, clearly taken with her impudence. She would not let the matter rest, however, and by the time the course was over she had persuaded him to oppose her in combat. "Merely to indulge you I agree to your rash scheme," he said chaffingly. As ever, his face betrayed his thoughts and emotions, and Asrăthiel could tell he was privately planning on letting her win. It vexed her slightly to perceive he was merely patronizing her, and the knowledge strengthened her resolve to show him her worth as a swordswoman.

Before dessert was served, the king welcomed Asrăthiel with a speech, and the guests raised their drinking vessels on high in a toast to the newcomer. As the diners prepared to assault a range of sweet dishes—seed cakes, jellies, custards, wafers, blaunderellys, pety pernaux and bake metes— William again steered his conversation with Asrăthiel to the topic of swords.

"Do you know," he said, "I first set eyes on Fallowblade as a small child, visiting Rowan Green with my father. When I actually saw the sword I was astonished."

"Many are astonished."

"Yes, but I was astonished in the *other* way. My father tells me I exclaimed, *'But I thought it was ten feet long and shining with its own light of a thousand suns!'* "

Asrăthiel smiled. "Ah, yes, I understand your meaning. Over time, legends grow. The subjects of romances become exaggerated, overwhelming the reality. As years pass, the telling of stories may change recollections—may even ultimately transform fact to pure fiction."

"I daresay you employ Fallowblade for your fencing practice," said the prince. "Unless you have brought him with you, in King's Winterbourne you will have to make do with a weapon of lesser stature. The blacksmiths of Narngalis are the finest in the Four Kingdoms, but we have nought to match the Golden Blade."

"I have never wielded Fallowblade in combat rehearsal."

"Why not?"

"I promised my grandfather I would not do so until Desmond, my swordmaster, judges me to be of sufficient merit. Fallowblade is perilous to wield, you know; almost as perilous to wield as to challenge."

"Nonetheless, you are the sword's owner, and you may do as you wish with it."

"I have given my word, sir, and I will not be forsworn."

"No," said the prince, observing her thoughtfully. He toyed with a crystallized plum on his plate. "Your sense of honor is surpassingly strong. For you, it is especially important to keep your word. I have always been aware of that. It is one of the reasons . . ."

"Reasons for what?" Asrăthiel was caught unawares. As soon as she asked the question she regretted it.

"I believe you know."

Discomfited, Asrăthiel took up her wine-cup and sipped, using the vessel as refuge. She had no wish for William's attachment to be openly acknowledged between them. Recognition would entail a host of problems. She hoped his affections would subside as time went by, leaving her free to be a friend to him, as before. He was a good-looking young man, there could be no denying. Many a damsel at court sighed over him; they flaunted their charms in his presence, batted their eyelashes, laughed extravagantly at his mild jests and demonstrated flamboyant interest in his every opinion and deed. Yet there was not, for Asrăthiel's part, a spark of anything more than fondness for the king's son.

William said dryly, "A sense of honor is very commendable in a lady," and with relief his companion noted he was indulging in banter to deflect the moment of tension. "Most women here at court would as lief stab their own grandmother in the back if 'twere to their advantage."

Asrăthiel pretended to rise to the bait. "Honor is commendable in anyone," she replied, as if scolding. "Furthermore, you underestimate the worthy ladies of the court. They are not so ruthless and scheming as you devise!"

"How generous you are, Asrăthiel," the prince responded with joviality, "forever staunchly defending womanhood!"

"In so doing so I am defending men, also, from the molds into which some people would press them. Men and women both can be honorable, or dishonorable."

"And for those who are honorable, it means more than keeping one's word," said William. "It means also that one's promise must never lightly be given in the first instance."

"Verily," she affirmed. "It appears that you and I are of one mind at last!"

"Of one mind in many respects," he said, suddenly earnest again.

Dinner was followed by dancing in the ballroom. King Warwick presided over the ball, viewing the energetic display from the high table on the dais, where he sat at his ease. He would not dance; had not done so since the untimely death of his wife, Queen Emelyne. In his long gown of velvet, dark purple and trimmed with ermine, he leaned on his elbow beside his friend Avalloc Maelstronnar and surveyed the scene, calmly pleased to see his guests enjoying themselves. Splendidly, the borders of the king's robes were jeweled with maroon beryls, tourmalines and almandine spinels. In the heat of the ballroom he had cast aside his mantle of dark blue wool, with its amethyst-jewelled strap across the breast and lozenge-shaped clasps and cords, but he still wore his heavy collar of closely interlocking S-shaped gold links.

Whenever the dancers needed to rest, they had the choice of walking out onto the terraces, where the north wind sang a high, thin song of ice, or more painlessly moving into one of the side chambers to partake of refreshments or watch a puppet-play produced by a troupe of traveling Slievmordhuans, which was intended as a divertissement for the young children of visiting dignitaries. After exhausting themselves in skipping to a particularly vigorous cotillion, Asrăthiel and the three daughters of King Warwick withdrew to the Mauve

Drawing Room. Partygoers clustered about the guest of honor and the members of the royal family, while keeping at a courteous distance. In the parlor across the corridor the puppet-show was enjoying an interlude.

The three princesses were interested in the discovery of the Sylvan Comb, which remained in Avalloc's keeping at High Darioneth. "After this momentous discovery," said Lecelina, "I daresay treasure seekers would be swarming all over the ruins of the Dome, except that they know the owners are weathermasters." The eldest sister was demure in a black satin dress with silver embroidery and buttons of ruby and pearl. Her inner sleeves were purple silk, and petticoats of crimson velvet showed from beneath her skirt.

"To what work will you put the Comb?" asked Winona, whose gold-and-red brocade bodice and skirt overlaid a longer underskirt of patterned cloth-of-gold edged with lynx.

"To no work, Your Highness," said Asrăthiel. "'Tis of no use to us. 'Tis of no use to anyone at all, unless—I hazard to guess—they were being pursued by an enemy and wished to throw it down to block his path."

"Then they would have to go back to retrieve it later," said Saranna. The youngest sister habitually looked vague and fey. She was resplendent in a gown made of cloth-of-silver embroidered in gold, green and crimson threads. The wardrobe of the princesses was, as protocol decreed, more ostentatious than that of the courtiers.

"Indeed," Asrăthiel replied. "Yet even if the enemy discovered it and picked it up, the Comb would be no use to him without the Word that activates it."

"And what is this Word?" asked Lecelina.

"'Tis a secret!" Asrăthiel said affably.

"How did you discover the secret?"

"'Twas not I who discovered it but a learned scholar, a friend to my grandfather."

At that moment the tootling of a tin-pipes from the parlor across the corridor interrupted their conversation; the puppeteers' way of announcing that their show was ready to resume.

"Is that a saraband I hear the musicians striking up in the ballroom?" asked William, who had just joined Asrăthiel and his sisters.

"No, it is another cotillion, as you know well," said Winona, turning towards him and shaking a pair of silk gloves in his face. "I am fully aware you detest puppet shows, and you are trying to escape. But you must come and watch it with us." Before she could rope them in, Lecelina and Saranna disappeared in the direction of the ballroom.

"I am certain it is a saraband," said Asrăthiel, who equally loathed dramatic performances involving grotesque effigies with squeaky voices. "Let us hie ourselves back to the dance floor."

"No, no!" cried enthusiastic Winona, seizing Asrăthiel by the elbow and leading her across the corridor to the parlor. "You shall not escape, either."

A bevy of courtiers trailed in their wake. Accustomed to being the focus of attention, Winona and William calmly ignored the constant surveillance, but it irked Asrăthiel. Several rows of velvet-upholstered chairs faced the puppet-theatre, many of them occupied by children and their nurserymaids. Everyone jumped up to make way for the members of the royal family and their honored guest, but Winona waved her hand in a gesture of dismissal. "Pray keep your places," she announced. "Allow the children to sit in front. We will take the empty seats in the back row." The princess guided Asrăthiel into a chair. "Let us watch this spectacle. It is sure to be diverting."

Behind Winona's back, William, who had followed, grimaced in disgust. Catching his eye, Asrăthiel smiled sympathetically. The show began.

The puppets, such outrageous caricatures that they overstepped the bounds of comedy and were better suited to tales of horror, were made to enact the story of "The Salt Box."

There were six main characters in the play: a family by the name of Reynolds—mother, father and child; their servant the cowman and a couple of hideous goblins. In the first scene the family was living on their farm at Gorsey Bank. It was a prosperous farm—so the narrator informed the audience—and the house was solid and comfortable, an ancient building that had, during the reign of a long-ago king, been a grand manor. Throughout the years it had stood, this mansion had unfortunately become haunted by the two goblins, who looked like a dwarfish old geezer and a crone. This pair harassed the Reynolds family without ceasing. Mounted on the back of a monstrous boar, they would gallop around the entire property—homestead, fields, yards and barns. No beast nor fowl nor human creature ever found any peace from their trouble and mischief.

The greater part of the juvenile audience laughed uproariously at the antics of the goblin-puppets as they upset milk-pails on Father Reynolds's head, or stole Young Eddy's toys, or jumped out at Mother Reynolds, scaring her so badly that she dropped a basketful of eggs. Mother Reynolds's falsetto tones were very squeaky indeed as she and Father complained—behind closed doors, so as not to offend the goblins—about the atrocious behavior of the little menaces.

The Reynoldses could not quit of these pests no matter what they tried. They fetched a puppet-carlin to oust them, but the goblins jeered at her and made all manner of mockery of her, sending the audience into hysterics. The frightened carlin soon made herself scarce.

Finally the goblins' tormenting became so unpleasant that the Reynoldses could endure them no longer. They decided to secretly escape from Gorsey Bank and go to live at a smaller farm they owned, a good three miles away.

The three of them colluded in a plan.

They gathered together their possessions, a few at a time, and whenever the goblins' backs were turned, they sent their baggage off to the smaller farm. At last one evening they collected the last of their belongings and departed with all haste and secrecy, leaving the wights in the empty house.

When they arrived at their new abode, feeling highly pleased to have got rid of their tormentors so cleverly, they began to unpack and arrange their possessions about their new home.

"Ooh, where's the old salt box, Father?" squeaked Mother Reynolds in her cracked upper register.

"I'm sure I don't know," said Father. "Young Eddy, have you got it?"

"Me not have it," shrilled quaint-ugly Young Eddy, provoking an outburst of coos and guffaws from the spectators.

"I am very fond of that old salt box," declared Mother. The rest of the family agreed that they were fond of it, too.

"We must have left it behind," Father said dolefully.

"Cowman! Cowman!" screeched Mother. "I am desperately vexed! Go back to Gorsey Bank this minute and fetch the old salt box!"

The cowman, a persecuted character of mournful countenance and pessimistic disposition, said hollowly, "I do not like that job at all. I will not go."

Mother boxed his ears. "Why will you not go?" she shouted. The audience hooted.

"I am afeared to go to Gorsey Bank on my own," said the cowman.

"Very well," squawked Mother, "then we shall send Young Eddy with you!"

The slow-witted cowman could think of no more excuses.

"But be very careful that the goblins do not catch sight of you," screamed bullying Mother as the cowman exited, stage right, in the company of her child, "or goodness knows what might happen!"

Raucous Mother and Father descended into the depths of the puppet theatre, while the tin-pipes began to tootle again. Presently Young Eddy and the cowman entered from the left side of the stage. They were bobbing along in a manner that approximated walking, when who should they spy approaching jauntily but the two goblins, the geezer and the crone, bobbing similarly along on the back of their huge hog. Before the cowman and Eddy could turn and flee the goblins had spotted them. "We've brought your salt box, we've brought your salt box," chorused the obnoxious wights, to the amusement of the onlookers.

There was nothing else the long-suffering cowman could

do but escort the dreadful nuisances back to the farmhouse. Mother and Father Reynolds were aghast when they saw the goblins coming but, fearing the vengeance of the wights if their ruse were to be discovered, they feigned innocence, and pretended they were pleased to see them again. They invited the nuisances in, offering them food and drink.

"You must come into the best parlor," twittered the Mother puppet, who was heaping papier mâché boiled beef on a platter, using both hands, as well as her jutting chin, to carry each piece. A thin curtain screened the best parlor from the brew-house, where Father, Young Eddy and the cowman were busy using the same method to bring in a large number of painted sticks and logs from the "wood-pile," with which they kindled a lively fire of starched red silk. Out of the goblins' view, Father made the downtrodden cowman stretch himself out in front of the brew-house hearth, and concealed him beneath a bundle of dried grasses.

"Come and warm yourselves by the fire," Father called to the unwelcome visitors, "for it is a right cold season. You may sit comfortably on this lovely truss of straw!"

"What do you think you're doing?" Mother muttered in a loud aside, which amazingly was not heard by the nearby goblins, possibly because they had ears of plaster.

"Wait and see!" said Father, somehow contriving to look shrewd despite his painted expression being fixed in a species of unattractive scowl.

In the brew-house the Reynoldses regaled the horrid little wights with beer, and conversed politely with them. All the while, in a low undertone, the cowman's dismal voice could be heard complaining about the fire's heat and the terrible weight of the goblins who sat upon him.

The watching children giggled at the cowman's discomfort and tittered in expectation.

Suddenly Father yelled, "Hurry, you old slowcoach!" and up jumped the cowman, tumbling the goblins right over into the fire, straw and all. To the delight of the more heartless spectators, there was much caterwauling and howling as the Reynoldses and the cowman set to work poking the hapless wights with pitchforks and brooms, keeping them ablaze in the flames of paste-stiffened red cloth until they shriveled up and burned to ashes—or at least, until they disappeared from view and a couple of handfuls of black sawdust jetted into the air.

Looking about, Asrăthiel noted differences in the way the children were moved by this gruesome comedy; some were vastly entertained, while others stared, agape with dismay.

"And the Reynoldses never saw anything more of the goblins after that," announced the narrator, "so they went back to Gorsey Bank and lived in peace and quiet."

The tin-pipes tweeted and the audience duly applauded with enthusiasm. Three Slievmordhuan puppeteers appeared from behind their screen, swept the hats from their heads and bowed flamboyantly. Winona rummaged in the aulmoniere that dangled from her belt and produced a few silver sixpences, which she tossed to the showmen.

"I don't think much of that as a story for children," commented Asrăthiel as she and her companions, trailed by various courtiers, left the parlor and drifted towards the Mauve Drawing Room. "When I was a child, that show would have given me nightmares."

"For shame, Asrăthiel!" cried Winona. "'Twas only a bit of fun!"

"I shall be forced to leave the bedside lamp burning until morning," said Prince Walter, who had joined their group halfway through the play. "For certain I will be having bad dreams about goblins tonight."

"Pshaw," his sister scoffed with a smile.

They emerged in the Mauve Drawing Room, where one of the more feckless royal cousins, who had imbibed a prodigious quantity of liquor that evening, was showing off to all and sundry a trick he had recently tried to learn from some wandering entertainer. "Look at me! Lo!" he crowed as he caught sight of the newcomers. "I can breathe fire!"

He swigged a mouthful of strong spirits, then plucked a candle from a sconce, held it in front of his face and expelled a great gust of air from his lungs. A jet of blue flame spurted from his lips and vanished almost as soon as it had appeared. The clown cheered triumphantly at his own trick, while several onlookers clapped their hands. "Wait, I can make a bigger flame!" he boasted, and proceeded to bury his nose in his cup, taking great gulps.

Asrăthiel, who had witnessed fire-eaters, fire-breathers and fire-jugglers galore at the many fairs and festivals held all across the Four Kingdoms, could not help being bored by the amateur exhibition, and allowed her attention to wander. A familiar prickling brushed the back of her mind; her brí-senses were picking up some natural disturbances in the atmosphere. Far away, beyond Wyverstone Castle, beyond King's Winterbourne, beyond the lofty hills and verdant vales of Narngalis, a northerly airflow was developing across Tir. A high pressure system was moving across the Southeastern Moors, and a low pressure trough was traveling into the Stone Deserts. She judged that the trough would reach Ashqalêth late on the following day, Sun's Day the twenty-sixth of Sevember, then cross the Four Kingdoms on Moon's Day, with a weak ridge to follow on War's Day.

The young weathermage perceived these distant conditions detachedly, and automatically made the forecast. To sense atmospheric phenomena was as much a part of her nature as breathing. She was always conscious of them with one section of her mind, just as anyone who reads a document or a book is distantly aware, despite being immersed in the narrative, of the surface on which they sit or recline, the sounds and odors of their environment, their own pulse, the texture of their raiment against their skin.

Lost in her reverie, Asrăthiel was transfixed by a rush of confusion when the screams arose all around. Next moment, someone had thrown a tablecloth around her head and shoulders, wrapping her tightly, partially muffling her face. Vainly, she squirmed to break away. William had her enfolded in his arms, and Prince Walter was calling for carlins and apothecaries. "Are you hale? Are you hale?" William kept demanding anxiously.

"Of course I am! Set me free! What has happened?"

"Forgive me! Forgive me!" wailed the fire-breather, staggering into a side table and knocking over several dishes. A couple of his comrades grabbed him by the elbows and marched him from the room.

"We have managed to smother the flames," William told Asrăthiel. "Your hair caught fire—pure carelessness on the part of that idiotic cousin of mine. I'll see him thrown into the Tower for this. We'll have a carlin to you straightway." The prince's comely visage was contorted in anger as he lifted Asrăthiel into his arms and bore her away into an antechamber, where he laid her upon a divan. His sisters, his brother Walter, many courtiers and a bevy of household servants followed, thronging about, the courtiers loudly voicing their concern.

"For goodness' sake, William, let there be no fuss," Asrăthiel insisted. A choking panic was rising in her chest. "I am hale. I felt nothing. Do you not recollect? *I cannot be harmed.*" The last phrase she hissed into his ear, hoping that no others would hear. Yet it was too late. The tablecloth, singed black and brown, and in places burned through, had been unwound from her person. All the people crowding into the room suddenly lapsed into silence.

They saw Asrăthiel's tresses, not a fiber demolished, coiling like dark ribbons down her back. In places her gown was scorched, but where it touched her skin it remained intact.

"The fire flared into your hair, m'lady!" exclaimed one of the courtiers.

"Yet it did not burn you!" another marveled, redundantly.

Asrăthiel was indeed burning now. Her face glowed with a fiery heat. Her superhuman invulnerability, the secret she wished so ardently to keep private, had been made glaringly obvious to everyone. Now, surely, she would generally be regarded with awe and suspicion. Feeling utterly wretched she could think of nothing to say, and only wished she were far from that place. She sat on the divan, staring hard at her own hands as her fingers tied themselves in knots, unable to force herself to lift her head and meet their stares.

"Depart, one and all!" shouted William. "Tell the carlins and apothecaries they are not needed. Go, now!" And they went with a rustle of silk and a clatter of shoes; all bar the two princes and their sisters.

"We were worried about you, Asrăthiel," Winona said gently, wonderingly.

"No need."

"No. Of course." Winona dabbed at her forehead with a lace handkerchief.

Saranna gazed in awe at the Storm Lord's daughter. Nonplussed, neither she nor Lecelina, who stood at her side, uttered a word. The royal family had long shared Asrăthiel's confidence, but never before been audience to its ramifications.

Presently Walter said, "We had forgotten you are invulnerable, forgotten you cannot be harmed or die."

Making a valiant effort, Asrăthiel raised her eyes. It was immediately clear to her that these kindly people had become, if temporarily, uncomfortable in her presence. Since she was unhurt, they quizzed her no further about the extraordinary event. In turn she had no idea how to respond to them, but felt awkward, as if she were some misfit, an outcast amongst them. It seemed strange, so strange; just a moment ago she had been part of the group, and now she found herself as isolated as a far-flung atoll in some shoreless ocean.

After his brother and sisters returned to the revelries to reassure their father and the guests that all was well, William seated himself on the divan beside Asrăthiel and took her hand in his. She was grateful for this sign of acceptance. His touch was warm.

"Forgive us," he said gravely. "As our dear friend, you have been our guest many times, and we have been yours. Over years of good fellowship we have come to perceive only the qualities we have in common with you, and to overlook your singular virtues. We are but blind fools. Your pardon, prithee."

"There is naught to forgive. Pray, do not distress yourself."

William spoke hesitantly. "You must be apprised—I must tell you—these gifts of yours do not affect my family's affection for you, adversely or in any other way."

"Of course not. Yes, I know that." It came to the damsel that he had noted her embarrassment, and pinpointed the source, and was endeavoring to ease her mind. His solicitude was genuinely touching, yet at the same time it unsettled her further. There would be no need for sympathy if she were not set apart.

"Are you certain?" he asked.

"Yes."

" 'Tis only that—if you should believe we look upon you as, well, exotic or anything, you would be mistaken. You understand?"

"Indeed." Asrăthiel nodded, and composed her features into a pleasant smile. "I know you could never consider me an outsider, sir," she said, putting as much conviction as possible into the falsehood.

"That is well. Come, let us return to the dancing."

His emotions and desires were easily gauged. She could tell he disbelieved her words, and planned to take time to convince her.

❧

The weathermaster coterie that had accompanied Asrăthiel on her journey to King's Winterbourne sojourned for a few days at the castle, enjoying King Warwick's hospitality. The following Moon's Day, with its low pressure trough, proved clear and bright, although the breezes were brittle with the chill of the northern latitudes. Enjoying this respite before she had to return to The Laurels to begin her duties, Asrăthiel found a sunny nook in the castle gardens, where she seated herself on an elegantly carved wooden bench, arranged the draperies of her gown of dark blue linen-velvet, and resumed reading a book she had brought with her from High Darioneth.

In front of her, crescent-shaped beds were formally laid out around a circular central display of roses. Low, neatly clipped hedges bordered each plot. Here and there, bell-shaped topiaries stood up, like quaint toys scattered by the children of giants. Walkways led through arches covered with greenery, or curved past latticed trellises entwined with creepers. Late in this northern Summer, the gardens were brushed with the vertical amethyst of lavender, the blush of floating poppies, the gold of daisies. Two gardeners were pruning shrubs, working with long shears. Boys followed after them, gathering up the cut twigs and piling them into wheelbarrows to be taken away.

Beyond the formal garden green lawns swept smoothly away to the right, towards the park with its bowery trees. To the left, the lawns led to the massive stone walls of some of the outbuildings that nestled amongst foliage, traced with ivy. In another direction the glazed roofs of the glasshouses glimmered like great cut-crystals, transparent white against a backdrop of dark green conifers. On the far side of the garden walls rose the gentle shoulders of tree-clad slopes, giving way to the sudden spectacle—always breathtaking, even when familiar—of the Northern Ramparts; colder, sharper, clearer, higher, more imposing than even the storths of High Darioneth. And above the mountains, only the vivid indigo sky, dramatic, swirling with feverish cloudscapes whose shadows fled across the world below.

Asrăthiel was engrossed in the perusal of her book when William came by. "I have been seeking you," he said, seating himself beside her. "There is news from Slievmordhu."

"Oh, news," the damsel said with a sigh. "I had hoped to shut out the world for a while and lose myself between these pages."

"Is it so interesting, your book?" The prince tilted his head in an effort to see the title. Strands of his hair fell across his face, and he swept them back with both hands. Asrăthiel closed the book and showed it to him. "*The Other*

Inhabitants," William read out loud, "*Our Neighbors That Dwell in Wood and Hill.* 'Tis all about eldritch wights, I suppose."

"It's not about wights. It is fiction with nonhumans as the protagonists.

"Nonhumans?"

"What you would call animals. In this narrative the animals are acting as they would truly act, not as human beings would behave."

"I do not know how you can bring yourself to read such tedious stuff!" William scoffed gently. "Honestly, Asrăthiel, it cannot be any good! How can there be a story to it? I can show you some really interesting books. All the best literature is concerned with exploring the human condition, the nature of the human spirit." He leaned against the back of the bench and folded his arms across his chest.

"Why?" she said simply.

"Because—and I know you will upbraid me for saying so—humankind is the highest life form."

His eyes rested contemplatively upon Asrăthiel. Carefully avoiding his gaze she said, "Our world, William, is one of many worlds amongst the stars. So is our race only one of many races within this world, all with rights of their own."

"Ah yes," said William. "I have never understood this unusual philosophy of yours. Tell me more."

"Nonhuman animals are not ours to use for food, clothing, entertainment or any other purpose. They deserve consideration of their best interests regardless of whether they are endearing, or useful to humankind, and indeed regardless of whether any human being cares about them at all—just as the madmen who dwell in the Asylum for Lunatics have rights, even if they are not agreeable or useful and everyone detests them."

Asrăthiel laid her book on her knees and stared pensively at a stunted sprig of crowthistle that was sprouting in a crevice between flagstones. Even in the cool northern climes, it survived. Apparently the dratted weed grew everywhere in Tir, undaunted by harsh climate, keen gardeners or any other adversities.

Her companion leaned towards her, his eyes sparkling with merriment. "You with your strange ways," he said teasingly, "refusing to wear furs and silks, accepting wool purchased only from certain kindly shepherds, forever nibbling herbs and worts, and decrying the noble sport of horse-racing! Race-horses at least are happy, I daresay. Trainers treat them well, so that they will perform well."

"With respect, sir, you are mistaken!" Asrăthiel exclaimed. "When large amounts of money are at stake, men will do anything to make a horse run faster. If the poor beasts are not fleet of foot and the quacks' compounds fail to work, the owners have the horses slaughtered. Even if the unhappy creatures avoid injury, when they can no longer run fast they are most often sold to the butchers."

"True enough," said the prince musingly. "I had never deliberated much about that side of the so-called sport of kings, but now I shall loathe it as much as you do. However, I shall continue to wear boots and belts of leather in good conscience, for leather is merely a by-product of cattle that are going to be slaughtered in any event."

"On the contrary, the success of slaughterhouses depends on the sale of skins. Wear boots of canvas, and save the lives of innocents!"

"You are as passionate as ever on this topic, Asrăthiel! Yet, it is natural for nonhuman animals to consume meat, so why not us?"

"Well, sir, humankind has the ability to eat the flesh of things that have eyes, but for ethical reasons we may instead choose not to do so. In any case, we thrive better on breads, fruits and suchlike."

"You are convincing. Let us not argue—" William broke off, and they both looked up as the sound of harsh cawing erupted in a grove of firs that stood like a cluster of dark green cones to one side of the glasshouses. A black-and-white bird took off from the topmost branches, leaving the twigs to bounce and swing. The repetitive noise arced across the gardens like a bridge of invisible steps as the bird flew away. "Those magpies make a terrible racket," said the prince, grimacing.

"Magpies?" repeated Asrăthiel. "That was no magpie. It was some bird I have not seen before. Magpies have the most melodious song; many's the morning I have woken to their glorious warbling."

"Ah," her companion answered, "magpies such as he that flew away are a type unique to northern Narngalis. It's possible there is another species you call 'magpies' at High Darioneth." In a while he added an afterthought that Asrăthiel scarcely noted as they sat there together, but recalled later, at a moment of staggering revelations, as being strikingly pertinent, unknown then to either herself or William: "I have heard my old tutor say that in some cases the same name is applied to entirely different birds in different parts of the country, and thus confusion reigns." The prince laughed. "Conversely, the same breed of bird, or beast, or fish may be given various names in various regions. We are most of us too stubborn or too lazy to change our habits, and stick to the names we are used to!"

"Such are the eccentricities of human nature," said Asrăthiel, breaking into smiles. "But prithee," she added, recalling her companion's original mission, "divulge your message from Slievmordhu."

The prince's pleasant countenance became grave. "I am afraid it is not good news. We have heard that rumors are spreading amongst Uabhar's subjects, kindling flames of discontent against the weathermasters."

"Against weathermasters!" Asrăthiel suddenly sat up. Before she could catch it, the book slid from her lap to the ground, and she was vexed with herself for once again forgetting to safeguard a precious object. "But why? How?"

William picked up the slim volume and placed it on the bench. "At first the gossips merely leveled unfounded accusations of indolence and avarice. Now they accuse your kindred of stealing items of gramarye from the site of the old Dome of Strang. Tidings of the Sylvan Comb's discovery have, quite naturally, spread throughout the Four Kingdoms. According to Uabhar, the Dome belongs to the kingdom of Slievmordhu, and the weathermasters have robbed the populace of their rightful property."

"B'thunder! What can Uabhar be playing at?"

"One may only guess. The man is far more ingenious than most folk comprehend. I confess I am baffled."

"The Dome belongs to the descendents of the Sorcerer. This fact has been legally established. If Uabhar is claiming he owns it, he has become a law unto himself."

"He reigns. He *is* the law in Slievmordhu."

Asrăthiel shot a quick glance at the prince. "Of course. As sovereign he may alter his kingdom's legislation at a whim. And I daresay his whims have led him to employ some quirk of his own legislation to claim the Dome. Having heard of the newly discovered Sylvan Comb, he is jealous of the find."

"Not all kings are equally capricious," murmured William.

"Sir, you must never place your own family in the same class as that of Uabhar!" Asrăthiel cried, with characteristic bluntness. "The Wyverstone code of honor and fair play can never be questioned! Ó Maoldúin is another dynasty entirely. There have been virtuous kings amongst that lineage in days of yore, but Uabhar's generation is made of different metal, if I may speak plainly."

"I would not have you speak otherwise to me. And again, I am of like mind."

"I do not want this magickal comb in our possession if it is going to precipitate trouble," said Asrăthiel. "Since Uabhar desires it so much, I shall ask my grandfather to give it to him. Then Slievmordhu can have no quarrel with my kindred."

"If Uabhar desires a quarrel," said William, "I daresay he shall find one."

"Anyone would be mad to estrange Rowan Green."

"I, for one, would be unwilling to vouch for Uabhar's sanity," the prince said sardonically.

The two joined in laughter, but a cloud passed across the face of the sun and a cold wind swept across the gardens. All at once the day seemed grey and drear, the sunlight leached out of it. The young man shivered. "It has turned chill out here," he said. "Let us go indoors."

Unwilling to remind him that she was impervious to the privations of weather, the damsel rose to her feet, tucked her book beneath her arm and accompanied the prince into the fire-bright halls.

꙰

Asrăthiel would not allow William to overlook his promise to encounter her in combat; therefore in the afternoon of the next day they met together in the castle's drill hall, geared up and ready for the contest. The hall had been cleared of its usual assortment of men practicing their fighting maneuvers. Only a select, discreet group of spectators had been invited to watch. William made no effort to conceal the fact that he felt ill at ease pitting his skill against a woman, and he had only agreed to do so at Asrăthiel's insistence.

The Storm Lord's granddaughter had brought her equipment in the aerostat from High Darioneth. Like her opponent, she was wearing the armor customarily used in longsword training. She and the prince stood face to face, their feet placed shoulder-width apart, their heels on the ground, knees bent, hips twisted, front foot pointed directly at the adversary.

The swordmaster shouted, "Lay on!" and the combatants began circling. They feinted and pondered, each noting the movements of the other's feet and the direction of their gaze, as best they could through the visors. They held their swords in guard position, resting on the right shoulder. All of a sudden they rolled their weapons off their shoulders and the wooden practice-blades were flying in a rapid exchange of blows. Like water in motion flowed the actions of these skilled adversaries. Their feet seemed to float in complicated patterns of footwork; small, shuffling yet poised steps diagonally forward, sideways, or in retreat.

The habits of a lifetime die hard. Blows cause pain, as any child soon learns; and to scathe any woman contradicted William's nature. To begin with he moved diffidently, almost timidly, reluctant to seriously engage. In contrast Asräthiel thrust diagonally forward, using her shoulders, hip and thigh to give impetus to the strike, pushing her body-weight through behind the weapon to deliver it with utmost force. Using the edge of the shield, William blocked the blow. The impact of her blade on his shield jarred right through the bones of his arms and into his frame. He was surprised at her strength, for the wooden swords weighed four pounds, and their fulcrums were forward of the hilt. Without pausing, Asräthiel drove another long thrust towards her opponent. William countered with a crosswise thrust. She feinted, distracted him for an instant, and delivered a hard thwack to his unguarded shoulder on his shield side. Even after that, William was reluctant to do more than defend himself. Shrewdly, Asräthiel kept herself at full range and would not allow him to close in. When he approached she darted quickly aside, fetching a blow to his helm before he had a chance to spin around.

Although he was slightly dazed, it occurred to the prince that her unstinting hits must surely be making him appear foolish in front of the spectators. Since it was clear Asräthiel could take care of herself, he halfheartedly began to attack. The damsel parried his moves skilfully, effortlessly, always blocking his blade with the forte—the lower third—of her own sword, but as close as possible to the tip of his blade. It was an effective trick, because all blades were stronger close to the hilt. If a sword were struck at the tip, it was easy to brush aside. If it were struck at the base it had more of the wielder's weight and strength behind it, and was harder to deflect or break. As they dueled, William came to understand that he was indeed confronted by a formidable opponent, and he commenced to engage in earnest.

The aim of the trial was to knock down or disarm the adversary. Asrăthiel attacked with a plunging cut and William counterattacked with a shifting cut. They hacked and slashed, whaled and clashed, sweated and panted, occasionally falling back for a few moments to deliberate, wipe the perspiration from their eyes and renew their grips on their weapons before waging battle afresh.

At last William dealt a solid blow to Asrăthiel's shield, pushing her off balance so that she staggered. While she was trying to regain equilibrium, she let down her guard, whereupon he rushed her, pushed her sword out of the way and sent her sprawling on her back.

The victor let his own weapon drop from his fingers, offering his gloved hand to help the vanquished one rise to her feet. She accepted with dignity, stood up and bowed.

"I salute you, sir."

They were both breathing like bellows.

"You are nineteen," he said, "and I am twenty-four. Yet I have not fought such a long battle, except against my own swordmaster, or warriors with twice my experience."

"Do not congratulate me," she said softly, her eyes downcast. "William, to cross swords with me is no fair contest."

At first he did not comprehend her meaning, and then there arose before his mind's eye a vision of her tresses alight, and where there should have been charred peel, bald rind and weeping raw flesh, there was only her flawless skin and her hair like some wondrous vessel of spun jet filaments, embracing incandescent flames of bronze and gilt and carmine. It could be no fair contest to battle one who was unscathable. Yet he laid aside the mirage, and squeezed Asrăthiel's hand, which he was still holding.

"You fight well," he murmured. Then a grin quirked the corners of his mouth. "You are a most proficient swordswoman. Indeed, I suspect you held back, because you are a true diplomat who would rather not defeat a member of the royal family."

"Not at all!" The damsel knew he was joking and smiled

as they both stripped off their gloves and helms, and shook out their sopping hair. Footmen bore away their accoutrements. Pages handed them towels with which they might wipe their faces, and cups of cool water to drink.

"Ah, you deny it, Asrăthiel, but I shall never be certain. I will not contend with you again, because I shall always doubt whether you fight fairly."

"As you wish, sir!" Asrăthiel swept him a second bow, grateful he had devised a way to forestall any future encounters. It had been her pride that had motivated her to challenge him in the first place. She had not properly thought the matter through.

Customarily, men had the advantage over women in contests of the longsword. A heavier, taller and stronger swordsman possessed a huge advantage over a slighter adversary. There was also much profit in having a longer reach. In order to best a man, a woman must be faster, better balanced, more thoroughly trained, defter, luckier. She must own greater endurance, and tolerance of pain. She must be more cunning. Asrăthiel guessed that if she were to truly acknowledge her native invulnerability, and throw off the shield and armor that slowed her movements; if she were to dare to fight unprotected, shedding the redundant fear of scathe she had taught herself in order to appear unexceptional, she might have a good chance of defeating even an expert and mighty warrior. This she surmised, but would not dare try. Her desire to be accepted as an ordinary citizen, as susceptible to injury as anyone, overrode her hankering for martial triumph.

As they walked side by side out of the drill-hall, William asked, "It perplexes me why you train at swordsmanship, for I know it is not in you to cause harm to living things. I would have imagined that hitting and hurting were foreign to your nature."

"To my mind, it is admissible to fight an opponent who is on an equal footing and who has freely agreed to the contest," she replied, "or to wage battle in self-defense. There is justice in those circumstances. On the other hand there is no justice in slaughtering creatures that have been born in captivity, with no chance to flee or fight back, or hunting wild beasts that have no weapons other than their four legs to make them fleet, or their own teeth and claws to defend themselves at close quarters. But you ask me why I practice with the sword. It is because I desire ardently to make myself worthy of wielding Fallowblade; employing him as he is intended to be employed, according to my birthright." There was a catch in her voice as she added, "My father would have wielded Fallowblade, were he still amongst us."

"To what purpose? No one would threaten war against the weathermasters!"

"Aye, and no one marches against Narngalis, either, yet your father keeps his defense forces in trim. Besides, Fallowblade deserves to be taken seriously as a weapon, and not treated as merely a mantelshelf ornament."

"Have you brought the Golden Sword with you?"

"No. He remains, as ever, in my grandfather's house." Catching a glimmer of mirth in William's eye, she laughed, admitting, "As a mantelshelf ornament."

William said, "Since you have no swordmaster in your new household, you are welcome to employ the services of one of ours whenever you wish to practice."

"Gramercie, sir," the damsel said, giving him a quick smile. "That is well. Methinks I shall take the tutor out into the field. I have promised myself to rehearse my lessons on rough terrain, as I am too much accustomed to the level floors of armories and drill halls and the smooth flags of training yards."

"A first-rate notion."

❧

Shortly thereafter, Asrăthiel removed to her lodgings in Lime Grove. It was early in Otember, the middle month of Autumn, and the time of the Lord Mayor's Show, a popular annual spectacle in the city. Crowds of Narngalish citizens milled throughout King's Winterbourne's labyrinth of mean-

dering streets and lanes. Amonst them mingled flamboyant
Ashqalêthans, their clothes dyed in soft citrus colors, muffled beneath the layers of furs in which they swaddled themselves against the northern cold; blunt sea-merchants from
Grïmnørsland, their faces chafed by wind and weather;
crimson-clad aristocrats of Slievmordhu decked with bronze
ornaments; peasants and craftsmen from all over Tir, clad in
nondescript outfits of drab homespun; knights in their
tabards, druids in their robes and carlins with woad-blue
discs painted on their brows.

The majority of houses and inns in the city were half-
timbered, or wattle and daub, whitewashed with lime, roofed
with slate. The Laurels was no exception. Behind the high
walls of the estate, the house was triple-storeyed and spacious, containing rooms more numerous than Asrăthiel and
her retinue would ever need. Protocol, however, demanded
impressive lodgings for the representative of High Darioneth. The premises suited Asrăthiel's requirements. There
was no incumbent brownie, but that was not extraordinary.
Brownies were an uncommon luxury. Most households relied on human domestic servants to perform the chores.

Mistress Draycott Parslow proved to be an accommodat-
ing landlady, benign and somewhat eccentric. She was fond
of recounting the story of how she had obtained her wealth,
for she had not always been well off. She used to dwell alone
in a remote house on a hilltop in one of the mining districts.
Her husband had been killed by the collapse of a shaft, in
one of the old "coffens," or mine-workings, in the hill. Conceivably attracted by the widow's seclusion, the local spriggans used to gather in her cottage almost every night to
apportion their plunder. Small in stature, with upstanding
and pointed ears, wide mouths and broad noses, these eldritch incarnations would creep in, accompanied by a strong
odor of leaf-mold. In return for the use of Mistress Draycott
Parslow's premises, they would leave a small coin by her
bedside. The money, meager though it was, helped to make
the dame's life a little more comfortable. Yet she was not
content; from beneath the bedcovers of a night, she would

secretly peer out at the wights and long to possess their treasure. There was silver plate, and gold, and jewels—all real, she had no doubt; perhaps unearthed from ancient barrows.

Eventually, one night, when they had snared more than the usual amount of loot, the spriggans began to dispute angrily about the distribution of it. There were seven wights but only five gold cups—as well as plenty of other wealth—and all the spriggans wanted to own a cup. They dickered and debated, disagreeing on the value of the vessels, and who should have one, and how the rest of the goods ought to be shared in compensation. Their slits of eyes glittered with malice, while their barbed, whipcord tails switched angrily back and forth.

Mistress Draycott Parslow, spying from under her blankets and pretending to be asleep, seized her opportunity. Surreptitiously, beneath the bedcovers, she doffed her shift, turned it inside out and put it on again. Turning one's clothes was, of course, an authenticated ward against minor wights such as spriggans. When she had protected herself against their powers, she reached out and grabbed a gold cup, boldly crying, "You shan't have a single one of them!"

The startled spriggans fled, but the last one, as he departed, swept his bony hand over the old woman's shift.

The wights abandoned all the treasure and failed to come back on the following nights. To the astonishment of the local inhabitants, Mistress Draycott Parslow became a rich woman. Gnawed by a niggling fear that the spriggans might eventually return seeking revenge, she soon left the cottage and went to live in King's Winterbourne, where she purchased The Laurels and settled down in the cottage in the grounds, which was far more sumptuous than her old abode. When asked why she dared to tell the story, when everyone knew that if you revealed you had obtained wealth from wights that wealth would disappear, she would explain, "Well, I have spent all the treasure already, so if I ain't got it, it cannot banish. Besides, it were real bullions and jools; it were not just some wafty glamor cast over a pile of hay-corns and leaves."

And she always added this coda: she was unable ever again to wear the shift that had brought her good fortune, without suffering intense torment. "Nobody knows how it can be, that putting on a shift can bring me such agrimonies," she would say wisely. "But I knows. 'Tis the work of the spriggans!"

Privately, Asräthiel wondered why the old woman did not simply throw out the threadbare shift. Perhaps she kept it for luck.

Once the weathermage had settled in to her new home, her work proceeded uneventfully. It was second nature for her to forecast the weather; no difficulty was involved. Each day she would send a messenger to the castle with her latest predictions. Sometimes she walked to the royal residence herself to deliver the news, for it was less than half a mile away, and while visiting she would avail herself of the king's private library, or practice swordplay with one of the weaponmasters. It was not until the middle of Otember, on a King's Day, when her brí-senses detected the approach of a violent electrical storm, that she was asked to actually intervene. She had become aware that a weak cold front, associated with severe thunderstorm activity, would clear from the east that night. A high pressure ridge would extend across Tir the following day, with a center strengthening to the east of the Four Kingdoms on Love's Day, bringing fine weather.

When this was reported to King Warwick he called for the young weathermaster and asked her for assistance. "The apples hang ripening on the trees," he said, "almost ready for the harvest. If strong winds and rain should batter the orchards of Narngalis at this season, the fruit crop will be in danger of failing. Pray avert this storm, Lady Maelstronnar."

Thus it was that Asräthiel went straightway and climbed a spiral stair that led to the rooftop of the tallest turret of the castle. At the king's command, nobody came near to distract her from her task. She gazed towards the east, and reached out her faculties like invisible tendrils on the wind, feeling her way through the pressure fluctuations, the differences in humidity and temperature, the flows and eddies of atmospheric rivers, until she discovered the core elements of this pattern, the essential forces brewing the storm.

Distant air currents, like gossamer streamers, rustled through the awareness of the weathermage, coiling in cyclones and anticyclones. Alive with boundless energy, sometimes they smelled of electricity, sometimes of salt, and sometimes they were tinged with the fragrance of new-mown hay. Always the currents smacked of freedom and excitement. As Asrăthiel breathed, she could scarcely tell where her own exhalations ended and where the gusts began. She knew faraway clouds, pouring like cream, and comprehended the flux of humidity like fine-grained banners of hyaline tissue, smoother than silk. Vapors sighed in her ears, tasting of purity and distilled freshness, scented with tranquillity. Perspiring with exhilaration, the girl on the turret could scarcely differentiate her sweat from raindrops, her heartbeat from thunder, her own voice from the cries and whispers of the wind.

Heat and cold undulated through the troposphere, driving forces invisible to the human eye. Hot winds like tatters of crimson velvet, raw as liquor and roaring; cold tides, piquant as green apples, chiming or piping thinly; the butter-mellow tepidness of hot and cold colliding in transition. The damsel on the roof perceived the remote workings of temperature, and it seemed hard to distinguish between her own pulsing blood-heat and the energies unleashed by the furnace of the sun. Her mind grasped faraway ligatures of lightning, and she did not know whether the high-powered levin bolts were discharging between the heavens and the ground, or in the snapping synapses of her own nerves.

Above Asrăthiel the atmosphere churned. Updraughts caught her hair in billowing strands, threading them along their paths. Her eyes, shining, reflected the streaming clouds, so that they seemed no longer eyes at all but long oval windows opening onto the roiling skies behind her head. Winglike, her sleeves and mantle flared from her shoulders. Standing on that height Asrăthiel spoke the words and performed the gestures, working with air and water and fire in far-off places; summoning, deflecting, coordinating; diluting the ferocity of the elements, turning them away from the cultivated lands of the north to expend the remnants of their rage on the mountains.

When at length her work was finished, she descended the stair, a little weary, perhaps, but not visibly exhausted, considering she had single-handedly thwarted a portion of the atmosphere's might. In fact, as always after she had weather-worked, she felt profoundly at peace.

Throughout that night the people of Narngalis had watched the lightning flicker and blaze on the heights of the Northern Ramparts, hearkening to the crash of airs riven asunder, the howl and boom of thunder rocketing from rock-face to chasm. The tumult seemed to split the very foundations of the world. And they knew, then, what a great weathermage they had in their midst, who could protect their kingdom from something so unimaginably puissant. On her own the Lady Maelstronnar had achieved a task that commonly demanded the united skills of many brí-wielders.

Everybody was grateful to Asráthiel; nonetheless their gratitude came from a distance, as though they revered her as someone not quite human. Indeed, at times she herself wondered whether her essential character had lost some qualities of humanity. She only ceased to feel hurt by the silence of those who entered her presence when she came to understand that it was not indifference or animosity that made them tongue-tied, but awe. Even William now seemed reserved in her proximity, trying unsuccessfully to conceal his wonder at her deeds. More than ever, she felt alienated and alone.

It was with relief, therefore, that she received an invitation to attend the celebrations for the official betrothal of Uabhar's eldest son, Kieran, to King Thorgild's daughter Solveig. Her fellow weathermasters had also been invited, and this was a welcome opportunity to enjoy their company again. In the month of Ninember, accompanied by her crew, she piloted *Lightfast* from King's Winterbourne to Sliev-mordhu. There she rendezvoused with Dristan, Albiona, her aunt Galiene and Ryence Darglistel at the city mansion of Calogrenant Lumenspar, ambassador for High Darioneth in Cathair Rua.

Great rejoicing took place at that reunion, and much animated discussion. Asrǎthiel learned that for several weeks past, aircrews on weather missions over Ashqalêth had been sighting columns of King Chohrab's soldiers marching eastwards, while in Slievmordhu, King Uabhar's troops had been involved in an unusual number of regimental reviews and training exercises. When asked about their intentions, spokesmen for both realms had stated that their armed forces had joined in alliance to combat the Marauders when they reemerged from their lairs in the warmer months. With this explanation the weathermasters had to be satisfied. Their curiosity, however, was aroused; and they felt the first twinges of apprehension about this unwonted buildup of military strength in peacetime. Long had they watched Uabhar with a wary eye, but now it seemed they must also be cautious of Chohrab, who had hitherto appeared to be a mild-mannered monarch possessing no exceptional wit or ambition. At length, putting aside their disquiet, they spoke of matters to hand. After consultation with Asrǎthiel, the Councilors of Ellenhall decided to take advantage of this festive occasion to officially hand over the Sylvan Comb as a gift to appease the jealousy of King Uabhar. No notice was given—it was to be a pleasant surprise.

Cathair Rua was decked with garlands of red and yellow Autumn leaves for the betrothal celebrations. The weathermasters rode through the streets in carriages, or enclosed chairs carried on poles, flanked by an honorary escort of Knights of the Brand, captained by Conall Gearnach. It seemed the city was in the grip of a high good humor; but some amongst the visitors noted a change. It was not a change of weather; rather it was an alteration in the attitude of the populace. Usually, citizens greeted weathermasters with respectful cheers and a doffing of hats, and smiles, and bows. This time, there were, amidst the cheering welcomers, a few who merely watched the weathermasters' progress stone-faced, or skulked away when the procession approached.

"Something is amiss," said Asrǎthiel, peering through the lace curtains of her chair and past the broad back of one of the four bearers. "I discern the citizens do not welcome us as is their wont."

"Nonsense," stated Albiona, whose conveyance was being carried alongside. "They applaud us. See, over there; a band of craftsmen waving their caps in a gesture of respect."

"Many behave as ever," said Asrăthiel, "but others turn away, or scowl."

"I do not see why they should."

"I wonder whether they are envious that Narngalis has its own weathermage."

"Balderdash! You are Warwick's subject, not Uabhar's. It is your duty to serve your sovereign. They ought to know that."

"Mayhap they resent our privileged position."

The chairs passed a charcoal brazier on a tripod set up on the footpath. A street-vendor was selling eggs he had robbed from larks' nests and pickled, and baby quails, threaded on a spit and roasted. Asrăthiel closed her curtains.

"Balderdash again." Albiona's voice carried through the lace. "Our kindred have always been privileged, and with good reason, for we provide indispensable services to the Four Kingdoms. Our prerogatives have never seemed to bother anyone in the past, and there is no reason why they should bother people now."

"I am uneasy."

"Only recall how courteously Gearnach gave us salutations upon our arrival, and observe how nobly his Knights of the Brand conduct themselves towards us! Their esteem is clearly as great as ever."

"Upright men, such as they, ignore scandal-mongers. Prince William told me that gossips in Cathair Rua are spreading nasty rumors about us. I did not think the citizens would listen, but I see I have been proved wrong."

"I expect you are mistaken, Asrăthiel. No ill-natured hearsay could turn popular opinion against us."

But the chairs lurched on, and Asrăthiel was convinced she was not mistaken.

Peering at the procession through a spyglass from a high, narrow window of the Sanctorum, Primoris Virosus observed all that went on in the streets below; the stately files of chivalry led by Commander-in-Chief Gearnach, the elegant vehicles conveying the weathermasters, the mixed reactions of the onlookers.

"Ah, how the loyalty of Two-Swords would be tested," he muttered to himself, "if he knew who had introduced the slander that disturbs the crowd! The royal perpetrator is wise to keep the truth from him. Between fealty and honor, the valorous knight would be torn in two." He sniggered dryly and continued to watch until the convoy passed out of view.

Dignitaries from all over Tir had been invited to attend the festivities. The betrothal of Prince Kieran of Slievmordhu and Princess Solveig of Grïmnørsland took place with much pomp and strict observance of formalities, but between rituals the guests indulged in a good deal of easygoing merriment. The banquet in the Great Hall, marking the closing of ceremonies, was particularly jolly. Resplendent in colorful raiment, the diners sat at long tables loaded with a variety of delicious and spectacular dishes. Banners and pennants and all manner of war gear decorated the walls of the vast chamber. King Uabhar displayed his celebrated personal armaments in pride of place above the high table; his shield, Ocean, his dagger, Victorious, his spear Slaughter, and his sword Gorm Glas, the blue-green.

As the occasion was a betrothal—the official confirmation of an arrangement made during the couple's infancy—and not a full state occasion, only representatives of Narngalis and Ashqalêth attended, rather than the monarchs of those realms. Had it been a wedding, the principal members of all the royal houses would have been present. Naturally the parents of the bride-to-be, King Thorgild and Queen Halfrida, were amongst the guests, along with their sons Hrosskel, Halvdan and Gunnlaug; also King Chohrab II's brother-in-law, Duke Rahim, and King Warwick's second son, Walter. Druidic delegates from the Cathair Rua Sanctorum graced the occasion on behalf of the greatly revered Primoris Asper Virosis, who, being particularly averse to jocular crowds, had absented himself and was taking his supper alone in a private room.

Uabhar's sons were determined to enjoy the occasion as it deserved. The elder two deliberately put aside their uneasiness about the popular smear campaign against the weathermasters, their alarm at the inexplicable rise in success of Marauder raids, and their tentative uncertainty about their father's political affairs, focusing instead on the joyfulness of the celebration. Prince Ronin, alone, appeared a trifle less than lighthearted, but that might have been for personal reasons.

The four most blithesome persons at the feast were the affianced couple—who were clearly deeply enamored of each other; Halvdan, Kieran's favorite comrade and the brother of the betrothed princess; and Conall Gearnach, who was delighted at the opportunity for companionship with his friends, the princes of Grïmnørsland. No one was happier for Kieran than Halvdan Torkilsalven, who sat close to the feted couple at the high table. During the breaks between courses the two young men flung jests back and forth, and swapped stories of shared adventures during their boyhood, to make Solveig laugh.

"Once," Kieran said to his bride-to-be, "in the days when I dwelled with your family at Trøndelheim, Halvdan and I slipped away from Two-Swords, ran off to the marketplace and hid ourselves in a wine-merchant's wagon. We broached a cask, drank the wine and fell asleep. By the time we awoke, night had fallen. We discovered the wagon had exited the city, and we were miles away from home!"

"Aye, and it was a hogshead of trouble you two landed me in over that escapade," said Gearnach good-naturedly. Tankard in hand, he had wandered over from the knights' table, where he had been seated with other warriors of the Red Lodge, and took up a position standing behind the tall, gem-studded backs of the princes' chairs.

"I do not remember it," said Solveig. "You boys were always skylarking so much that one prank seemed no more prominent than the others. I only recall being helpless with laughter every time I heard about your latest scrapes. It is fortunate that Conall was there to rescue you or neither of you would have lasted past your fourteenth Winter!"

"True indeed, Your Highness!" affirmed Gearnach, raising his tankard and bowing in a salute to the princess.

"One of the best jokes," said Halvdan, lowering his voice so that the other three must lean closely to hear him, like conspirators, "was when Gunnlaug challenged Kieran to walk through the cemetery at midnight on Lantern Eve."

"You would never refuse a challenge," Solveig said, bestowing dimpled smiles upon her betrothed. "How characteristic of our brother to suggest such a test of courage. He himself was terrified of that place. What happened?"

Halvdan said, "In secret, or so he thought, Gunnlaug draped himself in a sheet of bleached linen."

His sister could not contain her glee. "That must have been a pretty sight!"

"Then," continued Halvdan, "when Kieran was walking through the cemetery, our dear brother jumped out at him!"

"I assure you, Gunnlaug in a sheet is about as fearsome as a milk jug," said Kieran.

Halvdan chaffed. "Sister, Kieran is only pretending to be brave. He would have fainted, had I not forewarned him."

"Dan, you'd faint into your porridge if your nurserymaid said 'boo,'" Kieran returned affably. "But that is not the end of the story, Solveig my love, for I walked up to this strange white figure in the cemetery and I wished it good evening, which flummoxed it no end. Then I suddenly pointed a trembling finger over its shoulder, like this, and yelled, *'What's that behind you? By Ádh's Fortune, 'tis a black ghost!'* The white figure jumped pretty high, I can tell you—for I daresay Gunnlaug was fairly jittery after spending all that time in a graveyard—and when it touched the ground it was running in the other direction. So I shouted after it, as it fled into the darkness, *'That's it, black ghost! Catch the white ghost and carry it away with you!'*"

Solveig giggled into her hands, while Conall Gearnach

looked on with benign joviality, his elbow bent, his drinking-vessel held close to his chest.

"What's more," added Halvdan, "the white ghost was running so fast in the dark that it tripped over the sheet and ended up flat on its face in the mire. Gunnlaug never knew we had tricked him, so be certain you keep our secret!"

The princess nodded assent, pink-cheeked and laughing too hard to be able to speak.

Noting that Gearnach had just drained his tankard, Halvdan gestured to one of the butlers, bidding him refill the vessel. "Drink up, Two-Swords!" he cried. "I'll not have you going thirsty, especially when it's Kieran's beer we're all swallowing." Turning to his sister he said loudly, so that the knight would overhear, "You have heard about Two-Swords's fiery temper of course—" At this, Gearnach's stance stiffened, but in another moment he had relaxed into joviality again as the prince passed over the topic "—however did you know that he sometimes suffers from unfortunate lapses of common sense?"

Solveig shook her head, her eyes shining.

"When he was a youth," Halvdan continued, "Two-Swords moved out of his mother's house into a farm-cottage. A bit later his old mother asks him how he likes his new home and he says, '*The house is all right, but the next door neighbor's rooster starts crowing hours before sunrise, and it keeps me from getting any sleep.*' So his mother says, '*Well that's a pity because you cannot do anything about it. Your neighbor has a right to keep roosters if he wishes.*'

"Not long after, Two-Swords tells his mother he has fixed the problem of the next-door rooster's predawn uproar. '*How did you fix it?*' enquires his mother.

"'*I bought the rooster from my neighbor and put it in my own garden,*' says Two-Swords. '*Let it keep* him *awake now.*'"

The four friends guffawed at the joke, particularly Gearnach, who had never in his life dwelled in a farm cottage or purchased a rooster. He then riposted with an equally ludicrous fabrication about Halvdan. Their laughter was interrupted by a disturbance further down the table, which caught their attention. Prince Gunnlaug had lumbered to his feet, upsetting a stand of sweetmeats at his elbow. He surveyed the hall, loosened his belt by several notches, and thrust out his swollen belly. "By Axe and Bell, I have eaten so much," he declared to all and sundry, "that I am on the point of exploding. I hope everyone likes roast beef, ha ha ha!"

His father King Thorgild, a stalwart red-bearded man of forty-five Winters, had been watching this display. He spoke quietly into the ear of his page, who hurried off to pass the message on to Gunnlaug's personal butler.

While Thorgild's attention was focused on his youngest son, King Uabhar beckoned to Duke Rahim, the brother-in-law of Chohrab II, who sat nearby. The duke inclined his head towards the king, waiting to hear what he had to say.

"And will your esteemed brother soon be sending more troops from Ashqalêth to Slievmordhu to join us in war games?" Uabhar asked in an undertone, using one fingertip to draw patterns in spilled crumbs on the tablecloth. "We must all be well prepared to do battle against Marauders in the Spring, when the thaw releases them from their ice-bound caves in the eastern ranges. Unseelie wights, too, will continue to plague us, no doubt. Best to be ready."

The duke's face fell. "Chohrab's enthusiasm flags," he admitted. "It is a long journey, and costly, and displacing so many soldiers leaves our lands largely undefended."

A brief spasm of rage flitted across the countenance of Uabhar, and was as quickly erased. "Come with me to my apartments after the feast," he said smoothly, playing with his knife, "and I will give you a message to take to your sister's husband. It will be highly confidential. I can trust no other than you to deliver it."

An expression between complacency and conceit warmed the ruddy features of the duke. "Indeed I am the very essence of discretion, as you judge, Your Greatness," he said. "Pray tell me, what matter will this message convey?"

"This is no fitting venue to impart news of such consequence." Uabhar glanced furtively over his shoulder as if he feared eavesdroppers in his own hall, then leaned even closer to the duke. "You must not breathe a word of this to anyone except your sovereign," he said, picking furiously at the embroidery on his sleeve, "but reports have come to hand this very hour. I have been impatient to speak with you, but with all these public commitments, you understand, it has been impossible. My spies have confirmed that Narngalis and Grïmnørsland are indeed seeking to invade and conquer Ashqalêth, just as Chohrab, with inimitable foresight, suspected."

Stifling an exclamation the duke buried his face in his hands. "I was afraid it would come to this," he whispered.

"You are shocked, Rahim, but you do not seem surprised!" Uabhar muttered. "Can it be that you too have had indication that such an assault was being planned?"

"Even so. Ashqalêth is not lacking its own sources of information. What you have just told me, Your Magnificence, substantiates the intelligence that we have been gathering in Narngalis for months. I shall despatch post-riders to Jhallavad at once; semaphore is too easily decoded for sensitive communications. This revelation will certainly reinspire Chohrab to mobilize his armies."

"I am grateful for your swift action, my dear Rahim!" Uabhar said.

"But pray, tell me all," the duke said anxiously, "that I might better inform him. Let us not delay our private discussion!"

Uabhar readily obliged. After advising their courtiers that they were not to be disturbed and would return forthwith, the statesmen rose from their seats and made their way out of the hall, bodyguards in their wake. Without them at the High Table the laughter and joking of Kieran's convivial group grew even more high-spirited, contrasting agreeably with the amiable conversations of the two queens whose children were handfasted, and the comradely discussions between Walter of Narngalis and Crown Prince Hrosskel of Grïmnørsland. From their seats around their own table the weathermasters observed this. They were glad to witness the cordiality between royal families and the joy of the young couple, but their pleasure was marred by the discomfort engendered by the hostile stares, resentful sidelong glances and cold indifference of a number of Slievmordhuan nobles. These signs of disapprobation were plain, yet no word was spoken aloud against the guests from Rowan Green.

"I acknowledge that you were right, Asrăthiel," said Albiona. "You said you noticed a current of ill-feeling against us, and I see it now."

"I wish I were *not* right," replied her niece.

"One comfort," said Dristan Maelstronnar to his companions, "is that Conall Gearnach and the Knights of the Red Lodge display no evidence of turning against us. They have shown us nothing but courtesy and goodwill."

"Verily," replied his elder sister Galiene. "Two-Swords is an honorable man who will not be swayed by mere hearsay. I'll vouchsafe he has no notion whatsoever of why this scandal was spawned, or by whom. Surely he would take reprisals if he did."

"Gearnach's integrity is unquestionable," said Asrăthiel. "He has ever esteemed our kindred, and the respect, of course, is mutual."

"Yet," said Galiene, who was idly throwing a small apple from hand to hand, "he is a fiery-tempered fellow, for all that, and subject to bursts of insane wrath. I have heard it said there is some switch in his brain that can transform him suddenly from chivalrous knight to madman, when triggered by some event that angers him. At such moments he is capable of doing deeds he later regrets so profoundly that he goes to the Sanctorum and makes liberal offerings, begging the Fates for forgiveness, heaping coals of mortification upon his own head. Have you heard what happened to a horse he owned?"

"Pray tell," said Dristan, setting down his wine cup and wiping his mouth on a serviette.

"He used to have a couple of fine racing-steeds. One was undoubtedly the best in the Four Kingdoms, while the other was nearly as good. He entered them both in the Slievmordhu Cup. Everyone was certain Gearnach's best horse would triumph, and the knight himself wagered a great deal of money on the outcome. During the race, however, the second-best steed accidentally bumped against the best, costing it the win. After the race, as the riders were trotting off the track, Gearnach, in a fit of rage, seized the bridle of his second-best horse and slew it, in revenge for what the beast had done. He had lost money and credibility, and in that black hour he believed, irrationally, that the horse had betrayed him."

"That man will never be a friend of mine," remarked Asrăthiel. She pushed some cake around her platter with the tip of her knife.

"Oh, he waxed repentant enough after the deed," said her aunt, Galiene. "He was devastated, in fact, and mourned grievously for the horse, and censured himself for his rashness. He is his own harshest judge. His temper gets the better of him sometimes, which I daresay is useful for a soldier in battle; but I fear it might some day cause even greater misery."

"King Thorgild holds the Red Lodge's Commander-in-Chief in the highest esteem," said Dristan. "Last time he was in Grïmnørsland Gearnach saved the life of Prince Halvdan when their hunting party was embroiled in a mêlée with a band of Marauders. In gratitude, Thorgild swore an oath never to refuse Gearnach's hospitality."

"It is a weighty matter for a king to make such a pledge to a warrior," said Ryence. "I confess, I am greatly impressed to hear this."

"Weighty indeed!" agreed Galiene. "A supreme honor for a duke, let alone a knight."

"There exists a strong bond of friendship between Gearnach and the royal family of Grïmnørsland," said Dristan. He mopped up some gravy with a crust of bread and began to chew on it.

"I consider it a strange vow," said Asrăthiel. "Why is it deemed a sign of gratitude, to promise to sit at another man's table and eat his meat?"

"In the traditions of Grïmnørsland," explained her uncle, "if a man swears never to refuse another's hospitality it signifies he trusts him as a close friend. To refuse an invitation to dine with someone can be construed as a sign of mistrust or dislike."

"They maintain sundry such prohibitions in the western land," said Galiene. "They are great ones for binding themselves with oaths." After shaking crumbs from her fingers, she gestured to a waiting ewerer, indicating that he should refill her cup.

A scuffle at a side door of the hall drew the attention of the merrymakers. From the vicinity of the High Table, Prince Kieran's tones cut through the barrage of raised voices. "What is going on? Is someone trying to enter? Why is his way being barred?"

The guests ceased their chatter, and instead turned to stare inquisitively at the side entrance. A man-at-arms in the uniform of Uabhar's household guard stepped through the portal and bowed towards the Crown Prince. Into the hush he said, "Your Royal Highness, here is a beggar demanding provender from the High Table. He claims it by right of the ancient Slievmordhuan tradition that twelve paupers are entitled to victuals from the table at any royal handfasting."

Kieran frowned, hesitating. The assembly waited for his pronouncement.

"Is that so?" Princess Solveig softly asked him. "Is that in fact a tradition in your realm?"

"It is," Kieran responded, "however, my father has expressly forbidden it. He put an end to the practice soon after his coronation, but it appears that some of the common people are still unaware of the change. Or else they deliberately flout it, but who could blame them?"

"'Twould be feat to maintain such a generous custom," Solveig said, while in the background Queen Saibh whispered into the ear of one of her courtiers, who shortly quit the hall. Lowering his voice so that his betrothed alone could hear him, Kieran said, "Fain would I uphold the old tradition, my love, for nobility is characterized by generosity. I will resurrect it when I accede to the throne, yet for now I must honor my father's wishes."

Solveig favored her future husband with a look both reproachful and tender. "But it is *our* feast, not his!" she said, mildly piqued.

Gently but resolutely the prince replied, "A worthy son must obey his father. Dearest, pray let us not quarrel!" He kissed her hand. Turning to his manservant he said, "Send the claimant away." His order was presently followed by another scuffle at the side door, after which the disturbance subsided and the diners returned to their previous pleasant occupations.

Meanwhile, King Uabhar and Duke Rahim returned to the high table from their impromptu conference. The king leaned back in his seat, beaming benevolently at his happy guests, while the duke ran his fingers through his beard, chewed his knuckles and stared dismally into his wine-cup. He seemed to shrink into himself, but most of the other guests were too preoccupied with revelry to take note.

"Prince Halvdan makes merry tonight," said Asrăthiel, as the prince's laughter rose above the renewed hum of conversation. "I deem he is one of the happiest of men. Not only is he delighted that his closest friend is to wed his sister, but it is rumored in King Warwick's court that there will soon be an announcement; Halvdan himself is to be betrothed to one of Kieran's fair cousins, a daughter of the queen's sister. Thorgild is not the kind of man who would force his son into a loveless alliance."

"Kieran too is a dutiful son," said her uncle Dristan, "and I daresay he would have married for the sake of politics rather than for love, if his father asked it of him."

"After which, no doubt, he would try to love his wife as best he could," said Asrăthiel.

"Fortunately the young man is not in such an unenviable position," said Albiona. "His affection for Solveig is obvious."

"And his brothers' approval of the bride-to-be is also clear," said Galiene. "Ronin, for one, is all gallantry towards her."

"Enough of this women's talk about love!" grumbled Ryence Darglistel. "Who can trust all these alliances of power? Who knows what goes on behind the closed doors of palaces? I want to know why columns of soldiers are marching east from Ashqalêth. I want to know why Uabhar's battalions are simulating military operations all over the countryside. I do not give tuppence for their official explanations—'gearing up to wage battle against Marauders in the Spring,' indeed! Do they think we are still wet behind the ears? Some conspiracy is afoot."

"Recall whose roof shelters us, and be discreet," warned Galiene.

Ryence said abruptly, "As soon as we can be assured of some privacy I shall ask Thorgild what he knows of the situation."

A flurry of loud guffaws from the high table interrupted their conversation, and then a troupe of musicians and performers tumbled into the center of the hall to provide entertainment.

"By the rains of Averil," muttered Ryence, "I hope they will not sing that tedious ditty that the king seems to dote on."

"What song is that?" enquired Galiene.

A musician strummed a chord and opened his mouth.

"There is virtue in allegiance to one's comrades,
And love's loyalty, all honest folk admire.
But of all the deeds that prove him to be worthy,
A man's honor lies in duty to his sire. . . ."

Ryence groaned, and stuffed bread in his ears.

Towards the close of the feast, the Maelstronnars publicly handed over the Sylvan Comb to Uabhar as a surprise gift, along with a newly fashioned book containing a single leaf, on which was inscribed the Word that controlled the magical device. The book, whose silver-gilt covers were splendidly embossed, could be fastened shut with a lock and key of gold. To their astonishment, the presents were not received with the joy they had expected. On the contrary, the look on the face of the king of Slievmordhu was infused with as much choked-back sourness as his words of thanks dripped with syrup.

"There is some grievous undercurrent here," Dristan muttered, "some hidden intention. Uabhar is plainly displeased. I intend to get to the bottom of his games. My father has friends in this kingdom who might ferret out the truth."

A druid tertius of the Sanctorum, one of several who had been commissioned to make note of all that passed at the banquet, left his seat and immediately reported the king's re-action to Primoris Asper Virosus, who was finishing his soli-tary repast in secluded apartments. The news evidently tickled the primoris. Had the snitching tertius possessed su-pernaturally acute powers of hearing he might have caught the words of his superior who, after the informant had left the stuffy dining room, could not resist muttering behind his yellowed paper-kite of a hand. He was heard only by the per-sonal attendant waiting at his elbow, an illiterate but well-favored lad who lacked the power of speech and thus made a good repository for confidences that must never be revealed. In his declining years the primoris insulated himself so fre-quently from society that he had fallen into a habit of talking to himself.

"I find it amusing that Ó Maoldúin considers the Dome of Strang to be his possession," rasped the venerable druid. "He only decided this after the weathermasters showed interest in it. He never cared about the place before that." He chortled— a sound resembling a dry pea stuck in a hen's throat. "What a nasty surprise it was for him, when this Comb was found! He never guessed his henchmen had overlooked anything of value! Our honorable sovereign is intrigued by the object, and jealous, and has convinced himself it is rightfully his. Sprin-kle nutmeg." The dumb page obeyed with alacrity, while the druid, his lips elongating in the grimace that was his version of a grin, continued to savor evidence of Uabhar's barely dis-guised rage. "It is a liability of confidence tricksters," the sage gloated, "that in order to convince others they must first con-vince themselves. Ha ha! The king is discomfited by a snare of his own device!" He tossed a half-picked hare's leg–bone on the floor. "More nightingales' tongues, Lack-Tongue, and be quick about it."

After supper that evening, just outside a postern near the

palace kitchens, a flaxen-haired man in the queen's livery was distributing foodstuffs to a group of ragged men and women. Having received their bounty from the servant's capacious basket, the recipients trudged off, toting bulging packages. The last of the beggars carefully tied a knot in his bundle and hoisted it onto his skinny shoulder with a "May the Fates reward you for your kindness, Fedlamid macDall, and your mistress also," as he stepped away.

"Good night, Cat Soup," the manservant said with a smile, and he closed the small gate.

Later that night, when most folk were abed, yet another secret meeting took place in the palace.

In addition to a raft of courtiers, a team of body-servants, a legion of domestic staff and a host of other lackeys, King Uabhar employed certain assistants who did not officially exist. These included a conspiracy of spies, a den of counterspies, a gaggle of scandalmongers and a murder of assassins.

Most of these men had evolved to become nameless, except for sobriquets given them by the king. One of these servants, "Gobetween," a highborn member of the Slievmordhuan court who led a double life and was called Lord Genan of Áth Midbine in the other, regularly rendezvoused with his master after midnight, in the king's private apartments where no one could eavesdrop. If any of the household guards noticed the masked, cloaked and hooded figure of Gobetween glide past, they swore, even to their mothers, even when in their cups, even in their dreams, that they had seen nothing.

After receiving instructions—and sometimes, clinking purses—directly from the king, Gobetween would glide forth. An hour or so afterwards, still masked but now clad in the clothes of a peasant, he colluded with a second agent; "the Scandalmaster." The Scandalmaster's job was to relay the instructions—and sometimes a few of the purses—to the scandalmongers; a flock of assorted scoundrels, actors, tricksters, accomplished tattlers and desperate aristocrats with huge gambling debts, whom he always interviewed one by one, so that none might learn the identity of the rest.

If Gobetween's nights were spent gliding and masked, his days were spent unmasked but disguised as a commoner, for he frequented taverns and cockpits and marketplaces; he loitered about city gates and other public gathering places, listening and encouraging people to speak, generously buying drinks for strangers, asking discreet questions. In his nobleman's persona he attended aristocratic parties and did his listening there; indeed, he could find very little time to sleep, but he enjoyed much wealth in his coffers, much prestige as the scrupulous Lord Genan of Áth Midbine, and much perverse satisfaction.

When Gobetween's enquiries had assured him that a particular propagator of lies had successfully inculcated his message in the desired quarter, he would direct the Scandalmaster to give a purse to the tattler. On past occasions some quarreling and resentment had bubbled up from the gossips when payment was withheld. But no longer; those who quibbled were soon found in gutters with their throats slashed, or were never seen again. After the Scandalmaster notified the others of the reason for the killings, they discovered in themselves a strong sense of diplomacy when dealing with him, and became earnest proponents of the virtues of cooperation.

Thus in shadows and darkness Uabhar's assistant Gobetween glided on his clandestine missions.

❧

On the morning after the betrothal party, Asrăthiel and Ryence hastened to attend an audience with King Thorgild. The ruler of Grïmnørsland, accompanied by Crown Prince Hrosskel, heartily welcomed the son and granddaughter of his good friend Avalloc to his sumptuous lodgings in the west wing of Uabhar's palace. Bright sunshine streamed through the windows of the drawing room, a lofty chamber overlooking the grounds; the light glanced off multitiered chandeliers, gilt picture-frames, polished mahogany furniture and tall mirrors. A portrait of Uabhar, twice the height of a man, loomed like some prying disciplinarian on the wall above the mantelshelf.

Thorgild, with his broad face coarsened by salt winds, his bushy eyebrows, sea-waves of coppery hair and luxuriant beard, was like some manifestation that had arisen from the russet kelp-forests of the ocean; some chieftain of the mer-folk. His eldest son, Hrosskel, was the very image of him, matching him in height, but with close-trimmed beard and mustache, and golden streaks through his auburn locks, like his two brothers. Both were attired in costumes of rich fabrics dyed aquamarine, turquoise and the blue-green of verdigris. Embroidered peacock-feathers adorned the prince's tunic, and the king's splendid surcoat was stitched with the ancient emblem of Grïmnørsland—a square-sailed longboat.

The weathermasters, less striking in their grey robes, cordially greeted father and son, after which all four seated themselves around a low table laden with refreshments. Thorgild dismissed his attendants. Following the initial exchange of pleasantries Ryence enquired what the Torkilsalvens thought about the Ashqalêthan military columns heading east, and the Slievmordhuan army's sudden flurry of regimental reviews and training exercises.

"The troops of Chohrab and Uabhar," said Thorgild, deep-voiced, "are making ready to trounce the comswarms when they crawl out of their caves at the end of Winter. What else could they be at?"

Ryence, though inclined to be rash where matters of the heart were concerned, was more circumspect about political affairs. Unwilling to cast aspersions without evidence, he merely shrugged. "I have never heard of governments going to such great lengths to repel bandits. Perhaps Uabhar and Chohrab have decided to wipe them out once and for all."

"I myself would have contributed troops to the cause, had it been requested, however, I have been assured there is no need," said the monarch.

"Then you have set my mind at rest, sir."

Asrăthiel said, "My lord, may I ask your advice on another matter?"

Thorgild inclined his shaggy head, stately and dignified.

"It is a fact," said the damsel, "Ellenhall and Rowan Green are being vilified by rumor in this city."

"Truly?" The monarch was taken aback.

Prince Hrosskel turned towards his father. "It is so, unfortunately," he affirmed. "I myself have heard the whispers."

"I have never heard any ill spoken of the weathermasters," said Thorgild, speculatively stroking his chin with a heavily be-ringed hand. "I believed Rowan Green had no enemies."

"We believed so, too," said Asrăthiel, "but someone has kindled these rumors, and the fire continues to be stoked. Your Highness—" addressing Hrosskel "—do you know aught about the source of this hearsay?"

"Nothing at all, Lady Maelstronnar, but I will tell you this, in strictest confidence—I cannot be at ease about . . ." the prince hesitated, and then said with an expression of significance, "about our host."

"Hrosskel has never taken to Uabhar," boomed Thorgild, less guarded.

The prince glanced involuntarily at the portrait over the mantelpiece. "His behaviour is increasingly inexplicable," he said.

"You overstate. Uabhar is not a man I would have chosen for a friend," said Thorgild. "He can be cruel, and I do not hold with his practices, but he is my neighbor, and a powerful one at that. I, too, sometimes feel uncertain about what he is at, for rumors are legion, yet I have no *proof* of any underhand designs on his part, it is all unsubstantiated, all hearsay, and I know of no evidence that he wishes to denigrate Rowan Green or any reason why he should do so."

"Our host is a brilliant proselytizer," murmured Hrosskel. "It is little wonder his boys are thoroughly webbed in his nets of persuasion; they have been subject to his influence since infancy. I myself have only lately seen through his mask. Even now his manner is so convincing that he still induces me to doubt my own good sense."

"Notwithstanding, one cannot pin down anything to accuse him with," said Thorgild, addressing Asrăthiel and Ryence. "I would think twice about accusing him in any case, because I value goodwill between kingdoms, and especially that goodwill which is desirable between two families soon to be united. Solveig will eventually be settled in Cathair Rua, far from her parents. If any trouble were to break out between realms, it would bode ill for her; therefore diplomacy is the order of the day. Kieran will be a fine husband for my daughter and a fine king of Slievmordhu; on that I have no qualms. If his father's actions occasionally bemuse, I deem it best to practice tolerance. No man is beyond reproach."

Additional topics were discussed, and after sharing some food and drink with the Torkilsalvens Asrăthiel and Ryence took their leave, not entirely satisfied with the interview.

As soon as courtesy would permit, the weathermasters departed from Uabhar's palace. When they congregated at the house of the weathermasters' ambassador prior to the return journey, Asrăthiel and Ryence recounted their conversation with King Thorgild, and Dristan gave an account of what he had lately learned from his father's network of allies in the Slievmordhuan city.

"Evidently it is not enough that lies about our probity are being broadcast in Slievmordhu," Dristan began. "Now it is being whispered that we, the weathermasters of High Darioneth, are secretly and illegally plundering hoards of treasure hidden at the site of the ruined fortress of Strang, and that the Comb is the least of them, and that we are making ourselves unimaginably wealthy while officially disavowing our clandestine activities."

The other weathermasters listened in growing indignation. "Well, it is all my fault!" Asrăthiel burst out at last. "It was my desire to make public my claim on the Dome that sparked this trouble!"

"Nonsense!" exclaimed Galiene. "Your guilt is misplaced, Asra. There was no deliberate misdeed on your part. You cannot hold yourself responsible for Uabhar's unpredictable response." Everyone agreed with Galiene, reassuring Asrăthiel, so that eventually she allowed herself to be soothed.

Dristan continued, "Unfortunately the rumors expand; it is said that by seizing all this wealth for ourselves we are cheating the people of Slievmordhu of money that might be spent on hiring mercenaries to protect their villages from Marauders. I have left instructions for our friends here in the city to vigorously deny the rumors, but the damage to our reputation is spreading fast. We must immediately cease exploring the Dome."

"But I ask again, who is generating these rumors and how are they disseminated?" asked Albiona, scandalized.

"That is the vexing question. Nobody knows."

"Then it seems we have unwittingly made an enemy without a name! Such a foe cannot be countered."

"In my opinion," said Dristan, "the enemy is obvious. It is Uabhar; Uabhar whose paid gossips are doing this work." Several of his companions murmured their accord with this judgment.

"Gossips paid? By the *king*?" Albiona cried.

"Even so."

"This is outrageous!" she fumed. "By law the Dome site belongs to Asrăthiel. She may do as she pleases with anything that is found there. Has Uabhar meddled with the laws of inheritance without anyone's knowledge?"

Asrăthiel was pleased to hear Albiona defend her, given their previous disagreements. She recalled Prince William's warnings concerning Slievmordhu's capricious legislator, but trying to keep a cool head, said, "Albi, this is only a supposition. Nothing is proved."

Dristan said, "I have learned that the palace claims the legislation was changed some time ago. In any case, Uabhar can make these laws retrospective if he chooses. He is, after all, the highest lawmaker in his kingdom."

"Moreover he can be vicious and vindictive in the extreme," said Ryence. "He has an evil temper, and will stop at nothing to get his way. Recall the witnesses who disappear; the royal siblings who perish before their time; the unspeakable tor-ments his inquisitors inflict upon those whom he judges to have crossed him. Uabhar's ire is dangerous, to be sure."

"Dangerous indeed! For our own good we should act as if he is the promulgator of the lies, even if we have no evidence," said Albiona.

"We have given him the Comb," said Galiene, "and we shall stay away from the fortress of Strang. In fact, I propose that we publicly renounce all hereditary claims to ownership of the Dome, if Asrăthiel agrees."

"I certainly *do* agree!"

"That is well. What more can we do to mollify this unpredictable tyrant?"

"I would rather give the sly demon a taste of a levin bolt than mollify him," muttered Ryence.

"We can only try to disseminate the facts," said Asrăthiel, "and hope that truth will prevail."

With that, they took their leave of one another. Asrăthiel took off in her aerostat, and the weathermasters' convoy rattled through the streets of Cathair Rua, beginning their northward journey. Several people who watched them pass shouted, "Down with the weathermasters! Down with the thieves!" and shook their fists, and some made gestures of throat-cutting or hanging, and the weathermasters looked upon this and were shocked. Never in their history had they been treated thus. Notwithstanding these threatening displays, the visitors from High Darioneth manifested no evidence of distress, displaying no flicker of fear or wavering of purpose.

Far behind them, almost alone in a private chamber of the palace at Cathair Rua, King Uabhar was falling about in paroxysms of hatred. "This Goblin Comb!" he shouted, spitting foam. "That they should be seen to be giving me my own property! By Doom and bloody Ill-Fortune—that they should be seen to be extraordinarily generous! And I, forced to play the role of the humble receiver of a lavish gift which I am unable to publicly spurn!"

The voiceless page, terrified and bewildered, stood frozen in the shadows. In his hands he carried empty goblets he had been clearing from the tables. He dodged out of the way as a candelabrum smashed against the wall where he had been standing. "Get gone," growled the king, and the boy took to his heels.

VIII

Urisks

There was an old woman a-lying in bed.
She's pulled all the blankets up over her head
For every midnight the spriggans come in,
Dividing their plunder down to the last pin.
But one night they argue and cannot agree.
The woman peeps out from the bedclothes to see.
She slips off her shift while they squabble and fight
And dons it the other way, out of their sight,
(For inside-out clothing protects against wights.)
She leaps out of bed with the gold in her sights,
And seizes the treasure! They all run away,
She's rich but the shift's cursed to this very day.

— "THE OLD WOMAN WHO TURNED HER SHIFT"

*Asrăthiel sojourned briefly at High Darioneth before return-*ing to her new home in King's Winterbourne. Even with its steep gables bathed in the pomegranate glow of sunset, the house in Lime Grove failed to appear tremendously inviting as *Lightfast* descended over the driveway and across the graveled crescent before the front steps, making for its landing-place near the stables. The damsel missed the company of the other weathermasters, and was beginning to entertain doubts about the wisdom of her move to the city. Now she came to understand the reason her kindred so rarely migrated outside the Mountain Ring. Weathermasters possessed qualities that separated them from other people and united them with a strong bond. Yet she herself, immortal and invulnerable, wondered if she could ever truly belong anywhere, even amongst the weathermasters.

The porter hurried out to meet the dirigible and collect Asräthiel's luggage. Moodily she disembarked from the basket, leaving the two crew-members to stow away the aerostat, and made her way up the front stairs of the house. One of Mistress Draycott Parslow's footmen opened the door, greeting her respectfully as she passed through, followed by the burdened porter. Asräthiel's butler Giles had set supper on the table, and a hearty blaze flared on the grate.

After supper there came a knocking at the side door of the weathermage's apartments.

"Go and see who's at the door, prithee Giles," said Asräthiel, who was reclining in an armchair and staring meditatively into the gold and crimson dreamscapes of the fire.

The butler returned from the hallway saying. "Mistress Draycott Parslow is here to see you, ma'am."

"Show her in."

The widow hurried into Asräthiel's parlour, unwrapping her shawl from her shoulders. With a gracious bow, the butler received the wrap and hooked it on a coat-peg.

"Good evening, Mistress Draycott Parslow," said Asräthiel, sitting upright. "Pray take a seat. Giles, bring refreshments."

"I am pleased to see you have returned safely, m'lady," said the widow. She settled her trim frame into the armchair opposite Asräthiel. "They are wild lands, down south, wild indeed. I would never eventuate there meself. '*Never set foot out of Narngalis,*' that's my motley."

"Have you been keeping well?" Asräthiel asked politely.

"Well enough thank ye, m'lady, well enough. As you know I teach lessons once a week in my cottage. I show small groups of children how to knit and sew and crowsherray, and do all those useful things. Some of them pay heed to me but, well, with a few of them I start to wonder. I can talk till I am blue in the face but they never listen. Sometimes I feel as if I am fading away."

The butler came in with a carafe, some plates of food and two footed cups on a tray.

"Fading away?" Asrăthiel queried.

"Getting invincible. You know, I can talk and talk to them, but it's as if they don't see me, sain their little hearts. I think I must be getting more invincible every day." At Mistress Draycott Parslow's elbow, Giles poured a cup of wine and handed it to her. She sipped, and directed a meaningful gaze at her tenant. "Pray tell me when you cannot see me any more," she appended.

The damsel suppressed a smile. "Cake?" she offered, holding out a dish.

The widow waved the sweetmeats away. "Gramercie, my dearie, but I did not come here to eat you out of house and home. I came to warren you." She paused, directing another significant gaze towards Asrăthiel.

"To warn me about what?"

"Whilst you were away, a funny-looking little creation began lurking about the house. Some sort of wight. I don't suppose it's dangerous—at any rate, my dogs don't bark at it and the horses don't seem afraid—but I have never before seen its like, and I am not sure what it is, because it has only been spotted at nights, half-glimmered, you might say. I am just dimensioning it to you because I don't want you to get a fright if you see it. Anyway there's enough charms and wardrobes around here to scare away the king of the goblins himself, what with the iron horseshoes over every door— mercy me, one fell on me head the other day, I told Perkins to go around and hammer them all in proper-like—and red ribbons and rowan everywhere, and bells on the trees—I keep thinking I've a ringaling in me ears every time the wind blows—but dearie, we've got everything to keep unseelie wights away from the Laurels, so this one won't trouble ye. I daresay it will go away eventfully."

"Wait," said Asrăthiel, leaning forward attentively, "where was it seen?"

"Once by the well in the courtingyard, the oridgeling

well. And another time under the old ymp tree, the graftated apple that leans over the wall of the kitching gardens."

"Do not let anyone chase it away," said Asrăthiel, "until I have seen it for myself. It might be a seelie wight. It might bring good fortune to this house if it is treated well. I shall leave a bannock and some blackberry preserves out by the side doorstep for it this very night."

"Very well, m'lady, do as you please, but for me I'll not be having truculence with no wights meself in my cottage. I still wonder if them spriggans is a-looking for me. I will not let any wight over my freshold."

"I am grateful for your advice, Mistress Draycott Parslow."

"You're welcome, m'lady. Well now, I mustn't sit here gaberdining all night, you'll be wanting your rest after your long and weariful trip to them feasible lands."

"Good evening, Mistress Draycott Parslow. Giles will see you home."

"Good evening, m'lady."

The butler appeared bearing the shawl, and conducted the elderly woman across the grounds to her cottage. Meanwhile, Asrăthiel rummaged in the larder. She piled some foodstuffs on clean dishes, which she placed outside the side door, next to the threshold.

"Leave these here," she instructed Giles when he returned from his errand, "and tell the staff I am not to be disturbed tonight. You must all go to bed. If you hear voices during the night, ignore them."

"As you wish, my lady." Giles bowed, his face devoid of expression. Nothing a weathermaster could do or say would surprise or shock Asrăthiel's handpicked and devoted household.

Having removed the wight-repelling charms from the door's lintel, the damsel sat down in a wicker chair in the well-yard and commenced her vigil.

Hundreds of Mistress Draycott Parslow's thimble-sized bells dangled in the trees that surrounded the house and cottage. The ymp tree, the grafted apple, was the only one free from the dull tinkle of rusting metal. People did not like to meddle with ymp trees, because it was held that they were closely connected with eldritch wights. Some claimed that these trees guarded entrances to a world that was blissful and perilous beyond imagining, and that if you fell asleep beneath them you would be whisked away to that other world, never to be seen again.

The side-courtyard of The Laurels was small and paved with flagstones in a herringbone pattern. An old well stood in one corner, the coping mossy and overgrown. Stone figurines of frogs crouched upon it, and the pitched roof was falling in. A new well had been sunk closer to the center of the court-yard, with a hand-operated water pump next to it. A carved dragon's head spouted water into the new well's basin. The old reservoir had long ago become choked. It was popularly believed there was a curse on it, which is why they had abandoned the shaft and sunk the recent one. Elsewhere in the well-yard a couple of cracked urns perched on pedestals.

Resting in the chair of woven cane, the weathermage let her senses drift out into her surroundings. The wind was in the west. "Sefir, the West Wind," she murmured, but she was not wielding the brí, merely caressing the name of the wind with her voice. Sefir drove thin clouds across the sky, vintage purple and dusted with lambent glimmers of constellations. The voice of the wind was a lullaby, and the tiny, soft chimes of the bells rhythmically hypnotic.

Asrăthiel awoke to the sound of bird-choruses greeting the sunrise. The dishes beside the doorstep were bare; not a crumb or morsel remained. While she slept the food had been taken. Her waiting had been futile. Vexed with her laxity she vowed to set out more victuals and repeat the vigil the following night.

She kept the vow. Next evening, seated in the wicker chair, she leaned back, letting the hours of sunlessness roll by while she watched the stars slowly wheeling and the clouds scudding past like ragged refugees. The night sky streamed in through her open eyes, filling her mind with a vast darkness speckled with silver. Thus it eventuated that she was barely cognizant of the difference when her lids closed, and soporific hallucinations of infinite silver-studded shadows enveloped her, drawing her into slumber.

Next morning the bannock and berries were gone again, and the dishes were clean.

"Giles," she said to her butler, "I am unable to stay awake these past two nights."

"Apothecaries sell herbs that promote wakefulness."

"I wish to wake only, not be transformed into a maddened wasp."

"Wear thorns around your wrist to prickle you, my lady, so that you will get no rest."

"My tolerance of pain is exceptionally high." The servants were unaware she was invulnerable and consequently insensitive to suffering. Perhaps they guessed, but they did not know for certain.

"Sleep this afternoon, my lady," he suggested. "Then you will not be weary at night."

"An excellent idea."

So she slept. After sundown, when evening came shyly peeping around the corners of the world, she roused herself and took to the side-courtyard once more. Giles had removed the wicker chair. There was nowhere to be seated, except upon the flagstones or the well-copings. Refusing to allow herself to sit down, she walked, sometimes singing in a low voice. She carried three wooden balls, with which, from time to time, she practiced juggling in an effort to keep her mind alert. Moths gusted soundlessly past, and possums skittered across the eaves. The tree-bells tinkled in long, languid waves when the deep-hued breeze breathed on them, and the copious folds of Asrăthiel's grey woolen gown swished as she moved. A strange bird hooted from the top of the ymp tree.

The weathermage walked round and round, and presently the moon rose. She tilted her head to gaze up at it.

A voice said, "To look into Space is to look back in Time."

Moonlight spilled with the shimmer of glycerine, and in the gleam of it the urisk was standing by the old well, leaning on the coping.

The damsel experienced a flood of relief and joy that surprised her. She had not understood how keenly she had missed the creature. His curly head and stubby horns were a welcome sight, and she greeted him warmly.

"I am glad to see you—" she was about to call him "thing," then hesitated. It was her custom to title him "thing" or "creature," but the terms did not seem appropriate for the occasion. "What is your name?"

"Ask no questions, be told no lies. You ought to know better," said the urisk.

"What can you mean?"

"Names are not lightly to be asked for, or given."

Of course, he was right. There was weighty significance in a name. Telling someone your name gave them power over you. In particular the names of wights were notoriously difficult to discover, as many of the old tales confirmed.

"Very well," she said. "You won't tell me your name but I shall tell you mine."

Name-telling did not matter quite so much with humankind. All the world might know one's name and no great harm done. Appellations were necessary to social interaction.

"I know it already," said the wight.

The damsel frowned. "I am overjoyed to learn you are as ill-mannered as ever. I would hate to suspect you had suffered any improvement. You have journeyed far. Will you take some refreshment?" She gestured towards the crockery by the door. Half a loaf sat on one dish, while the other brimmed with strawberry jam.

The urisk uttered a short laugh. "These past two nights the hedgehogs have devoured your feast and licked the platters clean," he said, "while you slumbered in the willow withies like a babe. Why not let them enjoy it tonight, as well?"

Even as he spoke, a family of three hedgehogs scampered

across the flagstones and began to nibble and slurp at the provender.

The urisk's cavalier attitude abraded Asrăthiel's patience. For some reason she felt insulted. She had intended to please him with a gift, but now she felt like a patronizing fool. Her pleasure at the reunion was marred by her irritation. "What—did you think I left that food there for *you*?" she scoffed. "Of course not. What is it urisks prefer? Worms and fungus and stolen leftovers?" Petulantly, she tucked the juggling balls back into the drawstring pouch that hung from her girdle.

"Prithee, do not confuse your own tastes with those of more fastidious diners," the wight said icily, turning his shoulder.

At this evidence of rejection Asrăthiel became suddenly penitent. After all, it was a long way on foot—or on hoof—from High Darioneth to King's Winterbourne. She wondered whether the wight had journeyed all that way just to visit her, or if he were calling on her while passing through on the way to some other destination. The question was best left unasked; in general, querying him only led to complications. If he had made the journey specifically to see her she would be greatly flattered and delighted. Were he only passing through, she would still be glad he had paid her the compliment of a call. The past connected the two of them. He meant more to her than she had believed, and the last thing she wanted was to estrange him, despite his infuriating manner. She hoped to entice him to stay at least a while longer.

Subdued, she clasped her hands in front of her and said humbly, "This house is my dwelling-place. No brownie is attached to it. I expect you know that already, since you seem to discover everything that goes on. There is no ward above the side-door. I invite you into my home. Come and go as you please." Alarmed by a sudden afterthought, she added, "But if you do cross my threshold, I beg you to refrain from throwing out my belongings or causing any mischief, as you did at the House of Maelstronnar."

The urisk, his curls silver-painted in the moonlight, gave no answer. She was not, however, discomfited; for at least he did not refuse, and he had, after all, traveled the long road from High Darioneth. If not to remeet her, then why? The little wight was inscrutable, and no doubt she would never understand his purposes, but for now it was enough to have his familiar company, even if he did vex her sorely now and then, and notwithstanding the fact that encounters with him stirred a curious sense of disquiet that troubled her from time to time.

"If you stay in my home," she said daringly, "you are welcome to dine at my table."

"I have no wish," he responded, giving every sign of impatience, "to dine at your table, despite that you seem to consider it some great honor for a wretched wight to be invited to sit at board with a witch-princess."

"Alas. I meant only to be agreeable. It seems nothing pleases you."

"Oh, many things please me, Weatherwitch," said the urisk, "and mayhap someday you shall find them out."

Unsure if his words were intended as some dire threat or some mysterious promise, Asrăthiel was poised between apprehension and fascination. When he failed to proffer any further information, she made an effort to put aside her disquiet, and began to cast about for some innocuous topic of conversation with which to divert her unsettling companion.

"The stars are bright tonight," she ventured. As soon as she had pronounced the words she regretted their inanity. Surely he would deride her for it.

"So it seems," her visitor replied, completely without ridicule, "even though the light you see was fashioned in their hearts millions of years before humankind walked on this world. By tonight, although their radiance twinkles, those same stars might in fact be no more than dully glowing embers, or they might no longer exist."

"How strange! 'Tis a melancholy concept."

"Old stars die, new stars are born." Still leaning casually against the well-coping, the urisk appeared content to indulge in calm discourse, for the moment. "The death of stars gives rise to life, for it is the dying stars, the supernovae, that manufacture all the heavy elements. Living stars make sulphur, and the iron that reddens your blood, and the calcium from which your bones are constructed, and the salts that propel impulses along the pathways of your body. From dying stars issue silver and cobalt, arsenic and iridium, copper and zinc. The energies of the universe remix them, minting them into infant stars, new worlds, plants, and living creatures. Supernovae are our forebears. We are all made of stardust."

"Oh!" Asrăthiel was spellbound, almost dumbfounded by the wight's extraordinary and partially unintelligible statements. It seemed, too, unusual for him to be so forthcoming. Again she wondered about the purpose of his visits. Could the unfathomable layers of his character ever be penetrated, the riddles of his nature solved? She stood with raised head, gazing heavenwards. "How old is starlight?"

"The light from Lucan, the brilliant red star in the west, is twenty minutes old. Those two blue stars overhead, the Andretes, are four light-years away. It took sixteen hundred years for starshine to reach us from that globular cluster suspended above the oak tree, and thirty thousand years before our world received the light from the most distant stars in the heart of our galaxy, those that appear to you as a haze. But even dimmer lanterns hang in the sky beyond the sky. If you observe with care, you might behold the lamps of the Meliodas Galaxy, two million years old, or the tiny fires of the galaxies in the constellation Galeron, fifty million light-years distant. When we look into the sky beyond the sky, we look back into the deeps of time."

After a few moments' silent and awed consideration, Asrăthiel said, "There is so much that mortals do not know."

"So much they *cannot* know," answered the urisk. Then he appended softly, "The roots of crowthistle delve deep; deeper beneath the surface than can be guessed by the weed's appearance."

A mournful hoot punched a hole in the night, breaking the spell.

"Now lo!" said the urisk, as if rousing from a reverie. He stood up straight. "The owl laughs in the ymp tree and the night is aging. It is high time for witch-girls to be abed. Good night."

"Will you come back?" Asrăthiel's cry sounded thin and small in the dark. She was only nineteen, and far from home, and night's web stretched out on all sides, seeming vaster than ever. The urisk had already vaulted over the wall into the kitchen garden and merged into the murk. His voice floated back; "Maybe."

After a while, fainter, "Maybe not."

The season's colors, intense in the month of Otember, waned as strengthening winds ripped foliage from birch and oak and hazel. Across the Four Kingdoms Lantern Eve had been celebrated on the last day of Autumn. Ninember heralded the cold reign of the powerful wight called the Cailleach Bheur, the Winter Hag.

There was plenty of work for Asrăthiel during this season, even though she spent much time arguing with King Warwick's advisors about what was truly necessary, and repeatedly explaining the way that alterations made in one area of the atmosphere inevitably engendered repercussions in other areas. Weather-wielding was never lightly undertaken. It was the responsibility of weathermasters to ensure that the atmosphere's balance was never destroyed, for that would bring incalculable catastrophe upon the Four Kingdoms and even affect the whole of Tir.

In the undercurrents of her mind, Asrăthiel was still haunted by the desire to explore the Northern Ramparts at some undefined period in the future; to investigate those forbidding mountains, and maybe even to venture beyond, into the lands where her father had gone journeying, seeking a remedy to waken her mother from the enchanted sleep. At present, however, there was no time for expeditions. When she was not working, or playing the role of diplomat, she was practicing swordplay, writing letters, reading, exploring the countryside of Narngalis, caring for the kitchen garden at The Laurels—a hobby that privately perplexed the servants—or attending the various concerts, balls and plays regularly staged at various venues in King's Winterbourne. Her presence was greatly in demand by high society, but at the close of a busy day she preferred to dismiss the servants, retreat quietly to the downstairs parlor and curl up in her armchair by the fire, reading a book.

It was there one late Ninember evening, to her joy, that she saw the urisk again.

She looked up to see him perched on the wide windowsill, poised as if ready to jump out of the open casement at the slightest provocation. Gently she spoke in greeting, wishing fervently that he would stay.

"Prithee, let us be friends," she said. Putting down her book she reached out her hand, but he recoiled and she quickly pulled back.

"Keep your distance," he said shortly. "I am not your pet goat, to be patted."

Asrăthiel gaped, dumbfounded for a moment, then could not help but burst into laughter. She tried to stifle her mirth quickly, fearing she must have offended him yet again, but to her astonishment she perceived that a grin brightened his quaint little face. It was the first time, in her recollection, that she had ever made the wight genuinely smile, and she was quite taken aback.

"Nor are you my scapegoat," she quipped. "Come, sit with me. I'll not harass you."

"I will sit with you," said the wight, without budging, "on this ledge."

"As you please." Casting about for an opening to conversation, she added, "It is a quiet night."

"Quiet enough to hear the mice singing. . . ." the urisk said. "But your storybooks keep you happy, apparently."

Asrăthiel fancied she detected a hint of contempt, but ignored it. "This is not a storybook. It is an account of an expedition to the highest peaks of the Northern Ramparts—purely nonfiction. Words on pages *do* bring me delight, but conversation keeps me happy, too. You have lived longer than anyone I know. I daresay you have a wealth of tales stored in your memory."

"Indeed."

"Do you ever allow others the privilege of hearing them?"

"If they ask nicely."

Asrăthiel swallowed the few vestiges of pride that remained to her. It seemed to be one of the prices she must pay for this companionship. "Prithee, will you tell me one of your stories?"

"Can you bear to take your nose out of your books for long enough?"

"Yes."

"Well, then."

And he did tell her a story, while behind him the uneven glass of the window panes distorted and smeared the shapes of the stars, so that the sky looked as if it were weeping.

The wight recounted a tale of ancient war and woe, concerning a captain and his lieutenant. Many battles had been fought over a long period, and the captain's armies had the upper hand against their foe, but the end of the conflict was nowhere in sight. Loyal was the lieutenant, and utterly devoted to his leader. Wishing to hasten the victory, he went before his commander and said, "Forgive me, lord, but I would ask you to change your tactics if we are to gain swift success."

Valuing his officer's opinion, the captain hearkened.

The lieutenant said, "Never have you deigned to bear arms against the weaker elements amongst our foes—the women, the children and the elderly, the sick and crippled. Always you have commanded your armies to ignore them, or merely to sweep them from our path if they block our way. But I declare, lord, that the enemy must be totally wiped out, if we are ever to triumph. We must slay them all, regardless of their strength or weakness."

The captain hearkened, but he did not agree, and said so.

Thereafter the lieutenant went away with a heavy heart. He esteemed his captain beyond all others but was certain that his leader's eyes were veiled to the truth. He believed also that he, the lieutenant, understood what was best for his commanding officer and for their cause. The longer the battles continued, the longer his worthy commander would remain at risk from the enemy. For a long time he agonized in his own thoughts, seeking an answer, and at last he hit upon a daring plan. In order to force the captain to come around to his way of thinking, he would betray him to the foe.

The lieutenant judged that if the proud captain were to be seized, imprisoned and humbled by the enemy, he would be persuaded to hate his captors so absolutely that he would agree to the lieutenant's ruthless proposition of genocide. He had no doubt that his clever and fearless commander would quickly escape, and that then he would unleash every power at his disposal to begin a thorough slaughter of the foe, leading his armies in triumph to utterly wipe out the enemy from every corner of the world.

Thus it happened that the lieutenant conveyed messages in secret to the foe, revealing certain information. He betrayed his commander, who was indeed taken prisoner.

"What happened next?" asked Asrăthiel, speaking in hushed tones during a pause in the urisk's story of passions and bloodshed.

"The plans of the lieutenant went all awry," said the wight, "for his commander was not given any opportunity to respond as he had envisaged. Indeed, the enemy was more powerful than had been guessed, and they destroyed their prisoner. Crazed with anguish because he had brought about the downfall of his champion, the lieutenant cast himself from the brink of a terrible abyss, thus ending his own existence. Leaderless, the armies of the captain were defeated— ironically, all due to one soldier's obsessive loyalty."

Presently Asrăthiel said, "What a strange tale. It has moved me."

"Even so."

"It is pure tragedy for a man to destroy what he loved through his own fidelity." The damsel brushed a wisp of hair out of her eyes. "And, how sad it is to think of all those slain soldiers lying in the cold ground. Conceivably, every day we living creatures travel over the bones of the fallen, buried in fields or beneath the roots of the forests. We walk above, in the sunlight, and have little concept of what lies below."

"Many things are buried in the ground," said the urisk, "some deeper than others."

"Things such as lost coins, I should imagine," Asrăthiel said musingly, thinking aloud, "and broken ploughshares, and shattered glass or pottery, buttons and beads."

"Those and more. The history of the world is written underground."

"How so?"

"Year after year, blankets of sediment are deposited over the world's surface. Each layer preserves a record of the atmosphere, the climate, the state of the biosphere, cataclysmic events and other conditions that prevailed in the era it was laid down. Those who dig underground, through the youngest layers to the deepest and oldest, knowing what they are seeking, will discover a wealth of knowledge."

"But surely," said Asrăthiel, "such underground annals would be destroyed during quakes and volcanic upheavals!"

"As I asserted," the urisk responded, "*know* what you are seeking. He who would study the strata must be aware that uplift, subsidence and deformation can interrupt even chronicles written in stone."

Asrăthiel said, "What wonders *are* written there?"

"The forms of ancient creatures now extinct, preserved in sand, or mud, or volcanic ash. Jewels and gemstones, shining ore, fire and water."

"Underground is the haunt of knockers, and the Fridean, and other such delving wights. I would have supposed urisks had no interest in the lightless places."

"That demonstrates your ignorance. Urisks are nocturnal, weatherwitch, or have you forgotten?"

Asrăthiel was about to make a comment when footsteps creaked the floorboards in the hall and someone knocked at the parlor door. The voice of the butler said, "Your pardon, mistress, is there an anything you might be needing?"

"No, gramercie. Good night, Giles."

"Good night, my lady."

And when she looked again at the window the urisk had gone. Giving a shrug, she murmured, "Typical."

As Giles's footsteps receded down the hallway, she wondered whether the wight had moved into her new lodgings. She was uncertain, fully aware that he was a wilful thing and could not be caged, and would remain with her only as long as it pleased him.

The unlatched casement swung slightly back and forth, then abruptly banged wide open, driven by a gust. Asrăthiel rose to her feet and walked over to the window to pull it shut. As she leaned out to grasp the handle she sniffed the air. The wind was changing. It had swung around. "Boreiss from the south," she whispered automatically, naming the wind as was her habit. "Boreiss, whither do you wander?" And she raised her eyes to the heights of the north, where the wind was going. Honed against the stars, the peaks looked so close she might have reached out and cut her fingers on them. Instead she pulled the casement closed against the night.

&

Winter crossed the year's doorstep, beautiful and stark. In the realm of Ashqalêth, where seasons had scant power to touch the rolling acres of dunes, parched and baking, a pear tree leaned over a splashing fountain. Its green leaves, crisp against skies of dazzling blue, stirred in the breeze. Both tree and fountain were sheltered from the desiccating winds of the desert within the high-walled grounds of King Chohrab's palace in Jhallavad, amongst olive groves and shady fig trees and statuesque palms.

Inside the galleries and chambers of the palace itself, columns of porphyry, colored marble and veined serpentine soared, like fantastic versions of the palms, from the richly colored flower-gardens of mosaic pavements. Enamel-work, cloisonné, sumptuous fabrics and long cycles of frescoes covered all walls and vaults. The frescoes, on backgrounds of lapis lazuli, illustrated historic episodes; magnificently dressed kings winning victories at the battlefront or excelling at the chase; famous warriors on horseback engaged in combat, or noblemen driving chariots, against landscapes of trees and flowers or architectural backgrounds. The personified Fates frequently appeared, aiding or rewarding the kings. Creatures of eldritch abounded, and dancing girls, musicians, and circuses of lions, eagles, phoenixes, unicorns and griffins painted with brilliant colors.

In the palace grounds, however, the leaves of the pear tree overhung the sparkling diamante arcs of the fountain. A short distance away, sun-bronzed workmen in white turbans and loincloths had finished pouring wet concrete into a circular metal form on the ground, and were smoothing it with trowels. They were laying the base of a new oratorium that King Chohrab had seen fit to commission for his parks and gardens, in spite of the fact that five similar structures existed there already. Of late, the king had been unusually attentive to the Sanctorum, and particularly eager to propitiate the Fates.

From their vantage point beside the newly poured floor base, in which they had been investing a considerable amount of interest, Princesses Shahzadeh—the eldest—and Pouri—the youngest—saw their potbellied father staggering across the lawns, partially supported by Uncle Rahim. It seemed that since King Chohrab's last return from Cathair Rua, he had not enjoyed a moment's happiness. More and more frequently he "took refuge at the bottom of a goblet" as the saying went; yet he complained incessantly that the wine sent from Slievmordhu was "not right, there was something not right about it." Semaphore messages of complaint on this distressing topic had ricocheted back and forth between the two realms. King Uabhar, initially mystified as to the cause of the beverage's alteration, had eventually suggested that perhaps his special wine "did not travel well," and "the road must have plundered it of some of its virtues." Close to despair, Chohrab had sought ways to distract himself from his misery.

As she watched her father, Shahzadeh in her patterned silks, graceful as the pear tree, lively as the fountain, heard her little sister observe, "I would very much like to draw a happy face in that concrete. May I?" Pouri's ephemeral attention had returned to the more interesting job in hand, and the child crouched at the rim of the unblemished surface, brandishing a short twig of pear wood.

The eldest princess, intrigued by architecture, alchemy and the application of mathematical principles to practical ends, had spent many of her leisure hours studying the way craftsmen created mosaic floors, in defiance of the convention that such study was unsuitable for women. She judged that the thick paste of tile cement to be applied after the concrete hardened would compensate for a few shallow scratches in the base. The workmen, however, might fear retribution from their masters if the smooth finish was marred. As Shahzadeh meticulously formulated a reply for her little sister, her father came up and stood beside her, panting and red-faced. His smile was that of an inebriate. His robes and beard reeked of smoke; in particular, smoke from a blend of herbs and weeds called "calea reveries," which these days he was wont to inhale from a special pipe apparently fashioned from some mysterious clay combined with volcanic ash, rare sands and distilled rainwater.

"Father, may I make a happy smiling face?" beseeched Pouri.

"Mmm, yes, yes," Chohrab slurred.

Shahzadeh greeted her father and uncle with due courtesy. The three engaged in shallow discussion about the progress of the work, while Pouri tentatively stroked the concrete with her twig. Presently Chohrab took half a step towards the spongy floor base, stubbed his sandaled foot on a stray chunk of broken stone and lost his balance. On the edge of the pool of soft concrete he teetered, bent forward almost at right angles with arms flailing, for an agonizing instant, until miraculously he righted himself and tottered backwards into the arms of Rahim. The turbaned workmen groveled in terror at having witnessed such near humiliation of their ruler.

The Princess Royal sighed. She leaned down to Pouri, who was poised, immobile, between horror and hilarity. "That would *indeed* have made a happy face," she whispered. The child brightened like sunrise and continued to sketch in the matrix, while Shahzadeh, having bidden the workmen to depart as if nothing had occurred, found it prudent to kneel beside her sister and become absorbed in the child's play. She could not help overhearing what passed between the two men, once her father had recovered his composure. Evidently they were discussing their earlier burning topic, in which the princess had been taking a keen though discreetly concealed interest.

"I repeat, there can be no doubt," insisted Rahim. "My own spies have confirmed it. We *must* preempt their attacks by striking first."

"Mmm, yes, yes," Chohrab said. "Yes, you are right. We must join him and make ready to fight. We must drink many toasts to victory!"

❧

On clear evenings in Narngalis vermilion sunsets flared, painting gorgeous backdrops behind fretworks of leafless boughs. Morning hoarfrost transformed trees into ornaments cast from solid silver, each twig defined with elaborate precision.

Tenember was a wet and stormy month in the northern latitudes of Tir, bringing flooding and strong winds. The chilly weather and scarcity of food in field and hedgerow drove an abundance of wild creatures into the parks and gardens of King's Winterbourne. Black-headed gulls and cormorants flew inland to roost by night on the sheltered waters of the river. The grounds of The Laurels were alive with birds and insects. Mistress Draycott Parslow scattered bread crumbs on wooden bird-tables in her garden, and at nights she left tidbits for the foxes and badgers. A robin frequented the well-yard, often sitting on the gatepost and surveying the surroundings with eyes as round and shiny as jet buttons.

Throughout the first weeks of the season Asrăthiel came to enjoy her new tenure as she grew more familiar with the city and its surrounding regions, and became acquainted with a wider circle of friends. There was, also, the ongoing company of the urisk. The goat-legged wight's presence made The Laurels seem a brighter, more welcoming residence, despite that he never stirred so much as a finger to help with the chores. *As a weatherwitch I seem to have acquired a familiar,* Asrăthiel joked to herself; but she did not share the jest with the urisk, temperamental creature that he was, in case he took it as an insult.

His temper could fluctuate without warning. On several occasions in the past she had seen him as blithesome and happy-go-lucky as a reaper celebrating the end of harvest; so clownish and irresponsible that the damsel wondered—as of old—whether this was, in fact, the same urisk. This merry humor was on him more often these days, and she was glad of it. He could be mightily entertaining, if he chose. He loitered so often about The Laurels in the evenings that she surmised he must have moved in after all, presumably having found some cozy sleeping-nook for daytime use.

When Mrs. Draycott Parslow's gardener noted some signs of disturbance in the hayloft above the empty stables, Asrăthiel guessed the wight had made his bed there. She instructed the groundskeeper and hands to leave the loft alone, and mulch the garden-beds with straw from the shed instead. When the occasional Winter vegetable went missing from the kitchen garden, and the bread she left out by the doorstep had always disappeared by morning, she smiled to herself.

A few days before Midwinter's Eve it came to Asrăthiel's attention that the urisk had *not* been making his bed in the hayloft as she had believed. Mrs. Draycott Parslow's coachman had discovered an old tramp sleeping there. He had spied the vagrant climbing down the loft's ladder in the morning, crossing the yard and slipping through a hole in the wall next to the gnarled oak, to go begging in the streets.

"The loft stinks," said the coachman, "pardon my bluntness, m'lady. He is a dirty old gaberlunzie. Best to get him out of there."

Asrăthiel ordered that the tramp be given a nourishing meal, as well as a warm coat and trousers to replace his threadbare rags.

"What is your name?" she inquired of the beggar when he was brought before her, a doughty stable-hand gripping each of his angular elbows in case he should make a break for it.

The vagrant blinked inflamed eyes. His cheeks were traceried with a fine network of capillaries, his arms and neck encrusted with senile warts. "Cat Soup, ma'am."

Carefully blank-faced, Asrăthiel said, "If you wish, Master Soup, you may lodge in the lean-to behind the gardener's cottage. It backs onto the fireplace-chimney, and is always snug and warm." She offered him the job of "gardener's assistant," but by the following night he had made off with a bag full of gardening tools, and was not seen again.

Temperatures were particularly low for the time of year, and Asrăthiel forecast that the Spring thaw would be arriving late. Concerned about the urisk's welfare, she combed the house from top to bottom looking for his sleeping-nook. She scoured the attic, the wine cellar, the cupboards under the stairs, the still-room, the henhouse, the garden-shed and an abandoned dog-kennel. So thoroughly did she search that she discovered secret passageways and hiding-places behind the paneling, obviously undisturbed for years; yet she found no evidence of any wightish lair. Snow glittered hard and bright on the summits of the Northern Ramparts. At nights she lay awake listening to the rain battering on the roofs, and the wind screaming of its lust to bite flesh to the bone, and bone to splinter.

The weathermage felt it would be pleasant to set eyes on her eldritch companion again. She had taken to frequenting the well-yard after sunset in hope that he might make an appearance. To the astonishment of the servants, who pretended not to notice, the intense cold did not bother her. In an effort to avoid appearing abnormal she wrapped herself in layers of thick velvet, but sometimes she forgot to wear shoes and trod the icy flagstones barefoot.

A sevennight after Midwinter's Eve she was wandering about the courtyard juggling the three wooden balls; a trick at which she was, by now, adept. It had rained incessantly throughout the day, but towards evening the clouds had thinned and drawn aside, like a curtain revealing a theatre of constellations. The night's fragrance was the scent of wet soil, and its music was the chime of dripping leaves, the chortle of fast-flowing gutters.

"Oh where are you, urisk?" Asrăthiel sang spontaneously, watching the balls as she spun them in the air. "Oh where might ye be? Come to me, urisk, come unto me."

"A pretty voice, but I fear you have scared away the screech owls," said the urisk, who was lying on top of the wall as if he had been there for hours, his elbow crooked and his head resting on his hand.

Asrăthiel caught the wooden spheres in her hands and let her gaze travel over the dwarfish figure. His clothes looked even more flimsy than she recalled, and perhaps it was a trick of the starlight, but the shaggy hide on his haunches seemed traced with delicate filaments of rime. Pity stabbed her heart. How could she have overlooked his plight?

"Wight," she said, "I daresay you are cold."

"And if I am?"

"Since I have recently discovered that you do not inhabit my hayloft, I wish to offer you a warm place to sleep."

A sarcastic smile played around the wight's mouth.

"Your bed, perhaps?"

Shocked by his insolence, Asrăthiel found herself at a loss for words.

"If not your bed, then where?" asked the urisk, languidly

raising himself into a sitting position. "A kennel like a hound? A hearthrug like a marsh upial?"

Asrăthiel struggled to frame a reply. It was tempting to throw the juggling balls at the creature and march indoors without a backwards glance. Was he intending to make some lewd insinuation, or was he merely being flippant? Was it simply her own train of thought that offended her sense of propriety, or was it his purpose to do so? Horror and squeamishness stung her like the brief flick of a lash. With difficulty, she mastered her own temper. It came to her that she ought, by now, to have learned her lesson never to offer anything to the wight. He inevitably mistook her good intentions as patronization.

"I only wished to help."

"How very generous of you."

"I daresay you have your own arrangements," she said sullenly.

"Perceptive, in addition."

About to fling back a matching retort, Asrăthiel reined in the impulse. No doubt it was some arcane code that dictated the urisk's provoking behavior; something perhaps related to the well-known and equally inexplicable brownie trait of departing forever after being given a gift of clothing. It was not for her to try to unravel the complexities of wightish precepts, and, besides, she wanted to coax him to stay awhile. He was annoying, but perversely, she generally found his company to her liking, at least by comparison to that of many people.

Perhaps, she thought, it was because she was more similar to the urisk than to her own kind. Wishing to deflect the topic but temporarily unable to conjure a substitute, she fell silent, toying with one of the juggling balls, scuffing her feet against the stone flags of the paving.

"Sulkiness fails to become you," said the urisk at length. He yawned, staring into the distance.

Indignant at his obvious boredom, Asrăthiel burst out, "I would not be morose if there were any entertainment to be had from you, jaded creature. All you do is tease. You appear dulled by surfeit of the world and incapable of merriment. Since you have traveled all the way here, can you not perform any amusing tricks?"

The wight's eyes glinted dangerously. The damsel caught her breath; for a moment she thought she had overstepped the mark. Nonetheless her stab of fear was heightened by exhilaration. Would this supernatural entity react in anger? Common wisdom held that seelie wights were incapable of doing harm, and yet . . . One of the balls slipped from her grasp and dropped onto the paving stones. She saw it roll away, but when she looked up she could no longer see the urisk.

Spinning on her heel, she gazed about in an effort to locate him. He had apparently vanished, and she was about to murmur scornfully, "Oh, so you retreat from challenges," when his voice issued from an unexpected quarter.

"Perywyke is an erbe of grene colour
In tyme of Mai he bereth blo flour
His stakys ain so feynt and feye
Yet never more growyth he hay."

The wight was holding forth from atop an urn on a pedestal. The urn contained a spray of evergreen foliage, in the middle of which he was sitting cross-legged, crushing the leaves flat, so that they splayed out around him like a circular fan.

Relieved at the release of tension, Asräthiel laughed at his impudence. Impulsively she tossed aside the remaining two balls, running to catch his hoof and pretend to pull him down, but he drew back his arm and energetically threw something across the courtyard. She turned around to see what it was he had hurled. Something was shining on the flagstones near the doorstep, but before she had dashed halfway across to reach it, the urisk's voice was already emanating from another direction. She stopped short, darting glances all around, and spied him now reclining on the head of the stone dragon that spouted water into the basin of the operating well. In high-pitched, artificial tones he sang,

"Good druid, I have sent for you because
I would not tamper with Sanctorum laws,
And yet I know that something is amiss,
For when I see the youths and maidens kiss,
I tremble and my very knees grow weak
Until my chamber I am forced to seek
And there, with cheeks aflame, in floods of tears,
I toss, with strangely mingled hopes and fears."

Asrăthiel found herself blushing, for the verse was bawdy; but to her amusement it lampooned the druids, reducing their sanctimonious counselling sessions, at which they dictated how people should think, feel and behave, on pain of misfortune and an early death, to the status of eavesdropping on the licentious daydreams of young women. The verse hinted also that the druidry might not be as chaste as their vows decreed.

Giggling with delight at the wight's tricks, Asrăthiel ran towards the fountain and jumped up onto its coping, but a cloud sailed across the starry theatre of the sky. The courtyard was shut into semidarkness broken only by shafts of chamomile lamplight from two high dormer windows.

"Where are you?" Asrăthiel called out. She dared not call too loudly lest the occupants of the house should emerge and spoil the nighttime fun. For an instant she was tempted to summon an upper atmosphere wind to broom away the clouds, but she resisted the unworthy desire.

The skies swiftly cleared of their own accord, and celestial light revealed the urisk at the far end of the courtyard. He was hanging upside down from a gargoyle that served also as a finial on a gable-end. Unperturbed, he continued to recite indecent poetry, mimicking the shrill tones of a young girl;

"And druid, strange to say throughout the night
Although my figure, as you see is slight,
I dream I have a ripe, voluptuous form,
And strong arms 'round me hold me close and warm,
Until at last, at last, I blush to say,
My very garments seem to melt away,
Until as nature clad me, there I stand,
The willing victim to a wandering hand."

Asrăthiel doubled over in laughter, heedless, now, that anyone might hear. She was young, and glad of an opportunity to abandon herself to frolicsomeness.

Her jollity was interrupted when her lady's maid poked her head around the door. "Is aught amiss, m'lady?"

Suddenly the urisk was nowhere in sight, but Asrăthiel fancied she could hear an echo of mocking laughter in the outer darkness. "No! No!" the weathermage said, between gasps. "Nothing at all, Linnet."

"There is a good fire going in the parlor."

"I thank you."

"Would you like me to make some tea with supper?"

"No, thank you."

The servant curtseyed and retreated into the house, closing the door. When Asrăthiel turned back she saw the wight sitting cross-legged on the pavement. His mood had changed once more, as the sky changed, and the weather. He was quiet now, and seemed pensive; she was reluctant to disturb him, and refrained from speaking. A movement attracted her attention; a small asp, the color of jade, slithered out of a chink in the wall nearby. As the reptile slid past the urisk's knee, it seemed to become aware of his presence and reared up, gazing at the wight with bright glass spherules of eyes. The urisk extended his hand in invitation, whereupon the asp glided onto his palm and traveled all the way up his arm. It coiled on his shoulder, flicking its tongue at his ear and curly hair as if quite at ease. After withdrawing his hand the urisk seemed to barely notice this passenger. He remained silent, staring straight ahead as if brooding, while the snake investigated the upper seams of his waistcoat, climbed up and down his other arm and generally made free with his person. Asrăthiel watched, fascinated. She presumed the urisk had forgotten she was present, but at the end of a minute or two he murmured, "I will make an experiment."

Asrăthiel started. For an instant she thought the wight was talking to the viper, but he was regarding her; directly addressing her. He murmured, "Let me tell you something, mist-maiden, frost-friend, storm-sister."

Lifting its narrow head, the jade-green serpent made its forked tongue flicker like a flame. The urisk hesitated, then made as if to continue speaking, but uttered no word. He appeared to be waging some inner battle. Asrăthiel waited, holding her breath in case even the slight hiss of an exhalation should drown out his impending revelation. Presently the wight shook his head and said, "Well then, perhaps you will never know. But it will do *you* no harm." He touched his fingers to the ground. The serpent wriggled down his ragged sleeve onto the flagstones and slipped away.

"What would you like to tell me?" Asrăthiel softly asked.

A series of curious looks passed rapidly across the creature's face; some indefinable expression followed by rage, bitterness and finally cynicism. Eventually he said cuttingly, "Look to your own affairs. Your servant comes to nursemaid you."

Footsteps approached the door, which swung open. Once again Linnet put out her head. "Supper is ready, m'lady." The maid's attention seemed fixed on Asrăthiel's feet. It came to the damsel that she was wearing no shoes. Feeling nonplussed by the urisk's behavior and overcome by confusion at having so carelessly highlighted her uncommon resistance to the cold, she stammered, "Oh, I will come in directly."

He was nowhere. After scanning the apparently empty close, Asrăthiel went into the house. The back of her neck prickled as she stepped over the threshold. While she sipped

her tea she repeatedly wondered what the urisk had been trying to say, and why he could not say it.

After supper she stole once again into the courtyard, inquisitive about the object the urisk had tossed onto the flagstones. It turned out to be nothing more than a worthless
fragment of slate.

A quiet mouse happened to be foraging on the pavement
beneath the fountain's lip. It continued to go about its business after the damsel retired into the house and went upstairs
to her bedchamber. Like a handful of cobwebs and mist coa-
lescing to form a living creature, the goat-legged wight reappeared from the shadows. The mouse reared on its hind legs
and sniffed the air. Overhead, strands of tenebrous cloud blew
away from the vista of the heavens. Falling silver flooded the
courtyard with soft but brilliant light. His eyes downcast, the
urisk paced back and forth as if deep in thought, or indeci-
sive, or angry. Once he glanced up at the high window of
Asrăthiel's bedchamber, from which lamplight streamed
forth between the curtains. As he looked down again his gaze
happened to alight on an unlit ground-floor window.

The slender lead cames framing one of the glass panes enclosed the portrait of a ghost.

Or not a ghost, but something else—a insubstantial image; a chimera; a *reflection* in the pane. A face, delineated by
astral radiance, which appeared to hover there in the
shadow-backed glass.

*It was a masculine face, pale and confoundingly hand-
some, framed by long hair blacker than wickedness. The
stars of the firmament seemed snagged in that pouring of
coal-gleaming hair. The eyes, of some color that was elusive
in the starlight, were chips of diamond, or perhaps slivers of
steel, outlined with lashes of a darkness so intense they
might have been rimmed with cosmetic antimony.*

Here, instead of the reflection of a curly-mopped wight
with stubby horns, was the very vision that Asrăthiel's
mother, Jewel, had witnessed long ago when she dwelled in
the Great Marsh of Slievmordhu; the unnerving, ephemeral

but preternaturally lingering reflection in the pool beside the old black stump where this same urisk had been wont to sit. It was, too, the image that nine-year-old Asrăthiel—then Astăriel—had glimpsed by starlight, mirrored in her silver hairbrush. Unknown to her, the elusive urisk had been watching as she dressed her hair, and had departed the moment before she glanced over her shoulder.

In the courtyard of The Laurels the wight scowled at the image in the window, and the image scowled back. His gaze lit upon the fragment of slate lying on the ground. He snatched it up, drew back his arm and with a flick of the wrist sent the stone spinning through the pane with one swift accurate motion. Startled by the crash and tinkle of shattering glass, the mouse darted into hiding.

When Giles came running out to see what had caused the ruckus, the courtyard was deserted and the wind was blowing sad tunes through the jagged hole in the window.

⁓

Miles above Asrăthiel's lodgings in King's Winterbourne, at the upper limits of the troposphere, the high-latitude southerly airstream blew fine skeins of tiny ice-crystals northward over the ranges.

Beneath the mountains the grave-cold underworld was dark, with a darkness so intense as might cause the very stones to bleed. Somewhere down there the persistent burrower kept on at its delving, but there was, at last, a difference.

Something lay ahead.

At last, *something*. What blocked the thing's path was a mystery, but a kind of subliminal premonition was vibrating through the substrata; a prescience of unusual danger. The thing that lurked there was truly terrible.

Danger meant little to the delving traveler, whose senses were mostly numb. Like an automaton it shifted rocks, seeking paths and scrabbling its way through the maze, sometimes unintentionally doubling back on its unmapped and obsessively pursued journey. It cared little that the suffocating pinches and gasping vaults of this subterranean realm were barely illuminated by the occasional strange lights of wights' little mining lamps. Though some of its mental faculties had dried up, there in its tomb, it possessed a sharp navigational memory. It had learned to memorize tunnels and dry watercourses and shafts and adits and all the underworld cavities in their various shapes and directions, so that it could recognize them even if the wights' mining activities altered their dimensions, which made it possible to continue, more or less, moving in the same direction, scratching and scraping with its damaged digits.

What did the worm-pale, sight-deprived, mutilated burrower hope to achieve by this?

On becoming aware of this portent of extreme peril in its path, if anything it delved a little faster and more keenly, now that something *else* lay ahead after all the monotony; some goal to interrupt the tedium of never-ending darkness, and abrasive surfaces, and sour molds, and eldritch miners with their unintelligible witterings, and coldness, and dampness, and loneliness, and the eternal *drip-drip* of mineral-filtered water. The burrower's brain held pictures of warm, yellow sunlight and blue sky. It remembered its name, although somewhere back in distant caverns it had forgotten the reason why it spent its time digging and seeking underground, and solving labyrinthine puzzles. Nonetheless it never lost its sense of purpose, even when the purpose itself had long ago come loose and fallen out of its memory to lie, forsaken, at the roots of the mountains.

It occurred to the burrower that miniature miners no longer worked nearby; this section of the underworld was blind and blank—devoid of twinkling lights and activities and sounds. The small creatures of eldritch had deserted the region. Abstractedly the burrower wondered whether the fear's source was such a hub of horror that even supernatural creatures were afraid to stray close.

Milky rock lined the walls; pallid crystal veined with gold, visible because of a watery luminosity that strained itself out of some fluorescent rocks. Sometimes, noises of agonized squealing and groaning came barreling out of the dimness, the only ruptures in the heavy silence. Yet they sounded very far off.

Also the smell of the air had changed. The burrower sniffed. It was a familiar scent, yet unnameable; some odor once familiar, known long ago. . . . The sense of menace grew so intense that even the burrower, with its nerves scoured to nubs, suddenly shuddered with fear. Alarmed, it tried to turn back.

Too late.

A feeling of being dragged along, an unbearable sensation of being pulled, had seized hold of the digger. The creature had ventured too near and, enslaved by a nameless force, was being drawn towards the source of the danger. All the weakness in the burrower's spirit was called to by the terrible strength buried amongst rocks and ores at the heart of the mountains.

And then the slave cleared away a heap of rocks, heaved aside a pile of boulders, and arrived at a partition of mica that appeared, in the faint radiance, to be paper-thin. Destiny waited on the other side. Its fist punched the wall—a bundle of bone and sinew, encased in scorched parchment skin—and broke through!

Instantly, slim spindles of strange brilliance, dazzlingly clear, shot forth from the opening. The burrower screamed in ecstasy; screamed to feel its eyeballs skewered by the light-spears of an avenging host on wings of bright silver. Sheer, lustrous whiteness flooded its head.

Every finger on the hand that had dealt the blow tingled as if a million pins sizzled in the flesh. Delight and excruciating pain arced through the burrower's body. Faster, urgently, it scrabbled at the fist-sized hole in the mica screen, tearing away sharp flakes, enlarging the aperture. All the while the pain-pins spiking its flesh burned like ice, and stung, and harped on the throbbing wires of its heart, and pulled taut every nerve, so that it screamed repeatedly in terror and exhilaration even as it continued to tear at the rock with the remnants of its nails.

It seemed the light itself—thin bars of pure silver splen-

dor, translucent, like the rays of some glaring, alien moon—
was singing long, high notes with the voices of an eldritch
choir that never needed to draw breath. It shimmered ethere-
ally in long diagonals, like virgin ice lit from within by some
numinous force, accompanied by a deep, deep rumbling as
of distant thunder reverberating underground, pitched so low
that the ear could not hear it, but the bones, from heel to
skull, resonated to the vibrations. . . .

The burrower ripped frantically at the broken rocks, blood
streaming from its eye sockets, showering itself with debris,
heedless of the pouring dirt and gravel, as in a frenzy of
dread and excitement it thrust its body forward, levered itself on its arms, and burst right through the fragile interface
of mica into the *other* cavern. . . .

IX

The Invitation

Where are the children of Springtime, fresh garlands atop their
    bright hair
All clothed in the green of new grasses, who danced in the
    raindrop-rinsed air?
Where is the gladness of morning; the sun rolling up like a
    drum,
When the wind from the east brings a promise of legends and
    greatness to come?

Where are the saplings of Summer, the maidens and youths in
    their prime
Who fearlessly ran through the meadows, paid no heed to the
    passing of time,
Rejoiced in strength, passion and beauty, and tasted youth's
    marvelous days,

While the sun at high noon burned so fiercely, all shadows must
    flee from its rays?

Where are the reapers of Autumn, the wisdom-honed goodmen
    and wives
Who gathered at harvest-time tables, recounting the tales of
    their lives,
With wine-cups a-brim at their elbows, and toddlers a-perched
    on their knees
While afternoon light warmed the window, as mellow as honey
    from bees?

Where are the dotards of Winter? The doddering greybeards and
    crones
Who linger alone on the stairway, while flesh shrinks from
    withering bones?
They shiver and shake in the evening, they yearn for sleep as
    darkness grows
Till Winter's cold hand comes a-stealing, to wrap them in
    shimmering snows.

    —"SEASONS OF THE HUMAN HEART," BY ALEYN CILSUNDROR-
        SKYCLEAVER, BARD OF THE WEATHERMASTERS

Time was spinning numerous threads for its tapestry, some to
be woven together, some to entangle or fray, others merely
to perish and pass away. Held in Winter's enchantment, the
lands of Tir appeared locked in a stasis. Appearances, however, are inclined to deceive. Even beneath voiceless mountains, outwardly as motionless as death, unimaginable forces
may be at work.

    At Bucks Horn Oak in Narngalis the men who had long ago
numbered amongst the comrades of Jarred Jaravhor, son of
Jovan, spent drowsy hours nodding beside stoves of glowing
coals, contented as they lived into their autumnal years, well
cared for by their kindly liege-lord, the son of their original
employer. Several guests enjoyed the duke's hospitality this
Winter, amongst them the wandering savant Almus 'Declan
of the Wildwoods' Agnellus, accompanied by his bookish as-

sistant. The Duke of Bucks Horn Oak, being fond of learning, was proud to play host to a gentleman scholar of Agnellus's reputation. On Midwinter's Eve the ex-druid had deliberately made a short excursion into the wilderness, hoping to meet the Cailleach Bheur, the blue-faced wight who walked over the frozen ground at this season. Every year he tried to find her, as yet with no success. The sage was tough and resilient, able to withstand the extremes of harsh climate. His long-suffering assistant, however, was the latest in a string of protégés who found it almost impossible to keep up with the old man's zeal and his unquenchable thirst for knowledge.

Further south at High Darioneth, the Miller family thrived, welcoming yet another infant into the new generation, while up on Rowan Green the weathermasters put forth their senses and explored the intricacies of the atmosphere. During the Midwinter festivities Ryence Darglistel, who despite being middle-aged declared he would never be too old for child's play, indulged in his usual pranks. From time to time Avalloc Maelstronnar sat by the bedside of Jewel, his sleeping daughter-in-law, keeping her company despite the fact she never stirred, his thoughts straying to bygone times, wondering if she would ever waken, wondering whether he would ever see his eldest son again. The councilors of Ellenhall discussed the deteriorating reputation of their kindred amongst the populace of Slievmordhu, but no matter what measures they took to redress the lies that were being broadcast, the resentment, fueled by paid sources, continued to grow.

To the west, in Grïmnørsland, a large family of peddlers had returned home for the Winter, the roads being too bleak and hostile for traveling. In society's higher echelons, the family of King Thorgild Torkilsalven spent much of the season in the capital city of Trøndelheim, where the princes Hrosskel, Halvdan and Gunnlaug passed their days in study, or Winter sports or wassailing with comrades. Occasionally they traveled to various locations throughout the countryside, or entertained guests. Most often those guests included Crown Prince Kieran of Slievmordhu, Princess Solveig's future husband and Prince Halvdan's closest friend.

If the rest of Tir seemed locked in an icy stasis Cathair Rua, by comparison, boiled in a lidded ferment. Undercurrents seethed. Hidden influences pervaded and intimations persuaded. Rumors flew back and forth like shuttlecocks in a fast game.

King Uabhar had seized control of the old rubble-strewn site where Castle Strang had stood. He commanded that a summer palace be raised there; a country seat he intended to give to his eldest son upon the occasion of his marriage.

Only a handful of caretakers frequented the Red Lodge on one of the three city hilltops, chief headquarters for Slievmordhu's Knights of the Brand. As so often recently, King Uabhar had sent his elite corps of knights away on maneuvers. Aware that Conall Gearnach and his knights resisted the tide of ill-feeling against the weathermasters, High Commander Risteard Mac Bradaigh had recommended their removal until such time as the king's plans were ready to be acted upon. Although the Winter was bitter, the knights were sent into remote locations to practice large-scale tactical exercises carried out under simulated conditions of war.

Meanwhile, in the eastern marches of Slievmordhu, a comswarm of Marauders huddled in draughty caves, coughing in the smoky atmosphere and chewing on dried meats. During Winter they avoided life on the road. They were waiting for Spring. Cooped as they were in close quarters, with little to do save keep the fires stoked and avoid the Spawn Mother, they quarreled often. Now and then one of their number would be slain in a fight, and there would be fresh meat for dinner instead of dried. The shrill-voiced Scroop and lopsided Grak spent many anxious moments sneaking out of everyone else's way and making themselves as inconspicuous as possible. Scroop put all three of his eyes to good use keeping watch for trouble.

Between Cathair Rua and Ashqalêth, the islands and causeways of the Great Marsh of Slievmordhu floated on their own misty waters like some enchanted land, dreaming their way through the cooler season.

On the morning of New Year's Day in Narngalis, pale, wintry light seeped from a sky dry-brushed with swirls of feathery clouds. By noon, tarpaulins were spread upon the grass in the gardens of Wyverstone Castle, that people might seat themselves on the ground without spoiling their clothes. A sweeping lawn, hedged in by ancient holly trees in full berry, was the place of assembly for invited members of the public, and New Year's Day was a time for leisure and further celebration.

The afternoon turned crystal-bright. Snow glistened on the Northern Ramparts, and bird calls went ringing through the limpid air. In accordance with tradition, aristocrats and members of the royal family mingled with commoners. Everyone was clad warmly against the cold. Noblewomen had dressed themselves in gowns of best quality Ashqalêthan camlet, wrapping themselves in cloaks of otter-fur and chinchilla. Their menfolk wore large, well-insulated hats with upturned brims, decorated by pheasant plumes. Long-sleeved and fur-lined, their ankle-length greatcoats were trimmed with russet fox-pelts at cuffs, lapels and collars. Beneath the greatcoats they wore calf-length tunics, thick leggings and black knee-boots with the tops turned back to reveal the yellow lining.

Visiting farmers and craftsmen had dressed themselves in belted tunics of soft leather, with cross-gartered chausses on their legs and clogs on their feet. Their hats were bycockets, or capuchons with liripipes worn like scarves around the neck. Some wore sheepskin jerkins, and their cloaks were made of thick, warm frieze. Their wives and daughters were similarly garbed, except that kirtles and gowns replaced tunics and jerkins, and their heads were swathed in woolen couvre-chefs fixed on with bands of plaited yarn. In addition to this cold-weather paraphernalia, the older folk and some of the children were wearing shapeless bliauts of weather-proof canvas on top of all their other garments.

Pet hounds frolicked amongst the crowds, and several young men were playing football at one end of the lawn. The main event of the day was "tilting at rings." In this competition, horsemen vied with each other to obtain any of three bracelets decorated with ribbons, dangling from a horizontal yardarm on embroidery-threads. One of the armlets was made of bronze, one of silver and one of pure gold. While galloping past the post at full speed, riders must try to pierce a bracelet with the tip of their lance, thus breaking the thread and carrying off the prize. Contestants were each allowed three attempts. Custom decreed that the winners bestow their prizes on a favored lady. It was considered a great triumph to win any of the trophies; therefore many horsemen entered the contest. The competition was fierce but good-natured, and the convivial celebration of the new year was enjoyed by all.

After New Year's Day, the urisk seldom appeared at The Laurels. On the occasions when he did manifest himself, he would say very little, and was not to be drawn. He seemed distracted. It was as if something had stirred him profoundly. Asrăthiel was unable to decipher his emotions, for he was such an alien thing; and she found his behavior even more inexplicable than usual.

The people of Narngalis drank much cider to celebrate Wassailing the Apple Trees on the sixth of Jenever. They sang the traditional Apple Tree Wassailing chant:

"Huzza, huzza, in our good town
The bread shall be white, and the liquor be brown
So here my old fellow I drink to thee
And the health of every other apple tree.
Well may ye grow, well may ye bear,
Blossom and fruit, both apple and pear,
So that every bough and every twig
May bend with a burden both fair and big.
May ye bear us and yield us fruit in such store
That the bags and chambers and house run o'er!"

On the following morning, semaphore messages arrived in King's Winterbourne from Slievmordhu, reporting that King Uabhar had taken delivery of a sky-balloon of his own, which had been manufactured in secret. Such aerostats did exist outside Rowan Green, but they were small and, being non-dirigible, used only by the wealthy for recreational flights. Because balloons without weathermaster pilots were at the mercy of the wind, their final destination could not be predicted. Ground-crew had to try to follow the aircraft across the countryside so that they could fetch them back from wherever they alighted. This enterprise was time-consuming, difficult and dangerous.

The king had exerted his considerable influence to gather craftsmen with the skill to make a large sky-balloon capable of carrying relatively heavy loads. In the past he had never bothered with "glee-flights," as he called them, wherefore he concealed the balloon's manufacture so as to avoid arousing the suspicion of the weathermasters. When at last he revealed the completed project, it was the cause of much public astonishment. "Soon we shall all have our own private sky-balloons!" cried some of the more optimistic and ignorant citizens.

At High Darioneth the weathermasters shook their heads, wondering how such aerial transport was to be steered without pilots who could master the winds. Could it be that Uabhar had discovered some new gramarye? Or was it possible that an unknown child out in the wide world had, unaccountably, been born with a talent for the brí and independently learned to use it? Their uncertainty, combined with the certainty of Uabhar's ill intentions, made them apprehensive.

Asrăthiel sojourned one War's Day in Feverier at Wyverstone Castle. Throughout the morning she practiced swordplay in the drill hall. The afternoon was dreary with rain, and she spent it playing cards with Prince William and two of his sisters.

"Incidentally," said the prince as they sat around the card table, "a message arrived for you today from High Darioneth. Has anyone passed it on to you?"

"Not yet."

"A plague upon lazy clerks! Then I shall tell you myself, here and now, for it was not marked 'private.' The Storm Lord informs you he lately received word from Cathair Rua. King Uabhar contends he has suddenly become aware that an inexplicable rift has appeared in the relationship between

Slievmordhu and Rowan Green. He says that although the cause of the disunion is beyond his knowledge—"

"Beyond his knowledge!" Asrăthiel interrupted indignantly. "Pardon my discourtesy, Will, but I cannot stay silent! What glibness, what *effrontery,* for Uabhar to deny this knowledge when we are certain it is *he* who pays for the gossip to be spread!"

"He is hardly likely to admit to it," William said mildly. "Shall I continue?"

"Yes. Please do. I apologize for my outburst."

"He says that although the cause of the disunion is beyond his knowledge, he wishes to make amends by publicly demonstrating concord, and he has invited all the weathermasters to a grand banquet at his palace, in official token of renewed friendship."

"What? Does Uabhar really believe my grandfather is naïve enough to trust in him? No doubt this is some further scheme."

"Avalloc harbors the same suspicions as do you. He declined the invitation as politely as possible."

"Which will doubtlessly cause affront to Uabhar."

"Maybe the King of Slievmordhu is looking for an excuse to declare hostilities against Rowan Green," mused Lecelina. Paying no heed to the conversation, Winona squinted ferociously at the fan of cards she held in her hand.

"He is far too cunning for such a rash move," Asrăthiel said. "His armies, though formidable, are hardly likely to prevail against the might of my kindred and our allies."

"In sooth," said William, nodding in agreement. "Yet I ponder on his subtle purpose."

❧

The days of Feverier opened and closed their eyes in the lead-up to another traditional annual ritual, Whuppity Stourie, which took place on the first of Mars, the very beginning of Spring. King Uabhar Ó Maoldúin, accompanied by his vast retinue, made the long journey to Grïmnørsland to celebrate the end of Winter with King Thorgild, to all ap-

pearances further cementing their relationship. In spite of
the plethora of jolly occasions at this festive season, the
usual popular merriment across Tir was somewhat marred.
By now it was common knowledge throughout the Four
Kingdoms that Uabhar of Slievmordhu was mobilizing his
armies in readiness to defend his realm against unknown
numbers of Marauders when the comswarms became active
again. Furthermore, several battalions of Ashqalêthan soldiers were on the march, bound for Slievmordhu, as reinforcements. Uabhar's spokesmen trumpeted the tidings that
King Chohrab II's armies were going to help drive the
swarmsmen from their lairs and wipe them out. The weathermasters, still the target of malign speculation in Slievmordhu
despite Uabhar's elaborate protestations and ostensible efforts to placate the masses, suspected both the southern
rulers of clandestine designs, and remained vigilant.

Late at night, on the day after Whuppity Stourie, a rain-
storm swept across King's Winterbourne. Asrǎthiel was
asleep in her canopied bed when above the splash and roar
of the deluge there came a clatter of hoofs on the gravel
driveway in front of the house. A horseman swerved to a
stop. Immediately he leaped from the saddle and began
hammering on the front door. A messenger arriving so precipitately at this time of night, showering blows on the main
portal as if he would break it down, must certainly be bearing tidings of great importance. The weathermage sprang
from her bed and threw a cloak over her shoulders. By the
time she had raced downstairs Giles had already admitted
the rider, who was standing in the downstairs parlor, breathing heavily and shaking sprays of droplets from his garments. The entire household had roused themselves and
begun to gather around.

The newcomer's royal livery proclaimed him to be a messenger from Wyverstone Castle.

"What news?" Asrǎthiel asked peremptorily. As she descended the last few stairs and approached him, she was unaware of how beautiful she appeared. Her plumate cloud of
midnight hair tumbled loose about her shoulders, framing

her fine-boned face, and she stared at her guest with a gaze like twin beams of intense sapphire.

Endeavoring to hide his wonderment, the bedazzled messenger swept the drenched hat from his head and bowed low. "Your Ladyship, I bring greetings from his majesty King Warwick, who sent me to deliver this information to you. This night our sovereign received a disturbing report from Silverton."

"Silverton? That village under the mountains?" Asrăthiel had expected that any peril would threaten from the south, not the north.

"The very one, my lady. It is usually a quiet hamlet, but these past weeks the villagers have lived in a state of terror, alleging they are 'under siege from the night.' His majesty sent troops to investigate, and they have now verified the claims. In Silverton, swift and violent death strikes during the dark hours."

"Marauders!"

"Nay, my lady, not Marauders; something new."

"Militant zealots? Feuding villagers?"

"On no account. Rather, something eldritch that has not been encountered before. Something purposeful and truly deadly."

Asrăthiel knew of Silverton, the village built in the shadow of the Northern Ramparts. It had been named thus because silver ore had been smelted there in olden days, when the mines of the north had operated in full swing, and the precious metal was excavated in great quantities from beneath the mountains. One of the smelters was still working, even though the lode had dwindled over recent decades, and most of the mines were closed.

"What action has been taken?"

"The king's household cavalry has been dispatched to investigate further and to provide security. Semaphore messages have been relayed to High Darioneth. His majesty wishes to alert my lady's weathermaster kindred to the possibility that some new scourge has arisen in our lands. My lady, as we speak his majesty holds an extraordinary council at the castle. He requests your presence."

Asräthiel wasted no time. After instructing Giles to order her chair and to ensure the messenger received refreshments, she sped upstairs, calling for Linnet. Soon she was dressed and coiffed, seated in the covered sedan chair and on her way through the pouring rain to Wyverstone Castle. Her stoic bearers splashed through the mud without complaint.

At King Warwick's midnight meeting with his knights and councilors the young weathermage learned more about the recent alarming events. Over the past fortnight a number of gruesome murders had taken place in and around the village of Silverton, yet none could say who or what had perpetrated the atrocities. On separate occasions, cottagers who chanced to be out of doors between sunset and sunrise, coming home late from the tavern or from visiting friends, had been murdered in the road. Yet the slayings evidenced no hallmarks of Marauder-work, and indeed no swarmsmen had been glimpsed in the vicinity for years. Aghast at the idea that some mysterious nightmare had descended on their hamlet, the villagers were too frightened to venture abroad after dark. They huddled in their houses, barring the windows and doors. Four nights previously, a party of fifteen armed villagers had gone out to hunt for the ill-doers. In the morning their corpses were found; pierced through with surgical exactness, prostrate by the roadside.

In each case the murderers—for judging by the numbers who had been killed within a short period, there must be more than one—had struck swiftly and silently, leaving no trail, no evidence of their presence. They slew using bladed weapons, cleanly and efficiently, and with such lethal speed that the victims had no opportunity even to cry out. Nobody in the village had heard any disturbance. And every cadaver lay unpillaged, with budget and other belongings intact. Not so much as a copper coin or a belt-buckle had been stolen.

"I have never heard the like," said King Warwick. Grim furrows had carved themselves deeply into his visage. The king's chair was the most ornate at the circular table, its high back carved with emblems of Narngalis. He leaned against the upholstery, balancing his elbows on the armrests. His voluminous outer sleeves, lavishly lined with ermine, fell back to reveal the patterned brocade of the inner garment. Only the restless tapping of his fingers betrayed the sovereign's agitation. "Marauders do not operate in such ways. Their methods are more brutal, and less precise. They kill or maim, and always rob their prey. Often they hack their victims apart." Warwick paused, inhaling deeply. "Nor does this suggest the work of militant Sanctorum offshoots, or neighbors bearing grudges. It seems to me that no human being could execute such appallingly precise handiwork as we have seen these weeks. After long years of relative peace in Tir, it appears certain we are confronted with some new menace. I believe these killings are, in fact, the handiwork of unseelie wights of an unknown cast. What say you, Lady Maelstronnar?"

Asräthiel spread her hands, palms upward, in a gesture of bafflement. "Such deeds are as much of a mystery to me as to anyone, my liege," she said, "and therefore I can suggest no cure in this hour. However, I must agree with you—they would appear to be the work of malevolent forces not of mortal ilk."

Warwick nodded gravely. The lord chamberlain was positioned at the king's right hand, wearing robes embroidered with stags and swans and geometric patterns. He ceased staring ruminatively into the fireplace and said, "Fortunately the villagers keep potent wards nailed above their doors and windows. For now, at least, although the terrors of the night besiege them, they can be considered safe in their houses."

"True enough, Hallingbury," said the lord privy seal, Sir Torold Tetbury, who was flawlessly garbed in raiment of muted hues. "Yet who knows whether or not this menace, if left unchecked, will spread?"

"Or whether its power might grow strong enough to overcome the protection of iron and rowan!" said King Warwick's lieutenant-general, Sir Gilead Torrington.

Asrăthiel gazed about at the well-dressed officials, as exquisite in appearance as wild cats glimpsed through dappled sunlight, or resplendent flocks of birds.

Prince William, still sleepy-eyed after being wrested from repose, said, "I am in accord with my father. There is no doubt some unket eldritch agency has wrought this ill work; for what purpose and to what end cannot be guessed. One final piece of strange news may help towards solving the puzzle. Since early this new year, trows have been seen more frequently. The Grey Neighbors appear to be moving northwards across Narngalis. Something has provoked them. I venture to propose this has something to do with the slayings in Silverton."

"Let me remind you, Your Royal Highness, trows do not commit slaughter upon humankind," said lord chamberlain Hallingbury. "They are not truly unseelie."

"Maybe they have changed. That's not impossible," said the lord steward.

"Not impossible but improbable, to my way of thinking," said William. "'Tis likely they are attracted to potent eldritch activities, in the same way they are attracted to silver."

"Of old," said the king, "trows used to dwell in great numbers in the Silverton area, but that was because of the mines. When the mines closed they drifted away."

"What can be afoot?" the king's private secretary wondered aloud, voicing everyone's thoughts. Nobody could provide an answer.

"Your Majesty," said Asrăthiel, "how can I be of assistance?"

The king turned his troubled gaze upon the weathermage. "You are erudite, Asrăthiel, and I had hoped you might be able to shed light on this circumstance; however, I now perceive that it proves beyond even your knowledge. At this time there is naught for you to do. We must be vigilant, search through the lore-books for clues, and guard the villagers; that is all. A large cavalry contingent, led by selected officers, has been sent to investigate and provide protection. They will report anon. My knights, the Companions of the

Cup, stand ready—" Warwick nodded acknowledgment towards his Commander-in-Chief "—and my troops are preparing for possible action." He inclined his head in the direction of the High Commander of the Narngalish Armed Forces. "The semaphore stations are on high alert. At the first sign of any significant escalation of these attacks, the beacon fires will be kindled on the heights across Narngalis."

"Then every precaution has been taken," said Asrăthiel, bowing courteously.

The crown equerry said, "Furthermore, messages have been sent throughout the cities and countryside. From this night forward, at the king's command, the people of Narngalis must stay behind locked doors at nights, and invite no stranger across the threshold."

After the meeting had adjourned, Asrăthiel joined the royal family in one of the breakfast-rooms. The chamber was awash with the golden light of many candles and lamps, as if by sheer intensity of radiance the castle's occupants might drive off the unknown foes that haunted the dark.

"Well," the damsel said to William as they wandered companionably up and down the room, watching the servants hastening to serve victuals and beverages at such an unusually early hour, "am I to go home tonight? The king commands us all to refrain from venturing outdoors."

"You must abide here in the castle," said William. "You know I should be partial to that." He stood so close to Asrăthiel that she felt engulfed by his presence. His shirt, lace-edged, was faintly scented with lavender.

"After all the excitement it is hardly probable I shall sleep a wink in any case," said Asrăthiel.

"Then stay with me here in the breakfast-room, and together we shall await the dawn."

They reached the far end of the room, turned around and began to stroll back.

⤝

From King's Winterbourne the river ran southwest, through a gap in the mountain range, and into Grïmnørsland, where it flowed, growing mightier all the time, to the coast. Along the way it passed Trøndelheim, where King Thorgild was hosting a feast for Uabhar of Slievmordhu, in honor of the forthcoming wedding of Kieran and Solveig.

Close to four hundred guests occupied the hall of the western monarch. The notables of the realm were present, and every guest partook of his fill of food and drink, until all were mirthful and blithe. At Thorgild's command, his bards performed songs and recited sagas accompanied by musicians playing horns or striking the tuned percussion instruments peculiar to that realm.

At the climax of the celebration Uabhar rose to his feet and began to speak. His ringing tones carried above the joyful buzz of conversation, so that a hush immediately fell upon the concourse. "Two royal families shall be joined as one!" proclaimed Uabhar, raising his glass in an impromptu toast. "Here's health to Grïmnørsland and Slievmordhu!" After the cheers had died away, Uabhar continued his speech. "I am grateful to our host Thorgild," he said, "for his limitless hospitality. In Grïmnørsland I have not only a staunch ally but also a beautiful bride for my son. Can anyone think of anything that is lacking to complete my happiness?"

The assembled guests answered, no they could not.

"Surely, my friend, your happiness is complete!" said Thorgild, his rubicund cheeks shining in the lamplight.

"Yet there is one great lack," said Uabhar, and at this unexpected announcement the crowd fell silent, some in wonder, some in dread, most uncomprehending. "It pains me," continued the visiting king, "that some of my own people in Slievmordhu have unaccountably waxed bitter against the weathermasters."

A look of discomposure creased Prince Hrosskel's brow. He shifted uncomfortably in his chair, but his father shot him a warning glance.

"I maintain," said Uabhar, "that it is unfitting that the luminaries of Rowan Green be not held in highest esteem by all men. They have proved themselves worthy friends in the past, providing valuable service in stormy weather, averting the catastrophes that would have wreaked destruction upon our lands. In these dark days of increased aggression from Marauders it would be better if the weathermasters were fully united with my kingdom so that we may defend ourselves with utmost strength."

Murmurs of agreement rippled up and down the hall.

"It is time," Uabhar expounded, "to extend the hand of fellowship. I have requested that the Councilors of Ellenhall come to my table, there to enjoy my hospitality. Such a gathering would surely prove to everyone, once and for all, that the relationship is cordial. But alas, such an earnest invitation has been misinterpreted, having been transmitted by semaphore. Communication by carrier pigeon or courier is no better. Only the word of a man of eminence and honor is powerful enough to convey the earnestness of my invitation. Yet I fear that I myself would hardly be welcomed into High Darioneth at this time."

With all the attention of the assembly fixed upon him, Uabhar turned to King Thorgild. "I ask you, Thorgild my dear friend, to plead on my behalf for this reunion, which can only bring strength and joy to the Four Kingdoms."

And so it happened, as easily as that. In front of the applauding gathering, King Thorgild realized, somewhat to his own surprise, that he was agreeing to do his best to convince the weathermasters to attend Uabhar's reconciliation banquet in Cathair Rua, and to journey halfway across Tir to ensure this purpose was fulfilled.

Later, in private, Uabhar said to him, "Let us not waste a moment in notifying the weathermasters of your intended visit. Let us send a semaphore to Rowan Green at first light!"

And Thorgild, being a man who kept his word, granted consent.

➷

Dawn stole across Grïmnørsland. The glossy needles of the conifer forests glistened like tinsel when struck by the low-angled rays of the sun. Their softly bustling foliage came alive with fingers of light. A cirrus sky stretched all the way from the inland borders of the kingdom to King's Winter-bourne, many miles to the northeast. The clouds were wispy plumes, like goose-down strewn across the firmament.

Having passed the night at Wyverstone Castle, Asrăthiel returned in the morning to The Laurels. She slept for a few hours, and when she awoke her maid brought a letter on a silver tray.

"This arrived by post-rider just now," said Linnet. "It was dispatched from Rowan Green nine days ago. The rider was delayed."

Asrăthiel slit the envelope with a penknife and unfolded the sheet of paper. It was a message from her grandfather.

◈

"Unto The Lady Weathermage Asrăthiel Heronswood Mael-stronnar, at The Laurels, Lime Grove, King's Winterbourne, I, Storm Lord Avalloc Nithulambar Maelstronnar of Rowan Green in High Darioneth, do send thee Greetings.

"My dear Asrăthiel,

"I have received a message from our friends in Grïmnørs-land. King Thorgild presses us to accept Uabhar's invitation, in the interests of the unity of Tir. He has spoken with Uab-har and is convinced of his genuine desire for friendship. Thorgild gives his pledge to accompany us to Cathair Rua and guarantee our security, should we accept. Uabhar pro-poses to hold the banquet on Mai Day. Ten days from now the councilors will meet to consider the invitation. If you wish to participate in the meeting please come to us at High Darioneth within that period."

That allows me scant time, Asrăthiel thought, and the no-tion did nothing to soothe the sense of panic that had seized her as soon as she read the epistle. Uabhar, for reasons un-known, had developed a patent loathing of the weathermasters. He had also spread false rumors, turning the populace against High Darioneth; seized control of the ruined Dome of Strang and received the Sylvan Comb as if the givers had handed him a viper. Ominously, he had commissioned his own sky-balloon. The man was not merely a petty schemer, he possessed far more intelligence than he demonstrated. Furthermore she suspected, he was actually *mad*—therefore highly dangerous. There was no knowing what further plans he might be hatching, and to what end.

I must hasten to Rowan Green without delay and persuade my kindred not to go to Cathair Rua. Uabhar Ó Maoldúin's invitation might be couched in fair and flattering words, but my heart tells me he is false. I feel certain he plans to lure them into some trap.

"Tell the men to make ready *Lightfast*," she told Linnet. "But this time I will travel alone, for where I am going there will be ground crew to receive me."

Soon afterwards Asrăthiel's balloon ascended from the lawns of The Laurels. As it rose up the air became cooler, more rarefied, transparent as distilled water. Delicately suspended above a lake, the aerostat serenely drifted, the silver-white globe hanging silently, reflected in the water like a pearl on the throat of the sky. Asrăthiel murmured a command, and a sudden gust flurried across the water. The image blurred and the balloon was swept away.

At a height of five hundred feet Asrăthiel floated across the landscape of Narngalis. The forests, valleys, rivers, lakes and farmlands looked to be laid out in harmonious design; here slumbering beneath cloud, there basking in sunshine. After the hurly-burly of city life, the tranquillity of the lower atmosphere seemed hypnotic. Up here, there was no counteractive drag, nothing to retard the aerostat's effortless glide upon the shoulders of the wind. The balloon's airspeed matched the pace of every other windborne object; flecks of thistledown, a feather or two, smoke from cottage chimneys, rising vertically until it encountered the upper currents, where it dispersed to become the reflection of nothing.

The weathermage's airship rose higher. Shadows of topography and vegetation became indistinct, until at last the landscape adopted a hazy, veiled appearance, losing all detail. As the basket gained greater altitude, the vapors of the lowest cloud layers enveloped it. Moments of clammy dimness followed, after which the balloon broke through the ceiling of the layer. Above, the sky was the most profound and flawless blue imaginable. Direct sunlight glared brilliantly, reflecting in sudden lances off the sculpted cloudscape.

The sun-crystal glowed fiercely as Asrăthiel commanded it to produce more heat, lifting her higher over the mountainous country. Having reached Rowan Green, the aerostat dived down through the clouds. At first Asrăthiel was wrapped in a mist of miniature crystals like a saturation of sequins, glimmering and twinkling. The cloud of crystals merged into a moist, cool brume, a damp shroud that had the effect of augmenting sound. Asrăthiel heard her own voice louder in her ears as she muttered the brí commands. She caused the balloon to plunge rapidly, trembling and rotating as it accelerated. Below the basket the blurred tints of the landscape began to coalesce through the murk. Dropping out through the floor of the cloud layer, the balloon emerged into diffused sunlight. The instant the basket kissed the ground, the weathermage tugged on the rip line. A panel opened. The envelope's once-perfect symmetry became malformed, while the wicker gondola, still slightly airborne, was hauled across the ground. Slowly, as the warm air escaped, the envelope deflated. The basket lost speed and came to a gradual halt on the green landing-place, to be greeted by the ground crew.

As soon as she reached the House of Maelstronnar, Asrăthiel ran upstairs to the glass cupola, where her mother lay in a trance. After kissing the marble brow, she murmured, "Mother, I love thee. Yet I cannot stay, for I must speak with Grandfather. I will return to you before I depart."

Long, clear notes pealed from the belfry atop Ellenhall under Wychwood Storth, and in this gracious building atop the shelf overlooking the plateau, the councilors congregated. The Storm Lord entered, with Asrăthiel on his arm. Pouches of flesh sagged beneath Avalloc's eyes. His beetling eyebrows grew long, upswept like two wings, as if a giant grey-moth crouched upon the bridge of his aristocratic nose. Symmetrical troughs ran down from the inner corners of his eyes, beneath his cheekbones, as if a potter's thumb had impressed them in wet clay. Two more grooves began at the outer edges of his nostrils and vanished somewhere in the foggy tendrils of his beard. Three horizontal furrows ploughed his forehead. His troubles had graven their signature into his visage.

Outside, in the watercolor light of day, the grasses were spattered with the lemon-butter spangles of dandelion flowers. Indoors, brass lamps shed their mellow radiance against the paneled walls.

They all gathered; the councilors and more; prentices and journeymen garbed in elegantly decorated raiment of many tints, weathermages clad in traditional costume. Asräthiel's aunts Galiene and Lysanor came in with their husbands, and Avalloc's sister Astolat Darglistel entered the hall with Ryence and his siblings; Lynley and Baldulf Ymberbaillé accompanied their son Bliant; also Ettare Sibilaurë; Gauvain Cilsundror; Engres Aventaur; the carlin, Lidoine Galenrithar, and many others.

The Moot Hall was crowded.

Long waged the debate of the weathermasters. Strongly suspecting that Uabhar Ó Maoldúin harbored some deep and enigmatic resentment against them, the councilors were puzzled by the king's sudden rush of cordiality. For most of the day they discussed the topic of whether they should attend Uabhar's banquet as King Thorgild urged, or whether the risk of treachery was too great. Finally, after all voices had been heard and all votes counted, the Storm Lord summarized his opinion.

"There is no doubt that Thorgild is trustworthy," said Avalloc. "He is no fool, but his own nature is so artless that he fails to perceive deceitfulness in others. I fear he invests too much faith in Ó Maoldúin. Thorgild is not afraid of conflict, but prefers to solve it with dialogue rather than brute force. Always he has worked towards harmony within Tir, and reparation of political rifts. It is his hope to promote restoration of goodwill and accord."

"I would not like to disappoint him," said Engres Aventaur.

But Asrăthiel said, "Uabhar is treacherous. I say we should not go."

Lynley Ymberbaillé supported the Storm Lord's grand-daughter. "By the middle of Averil, Marauders will be well and truly on the move, hungry and eager for spoils after spending the long Winter cave-bound. It will be unsafe to travel by road."

"But what if Uabhar is in fact making a genuine attempt to demonstrate he holds no grudge against us?" asked Baldulf Ymberbaillé. "If we reject his invitation we shall appear at best ungracious, at worst cowardly and churlish."

"Baldulf is right. In any event, what have weathermasters to fear from Ó Maoldúin?" responded Ryence Darglistel. "We command forces greater than he can imagine! What's more, Thorgild's armed escort will be close beside us at all times. He has sworn to keep us from harm. I can see no reason to refuse. We ought to go."

A murmur of agreement arose on most sides. Immediately a pang of desolation struck Asrăthiel. She felt nauseated with horror. "What of this new eldritch menace near Silverton?" she demanded, grasping at reasons to stymie the expedition. This introduced topic diverted the attention of the gathering.

"I heard," said Ettare Sibilaurë, "that householders have been asking their domestic brownies for explanations, but the wights know nothing. Some folk have tried to interrogate other wights, but of course they are all so elusive. One man captured a trow who, when pressed, would only repeat, *"Sulver sir, sulver. That's what's a-calling me."*

"Silver!" exclaimed Baldulf Ymberbaillé. "We all know the Grey Neighbors are attracted to the metal, but this sudden flood of trows like nails to a magnet makes no sense. No new lodes have been discovered in that old region for years. It is practically mined out."

"Silver," said Avalloc ponderingly. "Of all metals known to humankind, silver is the one that best conducts heat and electricity. It has occurred to me, on occasion, that perhaps that is its power, somehow, over the trows."

"They seem to love it simply for its beauty, from all accounts," said his sister Astolat. "Trows compare silver to moonlight and starlight. We all know how much they dislike the light of the sun."

"Be that as it may," Asrăthiel said insistently, "some mysterious threat has arisen in Narngalis and we weathermasters must remain at hand, in case we are called upon for support."

"King Warwick has the situation under control," reassured Ryence Darglistel. "There have been no reports of fresh attacks at Silverton."

"Aye, but neither have the attackers been identified," said Asrăthiel. "Nobody yet knows who the culprits are—or *what* they are."

"I daresay they have been intimidated by the strong presence of soldiers," said Ryence. "They will have retreated to whatever gloomy lair they emerged from."

"We cannot be certain."

"But dear cousin, we need not *all* attend Ó Maoldúin's party," Ryence pointed out, returning to the main subject. "Some of us shall remain in Narngalis, obviously. Cloud and wind roll on—the weather will not excuse us from our duties!"

"I, for one, shall not go," Asrăthiel said stubbornly. "I am needed at my post."

"As Uabhar must surely understand," said Tristian Solorien, inclining his hoary head in emphasis.

In an endeavor to sway general opinion, Asrăthiel launched into an emphatic and impassioned series of arguments against the plan. The discussion shuttled back and forth until the damsel had exhausted all her objections and could conjure no further method of persuasion.

"It is time to make an end to discussion," said Avalloc. "Does anyone wish to make any further contribution?" Silence greeted his invitation. "Then, all in favor of this enterprise, raise your hands."

Hands were thrust into the air like pale flowers in some curious garden. The clerks and scribes muttered as they counted, and their eyes flicked from side to side, as busy as shuttles. They tallied up their scores, compared them and agreed.

"The weathermasters," announced the chief scribe, "will go to Cathair Rua."

"The vote has been cast, the decision has been made," said Avalloc. "The journey to renew the bonds of friendship will be undertaken by the Councilors of Ellenhall and those who choose to accompany us."

Submerged by a sense of helplessness, Asrăthiel wished herself free of the constraints and complaints of the world. As she accompanied her kinsmen on their way from the council chambers she let her brí senses issue forth, deep into the atmosphere, so that she might alleviate the feeling of impending doom and lose herself temporarily in the wild patterns of the elements.

X

Plots and Schemes

If lilac blooms remain tight-shut fine weather is at hand
But if they open rapidly, soon rain will drench the land.
If lilacs quickly drop and fade next Summer will be hot,
And if they flower late, then Summer rain will be our lot.

Another sign that forecasts rain as everybody knows
Is when the trembling poplar tree its silver lining shows.
When weeds in garden, field and roadside large and lofty grow
Next Winter will be bitter cold, and deep will drift the snow.

To learn this useful wisdom, look at nature's signs together.
The codes of flower, leaf and tree predict the coming weather.

—LOCAL WEATHERLORE IN NARNGALIS

Dimly underlit by the red glare of sunset, a cold front was passing from west to east across the kingdoms of Tir. Its undulating pressure gradient formed a line invisible to the eyes of most human beings, although apparent to nonhumankind and weathermasters. The turbulent band of moisture-rich cumulus associated with the leading edge straggled southward from the vicinity of the Mountain Ring as far as the Border Hills, and further, where it tapered to milky veils of cirrus. Beneath those veils a beggar, staff in hand, was hobbling along the highway in the direction of Cathair Rua. The wind tweaked at his garments and toyed with the rat-ends of his beard.

Cat Soup had sold the equipment he stole from The Laurels. Having once again violated the law in King's Winterbourne, he decided to leave the city until any hue and cry had died down, and continue his random wandering about the countryside. With coins in his pocket and a sturdy coat on his back, he trudged off in the direction of Cathair Rua, where the weather was warmer, hoping to hitch a ride and pay for it with his far-fetched and increasingly incoherent stories.

The old man was hoping he might find shelter before nightfall. His usual luck seemed to have deserted him. He had not chanced upon a single wagoner or carter willing to take him aboard, and there were no hamlets for miles ahead. The inhabitants of the villages along the highway had treated him with greater disrespect than was their wont, shooing him from their stables and byres when they discovered him attempting to bed down in the hay overnight. The threat of Marauders hung heavily along his route, like a fog. All said, his current peregrination had been a gloomy one. As so often before, he wondered if he was growing too old for life on the road. Yet a settled life would pall—he had tried it once or twice. When you lived in one place people came to expect things of you. They expected you to work, and to wash, and to be *responsible* for things. Besides, it was always so dull, remaining in one location. Life on the road had its extreme discomforts, but it was always full of surprises. For example, on the preceding night, while taking a little-known shortcut to avoid a loop in the highway, he had witnessed masses of Slievmordhuan soldiers on the move, traveling northwards under cover of darkness. It was obvious they sought secrecy, so he hid himself in a thicket of hazel and watched them go by, sweating with terror lest they come upon him and execute him for spying. Without noticing the observer they passed in relative quietude, their warharness and the hooves of their horses muffled.

The beggar had seen many peculiar things during his lifetime. He had also learned that it seldom paid to speak of them without a great deal of forethought.

The sun went down behind the hills, limning the cirrus wisps with rose-gold afterglow. Twilight was drawing in and the wind was rising. Emerging from a cutting, the road crossed a bridge over a fast-flowing rivulet and began to climb, bordered by flowering hedges of raspberry briars, interlaced with wild parsley. To either hand, vast meadows lay open to the sky, broken by distant lines of trees. The landscape was darkening, caught in a tumbler of grey-stained glass. The old man's threadbare cloak whipped about his gaunt form as if trying desperately to break free. As he limped along, lost in his reverie, he became aware that he was listening to a sigh.

The sound, a long-drawn whisper, was gushing from the fields, the hedges, the very ground beneath the old man's feet. It was not the moaning of the wind, although the wind might be its sister. The shadows of evening were rustling like pouring grains. Overwhelmed by stark fear the wanderer stood stock still, not knowing what to do.

A tidal flow of movement flickered at the edges of eyesight. He rotated his neck and stared. And then he saw.

A troupe of trows was passing by in the gloaming, hushed and ragged, trailing translucent grey scarves. No more than three and a half feet tall, with disproportionately large heads, hands and feet, they flitted across the road through some hitherto unnoticed gap in the breeze-tossed hedges and into the meadows, some muttering quietly in their own language. Flashes of silver twinkled amongst their dreary tatters. The old man caught a glimpse of long, drooping noses. Stringy locks dangled limply from beneath head-scarves or floppy pointed caps.

They were streaming towards Narngalis.

Though the beggar was in full view of the wights they neither turned their heads nor acknowledged him in any way, so intent were they upon their own business. When they had vanished from sight, merging into the grassy hills like water, Cat Soup took to his heels.

He was terribly frightened. All the trow-stories he had ever heard came flooding back to him; tales of people stolen by the Grey Neighbors, becoming trow-bound and enslaved, forever lost to the world of mortalkind. Never had he beheld trows in such great numbers, traversing the open lands. What else might be abroad? Duergars? Spriggans? The dreaded fuathan? Without pausing, he made a sign to ward off evil.

On the other side of the ridge the road dived into a valley. It was here, around a sudden bend, that the beggar's luck changed. First of all a crescent moon came slicing out of the hilltop, peeking between long shreds of cloud and softly rinsing the hills with streaks of wan radiance. Secondly, he came upon a grove of wild apple-trees, surrounding an open glade where no doubt some long-since crumbled cottage had once stood. A rushy brook flowed near the spot, and beneath the blossoming apple-trees a convoy of Slievmordhuan wag-oners had set up camp. Their fires glittered welcomingly. Fountains of sparks sprayed up, tossed by gusts and eddies. Flurries of white petals danced away into darkness amongst the wagons and the tethered horses.

Two armed men loomed in front of Cat Soup, challenging him fiercely, whereupon he dropped his staff and fell to his knees mewling like a kitten. "Have pity! Have pity!" he sup-plicated. "I am but a poor old man!" They prodded him with their spears. "I am mortal! I am mortal!" yowled Cat Soup. "I beg of you, let me but sit near your fires, for I am half per-ished. I have walked a long way. I ask for nothing more than companionship, for this night is warped and wefted with fell things, and I am afraid."

Reluctantly the men allowed him into their encampment. Retrieving his staff, the beggar crawled up to the nearest campfire, but someone said gruffly, "Move on!" and away he scuttled.

Then another man's voice said, "You may sit yourself down near our fire, *a seanáthair*," and the vagrant found himself amongst the members of a large family, none of whom approached him closely. Children eyed him with wary curiosity. When he had warmed himself at the flames, a woman handed him a bowl of pottage, which he devoured greedily and with gusto. The man who had proffered the invitation said, "Can you sing or dance, old fellow? Can you be tellin' tales? Or do you merely beg, and give naught in return?"

"I can tell a good tale," said Cat Soup, who could not help glancing over his shoulder into the darkness beyond the firelight.

"I recognize that voice!" said a woman in red skirts and an embroidered jerkin, striding into the lamplight. "That's Cat Soup! I've seen him on this road before. He does indeed tell a good tale! Go on, Master Soup—what wonders can you be regalin' us with on this windy night?" Companionably she seated herself amidst the group, whose members greeted her with smiles.

The beggar recognized the woman's face but could not put a name to her, which was hardly surprising, considering that his memory these days was playing him tricks. "Has anyone told you the one about the bockles at the Ransom Mine out Riddlecombe way?" he asked, before noisily licking the remains of the pottage out of his bowl.

His hosts were aware of the tale. "Some Grïmnørsland wagoners were tellin' it to us."

"Then, have you heard the one about the vixen and the oakmen?"

"Aye, that we have."

"What about the tale of the stolen swanmaiden?"

"We've a-heard it."

Cat Soup went through the list of his best stories, but the wagoners said they were familiar with them all. Finally, in exasperation, he delved into the cobwebby vaults of his nethermost stratagems, and came up with an idea. "This is no narrative," he said, "but it is true fact and you will not have heard it before because few are party to it."

"All right," said the wagoners, as intrigued as any entertainer could wish them to be, "out with it!"

After licking his cracked lips clean of food, their guest sniffed his empty bowl, sighed, and handed it back to the cook. "In Narngalis," he began, slipping into poetic mode, "strange artifacts of incredible workmanship can be found in remote places of the wilderness. Seldom discovered, they resemble pieces of amazing armor; greaves, cuirasses and the like. Narngalishmen call these artifacts by the odd name of *gypsy leather,* even though they are neither made of leather nor fashioned by gypsies. Of some curious black metal are they wrought, and covered with intricate silver intaglio, as if writhing with wicked serpents of hoarfrost."

"Have they been manufactured by mortalkind?" the wagoners wanted to know.

"Nay! For sure they have been crafted by eldritch wights," answered the beggar. "Some say that touching them brings ill-fortune. Others believe these pieces have influential properties, and can bring power to the possessor. Whether they are lucky or unlucky, for obvious reasons the pieces are kept hidden by whoever finds them, or else they are thrown away into inaccessible places."

Some among the audience looked disbelieving. "We have not heard of any wights that wear armor."

"Neither have I, but then I can hardly know *everything.*"

"What if a man collected enough pieces to clothe himself all over? What eldritch forces might protect him then, eh?"

"You might equally ask, *what eldritch forces might wither him to the bone?*"

"Have you seen this gypsy leather?"

"Aye, that I have. That I have indeed. It looks new but it is old, very old, for it has been lying about for years and years. I refused to touch it, for my flesh crept as soon as I set eyes on it, and the man who showed it to me fell from his horse the very next day and broke his neck, so his wife hurled the vambrace down an old mineshaft."

Clumped between the roots of the apple trees, the fragrant bells of lily-of-the-valley glimmered palely.

"What happened to the wife?"

The beggar pondered an instant, for he was never one to spoil a good story with accuracy. "Shortly thereafter she contracted a wasting disease, from which she perished."

Blazing sticks crackled. A buzz of conversation droned from a nearby campfire.

"Well that's a dismal tale and no mistake," declared the man who had invited Cat Soup to his fireside.

"Yes," said the beggar cunningly, "but a cautionary one. You'll thank me for saving the lives of your families, if ever you stumble upon a piece of gypsy leather. Is there any more of that delicious stew?"

"What is concernin' me," said someone as Cat Soup was helped to another bowlful, "is where did the armorers go?"

"What is concernin' me more," said another, darkly, "is what if they ever *come back*?"

A thoughtful silence supervened.

The wagoners allowed Cat Soup to spend the night at their camp, and in the morning he tagged along with the convoy, for he shared with them a common destination; the city of Cathair Rua. Seven days later they arrived safely in the metropolis, and he departed from their company.

It was almost noon. Leaning on his staff, the beggar moved haltingly—for his joints ached—over the cobblestones, through the crowded streets in the lower precincts of the red city. Meanwhile, unbeknownst to him and far above his balding head, a meeting was taking place within the stone walls of the Sanctorum on the hilltop. The King of Slievmordhu had recently arrived home from his sojourn in Grïmnørsland. Barely pausing to take refreshment, Uabhar secluded himself in a private apartment, and summoned

High Commander Risteárd Mac Brádaigh to his presence.

The soldier, a giant of a man, bowed on one knee.

"Are the preparations in hand?" demanded the king without preamble. "Are my battalions massed and organized?" He paced up and down, as was his habit when excited and impatient.

"They are indeed, my liege." Mac Brádaigh rose to his feet. "Your troops are ready for the great battle. They await your command."

"That is well. There is a little time yet to wait. As you are aware, one obstacle still remains in our path, but that shall shortly be removed, leaving us free to drive home our purpose."

"The weathermasters!"

"Even so. I rely on you to ensure they are captured and imprisoned with as little fuss as possible. They are not held in such high esteem as once they were, but the tide of public opinion would turn against me if it were perceived that I mistreated them. When they are closeted out of sight behind thick stone walls, their treatment will be another matter entirely."

"I take it my liege still intends to keep them alive?"

"In sooth. I comprehend your views on this matter, Mac Brádaigh, but I do not share them. 'Twould be a doltish act to arbitrarily order them slain and risk sparking bothersome insurrections. Ensure they are taken alive. They must be seen to receive a fair trial before their executions."

Mac Brádaigh swept his sovereign a bow so deep and gracious that the tip of his scabbard scraped along the floor. "Forever at your service, my liege," he said.

❧

Already, King Chohrab II waited as a guest at Uabhar's palace. He and his battalions had marched to Cathair Rua, as arranged, purportedly to practice 'war-games' in readiness for the imminent offensive against unseelie wights and Marauders. Having dined with his royal visitor, Uabhar departed from his residence and went swiftly to the abode of the druids, by means of secret passageways and curtained carriages, for a private audience with the Tongue of the Fates.

A red-robed novice touched a burning taper to a candle in a brightly lit room of the Sanctorum. As he attended to the lighting arrangements, he moved amongst richly embellished furnishings. Massive brass candelabra stood seven feet high, thick with crocketted pinnacles and tracery; the settles, bookcases and escritoire were diapered, chamfered and quatrefoiled. Cast bronze statues of the Four Fates stood in each corner of the chamber. A plaque attached to the plinth of Lord Ádh read: "Good luck favors the brave," while the inscription at the base of Lord Míchinniúint's icon declared cheerfully, "All ambition is doomed, yet men labor on."

A table was set beneath an oriel window. Marquetry-topped, it was bordered with a frieze of mouchettes. From each corner of the tabletop projected an ornate candlestick holder. Four slender beeswax candles grew thereon. At this table, in a rose-backed chair, sat the Druid Imperius, Primoris Asper Virosus. It was the same chair—in the same room—that had been occupied by the druid Adiuvo Constanto Clementer some twenty-six years earlier. The ancient sage seemed sunken into the framework of his own chest, shrunken and shriveled. Although clothed in robes of purest white baudekyn, appliquéd with costly samite, his person resembled the desiccated corpse of a rat from which the ichors had been drained. In the cellars of his cataract-filmed eyes an intelligence of indescribable cunning still coiled, yet perhaps it too had been altered by the passage of time, becoming colder, immoderate, more unbalanced. Even perverse joy at the misfortunes of his rivals hardly moved him as of old. These days there was nothing—no passion, no desire or compunction, that could move the machinery of this mind from whatever purpose it chose to pursue.

Garbed in a gorgeous doublet of crimson velvet stitched all over with golden dragons, the druid's liege-lord seated himself opposite him. Uabhar appeared gleeful. "I expect you have made further preparations?" he enquired of the druid.

The mouth of Virosus unzipped itself, like a razor-slash in a flaccid pouch. "My apothecaries have now got great store of this certain leaf, which they have dried in quantity. We have sackfuls, bushels. Leaf from the Lake District. They call it *fell noxasm*."

"Is it as potent as claimed?"

"Possibly. The effects are being extensively tested on caged animals."

"First the eldritch object and now another new weapon for my arsenal," Uabhar said with satisfaction, "and these strange reports from Silverton besides. Most convenient they are; the Starred One is, no doubt, favoring me." He nodded at the primoris, affecting gratitude.

The druid stared impassively. "Are the Silverton attacks some scheme of yours?" he asked bluntly.

The king laughed in his humorless way. "No! It is pure luck! As I said, Ádh is on my side!"

Uabhar had no reason to deceive him on this point, so Virosus enquired, "Have you any idea what is behind them?"

"Not at all." The king shrugged. "Have you?"

"No."

"I am merely gratified," said Uabhar, laughing again, "that it is Narngalis's problem and not mine. While the attention of Wyverstone is directed towards this new eldritch nuisance, whatever it may be, his southern defenses are weakened. I plan to use Chohrab's forces to my advantage, taking the opportunity to attack Narngalis by surprise. But first I must ensure that the weathermasters are no longer a hindrance, for I can never win in outright battle against Warwick's strongest allies. After I detain them in Cathair Rua under some pretext or another, a serious charge will be mounted against them, so that the tide of public opinion will conclusively turn, and there will be popular support for their imprisonment. Of course the meddlers will still be able to *feel* the weather—or whatever it is they do—even through walls of thickest stone, but they will be unable to work any mischief without the use of free hands and free tongues. Once incarcerated in my dungeons, the troublemakers will be unable to aid Narngalis." If Uabhar expected an accolade from his audience at this revelation, he failed to understand the druid.

"And what then?" Virosus asked aloofly. "What then? After we have won the war the mages will take reprisals."

"Not at all!" Uabhar refused to be beaten. "They are men of their word. I would not be so remiss as to set them free unless they swore a binding oath never to side with our enemies, and to obey me in all things. They will not break their oath, of that I am certain. There is no need for the Sanctorum to be frightened on that score."

The Tongue of the Fates scowled. "Hardly *frightened*. Sometimes, Uabhar, you appear to forget who we are, and who we represent. You speak blithely, but if any harm should befall the weatherlords as a result of your schemes, there are many who would seek vengeance."

Heedless of the ancient's offensive breath, Uabhar leaned towards Virosus, speaking softly, his eyes alight with an intense flame. Clearly and slowly spoke he, as if to a child, so that his confidant might make no mistake about his meaning. Sometimes even Uabhar underestimated the comprehension of the oldest of living druids. "Those who would return punishment to me on behalf of the puddlers will be powerless when this is over." Sitting back abruptly, the king began examining his fingernails in a preoccupied manner. "All is well. When will your industrious brethren be able to out-forecast the weathermages and render them redundant?"

The druid's eyes rolled like two veined eggs, each in a nest of wrinkles. He swiveled them to focus on the king. "That also proceeds according to plan. Come, see for yourself." As the primoris levered himself out of his chair, the novice rushed to assist.

Together Uabhar and Virosus made their exit from the chamber of gothic furniture and bronze statues. A party of eight senior druids, secundi, had been waiting outside the door. They now accompanied the king and the philosopher, remaining at a respectful distance behind them. "Acerbus," the primoris said to one of them, "King Uabhar wishes to observe the activities at the oracular workshop. To you I give the task of expounding upon the enterprise."

"The Primoris honors me," the secundus said smoothly, though the twitching muscles of his face betrayed nervousness. Like the others of his rank, he wore the traditional voluminous, deeply hooded robes of white wool. A long scarf of red silk was draped about his neck and shoulders, its tasseled ends hanging down to his waist, and the White Cockatrice insignia was embroidered on his sleeve beneath the sigil of the Burning Brand.

While they made their way through the corridors of the Sanctorum, Secundus Acerbus embarked on his task of instruction, speaking deferentially to the king. "When first your majesty's assignment was made known to us," he said, "we dispatched our agents to discreetly question the carlins, seeking to draw on their knowledge of weather lore. It is well known that the hags possess some limited ability to foretell changes in the air. Fortunately they are also stupid, giving away their knowledge freely, so that anyone might use it."

"Bah!" snorted Uabhar. "You need not have bothered with the blue crones. Who has not heard of their absurd little superstitions? They use weeds to predict the weather, and to *protect against thunder and lightning*! They declaim fatuities such as *In Autumn, if the tails of squirrels are very bushy, or if they gather big stores of nuts, Winter will be severe,* or *The first blossom on the horse chestnut tree means Spring has arrived and there will be no more Winter storms.* The dowager queen my mother used to believe all that twaddle. She'd repeat a rhyme—

" 'If the oak flowers before the ash,
We shall have a splash.
If the ash flowers before the oak,
We shall have a soak.' "

"This nonsense has been proved erroneous on countless occasions."

"Indeed, my liege," said Secundus Acerbus. Diplomatically, he cleared his throat behind his hand. "Perhaps the most gracious dowager queen, my Lord Ádh the Starred One shower bounty upon her, learned these rhymes from other sources. Certainly the carlins do not use them."

The king glowered at him. "What *do* they use?" he snapped.

"Begging my liege's pardon," stammered the secundus, recoiling, "as you say, they do employ some weeds as natural weather indicators. Scarlet pimpernel, for example, and morning glory. The flowers of both plants open wide in sunny weather but close up tightly when rain threatens."

The king laughed. "Most useful," he commented caustically. "What else?"

"Pinecones, my liege. In dry weather, their scales open out. When they close, it signals that rain is approaching. Carlins in Grïmnørsland, living near the sea, hang out strands of kelp. In fine weather the kelp shrivels and feels dry to the touch. If rain is in the air the seaweed swells and becomes damp. Strands of wool work the same way. When the air is dry the strands shrink and roll themselves into curls. If rain is expected the wool hangs straight."

"You bring me much amusement, secundus," said Uabhar.

As the noon-bell pealed from the city clock-tower, the party passed out of the main building onto a grassy plot, beyond which loomed the arched doors of a smaller edifice at the rear of the Sanctorum. The perfume of Spring flowers wafted from the ornamental gardens beyond the walls, and a blackbird perched, trilling, on a gatepost. In the center of the lawn, a glittering sphere of transparent glass balanced atop a stone pedestal.

"This is a daylight-measurer, sire," explained Acerbus. "It registers the duration of the day, as well as the path of the sun, and the intensity of its rays. The glass ball focuses the sun's rays onto this strip of thick paper, singeing it. As the sun crosses the sky, the scorch marks cross the paper, documenting the day's sunshine."

"Yes, yes," said the king, hardly sparing a glance for the apparatus. "Let us hasten to the workshop."

After entering the arched doors, the party of illustrious personages encountered a scene of arcane industry. Druids and their assistants moved amongst tables and stands laden with mechanisms. All work came to a halt when the dignitaries appeared, and the building's occupants made their salutations.

"Continue," said King Uabhar, waving his hand dismissively. Instantly his subjects busied themselves once more. "Secundus, what is this contraption?" The king indicated a hollow sphere measuring about two feet across. It was composed of metal rings, all circles cut from a single sphere, and set at varying angles.

"It is a bracelet orb, my liege; a model used to display the positions and motion of the sun and the stars as the year cycles. The weather at any given period is largely dependent on the sun's position in the sky."

"Indeed. And this?"

"A simpler version of the bracelet orb, sire, showing only the principal celestial bodies. Powered by clockwork, it replicates the world's motion around the sun, and how that journey affects the four seasons."

"Excellent. And do either of these devices control the weather?"

"Not *as such,* my liege," said Acerbus delicately, "but they do show promise." Beneath his ample sleeves he was wringing his hands. At the king's side the primoris leaned on one of the novices and stared impassively at the bracelet orb without comment.

"Permit me, my liege, to introduce you to the Official in Charge of Divining the Air's Invisible Moisture Content," said Acerbus, seeking relief.

A tall, gaunt tertius bowed to the two dignitaries and, walking in reverse so that he would not turn his back on them, obsequiously ushered them to a courtyard. There he demonstrated his four water vapor diviners. The Ice Diviner, supported in a three-legged wooden stand, was a ceramic vessel, tall and slender, lidded at the top, tapering to a spigot underneath. Ice filled the hollow core. "Invisible water vapor in the air turns into liquid water when it touches the cold outer sides of the container," the tertius explained with pride, "whereupon it flows down into this glass measuring tube. The greater the amount of water that is collected, the greater is the air's invisible water content. Over here, my lords, stands the Paper Diviner." He showed them a weighing device consisting of a rigid beam horizontally suspended by a low-friction support at its center, with identical weighing pans hung at either end. Soft paper discs were piled into one pan. "When there is little vapor in the air the discs become dry and therefore weigh less, pulling the pointer down. And of course the reverse is also true when the air is moist."

The Hair Diviner consisted of a brass case with an elongated vertical slit cut into the front. A strand of human hair could be seen through this slit. The top end of the strand was attached to a small wheel at the base of a pointer. The tip of the pointer rested against a flat brass disc incised with numbered intervals of measurement. "As the hair becomes wetter and expands, or dries out and contracts, it turns the wheel and the pointer swings," expounded the tertius.

Uabhar was growing bored. "What is the purpose of divining the air's invisible water content?" he barked.

"My Liege," gabbled the tertius, bowing repeatedly, "if there is much vapor in the air then we can be certain that rain is on the way."

"The rain has wetted your brain, Tertius." To the primoris, the king remarked, "It seems that during all these months of study at the expense of the treasury your scholars have hardly progressed beyond the carlins' pinecones." He walked straight past an amusing version of the Hair Diviner, which was built like a little wooden house with two front doors. At the center of the house stood a vertical axle, hidden behind a post. Attached to this axle was a flat plank, free to spin around. A woman-doll was glued at one end of the plank; at the other end a man-doll. A hair inside the house stretched or shrank, according to the invisible air vapor, causing the little man to come out of the door when there was rain about and the little woman to appear if the air was dry.

"Oh but my Liege, we have recently contrived a magnificently accurate Diviner," said the tertius excitedly. "In association with the Official in Charge of Heat and Cold we have produced what we call a 'Wet and Dry Bulb Diviner'—"

"Summon your estimable Official in Charge of Heat and Cold," Uabhar cut in. "Let us hear what he has to say for himself."

The king did not appear to be as fascinated with the two glass bulbs on the metal stand as the tertius had hoped. The Official in Charge of Heat and Cold hurried to obey the royal summons, and showed the king a Heat-Measuring Device. A knopped glass stand upheld six vertical tubes, closed at their tops and filled with clear water. Inside each transparent tube rested a bubble of colored glass shaped like an onion resting upside down. "When the day is hot," said the official, "these colorful onions rise in the water. When it is cold, they fall."

The king tapped his foot restlessly. His gaze roamed. "Tell me—what are those men doing in that corner, with one of your glass onion tubes, a mirror and a bucket of ice?"

"They are performing an experiment, my Liege," said the official, "endeavoring to discover whether cold, like heat, can be reflected."

"Leading to the possibility of using cold as a weapon?" quizzed the king.

"Well my Liege, that had not crossed my mind, but now that you suggest it . . ." The voice of the official petered out into the deserts of uncertainty.

Ignoring the man, Uabhar turned to the primoris. "Where is the gentleman of whom you spoke earlier?"

"The Official in Charge of Predicting Storms?" the druid enquired in rasping tones. His spindly frame looked to be in danger of collapsing, yet he did not falter.

"The very one. Perhaps his 'experiments' will prove to be of some profit to Slievmordhu."

The Official in Charge of Predicting Storms demonstrated

his "storm glasses," the first of which was the Water Storm Glass. It consisted of a fat vitreous bulb containing water. An upward pointing spout, marked with a set of intervals, jutted from near the base of the enclosed bulb. "We employ the water level to measure air pressure," said the official. "When the level in the spout is high, this indicates that air is pressing on the water but lightly. Low pressure means that storms can be expected."

"Interesting," said Uabhar.

"And over here," said the Official in Charge of Predicting Storms, gesturing towards a second glass tube, three feet tall and filled to within four inches from the top with silvery cream, "we have the Quicksilver Storm Glass. More accurate than the Water Storm Glass, it is, my Liege, arguably the greatest triumph of the oracular workshop." The lower, open end of the tube was immersed in a bowl of quicksilver. "It is the heaviness of air on the quicksilver in the bowl that prevents the fluid in the tube from dropping any further. When air pressure is high, the weight of the air pushes on the quicksilver in the bowl, forcing it further up the tube. The quicksilver rises or falls as air pressure rises or falls. In this manner we can actually predict storms!"

"I commend you," said Uabhar in tones of genuine approval, to the relief of Secundus Acerbus. "This is indeed an advance. Continue."

As he moved away from the benches supporting the storm glasses the king murmured to the druid Acerbus, "That last weather-measuring devices seems promising. However, if the oracular workshop is to outdo the weathermasters and make them redundant, we shall need weather-*controlling* devices. When shall you show such apparatus to me?"

"We are still working on them, my Liege," Acerbus said uneasily.

"Make haste, my good man," said Uabhar. "Make haste. Time flows swiftly. If the devices are not ready very soon, the repercussions will be—" he paused "—quite horrendous."

The druid bowed. He felt his heart race, driven by terror.

The fear soon dissipated; he was not a man of deep or enduring sentiments. At sunset, seeking solitude so that he might compose another speech for the benefit of the druidry, Secundus Acerbus climbed to the highest tower of the Sanctorum, where he seated himself at a small desk and gazed out over the city.

"Yea verily," he said to himself experimentally, "the beginning is but the end, and the end is but the beginning. He that laughs shall weep, and he that weeps shall laugh most heartily. The poor can be called the most wealthy, while those who possess riches are—" He paused, bearing in mind the royal treasury and the necessity of casting the king in a good light, and chose his words carefully, "—*sometimes* the poorer."

Lifting his quill pen from its stand he dipped it in an inkpot and began to write on a sheet of papyrus. *Hoard not your treasures, good folk, but give them unto the Sanctorum, that the druids may glorify the Fates. For unless you abase yourselves and compliment them without cease, they may well feel injured in their pride and turn their backs upon you.*

Having scribbled his notes, the secundus replaced the quill in its holder and raised his head. From his eyrie he could look across to the other two hills of Cathair Rua, crowned with the palace and the Red Lodge. He watched the cloud-boats fade from pink to grey, and presently he looked down at the roofs spread out below. Far away, quite at the city's northern edge, the ragged roofs of hovels were already blanketed in darkness. Here and there a window opened a flame-yellow eye, before being shuttered to keep out the shadows.

꣓

That night one of the slum's inhabitants was woken by a strange dream. Her name was Mairead, and by day she served in the kitchens of the Red Lodge. The child, no more than ten Winters old, looked out of the attic window. She saw countless stars, sparks of ruby, sapphire and topaz, and ethereal banners of diamond dust, pinned to the black backdrop behind the towers. The topmost towers of palace and Sanctorum could be glimpsed, hovering at the hem of the sky. People were saying the druids were manufacturing fierce machines that could master the winds. Perhaps they would also be able to gather the stars and make them into necklaces for the gentlefolk. If that were so, Mairead thought, they would be sure to charge an exorbitant price for such ornaments, for the servants of the Fates used every means at their disposal to gather riches. The contrast between the poverty of the slums and the luxury of the Sanctorum—and the palace, too, for that matter—could not be more striking. In private, Mairead despised the avaricious druids, and most of the wealthy classes, too. The Red Lodge, however, was a different matter—Gearnach's Knights of the Brand treated women with courtesy, no matter that they be scullery maids, floor scrubbers, or pail emptiers, and the wages were better than those paid by palace or Sanctorum.

Why were the druids learning to master the winds? she wondered. Did they wish to supplant the weathermasters? The child loved the weatherlords. Every time they passed through Cathair Rua they gave her some pennies and a smile. They were generous to the needy and they maintained no prisons or clandestine machines of torture, like the palace and the Sanctorum. If anyone spoke against them she turned a deaf ear.

The girl was thirsty, so without disturbing the small brothers and sisters who shared her bed, she tiptoed downstairs to creep into the kitchen.

Hearing the susurration of voices emanating from the kitchen, she hesitated on the stair. Wandering John habitually slept beside the hearth—perhaps he was awake and maundering. Her eldest brother was a harmless half-wit, and she had no fear of him. Yet there was more than one voice, and they sounded unfamiliar. The child's pinched, triangular face peered out from behind a newel post, and she beheld Wandering John's form huddled on the floor as usual, not stirring, but breathing regularly. In the corner, however, five child-sized creatures that looked like women were grouped about the family's wooden water pail, in which they were bathing their tiny babies. Mairead held her breath. The women-beings, smaller than she was herself, had such funny faces that it was all she could do to prevent herself from laughing aloud and alerting them to her presence. She had never seen anyone like them before, but she knew, from the stories told in the evenings by the fire, that they must be el-dritch wights. And she knew also that wights took offense to being spied upon, so she remained very silent indeed, hardly daring to move lest she cause one of the floorboards to creak.

After washing their infants, the shrunken wives dried them beside the fire and swaddled them in grey rags, all the while murmuring amongst themselves in a tongue the watcher could not understand. Then one of the creatures said, "Hoose an' all is clean then, as it should. Here's sum-mat tae pay for't." And she dropped something into the wa-ter pail, *ker-plunk*.

Just then a gust of cold wind blew in beneath the door, and banged at the shutters. The wights lifted their long, drooping noses and sniffed the air. They looked around the room and glanced at one another, but the watching child remained hid-den, and so quiet that apparently they did not notice her. They muttered as they quickly tied their shawls about their heads, wrapped up their babies and gathered up their scanty belongings. Then they slipped soundlessly out the door, closing it as quietly behind them. The girl ran to the window, her bare feet making no noise on the floor of beaten dirt. Peering through a gap in the shutters, she saw the queer vis-itors flitting like somber wraiths, away from the hovel, into the night, and the moon was a silver seashell rising before them in the north, and Mairead wondered what it could be that had called them away.

Her mother always said the child had been born with some form of intuition. Be that as it may, as she gazed at the moon she felt that this was not the first time such a phenom-enon had manifested; wights moving northwards as if at-tracted by some compelling gramarye. It had happened before—yet not in this place. Not in this world, perhaps;

somewhere far off, further than could be comprehended; yet also, in an inexplicable way, somewhere close by. Some place out there in the Uile, deep amongst the stars.

When she went to the pail to scoop out a drink, the water was clean and pure, and a silver coin lay glinting at the bottom like a tiny moon; a threepenny bit . . .

The trows meanwhile hurried along the road in the night, sometimes cutting corners, usually keeping to the verges, which were overgrown with briars and nettles and rampant wildflowers. To the eyes of many mortal passersby, their transit would have seemed little more than the wind blowing through weeds. Far ahead of the wights, their road meandered through meadow and field, across brook and stream, over hill and vale, past farmstead and hamlet. Through the village of Market Deeping it went, and over the Canterbury Water before passing between the Eldroth Fields and the Mountain Ring, then rolling on towards the royal city of Narngalis.

Nights and days winked on and off.

Late in Averil, the Councilors of Ellenhall with eight weathermages who were not on the council and six brí-prentices, arrived at the village of Market Deeping, traveling from the Mountain Ring. As prearranged, they rendezvoused there with King Thorgild and his retinue, who were to escort them down the Mountain Road to Cathair Rua, so that all might attend King Uabhar's Mai Day feast of reconciliation.

It was a magnificent cohort that followed the winding road southwards from High Darioneth on the following morning. The crack knights of Grïmnørsland, the Shield Champions, formed the greater part of Thorgild's suite, led by their commander, Sir Isleif. Sunlight glinted from their helms, and from the polished trappings of their horses, while their pennons, emblazoned with the west-kingdom's emblem of a square-sailed longboat, fluttered skittishly in the breeze. No chariot or carriage was to be seen; the weather-masters, too, had elected to travel on horseback. Their chieftain, Storm Lord Avalloc Maelstronnar, was not amongst them; nor was his granddaughter Asrăthiel. The former, never in full health since the departure of his son Arran, had contracted an ague and had taken to his bed, while the latter had gone to Silverton. King Warwick had requested that his weathermage help with the investigations into the uncanny carnage. Ordinary methods of enquiry had met with no success, wherefore Asrăthiel would employ her weather senses to try to extract clues from the atmosphere. She possessed the ability to alter the direction of local winds, bringing her scents and sounds from afar; moreover, she could fearlessly seek out eldritch wights and question them.

Thirty weathermasters, old and young, in the company of a king's cortege, made a splendid spectacle, with their fine steeds, their fair raiment and their rich caparisons. Folk in every village along the way rushed out to gawk and exclaim as the riders passed, and in later days they would say amongst themselves that they had seen the flower of High Darioneth on that afternoon, and some made songs about the noble progress. A merry company it was, traveling in good comradeship. Thorgild, accompanied by his sons, was in a high humor.

"I look forward to the wedding of my daughter," he said to Baldulf Ymberbaillé-Rainbearer, who rode at his side. At sixty-eight years old the weathermage was still spry, and although twenty-four years separated his age from the king's, he handled his steed with skill no less consummate.

"Indeed, 'twill be a blithe occasion," was the mage's warm reply.

"And I expect joy of this Mai Day Feast also," said the red-bearded monarch. "I am only too happy to help mend the friendship between Rowan Green and Slievmordhu. 'Twas a trifling dispute, after all, and not worth strife."

Ymberbaillé nodded a polite acknowledgement of Thorgild's words. Yet his head drooped, and his gaze seemed pensive, as if he dwelled on some inner trouble.

Noting his companion's downcast manner, Thorgild said, "Fear not, my venerable friend. I suspect you have not yet cast off your suspicions regarding Uabhar's invitation. I tell you, I am convinced of his sincerity. Why should he deceive Rowan Green? The work of the weathermasters is essential to the economic welfare of all kingdoms. Your kindred are loved and respected throughout Tir. And besides, he has personally assured me that no harm will come to you. His family is to unite with mine when Kieran and Solveig are wed—what better guarantee can there be?"

"It is solely because of your *own* guarantee that we have accepted Uabhar's invitation, Thorgild," said Ymberbaillé. "Everyone knows your heart is as honest as oak. Had you not pledged your protection, we'd not have come on this journey."

"Not that you'll need protection!" Thorgild said genially. "There is no threat from Slievmordhu, other than possible ambush attacks from Marauders. Between the swords of my soldiers and your thunderbolts we would make short work of them, don't you think?"

He laughed hugely. Buoyed by the king's cheerfulness, the weathermage smiled.

The highway crossed a water-meadow gilded with a swaying haze of buttercups, then ascended a wooded hillside. Pied flycatchers, tree pipits and nuthatches made the woodlands ring with their eerily sweet lyricism, and through the leaves a honeyed breeze was wafting from the south. Further on the trees dwindled, giving way to cultivated fields. High hedgerows lined the lanes, blowzy with flowers. The sky opened to immensity, strewn with unkempt clouds against which the wind carelessly tossed handfuls of flying birds. All along the way the cavalcade traveled blithely, with the sunny weather matching their mood. It was not until they had crossed the border of Slievmordhu that matters began to veer strangely slantwise.

They were traveling down a muddy lane hedged with elderberry and overarched by purple-bubbling crab apple, the approach to the village of Keeling Muir, when one of the outriders of their vanguard came galloping back to deliver news. "A troupe of knights and soldiers rides this way, led by the Red Lodge's Commander-in-Chief, Conall Gearnach."

Upon encountering one another the northbound cavalcade and the southbound turned off the road, so that they might meet together in a fallow field. It was there, knee-deep in a froth of lacy-headed umbelliferae, meadowsweet, cow parsley, wild angelica, hogweed and saxifrage, that Gearnach removed his helm and riding gloves, stowed the helm beneath his arm, bowed low to the king, the princes and the weathermasters, and respectfully conveyed a message from his sovereign.

"King Uabhar sends most veracious greetings to King Thorgild Torkilsalven and the illustrious weathermages of Rowan Green. On the site of the ruined Dome in Orielthir, not far distant from where we now stand, a summer palace is being raised. As is well known, his majesty intends this palace to be a gift for Prince Kieran and his future bride. The first part of the construction has now been completed, and it is my liege's wish that King Thorgild and the princes of Grïmnørsland will diverge from their course and accompany me there, to view the triumphs that have been achieved so far. Prince Kieran waits in Orielthir to greet you, and Prince Ronin also. A three-day feast has been prepared in expectation of the royal visit, and I myself am to be the host."

"Conall Gearnach," said the king of Grïmnørsland, frowning like a cliff, "surely you have left out some part of your message. Are the weathermasters not invited to this banquet?"

"Not according to my orders, my Liege," the knight answered steadily, though his look was strained. "The feast for the esteemed mages awaits in the royal city, where King Uabhar looks forward to giving them a magnificent welcome."

"This seems strange. I know you, Two-Swords," said Thorgild. "Your demeanor betrays you. It works ill upon you to give me this message."

"Have no fear, Majesty," the knight replied, keeping his expression blank, "for your companions will be safe along the road despite being without your protection. King Uabhar has sent these men of his own household guard to shield them from marauding highwaymen. He has given his word that his soldiers will see them safe to Cathair Rua."

"Then why have I not been invited to the Red City?"

"Thorgild King, you are invited. This earlier welcoming feast for you is especially on account of the betrothal. My sovereign wishes to bestow the summer palace upon your daughter and her future husband, but you yourself have never yet seen the site. The feast will be held there, in bright pavilions on the grass, so that Princess Solveig's esteemed father may behold the splendor of what is to belong to her. It is all intended as a pleasant surprise in your honor. The site is not far out of your way, therefore the detour will not take long, and afterwards you may rejoin the weathermasters."

"I have given my word to accompany them to Cathair Rua," said the king somberly. "Why has Uabhar sent you? He knows I cannot refuse you."

"I am acting under the authority of my liege," replied Gearnach, although a shadow crossed his face and a vein throbbed sharply at his temple. "It is not for a soldier to demand reasons."

The weathermasters watched this exchange, hearkening in grim silence.

"Conall Gearnach, you invite his majesty to a banquet he cannot spurn," Thorgild's lord chancellor interjected angrily, "since he has sworn an oath never to decline your hospitality. You are a man of honor. Are you really prepared to do this? To place my sovereign in the position of being torn between two opposing vows?"

For one instant, Gearnach looked unwell. Then he rallied. "I obey my liege's commands, Lord," he said, now holding high his chin and meeting the gaze of the courtier. "Such is my bounden duty as a knight of Slievmordhu." He seemed unflinching, proud and certain as a carved figurehead, but the chancellor noted that the knight's fist so tightly clutched his mailed riding-gloves that the metal rings bit deeply, bruising the flesh.

Thorgild, his face flushed the color of oxblood, said, "It is a ruinous request you make of me, Conall. Will you not release me from this invitation?"

"I hold you to your pledge," said Gearnach unfalteringly, the sweat trickling down his brow, "to turn aside, and partake of this feast with me in Orielthir."

"Then you are a knave." The shoulders of the king sagged. Weariness and defeat settled on them like two monstrous crows. "Very well. I cannot break my vow, knight, although I hold it against you—and your liege-lord—that you ask this of me at this time. I will go with you."

Gearnach bowed, averting his face.

Then up spoke Galiene Maelstronnar. "Thorgild King," she said, "would you rather forsake some revelries, or your friends from Rowan Green who have journeyed this far on your promise alone?"

"I will not betray my friends, Lady Galiene," said Thorgild, "for I will send my best knights with you. The twenty-four of my Shield Champions who ride beside us, with brave Sir Isleif as their leader, shall guard the weathermasters. Besides, Uabhar himself has pledged safe conduct. In truth I am convinced you will be secure on the last leg of the journey."

Gearnach's features tightened as if he were being tortured. It was plain that his mind was in turmoil. "King Uabhar has invited your knights to Orielthir also, Sire," he said stiffly. "He is most fervent that they attend. I beg you to reconsider and allow them to come with us to the summer palace."

"I have spoken!" roared Thorgild. "I will not reconsider! You already have your way, knight. Now do not haggle with me like some street vendor."

Again Gearnach bowed before the monarch. Beneath his short crop of sweat-slicked hair, his skin gleamed as pale as bone, and his aspect seemed haunted.

Sir Isleif leaned from his saddle to speak privately to Thorgild. "Be not dismayed, my Liege," he said in an undertone. "We shall represent you in the task of guardianship and thereby will your honor be retained unblemished."

"If I am wrathful I am also sorrowful," the king softly replied. "I have been made foolish this day, and I will not forget it."

As Gearnach turned away, he inadvertently cast a look of anguish at Thorgild, which went unobserved.

While the riders remounted and proceeded to take their places in the new configurations, Thorgild's lord chancellor took aside the Commander-in-Chief of the Red Lodge. The courtier's elegant visage was dark, his anger clearly simmering. "Conall Gearnach, I would that you had not delivered this message that has confounded the father of Halvdan and Solveig."

"What would you have me do?" Gearnach demanded harshly. "King Uabhar insisted that I employ the power of Thorgild's pledge to me; it was not *my* wish! Would you have me forswear my loyalty to king and country? It is not of my own desire that I came here to claim the fulfilment of your sovereign's obligation. I am sorry for what has happened, but you shall see that no harm can come of it, for both parties shall certainly fare to banquet in security and good fellowship." He paused, then muttered as if half-choked, "Even so it is an evil charge that has been laid upon me, one that a man of weaker loyalty might resent. I had harbored no inkling of this separation of Thorgild from the weathermasters. Of all the outcomes of Uabhar's command, those that grieve me most sorely are the wronging of Halvdan's father and the probable sundering of my friendship with the prince. I can only hope that Halvdan will forgive me."

The lord chancellor made no reply, but merely sat astride his steed, brooding. On either side of the two men, bridle and stirrup jingled as horses jostled and negotiated. Uabhar's soldiers arranged themselves about the weathermasters and the Shield Champions, while Thorgild, with his retinue, prepared to depart eastward with Gearnach and his Knights of the Brand. At last the honorable courtier of Grïmnørsland spoke abruptly, without turning his face towards Gearnach. "Well, Two-Swords, it is an ill day's work you have done and no mistake, but you in your turn have been caught in a cleft stick by higher powers. I shall advise Prince Halvdan the fault is not yours, for no blame can be attached to a soldier's obedience." With no other gesture or word he rode off.

Thorgild and Gearnach with their entourages started along a byway that branched off eastwards, in the direction of Orielthir. The Red Lodge commander led the way, galloping ahead of the rest that they might not look upon his face and read his shame.

The twenty-four knights of Grïmnørsland's Shield Champions led the southbound procession, their turquoise tabards and peacock feather panaches in sharp contrast to the blood-dyes of Slievmordhu. Behind and beside the weathermasters rode the cavalrymen of Uabhar's royal horse guards, in scarlet tunics, steel cuirasses and backplates, and white leather breeches. Snowy plumes nodded atop their helmets, and their red cloaks fanned out to cover the haunches of their mounts.

As they began to move off, one amongst the Councilors of Ellenhall, Galiene, murmured to her companions within earshot, "Uabhar is the one responsible for this. We should turn back. Some kind of treachery is afoot."

But they countered, "To turn back would be to lose face. Besides, we are proficient fighters. What man can stand against us?"

They debated at length, but the majority of the weathermasters were confident in their ability to defend themselves if any threat should arise. Notwithstanding, the Storm Lord's daughter took no comfort in their assurances, and faced the future with a heavy heart.

XI

Treachery

On gusting draughts the clouds rush in,
There comes a prickling of the skin,
As if some turmoil doth begin,
And weathervanes on pivots spin.
The wind abandoned leaves is strewing—
A storm is brewing.

Dire darkness creeps to veil the sky,
A flash of light explodes on high,
While thunder's rumbles amplify,
And dogs commence to bark nearby;
They know that something is ensuing—
A storm is brewing.

A sudden raindrop smacks your face,
The wind steps up its steeplechase,
And rapidly you seek a place
To shelter from this maddened race.
Now there can be no misconstruing—
A storm is brewing.

—A SONG FROM HIGH DARIONETH

Meanwhile Asrăthiel Maelstronnar, sojourning at the old mining town of Silverton, had been aiding King Warwick's officers and officials with their inquiries into the macabre nocturnal slayings.

Silverton lay north of the Harrowgate Fells, on a lush flat in the valley of the river Sillerway. Forests of oak and laurel, holly and maple clothed the slopes of the vale, bordering on fields of flax—blue-flowered in Spring—and rolling sheep-meadows. Falcons and kestrels, with pinions outstretched, hung suspended over the grasslands, or glided on the cool currents. Sturdily built to withstand the bitter north wind, the cottages and smithies, and the moot-hall with its clock-tower, possessed windows that were few and small, walls made of logs chinked with moss. The slate roofs, patinaed with sage-green lichen, were sharply raked to slough snow. Since the heyday of the silver-mines, the village's population had dwindled. Abandoned cottages had fallen into disrepair, their roof-slates salvaged to repair others, the lumber of their walls used for firewood. Numerous old chimneys, however, still remained standing, like a weird forest of brick trees, their disused fireplaces now merely rectangular hollows gaping on either side of their bases. Some were inhabited by the harmless wights called dunters, whom nobody ever glimpsed, and who inexplicably made repetitive churning noises in the chimneys at nights.

Behind the buildings the mountains towered, row on row stepping up against blusterous skies. Their peaks, unimaginably lofty like unmoored islands in the clouds, dwarfed the houses with their snow-mantled grandeur. About a mile from the village green, downwind of the prevailing breezes, loomed the hulk of the last operating silver-smelter, its black funnel a landmark for miles around. No smokes and sparks now gushed from that honking vent; the furnace had been banked, and the fires smoldered low.

Few workers were left to attend to the coals. Most people feared to venture outdoors at all. These days they either stayed at home, with doors locked and windows barred, or they piled their belongings on wagons and left the village in a hurry, during daylight hours, heading south. The normally tranquil hamlet was besieged by the terror that stalked the hours of darkness.

The weathermage had heard the tales from frightened villagers, had viewed the bodies—packed in snow and ice in the cellar of a derelict granary until their funerals—of the victims. Their deaths had been extraordinarily swift and violent. Sickeningly, the executioners had possessed the skill of expert surgeons. Heads had been severed with machinelike precision, throats cut with mathematical accuracy, vital organs removed with clinical exactness and left neatly arranged about the corpses like appalling jewelry.

"Something unseelie did this," the living continued to declare. "Something fell."

Of themselves, the killers left no trace.

Locked in their homes and tormented by apprehension, the remaining villagers could not help speculating as to whether the attackers would ever grow strong enough to overcome the warding influence of the charms nailed above their doors and windows. If that happened, Silverton's entire population would be doomed. The conjectures of the king's captains and reeves took a further step; would the scourge, they wondered, spread wider? Already half-a-dozen isolated reports of similar atrocities in the region had come in from the sparsely inhabited mining centers of Silver End, Cold Ash and Trow Green.

Across this landscape, largely deserted by humankind except for bands of Narngalish soldiers on patrol, multitudes of furtive trows continued to pass during the evenings. Anyone brave enough to peer through a crack between the shutters might glimpse the ragged wights moving through the valley in the gloaming, like ghostly grey waves, making for the mountains—trow-men galumphing with an uneven stride, trow-wives in headscarves, with their swaddled babies on their backs, trow-boys and girls skipping awkwardly. Some halted in the vicinity of the village, but to the relief of the inhabitants they generally moved on, usually as quiet as the wind, but occasionally accompanied by the clinking of earrings and nose-rings and bracelets and all manner of silver ornaments. "The Grey Neighbors do not murder humankind," the villagers reminded their own children, "but sometimes they steal us away. Do not venture outside."

"Where do they come from?" the children wanted to know.

"Who can say? Of yore they dwelled around here in large numbers, but when the mines were shut down they emigrated."

"Why have they come back?"

"Who can say?"

⨾⨾

Far south of Silverton the company of weathermasters, escorted by the twenty-four Shield Champions and the contingent of Uabhar's household cavalry, spent the night at Keeling Muir. Early next morning they rose and saddled their horses, then traveled all day.

As they jogged along, Ryence Darglistel began to denounce King Uabhar to those of his kindred who rode near him. "Ó Maoldúin is a sly demon, for all his proclamations of openness and honesty," he declared. "No doubt he deliberately placed Thorgild Torkilsalven in that embarrassing position."

Baldulf Ymberbaillé said, "Aye, we must call him to account for that when we reach the city. A curious gambit indeed. I cannot fathom it."

"Ó Maoldúin is treacherous and slippery," said Ryence. "'Tis a great shame that men such as he should have empery over others. No compunction exists within the cauldron of his skull. We've all heard tales of his ruthlessness. There is no fondness in him. Why, his madness for power even extends to his own family. He requires his wife to bear him progeny only that he might command their absolute obedience."

"Hush!" exclaimed Galiene Maelstronnar, glancing back at Uabhar's household cavalry.

"I will not hush. Many a time you yourself have heard that song he repeatedly makes his songsters parrot at the court of Slievmordhu!" Mimicking the affected pronunciation of Uabhar's royal minstrels, Ryence warbled,

"Loyal sons, show gratitude for your begetting—
Never question, quarrel, argue or inquire.
For your father's word is law. You must defend it!
A man's honor lies in duty to his sire."

"The ditty gives me nausea," he went on. "If it is sung during our sojourn at the palace this time, I'll be sure to lose my temper and hurl some handy object at the singer."

Galiene murmured, "Keep your voice down. Soldiers are eavesdropping."

"Let them hear! Let them go running to Ó Maoldúin with tattletales if they wish to behave like obedient little syco-phants. If they've any brains they'll be agreeing with me, and not telling him. Besides, Ó Maoldúin is likely to behead the bearer of any tidings that don't suit him."

"I'd rather not go to the city," said Galiene. "Let us turn back."

"We cannot now turn back," said Ryence, "for to do so would be a sign of cowardice. Recall, there is general agree-ment amongst us on this matter. We must exhibit no such weakness, or we will lose face and our kindred will become subject to general derision."

"It is true we must continue." Baldulf Ymberbaillé agreed grimly. "We have come too far to withdraw. To retreat would bring dishonor upon Ellenhall."

At sunset they entered the gates of Cathair Rua. In the street they were met by a group of Uabhar's stewards, who saluted them courteously and gave them greetings.

"My lords and ladies of Rowan Green, I bring unfortunate tidings," said the head steward. "You must not proceed to the palace, but instead take the route to the Hall of the Knights. This night you must abide at the Red Lodge, because the palace is currently occupied by the vast entourage of King Chohrab II, and there is no room."

The weathermasters were taken aback. "I am astonished," Baldulf Ymberbaillé replied with severity. "We are accus-tomed to being housed at the palace when the king invites us to Cathair Rua."

The steward evinced regretful obsequiousness. "I have been commanded to inform you that his majesty King Uab-har did not expect the weatherlords to arrive so early. When a messenger brought news that the watchmen had spied a cavalcade approaching the city, his majesty was caught by surprise. Every chamber of the palace accommodates guests this night. However, the Red Lodge is well-provisioned. His majesty grants that, as the Knights of the Brand are away from home, the weathermasters may have the lodge to themselves. Butlers and pages and servants of all varieties will attend you and make the lodge comfortable, my lords." The steward stared at the Grïmnørsland cavalry. "How now, I see we are endowed with some unexpected guests. Welcome, Sir Isleif. Silken pavilions shall be raised close at hand, to house the Shield Champions."

"That they shall not," replied Sir Isleif. "I am charged with the care of the Councilors of Ellenhall and I will not abandon them. They and I will shelter beneath the same roof."

"The weatherlords have no need of your protection," protested the steward. "As his majesty's guests they are under the protection of his vow of hospitality. Besides, the red fortress is a guarantee of security."

"The Shield Champions will abide with us," said Baldulf Ymberbaillé. "Where we take our rest, so shall they."

The head steward's mien became grim, and his gaze as hard as flint. "So be it," he said presently, performing a gracious bow. "My sovereign will be offended by your want of trust in him, but it is not my place to argue with my betters."

At the mention of the Red Lodge the weathermasters and their chivalrous escort had raised their heads and stared upwards. High atop the third hill of Cathair Rua perched the residence of the Knights of the Brand, its western walls painted magnolia-gold by the lingering rays of the sinking sun. Behind its angular roofs great clouds towered, like snow-covered glaciers cracked open by upwelling streams of liquid platinum.

"Tell us, fellow, where are Uabhar's elite fighting men?" Sir Isleif enquired roughly. "Why is the Red Lodge untenanted?"

"They are engaged in training, away out in the countryside, my Lord, save for those few who have accompanied the Commander-in-Chief to Orielthir."

"Are we truly to be conducted to an empty hostelry at

journey's end?" asked Ryence. "Is that the way Uabhar honors the weatherlords?"

"My king will come to you as soon as he is able to absent himself from his obligations to Ashqalêth. He offers deepest apologies. If it were possible he would have sent his sons to greet you instead of my humble self, but alas, the princes are all from home at the present. Cormac and Fergus were expected to return yesterday, in good time for the feast, but we have received word that they have been delayed."

Then schooling his expression to neutrality, Sir Isleif shrugged and turned aside. Ryence scowled. For his part, Baldulf Ymberbaillé looked displeased, but squared his shoulders. "So be it," he said to the head steward. "Escort us to the Red Lodge."

As they followed Uabhar's retainers up the steep streets, Galiene said to Ryence and Baldulf, "Even more, now, am I certain some treachery is afoot. No monarch of Tir would harm guests beneath his own roof, at his own table. But we have been sent to the hostelry of the Knights of the Brand, and no guest-protection awaits us there, I'll warrant."

Her companions could find no reply, but suspicion was marked clearly on their faces.

The Red Lodge appeared to grow vertically from the summit of the hill, its facades perforated by thin windows and capped by crenelations. Of massive oaken logs was it constructed, and the walls were double-thickness. Before entering, Ryence stood on the threshold and looked out across the city. To the west a jumble of roofs and streets sprawled across the two other hills. The lodge was built at the extreme eastern edge of Cathair Rua, and the city ramparts passed close under it, right at the foot of the incline. Eastwards, outside the walls of the metropolis, rose a fourth hill, lower, uninhabited and bracken-covered. Beyond it gentle, treeless slopes fell away into a shallow valley, now steeped in the deep gloom of evening.

As they entered the building Sir Isleif took careful note of the architecture. After his Shield Champions had explored the accommodations, the knight said to the weathermasters,

"To allay any fears that might trouble you, let me tell you that this place is stoutly built and well fortified, and anyone who was besieged herein could easily defend himself. It is built of sturdy oak, dense-grained. Neither barb nor blade can penetrate. Furthermore, as you will have noted, the entrance door opens into corridors too narrow to allow more than one or two intruders at a time, and if that intruder should be armed, he shall have no leeway to swing his weapons."

"Speaking of weapons," said Ryence, "there is not one in this house, despite that it is a dwelling-place for soldiers. Not a spear or sword; not so much as a knife, except a few blunt blades in the kitchens, perhaps tools for slicing butter."

"Strange," murmured Galiene. "One would have expected a few old notched swords about the place; a mended spear or two, perhaps."

"Now I too am growing suspicious," said Baldulf Ymberbaillé. "I, for one, will not sleep tonight."

They took their supper in the main hall. The walls were decorated with scarred battle-shields and stuffed stags' heads whose glass eyes stared with blind horror into an eternity they would never know. Uabhar's liveried servants waited on them; a staff of elderly butlers and aged footmen who, one might almost suppose, had been selected on the basis of their limited life expectancy. Galiene could summon no more than a meager appetite. King Thorgild's knights stayed quiet and vigilant, but many of the weathermasters grumbled about the insults heaped upon them by the King of Slievmordhu. Ryence Darglistel was amongst the most vociferous. By the time the meal was over he had invented a parody of the king's favorite song, which, without regard to proprieties, he began to sing.

"Even if it means forswearing other issues
Or denying what you selfishly desire,
You must never contravene your father's wishes
A man's honor lies in duty to his sire.

> Though you're forced to be unfaithful to your sweetheart,
> Or required to cast your kinsman in the fire
> Be assured your reputation stays untarnished
> A man's honor lies in duty to his sire!"

Some of his companions laughed, but their laughter was uneasy.

Beyond the oaken walls of the Red Lodge the sun incinerated itself, burning the sky to embers and ashes.

※

That same night, near Silverton, Asrăthiel was walking along a leafy lane in the broad valley of the river Sillerway. All her senses were a-tingle; beneath a clear sky that rinsed the meadows with the cool radiance of stars, she was looking for something wicked.

Wights, by their nature, must always tell the truth, but so far even they had not been able to explain the spate of unusual murders. King Warwick's officials had encouraged the people of the region to discover and question seelie entities—household brownies, hobgoblins of the hearth, lake-maidens, buttery spirits, siofra, and so forth—but to no avail. By various ingenious methods some folk had managed to detain and interview a few of these incarnations but, even when the wights' prevarications were unravelled, it appeared they genuinely had no notion of the agencies behind the killings . . . although one could never be entirely sure when supernatural beings were concerned.

Seelie wights had proved uninformative. Asrăthiel, however, being invulnerable, could seek *unseelie* wights, on condition she remained wary, and as long as she avoided the most dangerous. If she were seized by a carnivorous waterhorse, for example, and carried away to some underwater lair, immunity to hurt and death would not save her. Only her ability to summon the forces of nature could extricate her from such a predicament.

It was notoriously difficult to locate creatures of eldritch at one's own behest; they were secretive and elusive, intent on their own affairs. The unseelie kind were not only unwilling to aid humankind, they were actively hostile. Hoping to catch one by surprise and avoid being caught, the damsel, therefore, was moving as silently as possible, given that it was hard to see in the dark, and she must rely on her brí senses for guidance.

Night was a perilous time for mortalkind to leave the safety of threshold and hearth. Over in a meadow to the left, weird strings of tiny lights appeared without warning, and Asrăthiel saw a substantial feast laid out on the grass, attended by pint-sized revellers. When she stumbled on a stone, which rolled away under her foot with a clatter, the entire scene vanished. Surly, inquisitive, or baleful eyes peered at the weathermage from the tangle of shrubs and briars bordering the lane; sulphur-yellow, acid-green and cyanide-blue; some slitted, like cats' eyes, others round like the orbits of fishes. Her ears were assailed by bursts of monstrous laughter, screams, weeping, giggling and snatches of wild music. As soon as she stopped and reached out her hand, or called softly to the hedge-denizens, the eyes would be snuffed out like lamps and silence would abruptly fall.

Though they refused to cooperate, the wights had no hesitation in assailing the human traveler. Hands reached out from amongst roots and grabbed at her ankles; she kicked them away. Grinning hobyahs swung down out of overhanging trees and pulled her hair; she slapped them, sometimes muttering rhymes to drive them off. The difficulty lay in keeping unwanted attentions at bay while simultaneously inviting discourse; an exasperating conundrum. As a matter of course she carried wight-warding effects on her person, in addition to a covered basket for the purpose of temporarily confining intractable wights if the occasion arose.

The weathermage was approaching a bridge spanning the river Sillerway when all of a sudden a thin, stunted fellow wearing yellow breeches, a green jacket, and a pointed red hat sprang into the lane. He loped ahead of her, jumping and frolicking in the direction of the water, which could be heard gushing through the darkness beyond. Greatly surprised, Asrăthiel hesitated, wondering whether she ought to press on or retreat, given that the entity was clearly a pixie and therefore likely to be intent on leading her astray. People who were pixy-led might wander lost for hours, even in familiar territory—often until dawn, when cock-crow put an end to the spell. Resolved to carry out her important mission, however, and having faith in her own abilities and talismans, the damsel decided to walk on. As an added precaution she whisked her cloak from her shoulders and redonned it inside out, since reversal of one's clothing was said to be an efficacious ward against being pixy-led.

Boldly she continued on her way, the pixie always a few steps ahead. Having arrived at the river, the mannikin tarried at the bridge's entrance, where he was bounding back and forth and cutting ludicrous capers as if barring Asrăthiel's way. The weathermage, however, was not to be discouraged and she marched resolutely toward the wight, who never let up his nimble clowning. As she set foot on the bridge the pixie darted towards her, whereupon she swiftly leaned down, scooped him up with both hands dropped him into her basket. Quickly she secured the cover, delighted to have avoided the danger of being pixy-led while simultaneously obtaining a source of information.

Though capacious, the container was not big enough to allow the wight to move around, and he was obliged to sit without stirring. He was motionless, but not quiet, for as soon as the lid shut he began jabbering away in some outlandish tongue. The weathermage set down the basket, seated herself beside it, and attempted to ask questions through the wicker-work, but no matter how she cajoled she could get nothing out of her captive save for his continuous stream of babble, which she was unable to understand. At length the pixy's flow of gibberish petered out and Asrăthiel conjectured he had exhausted his speeches or withdrawn in sullen protest, or possibly nodded off. The mysterious silence was intriguing, and she could not help wanting to know what the wight was up to, so to satisfy her curiosity she carefully lifted the lid a fraction, and peered inside.

The basket held nothing.

She could only smile ruefully and acknowledge that she had somehow been gulled. How the dwarfish personage had extricated himself was a puzzle; perhaps he was a shape-shifter who could make himself small enough to thread his way through the woven canes. The damsel looked up at the clear sky and allowed the immensity of its glittering, sable dome to saturate her consciousness; then, with a sigh she rose to her feet, picked up her basket and continued on her mission.

The final ray of daylight twinkled through a flaw in the glass of one of the palace windows. Within a large and ornate chamber, portly King Chohrab II was reclining on a couch, surrounded by his courtiers. He was clad in robes colored tangerine and yolk-yellow, his curly brown hair caught in a jeweled turban, his fat fingers carapaced with rings of brass and red-gold. The Ashqalêthan emblem of the wheel patterned the rich fabric of his tunic. A goblet stood on a small table near his elbow, and an attentive butler waited nearby, carafe in hand. For the entertainment of Ashqalêth's ruler, dancers were flinging themselves about the floor.

Chohrab's interlude was interrupted by the precipitous entrance of his host. Startled, he hoisted himself to his slippered feet. "What's amiss?"

The musicians and dancers ceased their efforts.

"I bear news, my brother," said Uabhar, brushing invisible dust off his sleeve. Turning to his lord chancellor, who followed close at his heels, he said, "Dismiss these clowns."

The lord chancellor snapped his fingers, shouting, "Begone," and the performers scattered in retreat, bowing and scraping, hastily retrieving the silk flowers that had fallen from their costumes as they whirled.

"The Councilors of Ellenhall have lately arrived," Uabhar told Chohrab, "and reliable sources inform me that they intend to do us mischief."

The southern king gasped, clasping his hands in consternation. "Ill news indeed!"

"With Conall Gearnach and my Knights of the Brand away, I am poorly defended," Uabhar continued, running his index finger around the inside of his heavy golden collar. "I ask you, brother, to allow your matchless Desert Paladins to make camp around the Red Lodge wherein the weathermasters are installed."

"What? Are they in the Red Lodge?"

"Yes, yes. They demanded a well-fortified hostelry. The request seems strange to me, but as a good host I am prepared to go out of my way to indulge my guests, even when they plot against me. My only wish is to make everyone comfortable, but alas, I am so often rewarded with ingratitude and disloyalty. Well, friend and ally, will you deploy your knights around the Red Lodge?"

"Of course," Chohrab said quickly. "It is the least I can do."

"Keep your worthy knights well plied with liquor, at my expense. My coffers are open to you."

"Do you think it wise," Chohrab said nervously, "to let the Paladins get drunk? Matchless they are indeed, in battle, but they can be—" he hesitated "—they can be somewhat *unruly* when in their cups. Overexcitable, one might say."

"If your men's wrath grows, fed by rumor of the weathermasters' foul deeds and fouler purpose, there is nought I can do about it. I would be offended if you were to refuse my generosity."

"Even so. Then, let it be!" Despite his acquiescence, the desert king continued to wrinkle his brow in perplexity.

Uabhar noted this. "You were right, brother-in-arms," he said, sighing. "I ought to have hearkened to your advice in the first instance." Distractedly he scratched his ear.

Chohrab's eyebrows collided.

"Do you not recall? You advised me the weathermasters were becoming too dangerous," Uabhar explained. "And you were not mistaken. It occurs to me they must be stopped."

Between astonishment, righteous anger, excitement and dismay, Chohrab was lost for a verbal response. Instead, jowls quivering, he took a large swallow from his goblet.

Unseen behind a free-hanging arras stood Queen Saibh, thirty-five winters old, though her loveliness was barely tarnished by years and sorrow. A slender, glimmering shadow, she had entered the room alone, moments before, in her customary unobtrusive way. Her presence had not been marked. Now she paused, listening, her hand pressed tightly to her mouth. After hearing this exchange she glided away on silent feet, as quietly as she had arrived, in search of her most trusted courtier.

Fedlamid macDall was a brave man, named after the harper of a legendary king. He was of an age with her; indeed, she had known him since childhood. It was he whom she dispatched straightway into the starlit city, across the vale and up to the slopes of the third hill, whereon stood the knights' hall. Before midnight macDall returned with his report, presenting himself before his liege-lady in her private rooms where she sat weeping, attended only by two of her youngest handmaidens. Bowing on bended knee at her feet, the queen's confidant kissed her hand and told her, "The knights of King Chohrab are indeed setting up tents around the Red Lodge, and wineskins are passing freely amongst them, supplied by stewards of Slievmordhu."

Saibh appeared slight and frail as she leaned upon the arm of a massive chair heavily carved with foliage and grotesqueries. Her arms were two pale wands, and her tears glistened like pearls swinging from fine silver chains.

"It was impossible for me to convey your message to the weatherlords," her servant continued. His tone was gentle, and he looked upon the distraught woman with grave compassion. "Forgive me. I would never be able to pass unmarked through the pickets, for I am known as a member of your ladyship's household, not of Uabhar's, and I do not know the passwords. Besides, the lodge itself is sealed."

"*You* need never ask me for forgiveness," whispered the queen, and her countenance expressed more than words could convey. She handed macDall an envelope, fastened with her own seal imprinted in red wax. "My heart aches, Fedlamid," she said softly, "when I speculate upon what wickedness the king might be plotting this very night. Without delay you must ride to Thorgild at the site of the Summer palace in Orielthir. I will send no message by the semaphore, else Uabhar will discover me. Take my best horse. Ride hard, dearest of all friends," she said. "Ride swift."

MacDall bowed his blond head and kissed her hand again, most tenderly. "At your service, my lady," he said as he tucked the envelope inside his doublet. "The wind shall not outstrip me." His eyes reflected two bright flames of candle-light as he gazed upon his queen while taking his leave.

There was scant sleep to be had in the palace that night. Even as Saibh was bidding farewell to her messenger, her husband, far off in another suite, was in private conference with Primoris Asper Virosus.

"It is as I projected," declared the king. "The Councilors of Ellenhall have arrived, and are established in the Red Lodge. I have them locked in my very fist."

"The two best of them are not in your fist," said the druid, "the Maelstronnar and his granddaughter. They are still at large. What will you do about them, eh?"

"Avalloc is old, and diseased now, too, from all accounts. He's grown feeble. As for the chit, why, she's only a woman, Virosus! If the day ever dawns when a woman stands between the likes of us and the greater glory of the Fates, that will be the day men's brains turn into tweeting birds and take wing out of their skulls."

The primoris merely grunted.

"By morning," Uabhar progressed, "we shall have trumped up a charge against the weather-meddlers. Most importantly it must be publicly *seen* and *understood* that they deserve the fate of criminals. Soon they shall abide in my dungeons, unable to interfere in the affairs of Sanctorum and State, leaving the way clear for us to make our next move."

"Send someone to observe them," wheezed the ancient. "It would be best to know what they are at. What if they have grown suspicious, and are using their powers to call storms upon us?"

"I shall dispatch one of my servants and one of Chohrab's," said Uabhar. "Should the puddlers be at some activity that could be deemed treacherous, the buttermilk ninny of Ashqalêth will more easily be goaded to action if he learns of it from one of his own lackeys."

"Whoever is chosen, let them be nimble and circumspect," said the druid. "They must pass unnoticed to the walls of the lodge, and look upon the weathermasters without being seen."

"Whom would you recommend?" the king asked. "No doubt you are expert in selecting the most athletic and enterprising agents for this kind of work, since your own affairs require the gathering of much intelligence."

Apparently oblivious of the king's dig at his character, which, according to the precepts of the Sanctorum, ought to be the very model of shining integrity, the druid replied, "Two men with the cunning, speed and slipperiness of rats would be appropriate. I would recommend that fellow of yours who does your spying on the lord high chancellor. As for the other, let Shechem choose; it makes little difference."

Uabhar made no response, pretending to be lost in thought as an alibi for the snub; but later he did act on the druid's suggestion.

To the judiciously appointed agents Uabhar said, "Go discreetly and spy on the weathermasters. Bring back news of their doings."

Two men in dusky garments acknowledged their orders, bowed and slipped away with practiced stealth.

❧

A southwest wind blew the clouds over the river valley, near the hamlet of Cold Ash in northern Narngalis. Briefly, Asrăthiel paused in her climb. In the gloom beneath the cloud-blotted sky, barely tinged by starlight, she could hardly make out her surroundings. She was ascending a steep slope at the edge of the vale, heading for a rocky crag that loomed black against the feeble pallor of the heavens. From a distance, when regarding that crag, she had noted a certain quality that hinted at the presence of glamor. Few human beings would have picked up the clue; weathermasters were amongst those few. After doffing her cloak she looked again at the crag, and this time she saw something different.

Fragments of dried four-leafed-clover and hypericum were stitched inside the lining of her cloak, which meant that when she was wearing it she could not be deceived by common eldritch enchantments. Without the cloak, she perceived a faint glow emanating from the window of a rude stone hut perched high on the brink of a cliff, and instantly guessed she was seeing some unseelie trap.

A plan formed in her mind.

Deliberately she folded the cloak, placed it in her basket so that she would continue to see the illusion, and clambered up the hillside.

The feigned hut's single room, with its unlined stone walls, contained—or appeared to contain—a fireplace in which bright flames crackled, three stools, a pile of kindling, and some hefty logs for the fire. After entering, Asrăthiel loosened the strings of a pouch tied to her girdle and took out handfuls of a coarse mixture, which she strewed about the room's perimeter. It was *salisfrax* she was sprinkling, a carlins' preparation; primarily a blend of salt, iron filings, and ash-wood shavings. All around the seeming walls she scattered the compound, but not across the fake threshold.

Asrăthiel knew the night air was bitingly cold this far north, though being invulnerable she felt no discomfort. Nevertheless, she stoked the fire with fresh sticks, sat down in front of the grate as if she was warming herself at the flames, and waited.

Presently she drifted into a doze.

The door flew open with a bang and a duergar barged straight in, but though the damsel woke with a start she remained steadfastly in her seat, disciplining herself to show no sign of surprise, no evidence of alarm.

Dressed in a badger-skin coat, galligaskins of rabbit-skin, and a hat made of bracken adorned with a partridge-feather, the swarthy dwarf stood barely higher than a man's knee. He was barrel-chested and sturdy, with bedraggled, soot-colored hair and an even sootier beard. For a moment he glared at Asrăthiel, then he strode across to the stool on the other side of the fire and sat down.

The weathermage guessed what would follow.

Before the malevolent manifestation could begin to spring his trap she leaped up, slammed the door and dashed a quantity of salisfrax across the threshold. Uttering a cry of rage the dwarf lunged at his captor, but brandishing the bag of salisfrax in his face she warned, "Do not approach me, wight, for I have the power to overcome you."

"Ih siue arleske," the dwarf threatened in guttural accents.

"I am a weatherlord!"

Growling, the hostile creature drew back, while keeping well away from the strewn mixture.

"If you answer my questions," said the damsel, "I will set you free."

Impaling her with a look of hatred, the dwarf kept his mouth as tightly sealed as a snail in its shell, but neither did he move from the spot, so, without further ado, she proceeded to cross-question him, while the fire died down until it went out altogether.

An hour or so later the damsel was forced to admit defeat. The duergar proved as devoid of knowledge, or as intractable, as the rest.

"Go then," she said at last, sweeping the scatterings of salisfrax away from the doorway with a leafy branch from the bundle of kindling. The duergar hurled himself over the threshold and charged out into the night, spitting invective in some foreign tongue.

A light breeze arose, and far away an owl hooted. The damsel wrapped her cloak around her shoulders and looked about. She was standing at the summit of a crag, on the very lip of a gorge. The hut and the fire were nowhere to be seen; the four walls had not been walls at all, but empty air. On the ground, a scattering of salisfrax in the shape of a rectangle was the only sign of the glamor. Where the stools had been, now crouched three grey stones. To one side, exactly where the logs of firewood had lain, the gorge plunged fifty feet straight down to a rocky stream.

"How many human lives have you taken with your death-traps, duergar?" Asrăthiel wondered aloud. It gave her some small satisfaction to know that it would grievously provoke the dwarf to have been mastered by a human being. Kneeling, she scratched furrows in the thin soil within the non-existent walls. Then she withdrew a handful of seeds from another pouch at her girdle and planted them; the germs of four-leafed clover.

Vexed at her failure to extract a useful testimony from the wight, she set off down the hill to continue her hunt.

≈

It was after midnight. Within the Red Lodge, the Councilors of Ellenhall, awaiting the consideration of their royal host, rested uneasily. By unspoken agreement no one lay down to sleep. The sounds of a gathering of military forces filtered through the log walls from outside; men's voices, the jingle and clank of metal, the tramp of boots.

"Why do they bring men-at-arms so close to the Red Lodge?" they asked amongst themselves. "And why so late at night?"

"This is the Hall of Knights," answered Baldulf Ymber-baillé. "Perhaps those soldiers have recently arrived after some long march. I daresay they would be quartered here if it were not for our presence."

"Lord Rainbearer, let my knights bar all the doors and windows," Sir Isleif said suddenly.

"Whyfor?" asked Baldulf.

"My heart tells me something ruinous is imminent this night. Let us fortify this place."

"To do so would be discourteous to our host."

"Better to risk offending him than hazard the welfare of those who are under my protection," said the knight. "My charge is to guard you. Will you agree to this precaution?"

A vote was taken, after which the windows and doors were barred. Subsequently the entire company felt more at ease. As the night deepened, some of the weatherlords engaged in conversation, while others sat in contemplative silence, allowing their senses to wander out beyond the massive walls of oak into the currents of the upper atmosphere. Ryence Darglistel discovered a checkered board and a casket of heavy chess-pieces. Each piece was cast from bronze and finely detailed, spiky with weapons and crowns. He and Galiene arranged the toys in formation, and began to amuse themselves with a game.

Meanwhile, two figures swathed in drab raiment glided through the encampment of Chohrab's Desert Paladins, moving barely noted amongst the groups of carousing soldiers. Easily the spies proceeded, because they knew the passwords.

Far away, Fedlamid macDall on horseback, who had been picking his way through the streets at a leisurely pace to avoid attracting attention, burst at last from the city gates and began galloping full pelt towards Orielthir.

A cool breeze rippled the velvet cloak of the dark, and a few desultory panes of cloud slid across the stars. When the two spies reached the hill's summit, where the walls of the Red Lodge soared out of the barren ground, they prowled, keeping to the shadows cast by torch-flame and fitful star-gleam.

"The Hall of the Knights is well fortified," muttered Chohrab's henchman. "The door is barred, the windows few, narrow and bolted shut. I do not see how our task is to be accomplished."

A rod of yellow light beaming forth overhead caught the attention of Uabhar's man. "Look there," he said, pointing to a narrow window, high up, not much more than an arrow slot. Beneath the window an unyoked cart stood abandoned. "Clamber upon the cart's sides," Uabhar's lackey urged. "Try to reach that embrasure. I will help you."

Taking this advice, Chohrab's henchman vaulted up to the floor of the conveyance and began to climb.

On the other side of the wall, bathed in firelight and candle-glow, Galiene and Ryence played chess in silence. As her opponent picked up a barbed bronze knight and prepared to move it to another square, a movement caught the attention of Galiene, and she glanced up. Following her gaze, Ryence glimpsed a face peering in at a high and narrow slot. To add to the insults heaped upon them, they were being surreptitiously watched! Sudden indignation seized him and he hurled the chess piece at the spy. His accuracy was unerring. A hoarse scream ripped through the quietude, and the face disappeared from view.

"Someone was spying on us from that window," cried Ryence. He had jumped onto the table, scattering the chesspieces, and was craning his neck in an endeavor to stare through the lofty aperture. The weathermasters listened in consternation as the agonized shrieks faded into the night.

"What is Uabhar about?" growled Engres Aventaur. "He now sends hawkshaws to observe us secretly. One can only deduce that his intent is hostile!"

"I believe we are all in agreement," Galiene said vehemently, stepping forward and flourishing her clenched hand to emphasize her words. "He wishes us ill. I am certain this is some trap. We must break free from here as soon as possible."

Sir Isleif, who had by this time hoisted himself to the window by way of a couple of rusted wall-hooks and managed to obtain a good view of the surrounds, leaped lightly down to the tabletop. "The lodge is encircled by armies. They wear the harness of Ashqalêth. Their banners proclaim them to be the Desert Paladins."

Several voices were raised in alarm. "Chohrab's knights! How came this to pass? What can we do?"

"We must summon levin bolts," some cried.

"Stay! We have no substantial cause to take action against Uabhar or Chohrab," Baldulf Ymberbaillé said authoritatively. "They have not actually made any aggressive move against us. We must remain vigilant, that is all. Let us not allow passion to cloud our judgment. Neither of the two kings has reason to launch an attack upon the Councilors of Ellenhall. We have not wronged them in any manner."

"I ask again, do you truly believe that the madman Uabhar Ó Maoldúin requires reasons?" demanded Galiene. "It was foolish of us to come here. I suggest we begin weather-wielding without delay. It will take a long time to alter the patterns sufficiently to brew a squall with enough impetus to aid us."

The usual well-memorized admonition hung unspoken between them: *The first lesson learned by a prentice is that any upset to the natural equilibrium causes far-reaching consequences.*

"Such a course is not to be undertaken lightly," said Baldulf. "I urge you all to use caution. We must be certain there is a threat before we act."

"For myself," said Ryence, his gaze flicking over the spilled chess-pieces, "I am certain."

"I too," said Galiene. "But it is slow work we have before us. Let us commence without delay!"

❧

Through a forest of maples in the Sillerway Valley Asrăthiel wended her way, returning to her lodgings after a fruitless expedition. When she glimpsed furtive movement among the trees, some little way off the trail, she glided noiselessly towards it, hoping to spy some entity that would give her the information she sought. Her hopes dwindled when she saw that the small, stooped figures trudging through the forest were merely three straggling trows, probably amongst the last of their kind to journey northwards.

In desperation she bade them halt, which they did, peering at her with mournful eyes from beneath their ragged scarves and lank fringes of hair. Silver hoops dangled from their ears; silver rings glinted on their long, skinny fingers.

"Chile o' the Wind Laird's son, what with us?" they said.

"I beg you to tell me who is killing the villagers, and why, and how they can be defeated."

"Cannae tell what we dinnae ken," they said, beginning to move off.

"Stay! Why are you in such a hurry?"

"Sulver, madam, bonny sulver," they said. "Sulver's a callin'."

"Where is all this silver?"

"North," they said.

Asrăthiel would have asked the wights to be more precise in their description of their destination but at that moment her brí senses, which were extended far out into the night in every direction, picked up a trembling like the vibration of a cold, thin wire. Far away, something unusual was happening in the air. . . .

Refocusing on the task at hand, the damsel looked around for the trows, but only darkness lingered there with her beneath the trees.

※

An emaciated layer of vapor passed over the canopy of stars. Its dilute shadow flitted across the roofs of the Red Lodge, over the numerous houses and streets of Cathair Rua, and up another hillside, like a fleeing ghost. For an instant the cloudlet blotted the stars from the window of Uabhar's brightly lit salon, where he abided in the company of King Chohrab II and a bevy of courtiers whose customary languor was beginning to desert them. Whispers were circulating. The sovereign's attendants detected an undercurrent of suppressed violence, and their usual sense of wary tension was escalating.

"Prithee, dear brother, enjoy some more of my best wine," said Slievmordhu's king. With his own hands he decanted ruby liquor into a crystal chalice for his guest.

"My knights have successfully contained the weathermasters and there will be no mischief from *them* this night," Chohrab murmured indistinctly, his elbows sagging upon the arms of his chair. Propping his head on the heel of his hand, he yawned. "The hour is late."

"On the contrary, the night is but a pup," said Uabhar with energy. He lounged back against the cushions of his seat. "Allow me to call upon my favorite jongleurs to entertain you. I implore you not to deprive me of your cordial company so early in the evening." Slievmordhu's sovereign appeared to be afire with some kind of inner excitement, but his visitor was too overcome with weariness or doctored wine, or too unobservant to notice.

Chohrab raised a be-ringed hand in protest. "No more entertainment," he began, but his mumbled objections were interrupted by a disturbance outside the door.

"A plague upon't! Discover the cause of that annoyance," Uabhar barked at his gentlemen-in-waiting.

As a courtier opened the door, a figure came stumbling in. The man was clutching bloodied hands to his face. Glistening scarlet streams flowed between his fingers, down his arms and onto his swarthy clothing. Behind his shoulder a second visitor entered the room.

"Ádh! Ádh!!" howled the injured fellow. "They have blinded me!"

The court roused entirely from its fretting listlessness.

"Hold your noise in the royal presence, churl!" the king's secretary hissed into the ear of the injured man.

"What has happened, Balor?" barked Uabhar. He leaned forward eagerly, while the unwounded visitor, his own servant, answered the question, and the other sobbed and moaned restrainedly.

"One of the weathermasters threw something at him, and put out his eye."

A strange look passed fleetingly across the visage of Uabhar. Only his lackey, Balor, was in a position to witness it. The expression was at odds with the king's words; otherwise the servant might have construed it as a leer of triumph.

Uabhar leaped up, his eyes blazing. Flinging back his head he uttered a yell of wild laughter. "Hearken!" he cried. "At last the facts are revealed. It is apparent that the weathermasters have journeyed here not for the purpose of mending rifts, but in order to incite insurrection. See, they have seriously injured Ashqalêth's messenger, and no doubt they would have harmed my own man if given the chance. By this act the weathermasters have shown they intend to harm my country. King Chohrab, will you stand side by side with Slievmordhu?"

"Even so!" the inebriated monarch shouted virtuously, swaying in his chair and brandishing his chalice on high. Wine slopped over the rim and spattered his clothing.

"In that case," cried Uabhar, "let the soldiers of both countries encircle the troublemakers in the Red Lodge! I will command them myself!" He exited the chamber in a swirl of velvet and the furry husks of slain animals, shouting over his shoulder, "Follow me, brother Chohrab!"

Outside the palace, the north wind began to rise.

❧

Orders were relayed to the captains of the Desert Paladins and Uabhar's men-at-arms. Eager were the men, and avid for action. Their blood fired with potent liquor and malicious gossip about the weathermasters, they threw aside their wineskins, grabbing hold of weapons and flaming torches. Following their two sovereigns, they rushed en masse up the hill towards the Red Lodge. As they ran they uttered savage yells and shrill war-whoops, brandishing halberds and swords that threw off sudden glints of firelight.

Inside the building Sir Isleif ordered his knights to draw

their swords and take up positions of defense at the front door and every other weak point in the fortress. The Councilors of Ellenhall paused in their gesturing and expression of vector commands. They stood quietly, their hands at their sides, listening to the crescendo of approaching noise. After the din reached a cacophony, it subsided, tamed by the harsh shouts of the captains. The weatherlords did not require access to a window in order to know that a mighty crowd of men stood tightly pressed all around the walls of the Red Lodge, hemming them in with a forest of bright blades and incandescent brands.

Taking Sir Isleif's place atop the table, Ryence raised his head towards the narrow window and cupped his hands around his mouth, shouting loudly into the taut hush, "Who is it that confronts us in hostile fashion?"

"It is I, Slievmordhu," came Uabhar's reply. "My warriors surround you. Come out and surrender yourselves, and we will wreak no harm upon you."

"We have done nothing to merit such threats," roared the weathermage. "Of what offense do you accuse us?"

"You conspire with Warwick Wyverstone to overthrow the kingdoms of the south and the east."

As one, the weathermasters gasped. They gaped in amazement at each other, outraged at this accusation. "How dare Uabhar lay such perfidious charges against us!" they burst out. "Conspiracy? Schemes to throw down Slievmordhu and Ashqalêth? Either the man defames us for hidden reasons, or he is insane!"

"We deny your allegations," Ryence shouted in fury. "We deny them utterly."

"It is too late for protestations of innocence," came the king's reply. "We have proof of your guilt. You have betrayed your own schemes by assailing King Chohrab's loyal subject. Yield now and become my prisoners. I will treat you well, after you vow not to employ your powers in support of Narngalis."

Baldulf urged his companions, "For the sake of our lives, we must give ourselves up!"

"Nay!" hissed Galiene. "Uabhar is ruthless. He would not

settle for vows, even if we were prepared to make them. If he takes us captive there is no doubt he will fetter or cripple us to render us incapable of weather-wielding."

"You think too highly of him," said Engres. "He is mad. I daresay he would not hesitate to put us to the sword. I vote that we shall not surrender."

The other weathermages nodded and murmured in reluctant agreement.

"Your charges are unfounded," Ryence shouted to the slit window. "We will not yield you our freedom." To his companions he said aside, "Resume your labor! There is no time to be lost!" They took up their weather-working gestures and whispered commands from where they had left off.

"If that be the case," bellowed the king's voice from the other side of the walls, "you have condemned yourselves to death."

For a second time the weatherlords stood dumbfounded, transfixed by their dawning realization that they had been duped all along, and frozen by the sudden, chilling prospect of the fate that lay in store for them.

At length, standing tall upon the wooden boards of the table, his feet braced apart and the veins of his neck knotted like ropes, Ryence cried, "Uabhar Ó Maoldúin, you invited us to shelter beneath your roof as your guests. Will you violate the code of hospitality?"

The answer returned, "The roof of the Red Lodge is not mine. It belongs to my knights. Moreover, the code is not applicable when the visitor is no guest but an informer and agitator."

Understanding that the king's mind was set against them and no words would sway him, Ryence leaped down from his perch. To his people he said in a low voice, "Our only hope is to continue summoning wild weather as swiftly as possible."

❧

Outside the Red Lodge a contingent of druids elbowed its way through the crowd of soldiers, who fell back on either

side like waves before the prow of some relentlessly plough-
ing vessel. "Make way for Primoris Virosus!" a secundus
sang out. "Make way for the Tongue of the Fates!"

In a billow of white robes, the wizened sage stepped
through the midst of his bodyguard and confronted King
Uabhar. "To death?" he barked, his gimlet eyes snapping
fire. "You declare that the weathermasters have condemned
themselves to death? What are you playing at?"

"It is merely a threat to entice them from the shelter of
their burrow," the king replied.

"O King," said the druid, his face the color of sour milk,
"I am no fool. Has it been your intention all along to slay the
Councilors of Ellenhall, or do you really mean to imprison
them? If slaughtering is your object, I will not help you. I do
not love them, but neither am I out of my wits."

"I mean only to take them prisoner, of course!" Uabhar
retorted testily. "They will soon scamper forth like frightened rabbits. The Sanctorum must support me in this, or all
will be lost!" When the druid radiated cold disapprobation,
the king's manner abruptly mellowed. "Once rendered im-
potent," he said, "the water-worshippers will regret their be-
littling of the Fates. I will do them no harm, and the
Sanctorum will be restored to its rightful status."

"Have I your word, Ó Maoldúin?"

It was the king's turn to pale with censoriousness. "I am
Slievmordhu," he said aloofly. "I am not required to give my
word." The two men eyed each other with mutual contempt,
barely concealed. "But you have it in any case," Uabhar said,
"if it makes you happy."

As Uabhar turned away, the primoris gave his liege-lord a
look of intense dislike and distrust, but no further speech
passed between them at that time.

The night flickered with lurid light, like fires guttering in
a sooty lamp of red glass, as the soldiers of Slievmordhu and
Ashqalêth hoisted scaling ladders against the log walls of
the lodge, and hurled grappling hooks to the window ledges.
They clambered up to the high narrow embrasures, but the

bars held strong, and when the assailants leaned in, Sir Isleif's knights smote them with heavy blows and threw them down. Again and again the assaults were repulsed, with no loss of life on the part of the defending Shield Champions but many casualties on the part of the attackers.

Uabhar had ordered a high platform to be hastily constructed amidst the seethe of battle-hungry soldiers, on which he was standing alongside Chohrab to oversee the assault on the Red Lodge. The sumptuous garments of the two kings were beginning to flutter in a strengthening breeze. Around them clustered a conglomeration of personal bodyguards, courtiers, druids, advisors and officers; a melange of livery, gorgeous raiment, albescent robes and military uniforms. Mac Brádaigh was part of the concourse, and Chohrab's personal butler. A dozen message-bearers waited at hand. One of Uabhar's ran up to the foot of the platform and bowed on his knee before his sovereign. "Your Majesty, the Shield Champions and weathermasters have sealed the lodge. We cannot break in."

Uabhar frowned. He had felt the rising wind swerve and change direction. It whipped at his cloak and hair, and made the torches spew sparks. He spoke to his druids and commanders. "We must move quickly, before they have time to exercise the forces of weather. Bring up the ram!" Armored men hastened to obey.

"Your fine lodge!" Chohrab bleated as he stood teetering by Uabhar's side. "The door will be broken!"

"All in a good cause, brother!" shouted Uabhar. "All in a good cause! Do you suppose I would not be willing to sacrifice my good door in the cause of justice? It is the least I can do for you, considering how wisely you have helped me. I can only *try* to measure up! You showed *such* foresight by sending your troops to surround the weather-meddlers. Your wisdom *shone* when you advised me that they should be captured before they can do harm to our kingdoms!" Taking Chohrab by the elbow he pulled him close and hissed into his ear, "I was never so well advised as when I hearkened to

your counsel, O desert hero. I myself will see this dangerous
enterprise through, on your behalf. You will find me a loyal
ally, oh yes indeed. Loyal and faithful, as ever!"

Within the Red Lodge the occupants heard a new sound. It
was the deep-voiced boom of a battering ram crashing upon
the thick oaken door.

"By the powers!" said Galiene in disbelief, "the tyrant
means business."

"Indeed he does," said Baldulf, his face drained of color.

Several knights piled furniture in front of the portal as reinforcement, while the weathermasters retreated to the dining hall. Ryence and Engres armed themselves with short
flagpoles from the courtyards and roasting-spits from the
kitchens, where a couple of terrified young scullery-maids
huddled together in the inglenook.

Most of the Shield Champions filed down the narrow corridor to the door, where they waited—standing well back—for it
to collapse inwards, as it must, eventually, under that on-
slaught. Without pausing in their storm-summoning labors,
the weathermages listened while the ram roared again and
again, until at last the thunder of splintering wood and collapsing furniture announced that the attackers had broken through.

A mage-summoned flash of flame greeted the first couple
of fighters to burst in. They stumbled over broken woodwork
and rolled in fire, bellowing, until the blows of the Shield
Champions put an end to their agony. No sooner were they
vanquished than a second pair of warriors barged in to take
their place. However, no more than two soldiers could pass
through the doorway at a time, and each pair encountered the
wrath of Sir Isleif and his second-in-command who were vigorously defending the stronghold. Behind their captains,
more knights of Grïmnørsland waited with upraised weapons
in case one of the defenders fell. From beyond the ruined
door rumbled the tumultuous and throaty cries of armed men
clamoring for entry, howling for blood.

"Ó Maoldúin will never get in here," Ryence said to Baldulf, as they peered down the passageway and beheld Sir

Isleif dispatching another warrior of the desert, "and our storm is on the way!"

In the dining hall, Galiene stood, statuesque in flowing grey raiment, her eyes closed, murmuring the words that steered and drove the elements. Her senses traced the dynamics of pressure systems and temperature inversions, of wind currents, of the interfaces between air masses of varying temperatures and densities. Feeling a tug at her sleeve, she interrupted her labor and looked down, to see a young servant-girl cowering before her. The child's face was pinched and pallid, her eyes large, rimmed with dark smudges. "Let me help you," she gasped.

"What can you mean?"

"It is wrong, it is a terrible wrong, that weatherlords should be persecuted. I can help you." The scullery-maid was trembling.

"I thank you for the offer, child," said Galiene gently. "Nonetheless, if we can hold off our foes for long enough we will not need your help. You are risking your own life by siding with us. What is your name?"

"Mairead."

"Go back to your kitchen, Mairead. Stay out of harm's way, and do not trouble yourself on our account."

Child and weathermage held one another's gaze in a compassionate clasp, and at that moment the voice of Uabhar could clearly be heard, raging above the hubbub. "The knights collude with our foes. Set the Red Lodge alight! If anyone flees out of the fire, run them through!"

A cheer erupted from the soldiery; an ocean breaker smashing against a cliff. Ryence barked out an oath of incredulity.

"Wheel of the Hag!" the young servant girl screamed in terror. "They mean to slay us all!"

Presently the roar of cheering merged with another sound; the thud of branches being piled against the outer walls, the slurp of drenching oil, the crackle of torches, the windy murmur and lick of flames against the timber walls. Soon, by the garish glare at the high window and outside the disintegrated door, and by the change in temperature, the weathermasters knew that vast sails of flame were climbing the building. The lodge was ablaze.

"Uabhar is incinerating his own stronghold in his own country!" Baldulf shouted in horrified disbelief, as a thick cloud of smoke billowed along the corridor and began to fill the interior.

"It burns quickly. The flames will reach us before our storm arrives," cried Galiene.

Sir Isleif and seven knights came dashing into the dining hall, spattered with gore. "You speak truly, my lady," said the captain of the Shield Champions, panting as he caught his breath. "There is no time left. We burn."

Not one of the elderly servants or young scullery-maids was to be seen; they had rushed off somewhere in fright. The air was darkening with reeks, making breathing difficult. Many weathermasters were coughing as if they would surely choke. "Dip these cloths in water," commanded Galiene, handing out swatches of linen she had scavenged from the kitchens. "Wrap them around your mouth and nose."

Ryence scanned the smoky chamber with red-rimmed eyes, as if taking the measure of each person present. "Let us break out of here and die on the sword, or escape if there is any chance under cover of darkness," he said at last.

"Aye," said Baldulf. "Better to die by blade than fire."

"Unbar one of the back doors," said Ryence, "and pull those shields down from the walls. Let us arm ourselves with any weapon that comes to hand."

Sir Isleif wiped grime and sweat from his forehead with the back of his hand. "We shall enclose ourselves in a tight fence of shields," he said, "with the women in the center. Thus we shall make our exit, chopping a road through the briar-patch of halberds, to freedom."

All understood the hopelessness of their position. With so few trained fighters against so many, they had no chance. Yet even a vain shred of hope was better than despair, and both Ryence and Sir Isleif inspired courage in everyone.

"Very well," said Baldulf, lifting a shield from its hook, "let us make such a valorous assay as will long be remembered in song!"

While the Councilors of Ellenhall prepared for this desperate bid, Galiene once again felt a tugging at her sleeve. The pale, frail servant girl had reappeared. She whispered fearfully, "Mistress, follow me. I will show you the way. A hidden siege-tunnel leads from here. Our masters believe we have no knowledge of its existence, but we have always known. My fellow servants have already fled that way. Bring lights!"

"Gather, knights and kinsmen! Gather to me!" cried Galiene. Just at the point when all hope had taken flight, Galiene's spirits began to rise. Her companions clustered around her, carrying lanterns, and their guide led them from the smoke-filled hall. With naked swords at the ready, twelve of the knights strode ahead of the group, while the other twelve brought up the rear. Along cramped passageways they sped, and through fungous trapdoors, and down wooden ladders and many a spiral staircase that plunged deeply into the gloom of the cellars. The noise of shouting and the crackle of flames grew fainter as they progressed. Eventually they arrived at a damp and slimy tunnel hewn from water-glistening rock. This underground passage dipped still further, and they swiftly descended the slope, their path lit by the lanterns they had brought with them. One of the older weathermages stumbled. Baldulf set his shoulder beneath his comrade's arm, half-carrying him.

"Where does this lead?" Galiene quietly asked their rescuer.

"Right out of the city," Mairead replied. "Past the eastern ramparts."

The floor began to slant upwards, and presently the tunnel came to an end. In front of a small aperture amongst the stones, fringed with wild grasses and tendrils, the young girl halted. The opening looked out upon an ebony sky splashed with stars, and a fresh breeze blew against the faces of the escapers.

"Douse your lanterns," the scullery-maid said.

Slim ringlets of smoke coiled from the extinguished wicks, while the eyes of the weathermasters adjusted to night's dimness. Between the blowing silhouettes of the leaf-blades glittered the cold, silent stars, like phosphorescent fractures in black ice.

XII

Upon a Ferny Hill

I had a comb of silver to decorate my hair,
They said 'twas made by goblins; I said I did not care.
But goblin work's illusion, trickery and dreams;
And goblins can't be trusted—nothing's what it seems.

I had a comb of silver, I cast it on the ground.
A mighty forest sprouted and burgeoned all around!
For goblin work's illusion, trickery and dreams;
And goblins can't be trusted—nothing's what it seems.

—"THE GOBLIN COMB"

*The escape party pushed past the foliage, and emerged qui*etly to find themselves upon a draughty hillside. At their backs loomed the embankment and parapet of the city walls, behind which the hill of the Red Lodge towered, now crowned with fire and smoke. Before them rose a low hill covered with tall fronds of bracken-fern, soughing and bending in the wind. No observer was in sight. Even as the refugees began to hasten away from the burning hilltop, one of the Shield Champions fell, bleeding, to his knees. His comrades raised him to his feet, but Galiene, abruptly noting that Sir Isleif had also sustained injuries and appeared dazed, declared, "We have eluded our attackers, but there are wounded and weary folk amongst us. We must soon rest.

Make for the next hilltop. There we will lie hidden in the ferns for a short time, that we may at least bind some of our hurts.

"As for you, dear Mairead," she addressed the young serving girl, "blessings upon your next nine generations. Take this." She unpinned a brooch from her cloak and pressed it into the maid's hand. "It is all I have to give you by way of thanks. Now go."

"Wait!" Accompanied by one of the weather-prentices, Ryence strode up and squatted on his haunches to speak to the child. "This lad with me, his name is Cador. When you go, I pray you to take him with you. As soon as you are both clear and safe, direct him towards Orielthir. That is all I ask."

Solemnly Mairead nodded. Ryence smiled, patted her on the shoulder and stood up.

"You have played a worthy part," Galiene said to the child. "Put a safe distance between you and ourselves. Begone! Begone!"

Servant and prentice took to their heels, disappearing into the rustling foliage.

"You must not wait for the wounded," muttered Sir Isleif as he sank to the ground on the crest of the hill Galiene had pointed out. His face was haggard and wan, a smear of chalk in night's gloom. "Go on! Hasten! My task is completed."

"We are all weary," said Galiene, "and some of our people are no longer young and able. Besides, many of us have suffered greatly from inhaling smoke, and are struggling for breath. We are safe here, for the moment. We would rest awhile anyway, whether or not you were hurt. But you are injured, and I would fain bind your wounds while we have time."

She wound a strip of torn fabric about the gashed brow of Sir Isleif. The task was not easy; her hair was blowing across her eyes, while her cloak snapped and billowed like a loose sail in a hurricane. Driven before the blustering gale, the ferns swayed and hissed; a violent ocean. The air's severe turbulence heralded the mage-summoned storm that was racing towards Cathair Rua. Between bouts of coughing, Baldulf was still steering the atmospheric disturbances with hand and voice.

The weathermasters were of one accord—they would sojourn briefly amongst the ferns, gathering their strength, before making a break for freedom. Crouching in the tangle of tossing leaves, they and their chivalrous guardians stared out across the dark and restless slopes to the terrible blossom of fire that was the Red Lodge.

"It must be all they can do to contain the blaze, with the wind so strong and unpredictable," remarked Engres, before being seized by a coughing fit.

"I wish it would rage out of confinement and burn down the king's house," said Ryence.

Galiene said quietly to Ryence, below the wind's moan, "We must depart soon, before Uabhar suspects we have escaped. Yet even if we manage to leave the marches of the city undetected, I do not hold much hope for us. We are so far from home, and there is no refuge in this country likely to guarantee our security! We cannot travel as speedily as Uabhar's forces, and where shall we go?"

"Towards Orielthir," Ryence answered promptly. "I have already sent young Cador ahead, to warn Thorgild and to beg him to come swiftly to our aid. The lad is fleet of foot, besides being small and sly enough to have a chance of evading Uabhar's scouts."

Wind hissed through the bracken with the sound of myriad tiny bubbles fizzing through water, and fern fronds thrashed in a manic dance. The clamor of men's shouts wafted to their ears on a puff of wind, drawing the weathermasters' attention back to the vigorous blaze atop the opposite hill.

"This summit where we stand is a good vantage point," Ryence added. "From here we can keep surveillance for signs of attack. Soon we must move again. Meanwhile we ought to rest, and fix our attention on the weather. If we do not continue to drive and direct the currents, the storm might wander off the desired course."

"I wish fervently that the storm will reach us before Uabhar does," said Galiene. "It is our only real hope, our single weapon."

As she spoke her breath, unseen, was snatched away by the wind, which bore it down the hillside and across the shallow vale, dancing above the spear-tips of the howling warriors who surrounded the flames consuming the Red Lodge. The heat from the conflagration was so intense that the Desert Paladins had fallen back, leaving a wide vacancy around the perimeters of the blaze. Bathed in red-gold illumination, they were yelling and brandishing their weapons. Servants were unloading barrels of water from wagons. They broached the vessels and drenched the surrounding ground in efforts to prevent the fire from spreading.

As for Chohrab Shechem the desert king, supported by the officials of his household—by now he was in hysterics, stammering and shrieking, unable to tear his gaze away from the holocaust. He alternated between tearing his hair and yelling "Hurrah!," screeching "Drive them out!" and wailing, "Ádh, O Starred One, O Míchinniúint, mighty Axe-Lord, save me from the wrath of the weatherlords!"

From a cooler and more comfortable location beneath a canopy further back amongst the ranks, the king of Slievmordhu observed the proceedings with increasing discomposure. "All doors and windows are being watched, but the puddle-makers have not issued forth," he said to Primoris Virosus, who stood nearby, leaning on his staff. "Neither have the servants. Are they all such heroes that they have forfeited their lives for the sake of pride?"

"I cannot say," the ancient druid replied, somewhat sardonically.

His king was too intent on his own deliberations to take note of the sage's tone. "I find it hard to believe the puddlers would sacrifice themselves; harder to credit that they would not permit the scullions to escape the frying pan. There is some mystery afoot." Beckoning his lord chancellor, he said, "Is there any other way out of the Red Lodge?"

"Why no, Sire!" stuttered the courtier. "At least—that is to say—I believe there was once a siege-tunnel, but its existence was a secret known only to a few in the upper echelons—"

Uabhar stared at his noble retainer, the veins on his brow standing out like worms crawling beneath his skin. "Had you informed me earlier, we might have sent men-at-arms to attack them from within the lodge itself, you quatch-buttocks! For this oversight you will be hanged!"

The lord chancellor could only execute a deep obeisance as he struggled to disguise his dismay.

"Where does this siege-tunnel make its exit?" demanded his sovereign.

"Sire, I understand it issued forth somewhere beyond the city walls."

Uabhar, in fury, shouted, "Imbecile!" Then he suddenly checked his ire, and fell silent, as if cogitating. Perceiving this slammed-shut cliff of ice where lately a furnace had roared, the lord chancellor winced.

Presently Uabhar turned to a commander of the Desert Paladins and said, "Tell your brigadiers to remain at the burning lodge with their drunken braves." To High Commander Mac Brádaigh and other officers he gave a series of rapid orders. "Find the tunnel's exit. Select a few discreet men who can be trusted to hold their tongues and dispatch them there immediately. Let them stand guard. They must slay anyone who emerges, and scour the surroundings for signs of escapers. Muster the druids. Send guards to the city gates—should any citizens emerge in an attempt to gawk at our business, turn them away. Tell them they must not come near, or they will be subject to the death penalty. Bring down a curfew. Go at once!" Driven by the extremes of tethered rage, he gnashed his teeth until his jaw convulsed.

The storm was rapidly approaching. From the corner of his eye Uabhar caught sight of a flicker of light in the sky, and glanced up. Heavy clouds were flooding across the stars in a dark tide.

"The weathermasters do indeed live," he said, his lip curling in a snarl. "Behold, they are summoning a thunderstorm. Let us hasten to receive them at this secret sallyport!"

The king flung himself astride his charger. Surrounded by a cavalcade of bodyguards and officials, he galloped away, calling for Chohrab to follow. Several scouts, already mounted, had hastened ahead. When Uabhar arrived at the low bluff where the tunnel opened onto the hillside, the scouts informed him they had encountered nobody, but had discovered splashes of fresh blood upon the vegetation at the tunnel's mouth.

"Someone has passed this way not long since," they said. "Someone who was grievously stricken."

At that moment a runner dashed up to the king of Slievmordhu. "We have lit upon the weathermasters!" the messenger cried. "They are gathered atop that nearby hill, at bay. We did not approach, for they threatened to hurl balls of fire. But the soldiers have surrounded them."

"This I shall see for myself!" cried Uabhar, tugging on the reins so cruelly that his mount reared and squealed, its mouth torn. The king, a practiced horseman, remained in the saddle. "Is Virosus not here yet? Send a chariot for him!" he shouted, clapping his heels to the flanks of his steed. Away he rode, with Mac Brádaigh close behind, to confront the cornered weathermasters.

The low hill was limned by the glimmer of moon and stars, their radiance smoke-yellowed, like old paper. Fibrous bracken-ferns, almost waist-high to a man, surged like ocean swell, the greens and golds rendered tangerine and scarlet in the glare of the encircling torches. A knot of windblown figures crowned the hill, most standing up, others on their knees half-submerged in swaying foliage. Several were seen to be molding nothingness with their outstretched hands, crying out in an incomprehensible tongue, their lilting phrases rising and falling with the blowing of the wind.

Flushed with triumph, inebriated with vindictive joy, Uabhar witnessed the forsakenness of the weatherlords; castaways on a lonely isle with nowhere to hide and nowhere to flee. The troops awaited his orders, not daring to approach. Despite their mood of insobriety and relative abandonment, they remained in awe of the denizens of Rowan

Green, and besides, they had been well drilled in obedience. Uabhar's victory was almost complete. He felt he could afford to gloat before the final stroke.

And the stroke *would* be final. All along he had intended to slay the senior weatherlords, and now the opportunity was at hand. To Mac Brádaigh, who attended him, he said, "Most of the Councillors of Ellenhall are here. The missing pair, the chit and the dotard, will be easily taken care of when they no longer have the support of their kindred. Once all are gone, nothing stands between myself and absolute power, save for two armies unprepared for war. Aided by the Sanctorum, my allies both secret and acknowledged, the tricks of the goblin artifact and the advantage of surprise, I will sweep away all opposition. Dispatch someone to the palace to fetch some lethal adulterant, Mac Brádaigh; wolfsbane is my favorite. Order plenty. There shall be no witnesses to this."

"At once, Your Majesty," said Mac Brádaigh. "High King of Tir!" He bowed deeply to show his devotion, yet there was a certain look in Uabhar's eyes that made him uncomfortable. He had witnessed extreme monomania before in other men, and knew he glimpsed it now. After conveying his liege lord's instructions to an errand-runner and seeing the man off, he said sanguinely, "Our position is excellent, despite our original plan being frustrated."

"Ah, yes." Reminded of this fact, the king directed his gaze over towards the group on the hilltop. He frowned. "It is a pity we did not achieve our objective of driving the meddlers out of the Red Lodge and imprisoning them in my dungeons. After they were thus rendered powerless it would have been easy to kill them with slow poison, or by means of an 'accidental' fire; some tragedy whose blame could not be laid at my doorstep. Now it is a different kettle of fish, for they are here, on this open mound, in full view of my soldiers and Chohrab's knights. If only it had been possible to act without all this fuss!" Uabhar's elation appeared to be ebbing. "What is to be done now, eh Mac Brádaigh?" he said sharply. "What is the best course of action?"

"We could rush them," the High Commander suggested.

Above the dark distant horizon, a thin, dazzling crack opened and closed. Shortly thereafter, a low grumbling noise rolled across the skies. "Look at that!" the king shouted. "Thunder and lightning are drawing near!" He rounded on Mac Brádaigh. "Time is not unlimited, do you understand? If we rush the weathermasters they will drive us back, again and again, until their storm arrives to blast my troops and save them."

Mac Brádaigh bowed by way of acknowledgment. He began to fear that they might be losing control of the situation. It was clear that Uabhar's triumph was turning into panic as he started to comprehend their position. He seemed verging on hysteria as he shrieked again, "Where is Virosus? Where is he?"

The withered sage was duly fetched to join his sovereign at the foot of the ferny hill, clinging to the metal sides of a chariot as it bumped its way along. Two younger, stronger druids flanked him, and others followed in a convoy of conveyances.

As soon as Primoris Virosus stepped down from the chariot, Uabhar took him aside.

"You must help me now," he said, almost pleadingly. "We have trapped the weathermasters but they have not surrendered. They are making a stand, and with every moment that passes their storms draw closer, flying to do their bidding. If we wait any longer, the wild weather will be upon us. Against elemental forces no human army can triumph. If the weatherlords escape now, they will unleash dire vengeance upon us. Our foes will support them—Narngalis and Grïmnørsland—there will be no chance for Slievmordhu. Soon the lightning will be at the fingertips of the mages. Use your resources. Seize them, man, before there is such slaughter done here that our enemies from every land will descend on Slievmordhu in its debility."

The aged druid scrutinized the king from beneath his hooded lids. "Uabhar," he said, "although I have not hindered their entrapment I have never been party to any scheme to *slay* the weatherlords. Know that if you do this deed, as appears to be your desire, then the wrath of Ellenhall will hammer upon Slievmordhu in any case. Granted, the flower of Rowan Green is within your grasp, but there are others of that kindred who are not here amongst them—the Storm Lord and the powerful Storm Maiden Asrăthiel, to name but two."

"So you keep saying. Consider you, that the Sanctorum and Slievmordhu are no match for a dotard and a wench?"

The druid continued, "Your majesty has been remarkably ill advised in this venture. Or perhaps you have acted on impulse, I cannot say. Know also, Uabhar, that I am not fool enough to directly assault weatherlords. Should I do so, even the Four Fates would not protect me."

Uabhar seized the druid's scrawny shoulder in a powerful grip, murmuring rapidly and urgently. All the while his gaze roved the scene, flitting across the milling crowd of armed men, the stamping horses between the chariot shafts, the flaring brands and lanterns, the distant glare of the burning lodge across a vale of darkness and the dim outline of the ferny hilltop beneath churning clouds. His eyes coasted back and forth, while his free hand plucked at his own fur-lined garments, and twisted the rich fabric.

"Of course I will not destroy them. Do you take me for a fool?" he said in a low voice. "I pledge that I will wreak no harm upon the weathermasters if I can but imprison them in my dungeons, and bind them so that they cannot speak their brí-commands or make their gestures of power. I will not take their lives, Virosus, I swear it." The sage regarded his sovereign dubiously. Infuriated by this hesitation, Uabhar clenched his fist. "Most esteemed Primoris," the king said abruptly, "you bestow your advice freely. I can be equally generous. Know this: if you believe the wrath of the puddle-makers can be severe, you have failed to accurately observe the world around you. Perhaps the front of your cowl has been slumping across your eyes. The vengeance of Uabhar Ó Maoldúin makes that of Ellenhall dwindle to insignificance, and the palace is closer at hand than Rowan Green." He released his grip on the druid's shoulder.

The Druid Imperius was not unaware of the king's power

over his own person; nevertheless the expression on his puckered countenance did not alter. He was too wily to allow his true feelings to reveal themselves.

"Well," he said at last, "you have made a pledge, and I understand well that Uabhar Ó Maoldúin would never be forsworn. I am pleased to obey the royal command. Have more water-wagons brought up, and direct the men to arrange ramparts of brushwood around the hilltop where the weathermasters are holding out. Ádh's chosen ones will do the rest."

"Would you burn the storm-bringers, then, after all your lip service to gentleness?" Uabhar uttered a short, hard burst of laughter.

"Nay. Long have I harbored a better scheme, should such a pinch arise." The druid sucked on his own index finger, then held it high. "The wind swings now towards the east," he said. "Now, Majesty, if you value your senses you had better hie in the opposite direction." Without saluting, he vanished out of the king's sight, into the wind-battered shadows. "Hasten," said the Tongue of the Fates to his chief scribe, "and tell the acolytes to fetch great quantity of the Leaves of Sleeping."

Swiftly the king's servants did as they were bade and piled up brushwood in embankments, yet even as torchbearers set fire to them, the first sparse droplets of the oncoming storm commenced to patter down. Captains and overseers cursed the laborers for their imagined sluggishness. "Hurry! Hurry, ere the rains begin to fall!" The dry boughs quickly caught alight. For the second time that night newborn flames soared, the fuel crackling and spitting. Yet lightning flared in bluish sheets across the sky, and the clouds groaned.

Fire raced uphill through the bracken, but the weatherlords parried it with chill blasts, the effort costing them much of their failing strength. Huddled together on the hilltop, they pondered on their straits.

"Uabhar seems determined to roast us," Sir Isleif said grimly. The bandage across his brow was soaked with blood.

"Hold fast!" Ryence encouraged his brí-wielding comrades. He wiped his perspiring forehead with a soot-smudged hand. "There is yet hope!"

"I fear the rains shall arrive too late!" warned Engres. "The fire is swifter than the storm."

"Yet 'twould be bootless to change the local wind's direction," Baldulf rasped. "We are encircled. No matter which way it blows, it blows the flames to us."

"We can only wait," said Galiene, "and continue weather-working, and keep the fire at bay until the clouds loose the downpour and Thorgild comes to our aid!"

"What's this?" said Engres, squinting with watering eyes against the flames' glare. "Now they are piling green hazel branches upon the fires. What are they up to?"

Shadowy surges of asphyxiating smoke poured from the sap-filled hazel stems. Through the curding fumes the besieging host was blotted from view, and no one could rightly see them; only dim, choking figures emerging from the gloom or disappearing into it as they cast armfuls of callow boughs upon the pyres. Notwithstanding, the weathermasters bade the nearby air currents blow the worst of the fumes away in other directions.

Had they been able to penetrate the haze, the company trapped on the hilltop would have witnessed a strange phenomenon. After the hazel stems began to smoke, more men came, bearing bulky hempen sacks from which they extracted string-tied bundles of dried leaves and twigs; but after they had cast these offerings upon the infernos they fell down in a faint. Indeed, some who tried to approach were unable to do so, swooning before they reached their target. The weathermasters, however, were blinded to this.

"We may yet turn Uabhar's tricks to our advantage," Galiene gasped, breathing with difficulty in the toxic atmosphere. "Under cover of this smoke screen we might create a cool gap in the ring of fire and slip away."

"An excellent plan," agreed Ryence.

All the weathermasters and knights were of one accord, and those who had been lying exhausted amidst the bracken clambered to their feet, aided by their companions. After wrapping cloths about their mouths and noses, they renewed their grip on their weapons, holding them at the ready. A light pre-storm shower briefly brushed their faces as they commanded small, local puffs of air to clear a path before them.

Yet even as they stepped forward, uttering the brí-commands to drive the heat out of their way, the weatherlords faltered. The pall of carbonaceous particles pressed on all sides, engulfing them like acrid blankets, smothering them, irritating their eyes, infiltrating their airways, somehow penetrating—evidently—even into their bloodstreams. They became light-headed, and as they staggered down the hill it seemed to them that they were cast adrift upon an ocean of clammy combers, so that they were persuaded that they must swim, instead of walking.

"Alas," Ryence said to Galiene, in a voice that was scarcely more than a whisper, "this is no ordinary fume. We have been undone, after all."

"Dear friend," was all that Galiene could manage to say as she leaned against him, barely able to remain upright. Dazed, the entire company let fall their weapons and extended their arms like swimmers striking out, but instead of floating they crumpled to the ground, rendered insensible by some curious property of the vapors. They lay unmoving, slumped upon the hillside, And as they breathed, strange gases entered deeper into their bodies, and they succumbed to a profound slumber.

Darkness gave way to a dim, overcast dawn. Then at last, too late, the heavens let loose their flood. Upon and around the bodies of the fallen, the long-awaited rain began to pour in escalating torrents. Voluminous clouds of smoke and steam issued from the ramparts of burning brushwood. The wood hissed and fumed until the increasing deluge drowned all flame and spark, but even before the furnaces were extinguished, men had surged forth and borne away the sleeping forms of the weathermasters and their guardian knights without striking any further blow.

So it was that the senior weathermages—the Councilors of Ellenhall and others—were overthrown. Paralyzed and insensate, they and their guardians—the valiant knights— and the five remaining prentices were brought, bound hand and foot, before Uabhar, who waited in the company of his High Commander, the Druid Imperius and Chohrab Shechem. The desert ruler had grown quieter by now, his face as grey as spoiled oatmeal as he mumbled desperate pleas to Ádh, Lord of Prosperity, as well as the other three Fates for good measure.

Canvas awnings on poles, supported by footmen, sheltered the statesmen from the downpour. Most of Uabhar's soldiers and servants had been ordered to depart forthwith and return to shelter, along with all Chohrab's knights, bar one. Uabhar had carefully chosen those who stayed, and not a first-rate man was among them, save for Mac Brádaigh and the sole remaining Paladin. The rest, bedraggled in the deluge, were in the class of the lowest ranking, the weakest, the most useless of subordinates; the soldiers stupefied with inebriation, the servants dull-witted. Chohrab was in such a state that he failed to note so few of his household were left. With only his personal butler and a single knight left to him, he knelt upon a sodden carpet with his head in his hands, his eyes covered, and would not look up. A circle of wagons and horses fanned out before the kings, the entire scene lit by a feeble glow from the east, and flashes of lightning, and covered lanterns, every naked flame having been extinguished by the teeming rain. In the center of the circle, unprotected from the elements, lay the bodies of three-and-fifty sleeping weathermasters and knights.

"See what your *fell noxasm* has done," Uabhar said to the Druid Imperius, smiling silkily.

"We have gone too far. I wash my hands of these matters," said Virosus, and he swiftly returned to the Sanctorum with his attendants.

Uabhar looked a little put out, but the response of his ally was extreme. Aghast at the primoris's reaction, Chohrab heaved himself to his feet. He turned to Uabhar, screaming, "The druids have withdrawn their support! It has come to this! What will the weathermasters do when they awaken in your dungeons?"

Commander Mac Brádaigh stepped in, his tone soothing. "They can do nought, Lord. They will be gagged and mana-cled—"

Uabhar was not listening to either of them. "Deeds have been done, Chohrab, and the Sanctorum refuses to share the blame!" He chewed his lips in seeming agitation. "It is of no use to merely imprison the meddlers, because long as they lived, dear brother, they would be a threat. There would be rescue attempts, and they might become a figure-head representing your enemies. You and I must ensure that they are wiped from the face of the world forever. There is nothing else for it. The weathermasters must all be put to death."

As the full significance of this statement sank in, a stunned look grew on the face of the desert king. His butler shrank back in fear.

"Virosus, no doubt," Uabhar continued, "would have been unreasonable about it, for alas, he is a coward. It is well that he has turned tail for the nonce." In case the comment appeared irreverent, he appended, "All praise to Lord Ádh."

At the mention of the Druid Imperius, Chohrab gazed about with a wild look in his eyes. "But the druids have deserted us!" he exclaimed.

"Do not for one moment be deceived by the primoris's bluffing," Uabhar replied with urbanity. "He will return. Instead, be overjoyed! Your wish has been granted, and victory is ours!"

Chohrab chewed at his nails, darting sidelong glances at the mages, prentices and knights lying in a swoon amongst the ferns, as if he hoped they were an illusion that would disappear when he looked away.

"Behold, my dear colleague!" said Uabhar said genially, "all has turned out as you planned. Your enemies are within our grasp. I have played my role in this affair. In return for what I have done for you, you shall slay them."

The jaw of Chohrab flapped as if on hinges, but he uttered no sound.

"Your sword Hesam dangles at your side—as befits a military overlord—and a fine weapon it is, comparable only to my own blade, Gorm Glas," said Uabhar. "Use it, brother, to end these lives once and for all, that they may no longer support the northerners who would invade your lands."

The King of Ashqalêth failed to move so much as a fingertip.

"Come now! You yourself told me it is your wish that they should perish."

Chohrab appeared, briefly, to choke.

"Now it is time," insisted Uabhar, "for you to demonstrate that my loyalty is reciprocated. I have done my part. It is your turn. The time is ripe to prove your fidelity. If you truly mean to ally yourself with me, treat these foes as you promised."

Drug-addled King Chohrab, appalled by the atrocities he had witnessed, and terrified of the revenge of Rowan Green, had fallen completely into Uabhar's power. "Lord Ádh! Lord Míchinniúint!" he jabbered in fear and confusion.

Uabhar said, "You have cast down the meddlers and the druids have deserted you. Who now will stand between you and your foes? Who else but Slievmordhu? Would you refuse this deed and cause a rift between us?"

"I vow to do anything you command, if only you will remain my ally and keep me safe!" So saying, Chohrab drew his sword and handed it to his most doughty Paladin, the only one who remained. "Slay them," he said shrilly.

A murmur of horror went through the select few who had been permitted to remain and watch the proceedings.

Chohrab's knight stoically took the weapon and began his gruesome task, while the tears of the firmament fell down, and the skies mourned. The warrior hewed off the heads of the sleepers, and their blood mingled with the rainwater, flowing into the fescue and ferns, while those who witnessed this deed could not help but groan and sigh, as if they were in agony, each time a sword-stroke fell. It was impossible for them to comprehend the enormity of the atrocities being carried out before their eyes. Some of the observers turned their faces away and wept, their tears unnoticed in the deluge of the crying storm.

"Load the remains on covered carts, and carry them far from here, to some remote location," the King of Slievmordhu ordered his men. "Bury them. Let heavy stones be piled upon their graves."

Uabhar contrived, with the utmost cunning and ruthlessness, to have those who had witnessed the slaughter murdered immediately thereafter, that no whisper of what had occurred could enter into public knowledge. He bade them drink a toast to victory over the weathermasters, but Chohrab's personal butler had been made to surreptitiously mix wolfsbane with the wine. Shortly after the cups were raised on high and the liquor downed to the last drop—at the king's insistence—the doomed drinkers experienced numbness, giddiness and severe restriction of breath. They fell to the ground gasping, under the pitiless eye of Uabhar, who looked on as their heartbeats slowed and eventually ceased.

Mac Brádaigh was the only onlooker permitted to survive, other than Chohrab, who, a whimpering wreck, could speak no sense at all, and had developed a form of delirium. Mac Brádaigh slew the desert king's butler and his doughty executioner as well, stabbing them both in the back. The Paladin was the last to die, he having been the misguided agent of most of the other killings. The king of Slievmordhu had it bruited about that the dead had all fallen in battle against the weatherlords, and no one dared illuminate the inconsistencies in this story. It was a bloody night, a darkness of smoke and death and storm. Raw red gore mingled with the black rainwater swirling in ditches and gutters.

Thereafter, Uabhar was confident that he would be safe from possible reprisals, at least until he achieved his great ambition, after which he would be all-powerful, and no man would dare accuse him. To his knowledge, all witnesses had been accounted for.

Yet there was one other who had seen.

✣

At sunset on the previous day, the aged itinerant, Cat Soup, had stowed away on a wagon departing northwards from Cathair Rua. He had hoped to make his customary journey to King's Winterbourne in relative comfort, because lately his feet had been mightily sore. The wagon, however, had turned off the main road one league from the city, and struck out to the east along a narrow track leading deep into the countryside. Cat Soup deduced he had erred in his judgment, and had boarded a conveyance heading for some smallholding in a rural area. This circumstance, though not uncommon for a vagabond such as he, did not suit him. As soon as he reached this conclusion he slipped out from beneath the tarpaulin and began to make his way, hobbling, back to the metropolis.

There were unaccountable disturbances in the weather, which had earlier promised fair. The beggar sensed rain in the air. His joints ached, and a fractious wind niggled at his garments. He was glad of the oilskin cloak on his back, which he had stolen from a careless patron at a horse-race meeting that day—it was the very reason he was making a quick exit from Cathair Rua, in case the cloak's owner should stumble upon him.

As he made his painful way back to the royal city, trudging over the bracken-covered hills, he became aware that a fire had broken out atop the hill of the Red Lodge. Indeed, it looked as if the knights' stronghold itself were burning. This fact piqued his curiosity, and he plodded a little faster, spurred also by the sight of rain-clouds massing overhead. Some while later several troupes of horsemen thundered past, quite close, so that the old man quailed and hid behind the mossy trunk of a great oak tree that had fallen, several decades ago, amongst the ferns and nettles. A crowd of tiny grigs pinched him and pulled his hair for a while before scampering off, but he curled up and covered himself with the travel-stained oilskin.

Beneath stars and gathering clouds and veils of smoke the horsemen were gathering on a nearby hillside. Druids appeared amongst them, and laden wagons were driven up. Then more fires were kindled. Rough winds sprayed brilliant bursts of sparks through the darkness. The old man saw all this from afar, and wondered at it. "Trouble is afoot," he muttered to himself. He was torn between risking danger by creeping forward to investigate, and simply continuing on his path to the city. For a few moments he hesitated. Cat Soup had never been one to plunge headlong into peril; he had lived for so long by avoiding it. On the other hand, knowledge was power; he had often profited by spying, by learning other people's secrets. In the end his inquisitiveness bettered him, and he scurried towards the bonfires on the ferny hill.

One advantage of being a miserable beggar was that people rarely noticed you. Cat Soup, aided by his mottled garb, excelled at being unobtrusive. Thus it came to pass that he succeeded in stealing close enough to the scenes of royal felony to see everything, while remaining unobserved.

He witnessed it all; the mages of Rowan Green and the Shield Champions overcome by the fumes, their sleeping forms being dragged before the two kings, the exchange between Uabhar and Chohrab and the hideous denouement.

That the noble company of weathermasters and knights should be slain in cold blood seemed so incredible that for an instant the beggar entertained the notion he had contracted some fever, and was hallucinating. Revolted and terrified by the spectacle, he decamped with all speed, heedless of his aching feet. He rushed through the wind and rain, slithering and slipping, throwing himself flat on the ground whenever lightning smote the hills like weapons of steel, lighting the landscape with its cruel blue glare.

"Halt! Who goes there?" an Ashqalêthan knight shouted at him above the storm's noise, but Cat Soup crouched, cowering, beneath his cloak, hidden by the deluge and darkness, until he heard a second voice say, " 'Twas merely a coney. Do not dally." Whereupon the paladins rode away.

The ancient beggar dared not move. He scarcely dared to breathe. Water was running into his nostrils, but it could not wash away the stench of death.

He had seen it all. What now was he to do?

Far away to the north, in the village of Silverton that night, Asrăthiel planted her feet firmly on a mound of slippery scoria, and steadied herself. The weathermage, heedless of the local curfew, had quietly left her lodgings and fared forth, yet again, during the lightless hours. She had special dispensation in her position as weathermage to the king, and she feared no unseelie killers that visited in the dark. Besides, if the mysterious assassins should come tonight she would be able to steal a look at them at last, and perhaps blast them with a fireball or two to prevent them from wreaking harm.

The slag-heap, though old, had not coagulated much over the time since the ore had been smelted out of it. It was treacherous; still liable to give way and send her careering down. Over the years, dirt and dust had sifted into the nooks between the loose cinders, but few plants would take root in this vitreous aggregate. Only the weed crowthistle was hardy enough; here and there a prickly leaf stubbornly poked through.

Throughout those northern regions, curious mists had begun rising between sunset and sunrise, coiling in and out of the forests and pouring along the ground. They turned Silverton's river valley into a nebulous dreamscape, a flowing cloud-river that never rose high enough to obscure the sky. The vapours were supernatural; of that the weathermage was certain, for her brí-senses were numb to them and could not penetrate to their essence. She had never encountered such imperviousness before; it was a surprise, and an unpleasant one. Such phenomena, she conjectured, were probably connected with the unknown scourge. Still searching for answers to the enigmatic killings, she was putting forth her weather-senses to ascertain if she could pick up any clues from the atmosphere, when all at once a terrible shock went through the brí, as of some catastrophe. Immediately she knew that some kind of unprecedented turmoil had erupted in the troposphere towards the south. The patterns shifted in violation of natural laws. It was as though some careless weathermaster had inflicted sweeping changes, affecting every component of the meteorological system, yet too vast to be the act of a single mage. So violent and abnormal was the tumult that Asrăthiel had to assume it was due to some mighty accumulation of weather-working.

Reeling from the impact, the damsel barely kept her balance on the rocky heap. She struggled to regain her poise, both physical and mental, at a loss as to what had caused the anomaly. What could have happened? Perhaps something had gone awry with her senses. They might have been overloaded; maybe she had been too intent on extracting the maximum amount of information from her surroundings. Or else some phenomenon she had never encountered in her lifetime had occurred somewhere in the world; the near-collision of a comet or meteorite, for example, or a particularly strong and sudden bursting open of the world's crust beneath one of the great oceanic trenches. Asrăthiel felt unaccountably frightened, and also, suddenly, terribly alone and vulnerable. With all her heart she longed for High Darioneth. She had never been this homesick before. . . .

After slithering her way down from the heap with all speed, she ran towards her lodgings, hoping that a message from Avalloc would soon arrive from the nearest semaphore station to explain this new mystery.

❧

On the damp and dreary morning after the betrayal of the weathermasters, while the bodies were still being carted to their graves, a meeting of three men convened around a small table in a thick-walled chamber. It was then that the Druid Imperius discovered the truth.

"Where are the Councilors of Ellenhall?" he demanded of Uabhar. "What have you done with them?"

Wearing an expression of smug satisfaction, Uabhar informed the elderly sage of their fate, while Commander Mac Brádaigh leaned back in his chair and privately smirked.

On hearing of the deaths of the weathermasters Virosus could not contain his wrath. He jumped up with alacrity, astonishingly nimble for his age. Leaning across the table, he pushed his face into Uabhar's. "You are mad!" he shrieked, disregarding all royal protocol. "What of the vengeance of the Maelstronnar and his granddaughter, eh? What of the response of the populace if they find out? You are forsworn, Uabhar, forsworn and condemned for what you have done!"

"What *I* have done?" Uabhar said nastily. His attention seemed abruptly riveted on his embroidered sleeve, and he began ripping threads out of it. "You have misheard, druid. Perhaps you are getting deaf in your dotage, in which case I will forgive you for your offensive accusation. I remain a man of honor. I kept my word. It was not *I* who ordered the execution of the weathermasters, but Chohrab Shechem."

The primoris said, "Beware how you equivocate with me, my *Liege*—" he spat out the latter word as if it were some venomous insult "—for I am in a strong position. If I make known your secret, you will bear the blame. What would your sons do if they knew, eh? How would the peers of the realm react? They might rise against you!"

But Uabhar coolly replied, "If you make this issue public, druid, *you* will bear the blame along with Chohrab, for it was your *fell noxasm,* your Leaves of Sleeping, that brought about the weathermasters' downfall. By which you will see," he went on, paying no heed to the expression of hatred twisting the raddled visage of the primoris, "that your *fate,* ha ha, is closely bound to mine. If I fall, you fall with me. You have a choice: *'to fly with me or die with me,'* as the saying goes. Choose to fly, and when I am High King we will *both* govern the Four Kingdoms in our different ways—you by fear of death, me by justice and fear of pain."

Virosus's lust for power was strong, and he possessed common sense enough to know which side of his bread was buttered. He was also cunning enough to wish to distance himself from whole event. "So be it," he said after a pause. "I will not betray your black deeds, and I will support your invasion of the west and north kingdoms, but from this moment I will have no more truck with you in person, and—" he stood up as straight and tall as his hunched posture would allow, pointing a bony finger at his sovereign like a weather vane that has swung about to accuse the wind "—for your perfidy, Uabhar, I will pronounce a curse upon the house of Ó Maoldúin—a curse to endure for all time."

Mac Brádaigh, who had been lolling back and savoring the scene, sat upright and blanched conspicuously. After a moment's shock, Uabhar uttered a forced laugh. "Much good will it do," he sneered. "Lord Luck is on my side, and Lord Destiny also, and well you know it."

Without another word the Druid Imperius swept out of the room.

After the noise of his departure had dwindled, the king gave the table such a shove that it crashed over on its side. "I am closer to the Fates than the druids!" he roared, "and when I am High King I will destroy all the Sanctorums!"

But the Druid Imperius went straight to his strongrooms and collected his druids' hexing equipment. These shamanic tools, supposedly imbued with magickal powers bestowed by the Fates, comprised an assortment of fetishes and charms, totems and talismans, statues and idols. Accompanied by his unquestioning assistant, Acerbus, Virosus took a chariot out across the moors and fens, to an ancient lakeside Oratorium. There he drew circles on the ground, and painted signs on the air, and called out to the Fates, and made such ceremonies as the druidic lore-books stipulated, and more. Having bound all the good fortune of Uabhar's dynasty into four wooden statuettes—a star, a twibill, a cat and a wheel—he tied up the objects in a bag and cast them into the deep, black lake, which was haunted by unseelie fuathan, so that the objects could never be retrieved by mortal men.

"As these charms rot away, so will the House of Ó Maoldúin!" screamed the Druid Imperius. He kept his promise, however, and breathed no word of the weathermasters' demise to anyone.

❧

Many leagues from Silverton, the strange storm at Cathair Rua had petered out. Half dead with terror and the sweltering fever to which he had now truly become subject, Cat Soup finally managed to evade the forces of authority and smuggle himself aboard yet another wagon. It turned out that this one was indeed bound for King's Winterbourne, and as it rattled out through the city gates, the beggar privately vowed that he would never return to the red metropolis in the south.

Not far from the walls of Slievmordhu's capital, the vagrant's conveyance jolted past a certain spot that appeared superficially to be no different from any other leaf-embowered avenue of the highway. If any of the wagoners had peered into the rain-filled roadside ditch, however, they would have beheld a pale lily floating on the water, amidst delicate green traceries of duckweed and bladderwort. It was no pond-flower, however, but a face; that of Ryence Darglistel's slain prentice, Cador, who had been intercepted by Uabhar's soldiers on his way to Orielthir. The lad's lifeless form was suspended in the water, while loose petals of may-blossom and sweet-briar drifted down from the greenery that rustled above to alight upon his marbled cheek.

As for the other messenger, Queen Saibh's man, Fedlamid macDall, his mount had stumbled while galloping through the rain, and he had been flung to the ground. As he searched, calling for his steed, he had stepped upon a Stray Sod and been doomed, for the nonce, to wander lost. Soon afterwards he had come to the attention of a passing company of trows, who had abducted him, for they were attracted to human beings with yellow hair and wanted him for their own. MacDall's horse found its way back to Cathair Rua two days later, and when the queen saw it she wept, but would not say why.

No messenger had succeeded in arriving at Orielthir to warn King Thorgild of Uabhar's crimes. No willing man was able to tell him the truth, and no man who might have done so was willing.

Uabhar dispatched his own courier to Thorgild Torkilsalven, claiming that the weathermasters were safe and hale. That being the case—he wrote—Thorgild had accomplished his mission of escorting them to Cathair Rua and might now return to Grïmnørsland with an untroubled mind, being refreshed from his sojourn at the site of the Summer Palace.

"My liege begs me to inform you that your majesty's Shield Champions will soon follow," the courier said. "They will not be far behind your entourage."

The good monarch of the west kingdom harbored many suspicions, but he was convinced that even Uabhar would not stoop to scathing the beneficent lords of the elements. Furthermore, he trusted that the power of the mages and his own knights was sufficient to repel any who tried to do them ill. Numerous urgent duties of state beckoned him to return to his home. Casting many a backwards glance, he and his retinue struck out for their native land.

As for Conall Gearnach, Uabhar sent a message to him also. Even though the Commander-in-Chief of the Knights of the Brand could not learn of the executions, he would be certain to hear stories of siege and imprisonment. The high-principled but quick-tempered knight would inevitably be furious beyond reason when he learned how roughly the weathermasters had been treated, after he had promised them safety. His fury would be exacerbated by the news that Uabhar had burned down the famous Red Lodge, the home of his chivalry. Guessing that Gearnach would become unmanageable and troublesome should he return at that time to Cathair Rua, Uabhar decided to impose a cooling-off period. Gearnach's orders were to leave Orielthir without delay, take a company of knights, and strike out for the remote Southeastern Moors. The king issued these instructions on the pretext that unseelie wights were reported to be gathering on the moors in great numbers. It was necessary, the king declared, for Gearnach to gauge whether this mustering of malign forces would pose any threat to Slievmordhu.

Suspecting foul play, Gearnach was sorely tested when he received this command. Like all the Knights of the Brand he regarded keeping one's word of honor as the highest benchmark to which anyone could aspire, and he had sworn the oath of fealty to his sovereign, promising to protect and obey him. Yet he had uttered that vow before he began to understand the base nature of Uabhar.

His first feelings of apprehension on this matter had been sparked years earlier, and had grown gradually ever since, but he drew strength from harking back to the speech he had given on the inaugural Day of Heroes, which he still recalled word for word: "Loyalty in character means absolute obedience that does not question the results of an officer's command, nor its reasons, but rather obeys for the sake of obedience itself. . . ."

If followers were to renounce their masters because they no longer deemed them completely virtuous, there would be no purpose, no glory in oath-taking. Having resolved to do his duty by his country, Gearnach had sworn fealty to Uabhar on the understanding that the king was, by and large, a worthy liege-lord. Should it turn out otherwise, the knight would not besmirch the name of Gearnach by tergiversating. If he regretted the oath he would not allow himself to acknowledge it. He was determined to stand by his promise under all circumstances, because a truly honorable man could do no less. In the end, despite his sovereign's offenses, Gearnach remained unswerving in his loyalty to the crown of Slievmordhu.

So it happened that the knight departed from Orielthir with his chivalry, riding northeast into the region of the Great Lakes, and beyond. He went precipitately, nonetheless, so that he might return to Cathair Rua as soon as possible.

The fate of the weathermasters was hidden from public knowledge. In Cathair Rua the ambassador from High Darioneth was arrested on a fabricated charge and imprisoned, his household dismantled. The story was put about that the weatherlords had escaped the fire in the Red Lodge, and made peace with Uabhar. Any mention of conflict was suppressed. To prove their cordial intentions they had accepted his hospitality and were abiding concordantly in private palace apartments until further notice.

Uabhar concocted semaphore messages and sent them to the Mountain Ring, under the names of Ymberbaillé and Darglistel, declaring that all was well, and informing the Storm Lord that the weathermasters were happy to sojourn at the palace for a week or two before returning to Rowan Green. There was a hasty note about the mage-summoned storms; "All will be made clear in due course" was the only explanation given, and "no need to worry" said the letter.

Avalloc, still in a state of frailty, had been alarmed by the severe and inexplicable upheavals in the weather systems. On receiving the tidings from Cathair Rua, he grew more troubled. It was out of character for his kindred and comrades to act thus, and he could not help suspecting some form of chicanery. His first thought was to allay his granddaughter's anxiety about the atmospheric disturbances, which no doubt she had felt, so he sent her a calming message indicating that there was no cause for trepidation. Nevertheless he dispatched a band of riders south to Cathair Rua to uncover the facts, but they were waylaid upon the road by an unknown agency and never seen again.

❧

The wagon carrying Cat Soup jolted northwards amongst a procession of other horse-drawn vehicles. Before them the muddy road unrolled, here and there touching upon towns and villages linked along it like luck-amulets on a bracelet. Slowly the iron cartwheels turned. It would be many days before the convoy reached King's Winterbourne.

In Silverton and its neighboring hamlets Asrăthiel continued on her mission to throw light on the mystery of the eldritch slayings. Morning had dawned drear and overcast at Elpinstone in the Sillerway Valley, with not a puff of wind. So still was the air that plumes of smoke rose straight up from the cottage chimneys.

Asrăthiel paced the floor of her lodgings. She could not sleep, despite having been awake all night, traipsing across the countryside. Anxieties about the atmospheric disturbances and the unsolved slayings plagued her, and from time to time she was assailed by a desire to consult the absent urisk, who had become her font of eldritch lore. She missed his company—there was no denying it—with a disconcerting intensity; disconcerting because the feeling was unfamiliar, and because somehow it did not seem fitting or proper for any human being, let alone a weathermage, to form a strong attachment to an entity so utterly alien; a creature of gramarye, an incarnation of the very night. An urisk was a being with whom, by rights, she should have no association beyond the ordinary transactions—leaving a bowl of cream and a quarter loaf by the back door every evening by way of thanks for domestic services rendered. There was nothing ordinary about that particular urisk, however; nothing that fitted the mold.

The door's bolts squealed as the damsel drew them back. She stepped over the threshold into the open. An oak tree grew by the door, its far-flung boughs throwing a leafy canopy across the yard. Tiny bells hung from those boughs, silent in the stillness, and like the leaves, they were beaded with droplets. Asrăthiel stared into the distance. Along the valley great drifts of mists hung, like the sails of a vast fleet of ghostly galleons. The sun was veiled, yet, oddly, there was nothing dismal about the muted daylight and the floating vapors; rather the air was charged with a kind of excitement. The fogs might be concealing anything, Asrăthiel thought whimsically, as she began to pace restlessly beneath the oak. Wondrous things might be hidden behind those veils; they emanated from some supernatural source, after all. What might they hide—glimpses into other worlds?

Monsters? Faêrie castles floating on cloud islands? The weathermage contemplated the possibilities, but, inevitably, returned to her original concerns.

Apart from the proliferation of weird mists in the valleys north of the Harrowgate Fells, no tidings of trouble had come her way. During any spare moments she repeatedly perused the communications she had received from Avalloc, as if each new reading might reveal some overlooked word of reassurance. His assurances that to his knowledge her kindred were safe were intended to put her at ease, yet she remained anxious. She could not gauge what had caused the dramatic turbulence in the southern weather-patterns. Her grandfather had relayed to her the contents of the message he had received from Cathair Rua stating that all would be made clear in due course, and with that she had to be content. Knowing that Avalloc would send word if any dire event had occurred, she did not pursue the matter; nonetheless she could not help but be dogged by a sense of dread.

Uabhar wasted no time. He called for a grand assembly to be held at the palace, and while his closest military advisors and the senior members of his household were ponderously filing into the audience chamber, he paid a visit to King Chohrab.

Ashqalêth's ruler was in a bad way, suffering, no doubt, from shock and the effects of prolonged over-indulgence in certain items of pharmacopoeid. He had taken to babbling. His talk was unguarded; he seemed hardly to be aware whether he was in company or not, and his host sometimes feared he would spill every secret. It had been arranged that Chohrab should rest in the palace's comfortable Clover Suite, attended only by Uabhar's own handpicked deaf servants.

Finding his guest alone in his apartments, the King of Slievmordhu seated himself at his ease on the green velvet cushions of a tall-backed chair carved with intertwining four-leafed clovers, each lobe inlaid with malachite. Chohrab slumped bulkily in a window seat, his lids puffed up like bloated fish.

"I fear the retribution of the Storm Lord," the desert ruler muttered. "When he learns the truth, his wrath will be mighty." Unexpectedly, he surged forward and grabbed the arm of Uabhar's chair. "I have changed my mind!" he shrieked. "We must not attack Narngalis! 'Twould compound the other fell deeds we have wrought!" The flesh sagging from the structure of his face looked grey, almost translucent. "If Slievmordhu can assault one kingdom," he moaned, as if talking to himself, "why not another?"

Uabhar peeled the clawing grip off the oak and malachite embellishments. "You need have no fear," he said smoothly. "I am your ally, as you know."

Chohrab, however, merely fell back and gaped, his eyes wide but apparently blind to his surroundings, as if he were viewing the events of some older time, in some distant place, and as if the sight filled him with dread.

His exasperation getting the better of him, Uabhar jumped up. In his turn he seized Chohrab by the shoulders in what might have been a comradely fashion. "Brother!" he exclaimed, "have I not vowed to always shield you from suspicion? Now, come with me to the audience chamber, for we must present a united front, you and I, when we make our declaration. There is no need to tax your health by making a speech. I shall labor on your behalf. Come!"

All the grave courtiers and stern bodyguards and other members of Uabhar's grand assembly who had been brought together in the audience chamber were treated that day to the spectacle of two kings enthroned in majesty side by side upon the dais. After they had been sworn to utmost secrecy, Commander Mac Brádaigh fed the concourse with certain secrets and certain lies.

Conscious of Chohrab's distress, and fearing he would fail to keep rein of his loose tongue, Uabhar murmured into his fellow ruler's ear, "Recall, it was your own blade Hesam that did the necessary blood-work yesterday morning, yet in the name of loyalty, I breathe no word of it, nor ever shall." Adopting his usual volume he proclaimed, "It is a day for triumph and rejoicing! The way is now clear for us to attack

Narngalis and teach Wyverstone a lesson, before he and Torkilsalven execute their scheme to invade Ashqalêth!"

While the audience applauded and cheered, Chohrab said feebly, "How might we be certain of success?"

"How can you ask, when our armies, well accoutred, together outnumber theirs? Moreover, as you know I own a powerful eldritch weapon, the famous Sylvan Comb." Uabhar smirked. "I have other aces hidden within my sleeve, too, my brother, for I possess allies undreamed of."

"What other allies?" Chohrab looked alarmed and bewildered. "There can be no other allies!"

"My dear comrade, I have ratified a peace agreement with forces that, until now, have been unjustly despised by the general populace. They have pledged to support Slievmordhu."

"Of whom do you speak?"

Uabhar lowered his voice once more. "The Marauders, brother, none other."

"You have bargained with *Marauders*? But they are monsters, not men. . . ."

"Nonetheless, they can fight."

Again the southern king appeared to be on the verge of panic. "What have you promised such toads in return for their assistance?"

"Hush. Be at peace, Chohrab. You need not concern yourself with trifling details. We shall take Narngalis before Wyverstone strikes, and then turn our attention to Grïmnørsland. Rejoice! Ashqalêth will be saved!"

In front of the entire gathering Uabhar turned to his equerry, roaring, "Make ready my battle-gear—my shield, Ocean; my dagger, Victorious; my spear, Slaughter and my sword, Gorm Glas."

Brandishing his first above his head he shouted, "Slievmordhu marches to war!"

❧

On a lonely hilltop near the tiny village of Yardley Goblin, sixty miles from Silverton, Asrăthiel Maelstronnar stood lis-

tening to the songs of heat and water and the whispers of the
elemental gases of the troposphere, all the while observing
their intricate dances, and measuring their speed and direction.
The source of the eldritch mists continued to elude her. . . .

At length, withdrawing her brí-senses, she bowed her
head and lost herself in another reverie. During her weather-
search she had hearkened as always to the north wind; it had
murmured of icy peaks cupping frozen lakes, and limitless
leagues that lay beyond those peaks, unmapped. Somewhere
in those strange lands her father roamed. Would he return
one day, with or without that which he had been seeking?
Would he come back to his daughter, and to his bride who
slept among the roses? Or was he lost forever?

As the damsel's mind returned to her immediate surroundings, it came to her that she had been staring at a particular object without seeing it. It was a leafy sprig of
crowthistle, growing at her feet. A tuft of purple marked a
tightly wrapped bud, destined to blossom into a striking
flower whose shape resembled the unfurled wings of a crow.

The sight of this prickly weed put her in mind of the last
occasion she had encountered the urisk, and her thoughts
drifted away again. The memory returned to her with such
clarity that it was like watching it happen all over again
through the lens of time. As so often, he had been standing
before an open window, which framed a vista of the night
sky. He was positioned exactly in the center of the frame,
against a backdrop of brilliantly colored stars that shivered,
as if loosely nailed to the rippling fabric of the universe.
Within the room, his alien features were illumined by the red
light of the hearth-fire, but his expression was unreadable.

Behind the head of the urisk, the full moon was rising in
splendor, floating like a world cast from solid silver. The
sphere was so large that the parentheses of his horns could
not contain it. Unaccountably it came to Asrăthiel, watching, that the moon seemed subject to him, rather than an un-
connected body, remote and untouchable. For an instant she
had the absurd impression that the wight had commended
the moon to remain stationary behind him.

The orb of silver made him king of the night.

Before that instant of awe had passed and she had felt like laughing at herself for her fancies, Asrăthiel had, on impulse, asked him his name a second time.

He had laughed then, and cast her an odd glance that made her shiver, but had deigned to reply.

"I am called," he said, "Crowthistle."

Here ends
The Crowthistle Chronicles, Book 3: Weatherwitch.

The story commenced in
The Crowthistle Chronicles, Book 1: The Iron Tree
and
The Crowthistle Chronicles, Book 2: The Well of Tears.

It concludes in
The Crowthistle Chronicles, Book 4: Fallowblade:

A beautiful Lord of Wickedness, with hair as black as iniquity, is about to shatter the life of the weathermage Asrăthiel. Of this she has no notion as she prepares for battle against a tyrant who plans to seize dominion over the Four Kingdoms. The invading armies are pushing further north, and it seems that all is lost... until a new peril unexpectedly looms, a far more dangerous and deadly menace that threatens, not merely the balance of power, but the entire human race. It seems their only hope lies with the golden sword Fallowblade, and only Asrăthiel can wield that weapon. But what of this stranger, this perilous eldritch warrior whose beauty outshines the night...?

ACKNOWLEDGMENTS

MAY DAY RHYMES: "Pear for the fair,
   Hawthorn for the well-born . . ." etc.
   Aside from "hawthorn for the well-born," these are traditional rhymes repeated to this day during modern May
   Day ceremonies in Britain. Hawthorn flowers bestowed
   on one's threshold were considered to be a general compliment, which is why the extra line has been included.
   The celebration of "May Day," the welcoming of summer, is rooted in ancient pagan rites. In Celtic Britain the
   Beltane festival was held on the first of May, and marked
   by the lighting of huge bonfires on hilltops, perhaps in
   echo of the sun, or to encourage the sun's return.
FESTIVALS: Many of the festivals mentioned in this work
   are inspired by actual ceremonies and customs that persist
   to this day in Great Britain.
THE APPLE TREE WASSAILING CHANT: in Chapter 5 (which
   I adapted slightly) springs from Cornworthy in Devon,
   Great Britain. The original was recorded in 1805 and col-
   lected in *The Stations of the Sun: A History of the Ritual
   Year in Britain,* by Ronald Hutton. Oxford University
   Press, reprint edition, 1997.
JEWEL'S SLEEP IN THE GLASS CUPOLA: Jewel's long slum-
   ber in a chamber of glass netted by roses is inspired by
   two well-known fairy tales; "The Sleeping Beauty" and
   "Snow White."
CAT SOUP'S TALE: Inspired by "The Fairy Miners," in *Pop-*

ular Romances of the West of England, by Robert Hunt. Hotten, London, 1865.

THE PUPPET SHOW: The story told by the puppeteers is based on "The Salt Box," Burne and Jackson, in *Shropshire Folk-Lore: A Sheaf of Gleanings,* London, 1883. Collected by F. G. Jackson, translated by C. S. Burne from "The Saut Box."

MISTRESS DRAYCOTT PARSLOW'S GOOD FORTUNE: Inspired by the story "The Old Woman Who Turned Her Shift," in *Popular Romances of the West of England,* by Robert Hunt. Hotten, London, 1865.

THE BLACK GHOST AND THE WHITE GHOST: Inspired by "The White Bucca and the Black," in *Traditional and Hearthside Stories of West Cornwall,* by William Bottrell, Penzance, 1870.

JOKES TOLD AT THE BETROTHAL: Inspired by "Enoch and Eli," in *Anecdotes and Tales, Chiefly from the Black Country,* collected by Roy Palmer, Ms., 1966.

PERYWYKE IS AN ERBE OF GRENE COLOR: An anonymous herbal poem, apparently dating from about the time of Chaucer.

GOOD DRUID, I HAVE SENT FOR YOU BECAUSE: An adaptation of an anonymous erotic poem, possibly dating from the nineteenth century.

WEATHER LORE: This traditional rhyme was gathered from *Collins Eyewitness Guides: Weather.*

> "If the oak flowers before the ash,
> We shall have a splash.
> If the ash flowers before the oak,
> We shall have a soak."

THE OPPOSING PROHIBITIONS ON KING THORGILD, AND THE BETRAYAL OF THE WEATHERMASTERS: Inspired by part of the story "Deirdre," an ancient Celtic legend. This tale, also known as "The Exile of the Children of Uisnach," is often related as a prologue to the oldest prose epic known to Western literature: "The Cattle Raid of Cooley" (*Tain Bo Cuailgne*). It has existed by word of mouth since the first century A.D. and was written down by Irish scholars during the seventh century A.D. The story has been rewritten many times in the form of books and plays, and remains popular to the present day.

THE NAMES OF UABHAR'S WEAPONS: King Uabhar's weapons are named after the weapons of King Conchobar in the legend "Deirdre." "My shield Ocean, my dart Victorious, my spear Slaughter, and my sword Gorm Glas, the blue-green."

WHUPPITY STOURIE: This ancient custom is exclusively observed on 1 March at the Royal Burgh of Lanark in Strathclyde, Scotland.

THE DAY OF HEROES LOYALTY SPEECH: This is adapted from an actual speech by Rudolph Hess, in 1934, to the National Socialist Party in Germany.

PLACE NAMES IN NARNGALIS: Many of the place names in Narngalis are derived from locations in the British Isles. And what a delight they are.

THE INTELLIGENCE OF FISH: For fascinating information on the intelligent minds of fish, dogs, sheep, primates and other creatures, I recommend *New Scientist* magazine # 2451, 12 June 2004, pages 41 to 53.

ANIMAL RIGHTS: P.E.T.A., "People for the Ethical Treatment of Animals," have kindly permitted me to draw on information from their newsletter and from their Web site, which can be found at http://www.peta.org.

Thanks to Garth Nix, one of my favorite authors, for our discussion about character names. Thanks to the following writers for valuable information about swordsmanship: Elizabeth Bear, Mike Dumas, Elizabeth Glover, Steve K. S. Perry, Nancy Proctor.

ABOUT THE AUTHOR

A graduate of Monash University with a degree in sociology, CECILIA DART-THORNTON is the author of the internationally acclaimed Bitterbynde Trilogy and the Crowthistle Chronicles. Her interests include animal rights, wilderness conservation, and digital media. She lives with her family in Australia.

Visit Cecilia's Web site: http://www.dartthornton.com.